About the Author

Ian Evans was born in the city of Bath, England, enjoyed by and known to the Romans as Aquae Sulis. His parents were both Scots, despite the Welsh name, and probably descendants of the Scoti, one of the villains of this story. When he was a child, his family moved to Johannesburg, South Africa. He attended St John's College, which tried desperately – and ultimately failed – to teach him Latin, which is regrettable in the current context. His enjoyment of history, however, and his mother-inspired coin collection sustained interest in the four hundred years that Britain was a significant province of the mighty Roman Empire. At the University of the Witwatersrand, he majored in history and psychology, then returned to England for his PhD in experimental and clinical psychology at the Institute of Psychiatry, University of London.

His first academic position was at the strongly contrasting situation of the University of Hawai'i in Honolulu. With the now-established pattern of climatic and cultural changes, he, then, became professor and director of clinical psychology at SUNY-Binghamton, where he and his wife, also a professor, lived on a one hundred and seven acres disused dairy farm. On a whim, they abandoned this bucolic lifestyle for glorious New Zealand, where Ian taught clinical psychology at the University of Waikato and Massey University. On retirement as Emeritus Professors, they returned to their familiar Honolulu haunts. Here, influenced by his mother's successful career as an author of books for girls (pen name Jane Shaw), Ian turned his hand to writing novels – as one does.

The Last Villa is Ian's sixth novel and is a sequel to his fourth, *The First Village* (Pegasus/Vanguard Press, 2019).

His other previous fictional works are:

Forgive Me My Trespasses (Archway, 2025/2018) – a satirical look at political sexual scandals from the perspective of psychotherapy principles of compassion and self-forgiveness.

The Eye of Kuruman (Pegasus/Vanguard Press, 2017) is a romance set in Botswana and South Africa, in which a young public health nurse struggles with questions of love, cultural challenges and social injustice.

Menace (Austin Macauley, 2017) – a thriller in which an intern psychologist at a university counselling centre must judge the dangerousness of a student client.

Singing Grass (BookBaby, 2021) – a psychological mystery in which a clinical psychologist with a troubled past, now practising psychotherapy in Taos, New Mexico, encounters a mysterious client with an uncanny resemblance to the scout and pioneer of the old West, Kit Carson, embroiling him in past and present experiences with Native Americans.

When not at his desk or visiting lovely grandchildren on the continent, Ian enjoys wildlife photography in southern Africa, single malt Scotch whiskies, the beach, TV dramas, ranting about politics and wondering what to do with the large stack of books on Roman history. He still wonders why, as a schoolboy, no one told him that people once actually spoke Latin and were, in fact, interesting Romans, so he should have paid much more attention in class.

Look for Ian on Facebook, LinkedIn, ResearchGate and his website, www.ianmevans.com.

The Last Villa

Ian M. Evans

The Last Villa

Vanguard Press

VANGUARD PAPERBACK

© Copyright 2024
Ian M. Evans

The right of Ian M. Evans to be identified as author of
this work has been asserted by him in accordance with the
Copyright, Designs and Patents Act 1988.

All Rights Reserved

No reproduction, copy or transmission of this publication
may be made without written permission.
No paragraph of this publication may be reproduced,
copied or transmitted save with the written permission of the publisher, or
in accordance with the provisions
of the Copyright Act 1956 (as amended).

Any person who commits any unauthorised act in relation to this
publication may be liable to criminal prosecution and civil claims for
damages.

A CIP catalogue record for this title is available from the British Library.

ISBN 978-1-83794-464-4

This is a work of fiction. Names, characters, businesses, places, events
and incidents are either the products of the author's imagination or used in
a fictitious manner. Any resemblance to actual persons, living or dead, or
actual events is purely coincidental.

Vanguard Press is an imprint of
Pegasus Elliot Mackenzie Publishers Ltd.
www.pegasuspublishers.com

First Published in 2024

Vanguard Press
Sheraton House Castle Park
Cambridge England

Printed & Bound in Great Britain

Dedication

For Stanley Young (MA, Stanford; JD, Harvard), distinguished patent and civil rights lawyer, whose knowledge of and fascination with Roman history has been a source of stimulation, encouraging friendship and many constructive suggestions.

Prologue

This is a story of people and events in one community of Roman Wales – near the modern town of Caerleon and the village of Caerwent – at the end of the Fourth Century of the Common Era. Our story begins in the early spring of what was then known as the Year of the Consulship of Olybrius and Probinus (AD 395), the day in early February, which is the halfway point between the winter solstice and the spring equinox.

The story continues the tale told in *The First Village* of Galeria Arcadiae, a wealthy widow and *domina* of a magnificent villa, her intellectual son Flavius and his life-long friend Severus – both high-ranking officers in the Roman army – their impulsive junior comrade Caradocus, a Celtic-Roman centurion, and this young man's love for the beautiful Elen, daughter of a powerful Silurian chief, and their infant son, Dilectus. That story ended in September, AD 388, when news of the defeat and execution of Emperor Magnus Maximus came to Villa Arcadius. This new story begins with the death of another emperor seven years later and follows the threads of the first story to see what happened over the next fifteen years.

News by urgent dispatch had just reached Villa Arcadius that on January 17, AD 395, Theodosius I – the last emperor of an undivided Roman Empire – had died unexpectedly in Milan. According to his decree, his ten-year-old son Honorius became the Emperor of the Western Roman Empire, based in Milan, and his older brother Arcadius became Emperor of the Eastern Empire, based in Constantinople. Both boys were immediately dominated by powerful guardians appointed as regents until they came of age. In the East, this role was filled by Praetorian Prefect Rufinus, and in the West, by a half-Vandal, half-Roman brilliant *magister militum* called Stilicho.

Political intrigue, shifting loyalties, intense rivalry between the power brokers of the two divisions of the Empire and enormous pressure from nomadic tribes far to the east of the Empire's frontiers created dangerous instability and civil war for the next fifteen years. Stilicho managed to stem the tide as best he could. In AD 398, he is said to have launched a military campaign against the Picts, a mysterious group of peoples living in what is now northern Scotland, who were continually raiding the Roman provinces of Britannia by land and by sea. Claudian, the court poet of the time, wrote of the success of Stilicho's 'Pictish War' in strengthening fortifications, reducing threats from the 'grim' Scoti, the 'tattooed' Picts and the 'approaching' Saxons. Whether Stilicho led the campaign, however, is unclear. By AD 402, Stilicho was forced to remove Roman troops from Britannia in order to defend Italy from the 'barbarians', later known as the Western Goths or Visigoths. They were led by a former Roman army commander called Alaric, who had been elected king. Insecurity was heightened by the unreliable support from diverse Germanic peoples who had been allowed to settle within the Empire and now supplied most of the troops for the Roman army. In August AD 410, Rome, the Eternal City, was sacked by Alaric after three long sieges. This was the first time in eight centuries that Rome itself had fallen.

The remote provinces of Roman Britain, vulnerable on all sides to maritime raids, had been steadily disengaging from Roman rule. In reality, the effectiveness of what remained of Rome's military presence in Britain during our fifteen years had been compromised by frequent withdrawals of both field army units and garrison troops. In a one-year period, AD 406–7, the Roman army in Britain nominated and elected three different individuals to lead them and to oppose the rule of Honorius. The Fifth Century Greek historian, Zosimus, described the army in Britain as being 'insolent and irascible'. There are reasons why the troops still left on the island were so agitated. One factor was they hadn't been paid for two years. Another likely reason is the increased threat to Britain posed by neighbouring Gaul being overrun by Germanic tribes, Vandals, Alans and Suevi, crossing the Rhine frontier. The army believed the defence of Britannia required the defence of Gaul. Most importantly, their last officially appointed military commander had been killed in a skirmish in the summer of AD 406.

The troops in Britain first nominated one young aristocrat, Marcus, to be their new commander but soon regretted their choice and executed him three weeks later. They then picked on the wealthy city councillor Gratian as a possible usurper, but he met the same fate. Their third, more sensible choice was a soldier, Constantine, who took the decisive action in AD 407 that the field army wanted. For the second time in less than twenty-five years, all the nominally Roman troops were led out of Britain by a usurper. To the shock of the imperial court, he managed to set himself up in Gaul as Emperor Constantine III. Honorius, preoccupied with holding off the Goths, was forced to accept Constantine as a co-emperor. Constantine's success did not last long, however; by AD 409, he'd been defeated both in Spain and on the Rhine frontier.

With Constantine and his army fighting on two fronts, the only Roman forces left in Britain were small clusters of garrison troops, conscripts and auxiliary units of mostly local tribal men owing fealty to local chiefs. By 409, the people of Britain had had enough of Rome. The hoarding of gold and silver coins and clipping their edges had weakened the value of the Roman currency and was killing trade. Any remaining Roman magistrates were quickly turfed out of their positions. This finalised a process of disengagement starting twenty years earlier, with new alliances forged between important and wealthy Romano-Briton families and the traditional tribal chiefs, one example of which dominates the story in *The First Village.*

Because the native Celtic people of Britain were still being sorely harassed by the pagan Scoti from Hibernia (Ireland) and the Picts from Caledonia (Scotland), as well as by Saxons from the narrow sea to the east of Britain, the weakening of the Roman army garrison units left the locals even more vulnerable. There was pressure to now recruit Saxons as federated troops to help deal with the Picts – a controversial and ultimately disastrous policy. The chronicles record that Roman-Briton civilians who were still asserting their authority in the larger towns, then wrote to Emperor Honorius and begged for Imperial troops to return to protect them. This story seems implausible. Many ordinary Britons were delighted to see the end of the Roman military presence, especially the strongmen of the major tribal groups who were busily setting themselves up as kings. Those writing such a letter should also have known that by 409, Honorius was in no position to send troops anywhere. He was desperately trying to contend with Alaric's invasion of Italy, not to mention Constantine III competing for his imperial title. Honorius's sympathy for the most distant provinces of the Empire was at an all-time low.

Nevertheless, there is an obscure reference by Zosimus that Honorius wrote back politely to all the major administrative towns (the *civitas*) in Britain, telling them they would have to take care of their own defence. Known as the *Rescript of Honorius*, this communication is widely cited as fact, but modern historians tend to point out the original Rescript was probably sent somewhere in Italy. But it's a great story: the message 'you're on your own, chaps', coming directly from the Western Roman Emperor is a good way to mark the final end of any pretence of Roman control of Britain after AD 410.

Rome and her imperial institutions faded slowly into the next two hundred back-and-forth years of raids, then invasions, then settlements by Germanic tribes of Angles, Saxons and Jutes, eventually engulfing the Britons. Only the Celtic peoples of the more mountainous and less agriculturally productive parts of the country – Cornwall, Wales and Scotland – maintained some resistance to the steady Anglo-Saxon encroachment. The one exception to this ending of Roman influence is the staunch adherence to the Catholic Church by a significant number of the Celtic Britons. The influence and authority of the Pope in Rome extended to fragile places of worship in private chapels, converted pagan temples and churches, in addition to well-funded Christian clerics, institutions and organisations – parishes, bishoprics and monasteries. Religious influence was muted, however, by contentious theological divisions. While the Christian Roman Empire was being torn apart by war, massive migrations and invasion by pillaging and looting hostile tribes, the intellectual leadership of the Church was focused on bitter doctrinal arguments, heresies, persecutions, sects, cults and theological minutia. In Britain, many Celts had acquired a liking for the teaching of a leading preacher soon to be declared a heretic: a British monk called Pelagius. It is against this background that our story begins on the Christian feast day of Candlemas and the pagan festival of Imbolc, honouring the goddess Brighid.

Chapter 1: A Pagan Shrine
The First Night of Imbolc (February AD 395)

Two men, wrapped in heavy cloaks, squirmed on low, rough-hewn stools. They were miserably cold. It was a dismal place for a meeting. Probably why it had been chosen. A dank, stone-lined, square grotto – a neglected shrine with a crudely carved figure of a seated woman – was set among a foreboding cluster of ruined and burnt-out buildings. A space in the forest had been cleared long ago. Giant old trees – oak, yew and elm – some of them saplings four hundred years before the Romans arrived, had been turned to charcoal to forge iron ore into swords, spears and shackles. Shackles for the slaves who'd survived the Roman revenge for the Iceni queen's annihilation of the IXth Legion and who were brought to the coal mines here to work until they died of exhaustion, hunger and cold.

But Boudica was all ancient history. No one could really know what happened more than three hundred years ago. There were still signs of past coal and iron mining scattered around in bat-infested caves, open pits and collapsing tunnels. Gold and silver deposits had been excavated nearby, as well as red and brown ochre, so essential for the decorative arts of the civilised. But it was all long gone. Like any other colonising power, the Romans had plundered these raw materials – half the reason they were in Britannia in the first place. With Roman influence and those resources both so depleted, there was no indication of current human activity, and the forest, known to most as the Coedwig o Daneg, was already reclaiming the space.

On the outskirts of the forest, hunting was not uncommon but risky. It wasn't clear who controlled it or claimed ownership. Maybe Danes were still lurking about. Near the shrine, but never daring to enter it, raggedly dressed and malnourished local peasant children could sometimes be found searching for lumps of coal fallen from oxcarts in past years. But now, though the wind was still biting, the first hesitant signs of spring had lessened the need for extra fuel, and the children had little incentive to confront their fear of this intimidating place.

The table in front of the two men was covered in fine black dust. On it were soiled beakers of ale. They hadn't been touched. The mysterious official who had called the meeting had poured it out in front of them but hadn't sipped any himself. Poisoning was always possible. The two men shared the dread felt by the scavenging children. They'd seen crows circling overhead. That was an evil omen.

An imposing, well-dressed, grey-bearded man sat opposite them. The single candle, stuck on the table by its own dripping tallow, cast a shadow on the wall behind him, exaggerating his size. He stared at them silently, wondering if such nervous rabbits were up to the job. He shouldn't have started the meeting with a stern lecture on how tightly secret everything had to be. Seeing the promised reward might steady them – as emotions go, greed always overcomes fear in his experience. He reached suddenly inside his long leather coat. The two men jerked backwards. *Idiots! Did they expect me to pull out a dagger and kill them before they got started? Maybe afterwards.*

"Settle, fellows! I'm not going to eat you," he sneered. "I'm going to employ you."

He ceremoniously shook the bear scrotum pouch he had pulled from inside his jacket. Six shining gold coins fell, clattering onto the table. The two men were transfixed. *Perfectly calculated, enough to make them drool.* Two labouring men's lifetimes of earnings – if they were lucky – in one pile. He methodically separated the coins, lining them up in a row with a gap between the third and the fourth.

"Three for you." He nodded towards the taller, heavier-built man. "And three for you." He turned his eyes to the other one. "This is half what I had in mind. When you return with the boy, you will get the other six." He held up one hand with fingers splayed and one finger from his other hand. Although they were holy men, he wasn't sure they could count.

"Take your time. There's no rush. Locate him, observe him, keep him out of the way and do nothing until I decide the time is ripe. My lord has a plan. We cannot afford the slightest mistake. It may be next year; it may be the year after – I will send you a message. There will be no further contact – or gold – until you bring him to me."

"How are we going to recognise him and find him, your worship?"

"That's your problem. My sources tell me he moves between the Villa Arcadius and the Silurian tribal fortress of Garn Goch. But he's never alone. Getting into the villa without being questioned would be impossible. But the Chief of the Silures, who pretentiously calls himself their king, is old, fat and careless. People come and go from that tumbled-down rathole fort with hardly a challenge from the lazy guards. But maybe the boy roams outside with his friends, unsupervised – easy to grab him, kill the friends."

"Easy for you to say," the second man finally spoke up. "They won't think we're Hibernian slavers if we leave a pile of dead kids. We should take everyone he's with, and the Scoti raiders will be blamed."

"I don't give a horse's turd who'll get blamed as long as it's not us. Do whatever you have to."

"I've got another question. Sounds like we could be sitting on our arses for years waiting for you to give the order. What are we gonna do with a pocketful of gold solidi? No one will be able to give us change, and the moment someone sees us waving one around, we're dead men. The Romans were fuck'n swine, but at least they kept order. Not any more."

"I thought of that long before you fools did," the bearded man sneered. "I suggest you bury these coins somewhere safe for your future comfort, but give one of them back to me now, and I'll give you each the equivalent in silver siliquae; twenty-two of them, that's the same as all your fingers and toes and your two ears put together. That will allow you to get horses, food, lodging, women and anything else you need for as long as you need them without attracting attention to yourselves. Call it your *per diem* expenses for the mission."

"*Hmm.* That's fair. What's this boy called?"

"Dilectus."

"Dilectus? Funny name for a Celt. Doesn't he have a real name?"

"His parents were Celts, but his father was in the Roman army. They could speak Latin. Some say the boy is the son of Macsen Wledig, but it can't be true. He's heir to the Silurian kingdom, so-called, so don't piss around with him. I need him alive – you understand? My lord won't pay for a corpse or a skeleton. Take all the time you need. Don't take any chances. His disappearance forever and without a trace defines success."

"One more thing." The bearded man stood up to leave and glared at them. "You've never seen me before, never heard of me, and I never ordered you to do anything. Say otherwise, and I'll hunt you down like Cunomaglos and boil you in one of your odious cauldrons."

The shorter man made the sign of the cross, the other spat on the damp mossy floor. The man with the pockets of gold disappeared through the trees. An animal screeched in the forest – wolf, lynx, or bear, the two men didn't know. This time both men crossed themselves.

Chapter 2: The Villa Arcadius
Candlemas Day, Year of the Consulship of Olybrius and Probinus

Galeria tossed it into the conversation like a coin into the Aqua Virgo: "I want to go to Rome."

"Don't we all – oh, dear God, Mother, you're being serious."

"Flavius, darling, I wish you wouldn't blaspheme so much. But yes, our very 'Dear God' is the main reason I want to go. Another thing is that I'll be able to die happily after seeing the wonders of our immortal city, especially Apostle Peter's Basilica with the columns Constantine saved from the Temple of Solomon. Oh, and also to meet Pelagius again and try to intercede with Pope Siricius, who's so full of contrary opinions..."

"Stole the pillars, I'd say, knowing Constantine's reputation. And I'm afraid Rome won't prove hospitable much longer with Theodosius up and dying last month and his all-out stupid persecution of the pagan patricians backfiring. It's a mess. No grown-up heir. You'd most certainly die before you got there – and, oh, my god, you want to meet whom?"

"Pelagius."

"I thought that's what you said. Pelagius, our controversial monk? I've not read much of his stuff, but I've heard rumours of heresy."

"That's a matter of opinion, or rather malicious whispering. No one's ever made a formal accusation. I have an open mind, which is one reason to meet him. We've exchanged letters on and off, and he's sent me material he's written and asked me for comments. I've met him. I did tell you, but you probably don't remember – or weren't listening." Galeria gave a benign smile.

"Where?"

"Here. At our villa. He came for a couple of nights."

"Where was I? And what brought him here? I thought he was from the east, Cantium or somewhere further north?"

"I think you must have been off campaigning with dear General Maximus…"

Cecilia Galeria Arcadiae, the noble and elegant *domina* of the handsome Villa Arcadius, paused, staring mistily at the charming fountain sparkling in the tiled courtyard. It was a beautiful setting, surrounded by elegant murals, illuminated by shafts of the afternoon light. The February breeze was blowing drops of water onto the imported tiles, and pretending she had to wipe them up, Galeria bent down and dabbed at them with the end of her long silk shawl. Flavius wanted to say: 'Let the servants do that, Mother', but he knew her well enough to give her a moment to compose herself, and he kept his mouth shut, eventually just questioning:

"So, that must have been 69 or 70 when we were mopping up the Pictish hordes from the north?"

"No, no, the lad would have just been a child then. He came when he was about eighteen, so I suppose that would be the Year of Our Lord 378 or thereabouts. I don't remember what you were up to then." Galeria sat back in her chair, with its rounded back of exquisitely carved ebony inlaid with tortoise shell. She smiled again at her son. "Yes, his family is a wealthy Britannic family whose villa lies – or did – north of Londinium. I've never been, but I knew about them. Your grandfather Arcadius had some connection with them; don't ask me what. All I remember is he claimed the family were originally settlers who had fled from Hibernia generations ago."

"If they were Celts, why did they give him a Greek name, 'Pelagios', meaning 'of the sea'?"

"I suspected from what they wrote to me they had actually named him Morgan, but he used the Greek equivalent to fit better into the catholic world of Constantine's *Nova Roma*."

"*Hmm*." Flavius grunted. "Interesting. Go on."

"Well, they wrote to me wanting to know if we could accommodate their firstborn, who was on his way to Rome. They'd decided it would be safer for him to leave from one of the quiet harbours here on the Sabrina estuary. Those horrid Saxons, even back then, had been raiding the harbours on the east coast, and the Picts were still making trouble by sailing down that eastern side to avoid the Wall – despite your alleged mopping!" Galeria added teasingly. "But you know all that. You mustn't let me become a repetitive old woman. So anyway, of course, I said yes, and Severus helped find a suitable vessel going to Rome. The young fellow was on his way to study law."

"Severus! You and he are always cooking up something devious behind my back."

"Not true! You weren't here, and Severus was around, and he knows how to get things done."

"Unlike me!"

"I didn't say that! But you are a bit of a thinker while Severus, dear man, is a doer, which one sometimes needs."

Flavius rolled his eyes. "No matter. The fact is you can't go. It's now far too dangerous to go tripping off to Rome on your own, especially when we enjoy so much peace and prosperity right here."

"Actually, I was planning to take Dilectus along. Show him his heritage."

"Heritage! Funny sort of heritage, being the son of a Celt, even one who was a sworn officer of the Imperial army. Anyway, his mother, also a Celt, by the way, would never agree. Quite right, too."

"I'm not talking about bloodlines. I'm talking about cultural heritage. I'm saying he's been schooled in Roman ideas and customs, thanks to you and Severus, as well as to Elen. She's savvier about the world than you realise, and God willing, he'll be a king one day. I thought your whole mission was to help the Celts sustain the best of Roman civilisation even though so many Imperial troops and even some of the magistrates have gone?"

"You're impossible, Mother, bringing up my abstract ideas to try to win an argument about simple risk. He won't ever be king if the two of you – and whatever faithful retainers from the villa I can spare – are all dead in a ditch somewhere or captured by pirates in the *Mare Nostrum* and enslaved. Or fed to the fish. Seriously, the risks are too great. You'd better drop the whole idea."

Galeria gave her son a look anyone else would have recognised, meaning, 'I'll do precisely what I please. Thank you very much'. But Flavius did not. He was already back to the earlier conversation, puzzling over Pelagius and what on earth that was all about. And in any case, he thought it a safer topic to talk about than the ludicrous idea that an elderly woman, however indomitable, chaperoning a young Celtic prince, could get safely to Rome far less survive once there. He helped himself to a handful of plump black olives from a silver charger. God knows where his mother found such luxuries, given the chaos on the trade routes, and she wouldn't tell him if he asked her. So, he feigned disinterest, only murmuring appreciatively with each mouthful. His mother smiled to herself. She knew what silence implies. She would be going to Rome with little Dilectus and maybe one of her grandchildren as well.

"Tell me about Pelagius's visit, Mother. Did you talk to him? Question him? Presumably, he wasn't a heretic at eighteen."

"Naturally, I talked to him, but he mostly questioned me. He was a modest and serious young man. Except for how very tall he was, he reminded me of you when you were that age."

"Me?"

"He thought deeply about things, and he was willing to question orthodox ideas."

"A sure sign he's a heretic!"

"That's where you and he differ. He wasn't trying to be sarcastic, clever or witty all the time. He was kind of intense. In fact, I thought he rather lacked a sense of humour. I think that's true of a lot of pious young firebrands who have extreme ideas. I remember I was telling him about the beautiful new baptismal font I was having designed when he suddenly blurted out: 'Why would you baptise infants?' I was a bit taken aback and started to say, 'Well, because of original sin, of course', but before I got the words out, he said something like: 'Babies couldn't possibly have any sin, any more than they have a moral sense'. Well, you can imagine I was just thrown by this; it seemed he didn't understand anything about Christianity.

"I wanted to change the subject but made the mistake of challenging him: 'Don't you believe in original sin, one of our fundamental theological principles?' And he just laughed and said, 'Of course not, and neither would you if you read Genesis in the original or in the first Greek translation', and then he added, 'don't get me wrong; I do believe in baptism but only when children are old enough to understand what it's all about and that they are voluntarily entering the Christian community'. Well, I quite liked the sound of that once I'd got over the shock. In fact, I remembered his words when I persuaded General Magnus Maximus to be baptised here at the villa before he launched his misguided campaign to be emperor. He was a devout Christian believer but had never been baptised. I think it was by accepting God's grace that he became such a committed defender of the Nicene Creed and prosecuted those awful Priscillians. What do you think, dear? Surely *you* believe Adam's sin has stained all mankind?"

"Well," Flavius replied cautiously, not wanting to provoke his mother, "I like the sound of this Pelagius fellow, although I don't have any evidence of Maximus becoming any less sinful. But as to the Hebrews' story of Adam and Eve, I've always assumed it was just… a story. A good one, but purely allegorical, so you can't infer too much from it." He stopped abruptly, aware of his mother's worried expression. "Come, Mother, enough of this. You know, I prefer Greek philosophers to modern-day prelates telling us about the nature of man's soul, relying on scripture rather than observation and critical thought. Let's change the subject."

"All right, but I want to tell you one other thing that challenged me at the time. Pelagius later asked me why I hadn't married again after the death of your dear father at such a young age. My initial reaction was 'None of your business', but I held my tongue and told him what I've always told you and your sister: I'd made a promise to God that if He accepted your father's soul in heaven, even though he was a rich man, I would never marry another man and commit myself to use our wealth for the good of the community. At that point, a strange thing happened. Young Pelagius dropped to his knees, kissed the hem of my gown and said something like 'Lady Galeria, you are the most holy of women if that was your choice, of your own free will. You've given me new insights'. Something like that, anyway.

"I was a bit embarrassed. Didn't know what to say but got him off his knees by telling him supper was ready – wow, could that boy eat! I've never seen someone tuck away so much food. Cook told me Pelagius ate three bowls of porridge at breakfast before Severus got him out of there and onto a ship bound for Portus.

"Come, dear, it's getting chilly out here. Does the furnace need stoking? The floor is stone cold. When is spring going to arrive? Aren't you cold, son? I've got my shawl. We should go inside. The wind's getting up. Would you like some chamomile tea? You know, with the markets being so erratic, I've been growing my own chamomile flowers right here in the villa gardens? I got some *manzanillius* seeds sent from Hispania. They're superior to the Egyptian variety grown in Gaul, which was getting too expensive."

"Ah, my mother, the gracious Roman *domina* who discovered gardening in her dotage."

"Make fun if you like, but I must tell you I was deeply struck by young Pelagius being so intensely curious. At supper, he continued to ask me lots more questions about how I reconciled our obvious wealth with rumours of my interest in Mani's asceticism and the value of poverty, and I tried to explain that although we were rich, we were also thrifty and if Christ wanted us to treat each other with kindness, God must have given us the freedom of thought and action and self-development to be able to make a difference in the world. He admitted that because he came from a privileged family, he was struggling with the same issues himself, and I'd given him extremely helpful ideas to think about. I tell you, dear, he was very well educated. I congratulated his parents. His Latin was smooth; he said he could read Hebrew, and he claimed he was totally fluent in Greek, but I didn't dare test him because my Greek's so rusty."

Flavius stood up. There was one sheltered corner of the courtyard that still caught the late afternoon sun, such as there was. He stretched out his hands to help his mother out of her chair – lately she was always blaming the weather of Britannia Secunda for her aching joints.

"So, it was you, my lady gardener and lover of fine things, who was the inspiration for a heretic," he said as he started to shuffle the chairs. "I'll order some tea and see if I can call Flora to work her demiurgic powers."

Galeria put her hand playfully over his mouth. "*Shush*. It's not funny. There are wicked heresies everywhere these days; enough idle pagan chatter."

Flavius wandered off to find someone to make the tea but first quickly sidestepped into the villa library, where he did his work and his reading. There were two young men, students of his, who were busily filing books and scrolls away, and, in the corner, an older man was painstakingly copying a manuscript Flavius had managed to borrow from the local bishop.

"Hey, you three, stop what you're doing and do me a favour, please. Find anything we've got here in the library archives related to the monk Pelagius."

The scribe's eyes narrowed, and Flavius noticed.

"It's all right, Brother Molio, there's no need for alarm. My mother insists he's a pious man who seems to have been misquoted a lot. I'm interested in learning more and if he ever corresponded with my mother. Anything you can find on him would be excellent, any mentions in church documents, any letters he might have written, especially personal stuff, anything you can dig up."

A voice from an antechamber growled: "You've got bigger problems than some silly monk, old chap, however pious. Important news from the imperial court."

Chapter 3: News From the Empire

"Severus! You mad dog! When did you get back? And what are you doing skulking in the library – I didn't know you knew your way here. You only pretend you can actually read."

Severus grunted, coming out of the shadows and hugging Flavius, lifting him off the ground despite being a good foot shorter. "This ain't goddamned funny, old chap. I was waiting to talk to you while you were nattering to your mother like one of her cronies in the marketplace."

He looked around furtively and dragged Flavius by the arm out of earshot of the scribes in the library.

"I've got a letter. It came today from Mediolanum by special *cursus publicus*. Has the imperial seal. The real deal. It's from your namesake, Flavius Stilicho. He's been named Regent to the boy Honorius. And we know what that means."

Both men fell silent. Snatches of gossip, hearsay, rumour and many whispered stories raced through their minds. They knew full well it meant trouble. The imperial court in Milan was so remote it might as well have been on the moon. But they knew General Stilicho's reputation and his distinction in battle. Everyone of importance in Britannia had learnt that with Emperor Theodosius's death, the Empire was divided, and one of his sons, ten-year-old Honorius, had been named Emperor of the West. The implications suddenly became a lot more complicated now they'd discovered the commander-in-chief of the Roman armies was emperor in all but name.

"At least he's a Christian and follows the Nicene Creed," Flavius finally spoke, thinking of his mother's criteria for acceptability.

"I don't give a damn what creed he follows." Severus growled. "As long as he's willing and able to control the Goths. What's left of my family in Illyricum says those pigs in Moesia are constantly threatening them. Their leader is planning a campaign against Constantinople."

"I hear differently. I think Theodosius screwed those auxiliary Goth troops right royally at Frigidus River last year. Sent them into battle from a bad position. Half of them were killed. It's rumoured Theodosius did this deliberately. And we know he was devious enough to have done so. It's not surprising the Goths are furious. But anyway, Sev, as you are here and not in Illyricum, why the hell did *you* get a letter?"

Severus gulped, uncharacteristically shuffling his feet, and did not look Flavius in the eye. Even a friendship of his entire lifetime didn't allow him to predict what Flavius might think when it touched on his speciality of world affairs and matters of state and political tactics.

"*Um*... to be honest, he wrote to me himself. Personally. He wants to promote me to *Comes* and to reassemble and mobilise the army in Britannia in preparation for him coming here next year – or as soon as he can – with a couple of legions to deal with the Picts once and for all and drive them and the Scoti back across the Vallum Antonini, or what's left of it, to re-establish, as he called it, a secure northerly frontier for the Empire'."

"Jesus, Sev, that's brilliant! *Comes Brittaniarum*, resurrected! I salute you, sir! Congratulations, my dear old friend. He's picked the right man. What's the strength these days of the field army you'd be commanding?"

"Well, some of the best units have already been packed off to Gaul, but there are six regiments of cavalry and three of infantry – about six thousand men from every nation of the Empire. A rag-tag bunch, I tell you. They're going to need a shit load of training. I'm going to need your help."

"You know I've retired. You don't need a philosopher; you need a *primus pilus*. But there are at least three things wrong with what you've just said. There's no Roman province in any real administrative sense, and secondly, wild and dangerous as the fuckin' Picts are, they belong to these islands, they're ours, like it or not, and they're far less a threat than the foreign Saxons. The Picts have their traditional land so far up north that no one else of sound mind would want it, whereas the Saxons aren't just raiding – I'm worried their goal is to settle. And then take control. They'd be the new Romans but substantially less civilised. So, the general had better also appoint you, *Comes Litoris Saxonici*. And number three, I've heard the troops defending the lower wall, perhaps 'living in' is more accurate, are Frisii mercenaries and their women folk. God knows how trustworthy or combat-ready they are. Sounds to me like Stilicho is offering you a rapid entry to the underworld, presuming you can't be destined for Paradise on account of your never going to church."

"Not true!" Severus protested. "I took communion just last year in your mother's chapel. I'll admit she had to nag me to get me there. But I haven't agreed to the commission. That's why I'm here talking to you. He wrote that with Maximus dead and denounced as a usurper, he can see why we – he included you specifically – had refused to follow a traitor to Gaul, so there'll be no more talk of desertion. But if Stilicho comes here and realises what's actually going on and sees for himself what we've been up to… Well, shit, we're all going to be executed for treason or mutiny or insubordination."

"Or all of those combined," Flavius interrupted cheerfully, "since there's no word for what we've been doing, striking our own alliances and elevating a local chieftain to a sovereign position in the name of Roman law, which is about as fragile around here as your grasp of Christian theology and your once-a-year embracing of the blessed sacraments." Flavius was laughing now at his own gallows humour.

"Laugh all you want, but tell me what to do. You're the thinker. I just follow orders."

"Oh yeah? Since when? Maybe those that suit you. But you're right. This might give us an opportunity, especially if we can give the man a Pictish war if that's what he's hankering after. Of course, you must accept the honour of the promotion. No question. We must set you up in respectable headquarters; we'll dust off Isca Silurum. Let Stilicho come with some disciplined troops and something to pay them with. Personally, I think he'd be more useful standing up to the Goths, treating them fairly from a position of strength – Oh damn, I've totally forgotten about Mother's tea in all this excitement. Let me find someone to make it and then you'll have to join us in the courtyard if it's not too late to find your favourite afternoon sunny spot."

Once the hugging and exclamations of delight at Severus's appearance were over, the three of them were seated around a low marble table while a young serving maid hovered around with a plate of sweet almond biscuits and refilling their cups with tea, although Severus had begged for posca with a little cumin, thyme and salt. They'd switched to Latin, so the maid wouldn't understand. It was all too serious.

Galeria watched her son and his best friend slip into a classic male discussion style in which the fate of thousands was being planned the same way she would work with the villa's gardener to plan next season's herb plantings. They weren't ignoring her and would sometimes stop and explain a military detail to her or even – surprise! – ask for her opinion. But she was enough of a third chariot wheel to allow her own concentration to drift, pretending to follow the discussion while simultaneously reflecting on the two men and her feelings for them.

Her son, Flavius, lean and still handsome despite touches of grey in his wavy dark brown hair, impeccably dressed in a toga, was gesticulating with his hands and arms as though to guide his thoughts directly into the mind of his friend. Sometimes, he would bend down and illustrate a point by lining up some pebbles on the courtyard tiles, saying, 'Here's Stilicho's troops when he comes over, here you are with the army you've been able to muster, and here are some crazy Picts', as he scattered around the imagined countryside of northern Britannia the olive pits he'd earlier left in a neat pile on the table.

This was her complicated son: an army officer who hated fighting, a strategist who knew more about the heroic stand of the Spartans at the Battle of Thermopylae eight hundred and seventy-five years ago than he did about the true strength of Stilicho's auxiliaries, a man who was half Hispanic and a quarter Roman, who thought of himself a Briton. Although she was confident her intellect matched his, she recognised his privileged life and upbringing had given him a sense of confidence that allowed him to persuade others as well as himself of the inevitable correctness of his beliefs and opinions.

Then there was his friend, Severus. Blunt, uncomplicated Severus, who said what he thought regardless of his audience. Ethnically a Celt, but born on the continent, not Britannia; a soldier and a commander, hard as nails and a ferocious fighter, but showing his years far more than Flavius, though they were of the same age and had grown up together as boys. He grunted as he lent down to move some of Stilicho's pebble legions, revealing the scars on his outstretched arm, while his gut suggested his fighting days were now more given over to wine and steak-and-kidney stews, with more kidney than carrots. But Galeria loved him for all those features and most especially for his loyal defence of Flavius as boyhood friends struggling to survive life in military encampments. She knew he was utterly trustworthy, without guile, and his warmth towards her masked a well-controlled male urge Flavius showed towards no women. She loved Flavius as a son, and she loved Severus as a man.

Galeria re-focused on the discussion. She could guess what might be coming. She had quite some time ago decided the world she knew was galloping to an end. And while she felt no fear for herself – her time on earth was equally close to ending – she worried constantly about her daughter and her son-in-law and her grandchildren and the old family retainers of the villa and the community. Her community. A Christian community – on most days and on Sundays – which she'd helped create under the protection of her villa while the might of the Roman Empire was visibly crumbling over the past ten years. And as for Rome herself, Galeria knew the fate of the villa, indeed all the villas in Britannia, hung on the fate of that city. The villas were like acorns on a huge and powerful oak tree, green and thriving only as long as the Eternal City, the centre of the inhabited world, stood strong. If the tree became diseased, all the tiny acorns would fall to the ground and be carried off by squirrels or eaten by wild pigs rooting for food.

It had all been so different in AD 349 when she had come to the villa from the great family estates in Hispania as a new bride of fifteen. She had been totally devoted to her young husband, Arcadius. They had shared the same sense of humour and the same confidence in Christianity while taking the gospels as more a guide than a prescription. This was one reason, and she was willing to blame herself entirely, why her son had such disdain for dogma. She was always interested in ideas, especially around unanswerable questions. She didn't think one little Greek letter differentiating between *homoousios* and *homoiousios* could make much difference to her faith in the teachings of Jesus Christ. Same or similar substances? Who cared when it came to worshipping, He who promised salvation to all mankind? Surely, only opinionated men would ever insist on debating something so unimportant and, worse still, fighting over it.

She was grateful Arcadius's father had insisted on modernising the villa, as he had told her 'with my only son bringing home a refined Roman lady'. She was grateful that well before, the elder Arcadius had eliminated slavery at the magnificent villa and the surrounding lands, granted to their first Roman ancestor by Agricola himself, for outstanding bravery in the summer of AD 63. Agricola encouraged the development of villas throughout Britannia and educating the sons of the powerful as ways of Romanizing the tribes.

Galeria knew from Tacitus's account of these historical events that Roman bravery was matched by bravery from the Caledonians, who suffered fearful losses. She worried about the native tribes of her adopted country and whether civilisation would endure or whether the warrior chiefs would revert to barbarism. She worried whether Elen, heir to the adjacent united Celtic kingdom, had the strength of her dead husband Caradocus to enable her and her son, darling little Dilectus, to survive the uncertain future. The accord between the Silures and the Demetae had been engineered by Flavius using a Roman model of power-sharing, with Caradocus, a Demetae and a Roman officer providing the diplomatic savvy. How long could it last after the demise of King Conanus? Elen needed a second husband. Hopefully, she wouldn't make the choice that she herself had made – with any luck, the priest serving the Garn Goch community had never read anything by Jerome or heard of Augustine, the brand-new Bishop of Hippo. The combination of religious conflicts, imperial ambitions, and the irresistible pressure of Huns on the tribes of Germania, were threatening an already unstable world. The strength of family was more important than military conquest or religious schisms in her worldview. She had to interrupt and ask Severus if he had any news of her two grandsons.

"Severus dear, sorry to interrupt your big campaign strategising, but all this talk of war is disturbing. You may remember my daughter Aurelia and her husband Lucius grew a little tired of helping out with our village school and work in the parish generally and have taken the huge step of relocating to Londinium. They're starting up a mercantile company. There's so much trade coming through the River Tems now, and seven of our best roads converge on the town. They might be a good contact for getting supplies and provisions you'll need, especially if you'll be relying on the *Classis Britannica*."

"*Ha,* my lady! For once, I'm ahead of you! My two boys have been working in Londinium for years now, and because they're both in the Procurator's office, your son-in-law has already contacted them. The boys, as I foolishly still call them, were delighted to be in touch with folks from home who wouldn't laugh at their Cymru accents."

"Well, thank the Lord, that makes me feel better. But I'm afraid Aurelia's boys, unlike your sensible ones, were dead keen on a military career. I think it was partly their uncle's notoriety that influenced them (Flavius shook his head vigorously but didn't interrupt). Both Marcus and Rufus Lucius are now junior officers in some elite guard unit."

"I wish I'd known that earlier," Severus muttered. "I could have helped them. I wonder where they might be quartered. Do you know? We dismantled our fort in Londinium ages ago. A mistake. There are field army units scattered around there and there would be a *comitatus* unit for sure providing protection for Victorinus – if he's still governor – they've been disappearing faster than a flagon of ale on a hot summer's day. Anyway, once I take up my new commission, I can look out for them. I remember Marcus as a cocky kid around here. He should go far. I don't remember the other boy."

Galeria got up and kissed Severus on the cheek. "Thank you," she whispered. Severus was a rock. Like Simon Peter, the rock of the Church. Someone you could always count on. What Severus and Flavius were planning was clear. The two men would use their influence to martial a well-armed force from the militias of the local chieftains, assemble the Roman field army in Britannia and march to join Stilicho with his legions – hopefully plural – wherever he landed, presumably Dubris. They would then guide the general north, collecting additional auxiliaries as they went but not stripping the pitifully weakened garrisons of the nine 'Saxon Shore' forts. Once at the Wall, they would cross into the lands of the Novantae and the Selgovae – or what was left of them – and persuade them to join in one final subjugation of the unmanageable pagan Picts.

Galeria was horrified at the callous way they discussed these options, never suggesting a treaty or sending missionaries to convert them to the true faith. If the fragile hold of Christianity was to endure on this far-away green island, the serious effort had to be directed to preventing the pagan Saxons and their buddies, the Angles and the long blonde-haired Jutes, from getting a foothold on the land of the Celtic Britons. But the Romanized tribes up north had been constantly whining to successive emperors about Pictish harassment, and now Stilicho was going to come and take care of the situation once and for all. He cleverly selected Severus as the most capable local commander, past sins forgiven and promoted the one man who would be able to muster the total loyalty of what was left of the Roman forces in Britannia.

Stilicho, big on military detail and remembering how effective Celtic chariots had once been against the Roman army, had recommended in his letter that Severus assemble at least one chariot-based unit. But both Severus and Flavius, who had campaigned in the north as young officers, knew the rugged Caledonia highlands were not suited to chariot warfare, and the Picts had a habit of using guerrilla tactics, striking ferociously and then just as surprisingly fading away into the mists of the lakes and hills. Once the two men were discussing such details of supplies, weapons, horses and, most importantly, whether Stilicho's boss, the boy Honorius, could come up with the bags of money essential to stopping any conscripts from deserting or worse still, mutinying, Galeria decided she'd heard enough. With Severus back from wherever he'd been, she needed to slip off to the library and prepare a note to Senica, his loyal wife, inviting her down to the main villa and telling her the news that her sons and Galeria's own daughter and son-in-law were in touch. She knew Senica couldn't read; few women could, but she'd have one of the servants deliver the note. Someone who could be trusted to state its contents in clear terms. Stepping into the library, she bumped into a monk scurrying out with his arms full of documents. Many fell to the floor.

"Whoa, Brother Molio! You're in a big hurry! Let me help you pick those up."

"I'm so sorry, my lady, apologies, apologies. Please don't trouble yourself. I was coming to find Dominus Flavius. He asked me to find some manuscripts for him from the library, so I'll just rescue the ones I dropped."

"Wait a minute, young man, back up. I recognise some of those. Aren't some of them from my private correspondence? I recognise the velum I use. What was it Flavius wanted you to find?"

Molio hesitated. This was awkward. He did not want to get in the middle of a family conflict.

"Oh, he just asked casually if we had any material in the library pertaining to Brother Pelagius, including letters. I looked for the name only. I read nothing. I'm so sorry if some of these items are yours. I had no right."

"No harm, no crime. My son should have been more precise with his request. I'm just going to look through what you have and take out any personal items and letters that are mine and I'm going to pop them back in the library. Or, on second thoughts, I'm going to take them to my chamber. Let me hold everything while you go in there. Find me a leather binder or some good ribbon, so I can keep my correspondence neatly in one place."

Molio, looking more and more stricken, reappeared with a handsome leather folio. Galeria carefully placed a few velum pages and some rolled-up paper inside and smiled at the young monk.

"There you go, Bother Molio. Give everything else to Flavius. Just don't drop them again! But tell me, what do you know or have heard about Brother Pelagius?"

Molio now looked like a hare cornered by hounds. Everyone adored Lady Galeria and was terrified of her at the same time. He desperately tried to think of the right answer.

"Nothing, I'm afraid, my lady. I know he is a Briton, and he has been preaching in Rome. It is said his ideas conflict with those of Pope Siricius, especially the papal edict priests should leave their wives when ordained, but I don't know if this is true, and I do not have any opinion on the matter. I try not to have opinions," he stammered. "I myself am utterly celibate," he added, hoping that was the right assertion and would stop the questioning, despite his abstinence being due to lack of opportunity rather than any theological conviction.

Galeria smiled at him again, which scared him all the more, pursed her lips and nodded slowly, but it did not seem she was in complete agreement, whether about the need for clerical celibacy or the virtue of young monks having no opinions.

"You'll find Flavius in the courtyard, Brother Molio. I'm sure he'll be pleased with your research findings. It might take his mind off the Picts. They need to hear the Gospel, in *my* opinion. Would that not be wonderful? Why do these men never seem to think of negotiating with troublesome people – discover what they want and what it would take for them to agree to stay in one place?"

She moved down the passageway to her chamber, neither expecting nor wanting an answer. Senica's invitation would have to wait. Timid scribes like Molio were not likely to spread Christ's message. It was up to tall, hungry preachers like Pelagius to shape the world. She clutched the embossed leather folio filled with his letters close to her chest. She had to go to Rome to see him again.

And Molio, still shaking, moved stealthily down the passageway to find Flavius. But not before he had carefully taken a cluster of manuscripts out of the pile and tucked them inside his long, coarse, brown woollen tunic. He re-arranged its large sleeves to conceal any tell-tale bulges.

"Here you go, Dominus," he purred, handing a small sheaf of material to Flavius, who was still crouched over his plan for a military advance by an army that didn't yet exist. "This is all we could find in the library. I hope it is what you need." The serpent in the Garden of Eden could not have put on a more innocent look.

Chapter 4: Spies, Politics and Gold

Severus spent the next many months engaged in organising and training the army units gathering at the huge castra nearby, known as Isca Silurum to the Silures and Isca Legionis to the Romans. Being practical, Severus just called it the castra, or more frequently, 'my castra'. There was so much talk of Stilicho coming soon with men, weapons, and money that it had taken on the same expectations as the second coming of Christ. Severus used the excitement to motivate his men. Desertion was a chronic problem despite the severe punishments if caught. Intensive training, close-order drills and discipline had been the keys to Roman army success in battle, often against armies many times larger. But for at least the past hundred years, with the conscription of men from immigrant tribes with little allegiance to the Emperor or the Empire, winning only meant looting. Severus, aware of their many limitations, had decided that regular pay, encouraging personal loyalty and the legendary allure of Stilicho's name were stronger incentives than any thoughts of defending homes and families from raids which affected almost none of them personally.

Flavius was focused on gathering intelligence. The groundwork had been laid twelve years ago. Back in AD 384, after defeating Gratian, usurper Magnus Maximus had set up his imperial headquarters in Treverorum. This was also the seat of the Gallic prefecture, which had administrative control of the western provinces, including Hispania, Gaul and Britannia. With its impressive gates, comfortable palace, fine basilica for the bishopric, pleasant situation on the Moselle River, and superb local wine, it was a popular place for many different emperors over time. But it wasn't quite as important as the centres in Italy, like Milan, Rome and Ravenna. It was thus an ideal place for Flavius to post two well-educated young men. The two were in mundane mid-level civil service positions and Flavius doubled their basic salary as a retainer. Their only task was to keep their eyes and ears open, find out what was going on politically and militarily, and report back to him in Villa Arcadius, sometimes by dispatches, sometimes in person. Galeria knew something of the arrangement and had once called them, not inaccurately, spies. However, both Flavius and Severus, who were partners in the venture, had no qualms, knowing how important it was to have accurate information on the endless intrigues and power struggles that would eventually affect them and threaten their security.

The latest report that arrived, along with a collection of religious pamphlets and correspondence from some of his intellectual friends, was quite disturbing. The report detailed for the first time more information about the obscure new leader of the Goths. Something significant was going on. The man was an Arian Christian who had once held a senior officer rank in the Roman army. His name was Alaric. It was only now filtering through the news that the terrible casualties sustained by the Goth *foederati* troops at the Battle of Frigidis two years ago might indeed have been engineered or at least welcomed by Theodosius and his general Stilicho. Allies to Rome in name only, there were plenty of reasons to hate Goths after the Adrianople disaster, even if it was the snooty soldiers from the east who had been massacred. Whether the rumour was true or not, it is perception and suspicion that ignites ill feelings. Flavius's informants confirmed this Alaric person had resigned his commission in the Roman army, declared himself 'King' of the Goths and promised his men and his people that from now on he would seek their own kingdom rather than always being used, lied to and betrayed by someone else. They were going to look out for themselves in future. No more dutifully serving others, specifically Roman emperors.

Flavius immediately recognised the danger of an aggrieved and desperate tribal nation – some were calling them the Goths of the West or Visigoths – going on a rampage through Greece. It was not a happy thought. Anti-barbarian prejudice was spreading, not only in Rome but also in Constantinople, where they were referred to as 'skin-clad savages'. Without a settled agricultural homeland, Alaric and his Visigoths were obliged to pillage for survival. Sometimes, cities would happily send out provisions as an alternative to being besieged or attacked. Apparently, the tumult, as writers at the time described it, had proved to be too much and Stilicho had led a campaign against his former comrade in arms. He sailed from Italy to

Greece with his army, surrounded Alaric, and was in a position to destroy his power for good.

At this point, as Flavius explained to Severus later when they were pouring over the most recent dispatches, "My informants claim that everyone is amazed that Stilicho didn't finish Alaric off, there and then. Some say because he is a half Vandal; he's actually a Goth sympathiser. Others suggest Arcadius and his advisers in Constantinople are so threatened by Stilicho that they'd prefer to have a strong Goth presence in that region. So, that's why, they ordered Stilicho not to engage and even recalled some of the Eastern troops under Stilicho's command, forcing him to back off."

"Crazy fuckn'politics," Severus muttered. "It makes my head spin. They're all so devious. They're teaching this Alaric bloke not to trust anyone. Why don't they offer him what he wants or needs? Come to think of it, that wouldn't be a bad idea for dealing with the Picts and Scoti. My recruiting and training are going slowly. It's probably two years before we're ready to go north. I hope we can trust Stilicho. But I ain't counting my chickens."

"Are you and Senica keeping chickens now, Severus, dear?" asked Galeria, breezing into the parlour in a long silk dress and matching shawl, carrying her embroidery in a knitted bag with carved wooden handles. She settled herself in one of the cushioned chairs.

"No, Mother," Flavius answered, "we were lamenting the duplicity of our great and most divine leaders and their angelic henchmen."

Severus made his excuses and left the room. He didn't want his friend to go on one of his political rants, which he sometimes did to provoke his mother, who saw the good in everyone. She cleverly changed the subject.

"D'you remember, darling," Lady Galeria asked, looking up at Flavius from her embroidery, "that spring when I want up to Viroconium to see Bishop Viventius? What year was it? 384? General Maximus had just established himself as Augustus of the Western Empire."

"How could I forget! It was when you went secretly to meet with Elen."

"Not true! She sought *me* out. I had no idea that's where they were hiding. I needed to talk to the bishop about getting a priest and a schoolteacher down here."

"Correction! So?"

"So, what you may not remember is I stayed two nights with the biggest landowners in the region, the Vitalis family, in their gorgeous urban villa. They're linked with the Cornovii but as Roman as you and I."

"Oh, sure! Posers like us, you mean! I know their reputation – an ambitious and powerful family. They claim rights to that peninsula that points to Hibernia, and they have land near Glevum and Ratae. And some smaller estates quite close to us. What of it?"

"So, they were looking for a suitable wife for their eldest son, called Vitalinus – in Latin, anyway, after his grandfather. He would have been about twelve or so and showing promise scholastically. He didn't seem cut out to be a warrior, but they thought he might be suitable for some senior admin post in the Empire. They wondered if I had any connections with important Roman families. Well, General Maximus had told me a couple of times he was worried about finding husbands for his two daughters."

"Oh, Mother, the matchmaker! Not a likely conjugation at all. For sure, Magnus Maximus was constantly nattering me about how he was looking for husbands of high rank for his girls. In fact, as you know, he managed to marry off one of his daughters, Flacilia, to the Proconsul Africae. I don't know what happened to the other one."

"Well, I do!" Galeria exclaimed in triumph. "Give your old mother some credit. I knew Maximus would consider even a wealthy family of Celts to be far too lowly a match for his youngest daughter, Flavia Sevira, but after he was executed, the situation looked rather different, didn't it? Dead men can't be proud. I suppose I should be grateful Theodosius spared Maximus's wife and the younger daughter – they'd sought protection from Bishop Martinus of Tours."

"Mother dear, I don't have all day. Is this convoluted story going anywhere?"

"Rude and impatient, as usual, dear boy. Of course, it is. Knowing the family was still in danger, especially after you told me Maximus's young son Victor had been murdered, I sent letters to Bishop Martinus and my friends in Viroconium suggesting they discuss marriage between their son Vitalinus and Maximus's daughter, Sevira. Naturally, I sought her mother's approval as well – the poor woman has been through so much and is not at all well. She's living in a convent that Bishop Martinus started. It took a lot of negotiation, but my idea was brilliant. Sevira is a highly connected young lady but in dire financial and political straits, and the Vitalinus boy, now about twenty-two or twenty-three, still hadn't found a suitable Roman wife. Anyway, to cut a long story short."

"Slightly shorter!" Flavius chuckled, but Galeria ignored him and went on excitedly. "It's finally happened. I've just received an invitation to their wedding: Vitalinus and Sevira, the daughter of Magnus Maximus, the real Macsen Wledig! How about that?"

"Mother, you're amazing! When I think how hard I've been trying to preserve the best of Roman culture and way of life during these dreadfully troubled times, here you go with all your wiles and connections, maybe keeping the links between the Western Empire and Britannia alive. The poor girl won't have much of a dowry – Maximus's estate was confiscated."

"Bishop Martinus found a way to scrape up a respectable dowry. You know what incredible assets these prelates have. Fortunately, he himself is very frugal, but he also loves to share – you must remember the cloak story. And he's an old man now, in poor health, so I imagine he doesn't feel any need for the wealth he's managed to accumulate. Still, it was generous. The only sticking point in the negotiations was that young Vitalinus, much to his parents' surprise, is supposedly a Pelagian. Turns out Bishop Viventius up there is like me and has become quite enamoured of many of the doctrines and has influenced the young man."

Galeria smiled to herself as she pretended to concentrate on her stitches. Using the purist silver thread still obtainable if you had the money and the contacts with Hispanic merchants, she was embroidering a crucifix on a snow-white piece of the finest linen from Hibernia. It was to serve as a napkin to cover the chalice during communion services in the little chapel she had built for the villa. She wondered if she could stitch the words SANCTUS PELAGIUS into the hem of the napkin without offending too many people. Smiling even more broadly, she thought better of it, and even though none of the common folk and few of the servants in the villa could read, she started instead the letters in their native tongue: DUW CARIAD YW.

Flavius stared at her. His mother could never be described as inscrutable or enigmatic. Her facial expressions gave her away as readily as the spoken word, but the implications of what was being given away were never absolutely clear. Smiling clearly meant she was amused, but *what* was amusing her was unknowable, even to Flavius. Was it the thought of General Maximus's progeny living on, the spread of Pelagian thought or just the joy of a politically and strategically meaningful marriage that was amusing her? Her final words caused a flash of anxiety:

"They're an ambitious family, all right. The young man has adopted the Celtic title of 'overlord' – Vortigern. A little presumptuous, wouldn't you say? But an ambitious landowner with a wife from an aristocratic Roman family, however impoverished now, looks like someone to be reckoned with in the future."

"Are you going?"

"Where?"

"To the wedding."

"I haven't decided. An aspiring social climber like Vitalinus Vortigern is a potential threat to our villa and our community here. Do I want to try to get on his good side or keep him at arm's length?"

"Goodness gracious, you're beginning to sound like me! You're not usually suspicious."

Galeria gave her son, the philosopher, a quizzical look. "I'm not sure suspicion is the right word – strategic is more apt. Like you, I can anticipate the future by remembering the past. Ambition and lust for power has been the curse of Roman civilisation, and I've no reason to suppose an increasingly autonomous Western Britannia will be any different – after all, we keep telling the barbarians they should be more like the Romans!

"But I *have* thought of a gift to send. In the treasury, I have a golden torc of the most magnificent Celtic workmanship, with braided and twisted threads and beautiful lion-head terminals. I'm not sure you've ever seen it; it's strictly feminine adornment. I had once thought that if you ever…" Galeria's voice trailed off. She quickly got back on track. "Well, anyway, I don't imagine Sevira will ever want to wear it. It must weigh two or three *libra*. But if she does, it will help her fit in with the local culture and she'll never see finer workmanship. I think a gift like that will easily exempt me from attending the actual wedding unless sheer curiosity forces me to go."

Just at that moment, shrill children's voices could be heard from the villa's adjacent courtyards. There had been an audible conversation for a while, but it had suddenly escalated into a quarrel.

"That sounds like my granddaughter," Galeria said. "Who's she arguing with?"

"Dilectus, I'd guess. He's always bothering her because he doesn't have anyone else to play with when he's here and Severus hasn't managed to exhaust him with weapons practice. Sev gets worn out long before Dilectus, so he lets him off early. So, then he goes and finds Claudia Augusta. I'll go and sort them out. All that talk of your gold torc has got me thinking it's time for a lesson that would benefit both of them."

"Fine, go make peace, but don't forget dinner will be ready soon." Galeria turned and looked at the clepsydra hanging on the wall, squinting her eyes as she tried to read the level. "At least I hope it will be; my tummy's rumbling, whatever that silly clock says."

Across the villa, on the west side, the setting sun was still bright enough to challenge both the clepsydra's level and Galeria's tummy. Claudia had been trying to finish sewing a dress. Her grandmother's exquisite taste had made her conscious of the latest fashions on the continent, and she was struggling to gather the fine Egyptian cotton under the garment's bust line without success. The problem wasn't her needlework. It was being constantly interrupted and distracted by Dilectus, who was trying to get her to play a game with him. She usually enjoyed fooling around with the boy – he was pretty smart for a nine-year-old – but she needed to get her work finished. Her grandmother was surely about to summon them to dinner.

"Just scram, Dil, you're like a giant horsefly, buzzing around."

"But, Claudie, you *prom*-missed if you finished your work, we'd have time for something fun."

"I did, but you can see I'm *not* finished, so buzz off and take that whiney voice with you. Why don't you go practice throwing your little dagger at a tree trunk and see if you can ever get it to stick in the way Severus showed you? That could keep you happy for hours."

At that moment, Flavius entered the courtyard. He was carrying an oak chest with silver hinges and set it down with a loud thump on the table, gently pushing aside Claudia's dress-making supplies. Claudia and Dilectus had never seen the chest before and stared, fascinated, as Flavius blew some heavy dust off the lid. Claudia snatched her dress material out of range. Dilectus sneezed.

"I could hear you two bickering from the other side of the villa, and I thought I might rescue you, Claudia Augusta, by giving Dilectus a quick history lesson."

Dilectus grimaced, and Claudia smiled. Dilectus knew Uncle Flavius could drone on for hours once he got into a topic, and Claudia knew she could easily escape now – history wasn't for girls, even though her grandmother had insisted she be fully educated. But that was all years ago. Getting ready for marriage was her priority now. She started to gather up her material.

"Don't go, Claudia," Flavius said, "this will be useful for you too. You're soon going to need to know how to manage a household budget, my dear."

Flavius pried open the clasps, lifted the lid with a flourish, and removed a layer of red silk. The two young people stared transfixed. The chest was full of coins, gold, silver, bronze, large and small.

"I know you've both had experience of spending money at the market, but a large amount like this is a different matter. When you grow up and become king, Dilectus, your treasure, or should I say treasury, will determine what policies you can introduce to help the people of your tribal lands and how you can pay your fighting men for your and your family's protection. And for you, Claudia, your access to money will determine your family's lifestyle. The coins in this box represent some of the wealth of this villa. It's our security. There is more, much of it hidden away in safe and secret places. But this supply, right here, is what guarantees our ability to operate this villa. Let me explain."

Flavius's fingers ran through the clinking coins, flashing in the late afternoon sunlight. He found what he wanted and took out two coins. He placed a large gold one in Dilectus's outstretched hand and a similar-sized, silvery one in Claudia's palm. Neither of them had ever seen anything other than small bronze *assaria*, which bought them sweet treats or a rare piece of fruit in the market.

"It's heavy," Dilectus exclaimed. "Let me feel yours, Claudie. *Hmm.* About the same size, but a lot lighter. Why is that Dominus?"

Flavius smiled at the honorific title – not Dilectus's usual cocky style. "Because one is silver, and one is gold."

"I knew *that*! But why is gold heavier than silver?"

Flavius looked pleased. "What a good question! I don't know. Why are both of them heavier than Claudia's long, sharp bone needle she's been using? What makes some things heavier than others of the same size? I think it must be some special property of the substance, like its spirit or maybe its persona. Just like you, Dilectus are brave and curious and can be a nuisance, and Claudia is kind and, well, we all know it, a bit bossy! So, gold's persona is to be heavy and soft; it is its mystical, satisfying weight that's made it so alluring to all the peoples of the world since the dawn of civilisation. It's easily worked by craftsmen, never rusts, suitable for decoration, for jewellery, even for platters and goblets, but not for swords. To get a decent sword, you have to change the persona of iron by hammering it out repeatedly in a charcoal furnace, and the more you hammer it, the harder it gets, just like the Picts and Scoti. But you're both distracting me. I wanted to show you what is on these coins. Look at this gold one, Dilectus, and tell me what you see."

"Well, on this side, I see some old guy with a big nose and flowers in his hair."

"Good lord, you're a disrespectful young whelp, my boy," Flavius responded cheerfully. "They're not flowers; they're rosettes, and they're very grand. And that's a Roman nose, very aristocratic and greatly admired, not like your little Celtic snub nose! Read the writing and tell me who it is."

"D. N. MAGMA XIMVS, then more letters, P, F and A, V, G. I can guess AVG is short for Augustus, so this is an emperor. What does DN mean?"

"Good start. DN stands for *dominus noster*, and I know your Latin is good enough to know what that means."

"Our lord!" Dilectus exclaimed in triumph. "What about PF?"

Claudia, feeling a bit left out, piped up: "*Pius* and *Felix* – pious and happy. According to Grandmama, he was pious but not happy."

"So, you know who this is?" Flavius asked, visibly impressed.

"Of course! Magnus Maximus. Grandmother Galería told us you were hiding from him for years, although she liked him and cried when he was executed."

"I wasn't exactly hiding; it was more like avoiding. But let's not go there. I want Dilectus to explain what's on the other side."

"Two people in long skirts, sitting down and holding a round thing between them, and above them a little person with wings, around the edge more letters or words. Could be VICTORIA and then AVGG, and AVGOB at the bottom."

Claudia couldn't stop herself from giggling. "If it says 'victory', then that's no little person in the middle there. It's Winged Victory! Romans love that symbol, the pagan goddess of victory. Even though she was Greek!"

Flavius looked at her admiringly. All that education his mother had insisted on for all her grandchildren had paid off.

Dilectus was less impressed. No one likes to be outsmarted by a girl. "OK, smarty pants, why are the two ladies sharing an apple? And who's AVGG?"

Flavius looked at his niece quizzically. Should he say anything or let her work it out? He waited.

Claudia was a little more hesitant. "I'm only guessing, but I think they aren't ladies, Dil; they're emperors in togas like Uncle Flavius wears, and what they're sharing is the whole world between them. And the double G could mean two Augustus's. Two emperors sharing the world would be Magnus Maximus in the West and Theodosius in the East, but that can't be right because Theodosius was the one who put Maximus to death. They weren't friends. I've no idea who Augustus O B is, but those letters at the bottom."

"Clever girl," Flavius's admiration was genuine. "In the year this coin was minted – that means struck or made – which was the Year of Our Lord 384 – Theodosius had grudgingly accepted Maximus's claim to be Emperor of the West. I knew Theodosius; I served with him under his father who came to help us restore order after the guards on the Wall mutinied and allowed an army of crazy riffraff to run around the country killing people."

Claudia, seeing where this could go and worried they might miss dinner, interrupted.

"What about the letters AVGOB?"

"*Ah*, that's what I wanted to explain to you both. Very important. They tell you exactly where it was minted: Londinium. One of the finest mints in the Empire."

"Augob sounds more like someone spitting than Londinium," Dilectus chimed in.

"So, what you don't know is about a move to change the name of Londinium to Augusta, as in 'empress', in honour of its growing importance to the province of Britannia and the Empire. Because Claudia is such a take-charge kind of girl, we nicknamed *her* Augusta from an early age, didn't we, dear?

"Anyhow," Flavius continued, not waiting for an answer, "coin designers use codes because they can't write everything out. AVG stands for the mint in Londinium, sometimes called Augusta, O stands for the Latin word '*obrizia*', which I'm sure you won't know means embossed by, which for a coin is the same as minted or made by, and the B, being the second letter in the alphabet, means the coin was made by the number two man in the mint."

Claudia, again thinking this was all getting a bit out of hand, and Dilectus, who was shuffling about clearly losing interest, couldn't help butting in: "But, Uncle Flavius, you're always telling us you're a *Briton*, not a Roman!"

"I am what suits me at the moment," Flavius tried to interject, but Claudia was moving on.

"Show Dil the coin you put in my hand. It's silver, right? It looks a lot older."

"It is, my dear. Here, Dilectus, look at the emperor with a beard on this silver coin. It's Hadrian, so that makes it about two hundred and seventy-five years old. It looks brand new because someone in this family saved it for its silver, and the amazing thing about our Empire is that it's still legal tender anywhere in the whole wide world. But look at the other side, where it says 'BRITANNIA'. What do you see there? A woman is holding a spear in the crook of her left arm while her elbow is resting on a massive Celtic shield. Her right leg rests on a pile of rocks – maybe the wall Hadrian was building? – and her head is resting against her raised right arm. Pretty relaxed, wouldn't you say?"

"Who is she?" Dilectus demanded.

"She's us; she *is* Britannia. It was a Greek idea that in art, you could represent different countries as women. She's a Briton, ready to fight but relaxed, thoughtfully accepting, serving willingly as the newest province of the great empire. So, now, I've given you a lesson not only in money but in politics and in art. Hadrian must have been pretty sure Britannia was secure and pacified. One day, Dilectus, your face will be on the coins of your kingdom, not a Roman emperor's. I've been nagging your grandfather to set up a mint so he can issue coins for his kingdom instead of hoarding Roman ones."

"And Claudia will be the lady on the other side of the coin. I'll order it," Dilectus added grandly.

"Thanks, Dil," Claudia said, rather pleased, "I'll hold you to that promise, and the words around my gorgeous body can be 'Claudia Augusta'!"

"There' won't be any rulers, and there won't be any dinner unless we get to the dining hall," Flavius muttered, retrieving the two coins and closing up the chest. He was pleased, but his forehead was wrinkled into a frown. Dilectus was quick on the uptake and as sharp as a fox. He was already imagining himself giving orders and being in charge. But Claudia was more intelligent, or was it just that she was older and had had more schooling? He couldn't be sure. But without children of his own and with his two nephews, Claudia's older brothers, being off on military duty on the Saxon Shore, he suddenly realised his sister's youngest child was a force to be reckoned with. And thank God for that. The villa was going to need every resource it could muster, with his powerful mother fading in strength and vitality. It was exciting to see a new generation that could potentially continue his work of managing the transition from a Roman province to an independent, civilised Celtic nation – confident, free, self-sufficient Britannia with spear and shield and her foot firmly planted on the rocks of the land.

Chapter 5: Garn Goch

A year later, ten-year-old Dilectus was back at Garn Goch, the site of massive fortifications that were the seat of his maternal grandfather's kingdom. His mother, Elen, didn't know when her father's fortress was first built. Neither did he – nor his father, nor his father before him. In fact, no one could even imagine back four thousand years to when their earliest ancestors first climbed what they called 'the red hill' and built a cairn of stone at the very top. Something – most probably spiritual fervour for a majestic burial mound – drove the people to haul huge slabs of rock and then erect them, pointing to the clear sky by day and the brilliance of stars by night, so bright and dense that clusters of them looked like milk splashed across the dark sky.

But if, at first, it was the mysteries of life and death that inspired them, they soon recognised the practical benefits of settling their dwellings clustered on the hillside. Eight hundred years before the birth of Christ, huge earth mounds had been built around the crest of the hill as protection from the neighbouring tribe, the Demetae, though they were never that much of a threat to the fierce warriors of the Silures. Through songs and stories, everyone now knew that massive stone ramparts were then built on the earth mounds, and substantial wooden buildings were erected to house the local chieftain in considerable style: Y Gaer Fawr, the big fort, it was called. To accommodate new dormitories, luxurious bed chambers and a planned second meeting hall, a connected the smaller fort was started: Y Gaer Fach, the little fort. And then the Romans came.

Like all colonial powers, they came for the gold, the tin, the iron. Slaves were a bonus if anyone tried to challenge them. The Demetae saw the inevitable and formally accepted Roman sovereignty. The Silures, renowned for their belligerent spirit and their skill with horses and chariots, fought off the Romans longer than any other tribe. Inspired by Caratacus's staunch resistance in south-eastern Britannia, the Silures followed him to the last great battle against four Roman legions commanded by the governor, Publius Ostorius Scapula. A Roman army in that century was an unstoppable force. Inevitably, the Celts lost. Caratacus – called Caradog by the Celts – was betrayed and taken to Rome in chains. There, according to Tacitus, he pleaded his case before the Senate, and his eloquence moved them to spare his life: 'I had men and horses, arms and wealth,' he stated proudly. 'Are you surprised I parted with them reluctantly? If you Romans choose to lord it over the world, does it follow that the world must accept slavery?'

Like Caratacus, the Silures still refused to surrender. To discourage further active rebellion, another Roman governor decided to weaken their threat by demolishing the six fortified stone gates on Garn Goch. Roads and smaller forts were built at strategic points throughout the western region, and a large, permanent castra became the home of Legion II Augusta. A *vicus* was developed nearby.

With passing years came reluctant acceptance of the Roman occupation. Silurian chiefs, without declaring peace, became complacent. Other tribes were no longer a threat and Pax Romana had indeed delivered the promised prosperity. Extensive farming outside the walls ensured a steady food supply, with excess to sell to the legions at considerable profit. The Romans had introduced hornless white-faced sheep with superior wool and tastier meat, but the native horned sheep and goats were sturdier and could be allowed to roam freely. The small black endemic cattle of the region needed hedged or walled pasture to allow routine milking. Water was always available in low-lying bogs and small riths, and there were fat trout in the streams flowing into the Sabrina estuary and fat salmon and eels in the river itself. The wild mountains nearby were home to good-tasting boars and feral hogs, undomesticated sheep, hares and roe deer. When young men with something to prove could actually catch one, the brown mountain bears provided wonderful furry skins for bedtime comfort. Beavers were hard to trap, but when you were successful, their pelts made warm scarves and hats. Wolves were a nuisance because they scared the horses and sometimes the children at night, but their numbers had been declining recently, which no one regretted.

Living within the Empire for the past three hundred and fifty years, they had adopted Roman ways far more deeply than they recognised. The tribe had turned the *vicus* into their *civitas* capital and market town near the great Roman barracks of Isca Legionis, now often called Isca Silurum. Farmers, bakers, blacksmiths, potters, wheelwrights, horse breeders, carpenters, tilers, weavers, loose women were in constant demand and making good money. They learned to speak, read and write Latin well enough for the schoolchildren of the wealthier families to be taught from Tacitus's history the defiant speech the captured Caratacus gave in Rome that spared his life.

Though dominated culturally and militarily by Rome, everyone, including Elen, had to admit that being within the constraints of the Roman Empire meant that tribal warfare had been put on hold for centuries. And the people flourished. Trade increased. The Romans introduced exciting new fruits and vegetables that were easily grown, such as apples and plums, asparagus and carrots and happily imported figs, dates and olives. Grapes became popular, but cultivation was difficult, and all wine was imported from Gaul and Hispania. Luxury consumer goods flowed in from the east as Phoenician and other merchant shipping was protected by the Roman navy. Local craftsmen, not ashamed to imitate useful and attractive products, learnt how to make their own versions. Rich Celtic landowners and noble families hankered after the luxuries that Roman settlers enjoyed. Elen's father, with little effort of his own, was a wealthy man. His kingship had been negotiated by clever people from the villa, who had their own ulterior motives. Even her centurion husband, an up-and-coming officer in the Roman army, had, as a Demetae himself, contributed to the diplomacy – he had implicitly accepted Flavius's goals of working with, not against, those tribal chiefs who could be trusted.

Meirion, son of Rhonwen, father unknown, was teaching Dilectus serious riding skills, the kind you needed for jumping streams and ditches or using a slingshot or bow or javelin while at full gallop without stirrups. Meirion had known the boy since he was a new-born, when he, Meirion, was the right-hand man to the boy's father, Caradocus, one-time Centurion of the Imperial Army. Caradocus would have been surprised to hear the lad's status described this way, but Meirion was as skilful at self-promotion as he was at handling horses. In a more Roman context, when not surrounded by fellow Celts, he'd use the name Marianus and describe himself as master of horse, chief scout and herald to the one and only the great warrior, General Severus. There was just a smidgen of truth in all these appellations. Severus had indeed employed him in two of these roles, and as he usually brought life and death news back to the Villa Arcadius, you could, at a stretch, allow him 'herald' as well.

Regardless of title, the more consequential circumstances were that both Severus and the late Caradocus had paid Meirion handsomely for his services. Being a canny fellow, he had saved carefully and eventually bought himself several horses – quite cheaply, as they were yet to be trained for both hunting and combat. Being in good graces with the higher-ups at Garn Goch had also enabled him to move into a small but sturdy timber house within the great expanse of the ancient fort. As briefly an apprentice, could that person be considered a right-hand man? – to Caradocus's construction enterprise, Meirion had acquired sufficient skills in woodworking to make many improvements to the house, such that anyone observing his status in Garn Goch would not have judged him to be the son of the head cook but of having some nobility in his own right.

As is so common in self-important people, Meirion's harmless conceits masked a degree of insecurity, although it was concentrated in one area only. And that was what Elen thought of him. Capable, serene Elen, who had once nearly cut his throat with a dagger when he was at his lowest ebb in life, starving on the streets of Viroconium Cornoviorum. Now, being essentially master of the Garn Goch stables, where he also kept his own horses free of charge, gave him sufficient recognition to be widely accepted. Chief Conanus was undoubtedly the military commander, but his age and growing frailty allowed Meirion to be the one who gave orders. With everyone else except Elen, he managed not to take himself too seriously – he had a great sense of humour, often had adventurous ideas, knew the countryside like the back of his hand and could playfully tease the truly important people without offending them. Best of all, he was witty and kind, and Dilectus loved him as though he were a substitute father.

Caradocus had been murdered when Dilectus was only nine months old, and naturally, he had no memory of his father. His mother, Elen, told him lots of good tales about his father's bravery, goodness and loyalty to both Rome and his Celtic ancestry. If Meirion aspired to be a father figure, he had much to live up to.

As Meirion, on his slender Nabataean horse, bred for speed and cooperativeness, led Dilectus on a smaller, sturdy Cymru pony around the central courtyard of Garn Goch, Elen could see them both from her window when she opened the shutters. They didn't yet have glass windowpanes like at the villa, so she let in the fresh and not too chilly air of late in an April afternoon. It struck her how much Meirion had matured since she'd first met him, sick and starving and scared witless in the back streets of Viroconium. He'd grown a little taller now, although still half an *uncia* shorter than she was. And although he was still thin, he no longer had the lanky look of a teenage boy. She noticed how good-looking he was when confidently riding a beautiful horse and helping her son manage a shaggy and not overly friendly mountain pony.

Meirion looked up and saw Elen in the window. He gave her a cheerful wave, as one would to a close friend, not the heir to the Silurian kingdom. He then said something to Dilectus, and the boy turned, looked up, saw his mother and shouted to her. Elen couldn't hear, but she guessed he was saying, 'Look at me, Ma!' She waved with both hands in acknowledgement, feeling just a trifle guilty she had actually been staring most closely at Meirion, not at her son. She moved back from the window and closed the shutters.

Elen was widely recognised as the most beautiful woman in all of Britannia. That most people who had actually seen her had never been more than twenty miles from Garn Goch did not deter them from their certainty of this fact. However, wise people who had travelled far and wide, people like Flavius and Severus and even Galeria, who had come from Hispania as a young bride, all agreed with the assessment. Most of them were well-read enough to be able to make a comparison with another woman of the same name – allowing for the Celtic spelling of the Greek – one Helen of Troy, whose story went back fifteen hundred years. The name Elen, meaning beautiful, bright, shining like a ray of sunshine, certainly fitted this stately woman of twenty-seven years, who had just closed the shutter enough to allow her to continue reading the letters on her table.

One of the letters was from Villa Arcadius. It was in Latin, which meant the words were easy to read, but the meaning of some of them she did not know. The other was in Celtic but in Roman script, which made both the writing and the meaning challenging, even though it had clearly been dictated to a scribe. It had come from Ceredig, Chief of the Demetae people over on the west coast of the country and a man who was in a close and formal alliance with her redoubtable father, now frail and in poor health. As far as Elen could make out, it was a proposal for marriage. There seemed to be some claim that his household at the mouth of the Afon Teifi was most comfortable, and the coast from there to Mynyw was a rich source of delicious seafood and the deadly raids from Hibernia had largely ceased. Apparently, he assumed that linking the Demetae and the Silures by marriage would mean the administration of the kingdom would shift to where the Afon Teifi flowed into the Hibernian Sea. Chief Ceredig was at pains to remind her, at the very end, that his wife had died – not long ago but sufficiently distant to be seemly.

Elen, the widow with the stunning looks and glorious body and razor-sharp mind, had had plenty of offers of marriage once she'd returned to her father's household as his only surviving offspring. It had been easy to dismiss them out of hand. Her sadness at the death of Caradocus was still too raw. But now, seven or more years later, she could see the dangers of further hesitation. For greater security from the combined threats of Roman retaliation and the envy of other Celtic neighbours, the two tribes had managed to come together, under the delicate manoeuvrings of Flavius and Severus, to forge one unified kingdom. A marriage would tie everything together as tightly as a laminated bow and with the same strength and flexibility.

It was obvious to anyone that her world, relatively stable and even prosperous for over three hundred years of humiliating Roman occupation, was coming to an end. Unlike their Demetae cousins, her tribe had never formally made peace with Rome. But that didn't stop the Romans from demanding taxes, prohibiting the rebuilding of the fortifications of Garn Goch, or insisting trade and commerce were subject to Roman law. Flavius had convinced Chief Conanus, her timid father, a great bear without teeth, that Roman authority no longer applied, and they were free to form their own kingdom. They weren't, of course, not for a moment, but without any army muscle to enforce it, Roman authority had even less teeth than Chief Conanus. The fact was that being separated by sea from the rest of the Empire meant that the benefits of the Britannic provinces to the imperial centre rarely justified the costs of maintaining a presence there. The declining tax revenues had been a source of frustration to many emperors, especially as taxation was what they relied on to maintain an efficient

Roman military machine. Effective Roman control had ended in the spring of 383 when General Magnus Maximus had marched his troops off to Gaul. Some troops had returned but never this far west. 'What the fuck now'? was what everyone was asking, one way or another, and so they were all making it up as they went along.

Both the old compromises and the new agreements were painfully ambiguous. The new town magistrates collected revenues, regulated prices and trade, controlled the currency and imposed Roman law, but what about the traditional tribal laws and procedures? When a far-off emperor who had taken ill in Thessalonica, wherever that was, declared Christianity to be the official state religion, where did that leave the beliefs and practices of the common folk? And which Christianity anyway: Gnostics, Nicaean Catholics, Monarchianists, Arians, Marcionites, Priscillians, Donatists, Origenists, the list went on? Zealots who defaced pagan shrines were not very influential in changing the daily practices and beliefs of nonliterate people, but they successfully created many others who were simply confused and a few who were equally extremist in the opposite direction.

The lack of clear lines of authority and inconsistent enforcement created confusion despite their all being Roman citizens now. This pleased those with money, land and influence who could command retainers, but it confused a lot of the old people and the poor people. At the level of the powerful, who used religious beliefs for their own ends, the internecine rivalries and resentments of the tribes had not disappeared – some were poised silently like a pack of wolves being kept from the carcass by a great lion. And when, not if, this Roman lion was to weaken, they were ready to drive him off and fight among themselves for the pickings. Elen understood the situation in the symbols of the natural world around her that she knew, not in the political abstractions of Galeria. But their reasoning – or their vision – was the same and the anticipated consequences identical and equally frightening.

Elen was troubled by how easily that smooth-talking schemer Flavius Arcadius from the villa had persuaded her innocent father, Chief Conanus, to call himself a king and claim he was anointed by God. God was fine, but what about the ancient Celtic deities and spiritual beliefs? Was the Roman church going to decide for the uneducated which days were holy and work could be abandoned, or when the oats should be planted, and what needed to be done to ensure regular rainfall and sunshine for the farmers? Not to mention Lady Galeria's odd idea about everyone sharing in the farm labour as a community. Could people trust their neighbours to own the pigs jointly, and who was to decide who would feed the hens and how would the eggs be shared? There were many doubts, and if Elen, who was well-educated, shared them, she could see it was getting worse.

Her dear departed husband, Caradocus, was a Roman soldier. He had access to all sorts of intelligence about raids to the east, the out-of-control Picts and warriors from the other side of the world who fought buck naked, constantly encroaching on the Empire's borders – however much you hated Roman domination; the Goths sounded worse, and the Huns were from hell itself. And so, Elen was forcing herself to become worldly, wise and knowledgeable about extreme threats and how to anticipate them. What did she need to do to protect her son and the lands she was about to inherit from her father? She needed to be more decisive.

Elen looked again at the letter which had come from Lady Galeria. The messenger had brought baskets of goodies as well – Hispanic olives and olive oil, dates from the Holy Land, spices that were so hard to come by these days, and a collection of dried herbs she said had come from the Villa Arcadius gardens, which made Elen feel guilty. She knew she should be organising similar bucolic activities. She had been good at sending out some of the women folk to gather dandelion leaves and watercress and other edible plants, but they were just growing wild and hadn't been planted to help feed the families. She definitely should get more advice from Galeria about how to do all that sort of stuff.

But all this was trivial compared to what she could make out of Galeria's second paragraph. It sounded like Galeria was proposing to take Dilectus with her on a trip to Rome. Jesus Christ and all the Holy Martyrs, what was the woman thinking? It was pure madness. True, they had a good relationship. Dilectus had spent many hours at the Villa Arcadius. Severus was teaching him the basics of sword fighting, and Flavius was teaching him to read in two languages. Galeria would gather her grandchildren and other boys and girls in the community and tell them wonderful stories about the heroes of Rome, about Jesus's disciples and the early Christians who had been fed to the lions, and occasionally, she would add some wild tales from Virgil about the ten-year travels of a minor Greek king called Ulysses.

She was more like a grandmother to Dilectus than his true grandmother, Brangwen, who had died from severe gastric pains and fever when he was only two years old. He was quite comfortable with Lady Galeria, which surprised grown-ups who found her intimidating. But Dilectus had her wrapped around his finger, and, in Elen's opinion, she reciprocated by spoiling him rotten. And now she wanted to take him to Rome. Well, that wasn't going to happen. Never. Would it be reasonable to ask Meirion his opinion of such a foolhardy idea? She might need some arrows to her bow if she was going to resist any pressure from Cecelia Galeria Arcadiae, regardless of their past intimacies.

There was no escaping the obvious. She'd have to pay Galeria a formal visit. No point in writing about her objections. She wasn't as adept with the written word; when she spoke, however, she could command a room, even a great hall. She would take Dilectus along. He could show Severus how well he could ride now. He'd love that. So would Severus, although he'd be sparing with his compliments, if any. Meirion could come along, too. He'd be welcomed at the villa. But what could she take for the ever-generous Galeria, a woman who had everything and more? '*Wait. I have an idea*,' she said to herself.

Elen trotted down to the huge kitchen of the fortress to find Rhonwen. Rhonwen had been the chief cook for as long as she could remember and had always looked out for her as a little girl. It was Rhonwen who had helped engineer the elicit and dangerous liaison between her and Caradocus. She gulped, thinking of it, feeling a twinge of guilt she'd now been fondly contemplating Rhonwen's son, Meirion. But Rhonwen wasn't there. Her daughter Sioned was giving orders to some of the kitchen staff. She turned and saw Elen.

"Elen! I mean Milady! How lovely to see you! It's been days! What's happenin'?" Her warmth and pleasure were equally genuine. Elen hugged her.

"Stop with the 'my lady' nonsense! After all, we've been through together; we're sisters and a couple of soul mates. But, actually, I came down here to find your mother. I've just been watching Meirion give Dilectus a riding lesson and I wanted to tell her what a fine man her son has turned out to be – as if she didn't already know."

"Mum's taken the day off. She does that more and more these days. I keep telling her she should retire, but this is her domain, and she can't leave it. Your father might be the king now, but this kitchen is Mum's kingdom. I come down on days she's really tried to try to help out, but you know I'm a hopeless cook myself, so I just give garbled orders and hope the staff will improvise. I'm not so sure about Meirion, however, he seems too big for his breeches sometimes. If you were watching, I bet he was showing off. He's always trying to impress you."

"Spoken like a true big sister!" Elen wanted to get off the topic. "But if you *are* giving the orders, could you give some for me? I've got to make a visit to someone who keeps sending gifts, so I've been trying to think of something I can take that she won't have. Do you remember how Caradocus – may the Lord guard his soul – told us about how the men in his legion who were from near Rome used to dry strips of donkey meat? It keeps forever and is delicious."

"D'you think anyone will thank you for donkey meat? I've tried it when we were poor and it tastes awful, and it's tough as saddle leather, not that I've ever tried that."

"You idiot! I'm not going to take her *donkey* meat. You can do the same thing with strips of sheep meat or venison, and you can keep it tender if you take the strips from the top of its lower back. What did Caradocus use to call it? Something like a little couple, or *pauloduobus* in Latin because you join two strips together."

"Like a couple in bed together!" Sioned exclaimed.

"Shut up! How would I know anything about that? I've long forgotten."

"Well, don't look at me either. There's a serious shortage of suitable partners around here, and I'm very flexible – don't get me started. Tell me more about how to make the copulating meat strips, and I'll organise it for you."

"Thanks, Sioned, you're such a treasure – a grossly rude one! That's it! No more wisecracks. You're coming up to my quarters with me right now; we'll have some warm wine, and you can tell me why you're in such a giddy mood. Have you met a new—?"

"I wish! Someone, anyway. I'll be up in a moment. Let me make sure they know what they're doing down here, and I'll wash my hands and join you. Better be good wine; my tastes are getting more patrician."

Back in Elen's private quarters, the two women sat together on a wooden bench well covered with a thick sheepskin rug and four of five pillows of stitched calves' leather, filled with goose feathers and covered with a silk pillowcase. Elen had clearly come to appreciate some of the finer things in life. A servant brought in some warmed wine in a copper pitcher, but the goblets were made of wood. One of the consequences of the renewed attacks by the Scoti on unarmed Phoenician merchant ships bringing their famous glassware to remote Britannia.

Elen stroked the woolly white sheepskin throw and smiled. "Sitting here with you, I feel so Celtic and so proud of our people. But when I'm over at the villa – or what Galeria insists on calling the village – I feel and behave quite like a damn Roman. I've become bicultural thanks to living with an officer of the Roman army for three years. It feels weird. I don't think you are confused about *your* identity. You're so Celtic. One look at you, and everyone will know you're Silurian. Oh, and guess what? I've had a letter from Lady Galeria. Came today."

"Truly? The Roman tigress?" Sioned interrupted. "Lady *Formidulosa*! Is she the one you are going to tame with strips of dried mutton?"

Elen clapped her hand over Sioned's mouth, knowing her feisty, red-headed, freckled Celtic friend was joking. Sioned had put on a little weight but was toned and hard-bodied, so different from when they had found her in Viroconium, nearly dead from malnutrition and food poisoning. Why hadn't she found a husband? She didn't seem that interested. *Ah* well...

"*Shush,* dear, enough with the only Latin word you know! She's not that bad. She helped me – us – in direct opposition to her son; he's the scary one. I'll always adore her for that. She saved our lives by never revealing our hideout."

"Bold talk now, safe in your family stronghold. You used to be terrified of her. So anyway, what does she want, apart from a visit?"

"She didn't ask me to visit. But I'm going to have to, and you're going to come along. I've got to put a stop to a plan she's cooking up." Elen closed her eyes as if it would help her next words feel less real. "She wants to take Dilectus to Rome."

"In chains, like brave Caratacus and every other Celtic slave they have abused?"

"Don't be silly. We're citizens of the Empire now – or we were before my father unilaterally declared our independence – God knows what we are now. Anyway, Galeria is well connected – she's got relatives all over the continent, quite probably the world. But I can't let him go; it's too dangerous."

"You think? Good God, Elen, why are you even repeating such a mad idea? Is she finally away with the fairies?"

"No, I think it's a mixture of her fantasies of Rome as the Eternal City and wanting to indoctrinate him in Roman culture so that…"

She didn't finish her sentence. At that moment, Meirion burst into the room without knocking, panting and shaking.

"Is he in here with you two? Is he here?" he shouted, looking around desperately.

"Who?"

"Dilectus. He's missing."

Chapter 6: Boy Missing

Surprisingly, Meirion was too frantic to be helpful. Elen leapt to her feet, grabbed both his hands in hers and said calmly but firmly, "Look at me, Meirion. Take a deep breath. He can't be far. We'll find him. Have you checked with his grandfather? He loves to visit the old man."

"I did before I came here. I didn't want to worry him. I only asked if he'd seen the boy this afternoon. He hadn't. Oh Jesus!"

"Stop it right now!" Elen commanded. "Just tell us what you know. Slowly."

"After his riding lesson, I made sure he went to the stables to take care of his pony. When I went back to check, the horse was rubbed down and tethered properly and had a fresh straw and a bag of oats. But Dilectus was nowhere to be seen. One of the servants said he thought he saw him heading for the main gate. I grabbed my horse and rode over there and confronted the sentries. They're idiots. They said, sure; they'd seen two boys about the same height skipping past the gate and going down the hill. They didn't recognise either of them."

"Well, what in God's name are you so worried about? Dilectus knows some of the boys who hang around here and live on the local farms. He's gone off with a friend and will be back soon – as soon as he gets hungry, trust me." Elen allowed herself to sound relieved.

"But I rode out to find them. You know how dangerous the countryside can be. I rode around all the likely places, but there was absolutely no sign of them. And it's getting dark out there."

"You should have organised a proper search right away, not gone gallivanting about on your own," Sioned protested.

His sister's rebuke and Elen's reassurance finally allowed Meirion to kick into his usual take-charge mode of operation. He straightened his back, grabbed Elen's hand and squeezed it.

"I'll find him, Elen," he said earnestly, staring intently into her eyes. "I've got four good men saddled up and ready to ride. They've got torches lit – that won't light up the paths too well, but maybe the children will see them from afar. And one of the hounds is especially fond of Dilectus. I know they're not tracking dogs, but I thought if we gave him the lad's clothes to sniff and kept saying, 'Where's Dilectus'? nice and clearly, he'd get the idea and try to sniff him out. Worth a try. I'm going. Now, please keep calm."

Elen and Sioned watched him dash to implement his plan and rolled eyes at each other. The only person in the room most definitely not calm was Meirion. But to further reassure herself, Elen ran through in her mind the various things she – or more likely Severus back at the villa – had taught Dilectus about survival. The night wasn't cold, and it wasn't raining, which was unusual for April. He'd been dressed for riding did he have a cloak? She couldn't remember. Surely, he couldn't be lost? He had been out with her and other members of the household lots of times – just last autumn, for the Lughnasa festival at the beginning of the harvest season, they'd been roaming the surrounding hills picking bilberries. She looked out of the window. Damn. There was no moon. But Garn Goch was on the highest hill and could normally be seen for miles around. Meirion had a good idea about the torches. She called for one of the retainers she trusted and asked him, without causing a fuss or asking questions, to light one of the braziers on the highest point of the fort's ramparts. Doing something helped pass the time. Sioned poured her a large beaker of wine.

Their anxiety peaked again when the first of Meirion's men came clattering into the courtyard. He'd found nothing. Soon, the other three returned. Same story. Then, for one joyous moment, Elen saw Meirion ride in with a boy in front of him on the horse. But as soon as someone held up a flaming torch, she could see it wasn't Dilectus.

Meirion dragged the boy off the horse.

"This is the boy who ran off with Dilectus. His father found him hiding in one of his barns. Stupid little bugger was too scared to come clean, but his father and I persuaded him. Now, you rascal, tell the princess what you told us before I whip you again."

The mention of the princess was about as helpful as the threat of another hiding. The boy just stood there, his mouth tightly closed and tears streaming down his face. His sobs were punctuated by sharp intakes of breath.

Elen took his arm, and he flinched.

"This isn't going to work," she insisted. "Sioned, could you find some hot soup in the kitchen and a blanket? He's shivering so much that I think his teeth will fall out. Now, boy, come and sit with me. What's your name, son? Speak up. You aren't in trouble if you tell us everything."

"Caradog, miss."

"Well, my, my. There's a good, strong, brave name. Now, act like your heroic namesake and speak up and tell us what's happened."

"I found this little boat. Round like. Floats good. Rescued it from the marsh. Dil and I, we were going to go try it out."

"I think he means a coracle," Meirion interrupted knowingly. Elen nodded. She knew that would have interested Dilectus. But she suddenly panicked.

"Did you go out in it? Dilectus can't swim. Can you swim, Caradog?" Caradog shook his head.

"You didn't go out, or you can't swim? Where's Dilectus now? Did he…?" She couldn't utter the word drown.

Caradog shook his head more vigorously.

"We never went out, miss. We were looking at the boat to see how it worked and two men came up to us. They grabbed Dilectus, and I ran off. I thought they were men from the chief's house sent to find him. Dil was kicking them. They both held him. I went home and hid."

He started to cry in earnest again. Sioned, who had returned with hot milk, Elen and Meirion looked at each other. What did it mean? At that moment, panting hard, Caradog's father appeared and cuffed the boy hard.

"Stop your squealing in front of our princess," he yelled. Caradog cried even harder.

Elen addressed the father. "Have you heard of any men who do not belong here hanging around the area?" The man shook his head.

Meirion had another moment of inspiration. He crouched down to Caradog's level. "Think carefully, boy. Did either of the men say anything? Did they sound like foreigners or Celts? How were they dressed? Could one of them be a priest or a monk?"

"What's a monk?" Caradog asked. His father shuffled forward with bowed head.

"He doesn't know what a monk is. We're not... we're not... *um*... Christians. We're good folk, but we follow the old ways."

"That's all right. You don't have to explain yourselves to us. But," Elen turned and addressed the boy, suddenly realising what Meirion was thinking, "did one of them have a funny hairstyle?"

"I didn't see nothing," Caradog stammered, "it was dark. They had pointy hoods. I just saw them grab Dil. They said nowt. But as I ran off, I think Dil bit one of 'em, as the man yelled '*Ouch*' and then something 'bout a rat. He used a rude word my pa won't let me say."

"Fine. I think we get the picture." Elen turned to the others, amazingly composed. "This little boy ran off in the dark because he thought they were servants from our household who'd come to fetch Dilectus. That was his instinctive reaction. I think this means they *could* be locals, but not anyone he recognised, so not actually from around here. And one could possibly be our monk. If so, I'm truly worried now. They knew who they wanted. They didn't snatch this boy here. This was no random act of violence by brigands or slavers. Planned, not opportunistic. But we can't do anything more tonight. Mister, take your son home. Let us know if he remembers more. Don't punish him. We're all going to get some sleep. I'm going to pray. There's nothing more we can do tonight. And, at first light, we'll meet and come up with a plan if he's not in the kitchen getting breakfast, which I expect."

Trying to stay calm was a desperate attempt to control her anxiety; getting panicky wasn't going to solve anything. She'd been in tight spots and physical danger often before. But when it's your son, it's totally different. She didn't pray and she didn't get any sleep.

The next morning, Dilectus was not in the kitchen eating breakfast. Elen let Meirion organise the search. It would help him deal with his feelings of responsibility and the guilt of failure. She could best assist by keeping out of the way. So, while every available member of the Garn Goch household was out looking for Dilectus, Elen went to see her father. She had to break the news of his disappearance if he hadn't already got wind of it. But Chief Maccus Conanus – Elen couldn't get used to calling him 'King' – was so forgetful at times that she could never quite predict what he knew and what he didn't.

She found him resting in a big chair in his bed chamber. His eyes were closed, and he seemed to be asleep. Elen stood in the doorway, staring at him. He'd always been a big man, muscular but with a belly that proclaimed overindulgence. He was inclined to be pompous and self-important, especially after Flavius and Severus had managed to engineer his transformation into royalty. Yet his instincts were canny, and Elen was forever in his debt; he had recognised that his three children needed education despite being girls. But looking at him now, so feeble and tired, she suddenly realised that he was old, and like an old bear, he was retreating into a cave to die. His eyes were still closed, and his words took Elen by surprise.

"Well, don't just stand there, girl. Come on in and shut the damn door. You're causing a draught."

"Sorry, Father, I thought you were asleep. I've come to…"

"How can I sleep when the news is so bad?"

"You've heard?"

"I hear everything. I've got the best of the servants well trained. You seem remarkably calm. How can I help? If anything happens to that boy, I'll rain down destruction on whomever or whatever harms him. I can't take another disappearance in my lifetime." He glared at Elen, but she ignored the challenge.

"We're doing everything possible. And I'm only calm because panicking won't help find him. Also, I have faith in his survival skills. He has his father's ingenuity, you know."

"You're probably right. I trust in destiny. I haven't been praying to Lord Jesus. I don't think my faith is strong enough. Your mother was right. We were too quick to abandon our old gods. Jesus Christ can't be much assistance. He knew nothing about our green hills here – he was a desert chap, and he wouldn't know where to help look around here. But despite your increasingly Roman ways, the lad has pure Celtic blood in his veins, although the weak Demetae part might dilute the strong Silurian part. He'll know what spirits to call upon."

Elen gulped. She didn't think that asking for God's help meant that Jesus himself would join the men tromping through bogs and up hills to look for her son.

"I haven't heard you talk this way, Father, for a long time. You must be worried."

"Listen, girl, the lad will be back, believe me. But…" the old man's voice trailed off before recovering, "look dear, his disappearance makes me aware of what I need to do. Your precious mother is dead. Your two older sisters are dead. You and my grandson are all I've got to carry on our family name. I thought I'd have time to see Dilectus become a man and take my place, but this crisis brings home there's no time for that. Boys don't make strong rulers. So, until he's old enough, it will have to be you. That smooth-talking Roman, Flavius, told me long ago that a daughter could succeed and become Queen in her own right. 'Course, I knew that already. Think of Boudica, Queen of the Iceni. I'm going to… shit, I don't even know what to call it. Give up the throne. Step down. Hand over the crown. Make you Queen in name as well as in reality. You're running things here anyway, and damn well, I might say, especially for a rebellious little hussy like you."

"Oh, be quiet, Father. You know you forgave me long ago, and I got married and have been faithful ever since, even after Caradocus's death." Elen crossed herself.

"That's part of what I wanted to talk to you about. You need a new husband. Not just to protect you as queen but to give you more babies. Dilectus needs brothers, especially…" his voice tailed off and tears filled his old red eyes.

"Don't you dare say those words or think those thoughts, Father. Dilectus will be fine. But I *have* been thinking about marriage. My problem is the complete lack of suitable men – I'm still in love with Caradocus, and none can compare."

"*Hmm!* Yes, I forgave you; I never forgave *him*. But I always admired his balls. Excuse me. His courage and his confidence – and his good taste. You'll have to lower your standards. You need to find a new husband and not some old goat with land and self-importance. Someone young and virile, and don't be too picky. When you're hunting and you see a suitable stag, you put an arrow straight to its heart; you don't wait, thinking there's a bigger and better one just around the corner…"

"What a dreadful analogy, Father! Do you know certain of the important Christian leaders are saying second marriages aren't really a good thing? There's a bishop in Hippo."

"Where?"

"Hippo."

"Where's that?"

"I'm not too sure. Somewhere in Africa, maybe. Part of the Empire. Anyways, he says virginity is the most desirable state for a woman, followed by widowhood. A second marriage is a distant third, making it harder for a woman to get to heaven."

Conanus, grinned. "What a massive pile of horse droppings that is. However, remember I am a widower, and I have not remarried, although I've had offers, so I'm pleased to know I am destined for the Kingdom of Heaven. But, clearly, this African bishop knows nothing of the Celtic ways. What about children? What about heredity? I want you to marry and have more children to guarantee our dynasty. I know your friend Flavius was always trying to tell me the Celts elected their leaders, like olden times in Rome. He said that was better than the Romans now claiming their children to be heirs to nobility as well as the family fortune. But the family name is important. Don't you go listening to half-baked ideas from Africa."

"What profound reasoning, Your Highness and silliness! But I hear you. I'll keep an open mind. And believe me, I've had a barn full of suitors. The persistent ones are either very old or very obnoxious and arrogant. That one I rejected flatly just before Christmas a few years ago. I sent him away politely, although he was really offensive if you know what I mean, and he left angry and threatening. Meantime, I've got to get back to find out if there's any new information."

She bent down to kiss the old man's forehead. His eyes were closed. He might have fallen asleep again, but the fierce lines in his old face revealed the strain. Elen felt his abdication was already underway. When she reached the door, he recovered his spirit.

"Wait!" he commanded. Elen turned but didn't approach. "Ask yourself, why Dilectus? That's the key to finding him. Money or power. That's all some men care about. Either someone will demand a ransom soon, or someone wants him out of the way because he's the heir to this kingdom. Think who might benefit. Who are our competitors, even if not yet enemies?

"Elen, you, beautiful girl, there's one other thing you need to consider. You think I'm old and tired. It's true, but so is the Roman Empire. We've not sent the usual tax payments for years now and nothing has happened. Nothing; *dim*. Just think about that. Maybe Flavius is right when he claims we're now independent. But we seem to have exchanged one master for another. He and his cronies in the villa have a strong influence over us – me, certainly, you as well. Galeria is like an eagle soaring over us. Meirion – who I've put in command of security and who's a very good man, by the way, hint, hint – is in tight with and influenced by Severus. Are we trading one overlord for another? I want you to consider that our new Celtic kingdom needs to dominate the villa, not the other way around."

"Father, what I want is to emulate many of their ideas and make use of their know-how. I want a bathhouse and under-floor heating, but there are no craftsmen left who can build such things. I value their library, but are there scholars around who'll teach our children to read? I believe we need the villa and its resources, but we can't be responsible for protecting it. How will we ever be able to share its great assets?"

Her last few words were wasted. Conanus had again fallen asleep. But the final worry he had the energy left to express was an important one. Elen felt the weight of responsibility bearing down almost as heavily as the urgency of finding her son: you need a husband and more boy babies. And work out quickly who are our competitors.

Chapter 7: Captive

Dilectus was scared. More so than he ever remembered being before. He wanted to be sick. His head hurt. After he had bitten one of the men, the shit-for-brains had hit him hard across his ear and pulled a filthy, smelly hood right over his head. His hands were tied behind his back with some sort of cord that was cutting into his wrists, and he was lying uncomfortably on his side on the ground, which was cold. One thing he knew for sure. If he had any chance of escaping, he needed to do what his mother had often told him his father had done – stay calm and controlled and think. Don't panic. *Sounded great,* Dilectus thought. It was hard to do when you didn't even know what was going on, who these men were, where they were taking him, or why.

He stopped squirming around and tried to listen to what they were saying. But the heavy hood or bag or whatever it was over his head muffled the two men's whispered conversation. The few utterances he'd heard from them sounded Celtic but were barely understandable. Think. Fortunately, his good buddy Doggy would have run right back to the great fort on the hill and told everyone what had happened. That meant Meirion and all the armed men loyal to his granddad would be riding out looking for him very soon after his capture. They couldn't be far behind, but how would they know what direction to ride? He should have tried to kick off his shoes.

These two shitheads didn't seem to be in a rush or worried about being followed. They had ridden their horses through a marsh or a bog because he could hear the splashing of water. And lying face down across the back of one of the horses, he could feel water splashing on his bare legs. They were obviously riding so as not to leave hoofprints that could be followed – something else his father had once done, according to his mother's best story. How long has it been? Two days or maybe more. When it was light outside, they slowed down, probably to avoid running into anyone. They changed his position on the horse once or twice without saying a word. He may have slept or passed out. He knew he'd wet himself. This was the first time they had come to a definite halt. He wanted to cry; instead, he strained to hear their conversation as much as he could understand. They didn't talk like the men of Garn Goch and certainly not like anyone at Villa Arcadius.

"We've gone far enough. No one's following us," the taller of the men had decided, "let's spend the rest of the night here and head for the forest rendezvous tomorrow. These overhanging rocks will help if it rains. Dump the brat on the ground and light a fire."

Pulling Dilectus off the horse and onto the ground, the other man replied, "Sounds good to me, Brother Nec."

Nectan slapped him hard across the mouth. "Shut your stupid mouth. Blab again, you idiot, and I'll rip *your* tongue out."

"Ssorry," Petroc stammered, "I wasn't thinking about what the *curialis* told us," he whispered. "But shouldn't we feed him? I'm hungry. I'll start the fire if you're sure no one's on our trail. Where's the bread? Where's the goatskin of wine? I suppose we should give the boy something to drink."

"Why bother? He bit my fucking ear. Don't give him a damn thing. All right, maybe a drop. There's a stream down there. I'll water the horses and bring back a cup for him. We don't want him to die   not just yet!" Nectan let out a loud guffaw.

The two men busied themselves, preparing for the night. While Nectan went to water the horses, Petroc pulled the hood off Dilectus and sat him upright. "Don't fuckin' move, or you'll get no bread." He wandered around gathering sticks for a fire, kindling at first and then larger branches, which must have been too green because they made thick smoke. Eventually, the two men settled around the fire. Petroc held a small beaker of brackish water to Dilectus's lips; his hands were still tied behind his back. "Drink, boy. Now, take a bite of this bread. Chew it well, Dilectus; we don't want you to choke to death."

Dilectus munched on a large crust of bread. It was stale. Whoever these ugly men were or whatever they wanted, he knew they must be working for someone else. They weren't smart, and they certainly weren't important.

"Why d'you call me Dilectus?" he demanded suddenly.

"Cos that's your fucking name, you clod."

"No, it ain't. My name's Caradog."

"Horseshit," said Petroc, "we heard the other boy call you Dilectus."

"That was me. We look alike. You grabbed the wrong boy. Dilectus ran home; that's why no one is following you. No one gives a shit about me, little Caradog. My dad's a sheep farmer. He's probably happy to see me gone. He always says, 'It's time for you to go out to work, Caradog; I can't afford to keep feeding you here at home'." Dilectus stopped. He worried he was overplaying his hand.

Nectan got up and came over and smacked Dilectus hard on the side of his head. "Don't fuck with us, boy, you don't smell like a farmer's son."

"Leave him be," Petroc said. He sounded worried. He lowered his voice to a whisper and sidled up next to his companion. "Christ Almighty, Nectan, did we nab the wrong kid?"

"Don't be so fucking daft," Nectan replied, but he didn't sound too sure. The two men huddled together.

"So," Dilectus piped up cheerfully, "you might as well let me go and I'll walk home."

This time, he knew he'd overplayed his hand. "Dream on, squirt; it doesn't matter what your name is; we're going to sell you to one of the Hibernia raiding ships as a slave. They like little boys – they can play with," he added, leering nastily. "You're just trying to confuse us," he continued seamlessly in Latin.

"No, I'm not, I'm..." Dilectus stopped. He knew his mistake even before the large grin showed Nectan's missing front teeth.

"Well, Brother, how d'you like that? A miracle. A sheep farmer's son who understands Latin." He leaned over and hit Dilectus again on the side of his head, really hard. This time, Dilectus cried out in pain. Smirking at their own cleverness, the two men gathered piles of bracken and made themselves a sort of bed each, with their saddles for pillows. Wrapping their cloaks around them, they kicked some more sticks into the fire and lay down for the night, ignoring Dilectus.

"I got to piss," Dilectus shouted. Petroc sighed, got up and came over with a large knife.

"No more tricks." He grunted as he cut the cord around his wrists and used it to tie his ankles. "Hop over there and piss; make sure you're downwind." When Dilectus shuffled his way back, Petroc took another cord and tied his wrists together, this time in front of the boy. "You'll sleep easier that way," he muttered, checking the ankle rope, which was tightly knotted.

"Might as well try to get some shuteye – here, shift a little closer to the fire. It'll be out soon."

Dilectus closed his eyes but was determined not to sleep. He was scared like never before, but he was angry. He tried to think what Severus had told him about fighting. 'Remember, in a tight spot, anything you can hold and lift can be a weapon. The human body has weak spots – kick a man in the balls or punch him hard on the nose, even if he's a lot bigger than you, you can gain a moment of advantage…' How do you kick a man in the balls when your ankles are tied together, he wondered?

Raising his hands up to his face, he inspected the cords. He sniffed them. They smelled. A smell he knew. Horsehair. He tried biting into them, but they were so tight against his skin that he knew it was futile. Maybe a sharp rock. He felt around him. Nothing. He manoeuvred his bottom closer to the fire. It was going out. There were only embers. He poked at a stick that was partially out of the fire pit. It was poplar or beech, long and straight and hard, just like an arrow. He lifted it from the fire. The end was all that had caught alight, but there was no flame; only the end nearest the heat was still glowing. He carefully turned it around and laid it across the stones at the edge of the firepit, the glowing end facing him. Gritting his teeth, he held his bound wrists up to it and pressed down.

Dilectus didn't really have a conscious plan. He was acting not on instinct but smatterings of past observations and knowledge. He was only ten, but like all the other boys, he had never been protected from gory sights. He'd smelled burning horsehair when donkeys were branded at Garn Goch – Meirion disallowed branding the horses. He'd seen men with vicious wounds from fighting or hunting accidents being treated with red-hot iron; cauterisation was harsh but the only way to save a life or parts of a limb.

In the moonlight, he could see the cords starting to smoke and in the same instant, he felt the burning pain. He pulled his hands away reflexively. How many times had he listened to Flavius tell Plutarch's story of the Spartan boy and fantasised how he, too, would let the fox gnaw at his stomach without making a sound? 'I'm a Spartan,' he whispered and pushed down again on the tip of the stick. It worked. The braided hair smoked but didn't burst into flames. As he felt his wrist loosen, he jerked his hands apart and then clutched them to his belly. Excitement dulled the pain. With his hands freed, he grabbed the sharp stick, blew on its glowing end, and was now able to surgically place the tip on his ankle cords without badly burning himself again. He was free.

But what the bejesus now? Could he run without them waking and hearing him? With the horses, they could easily catch up with him. The horses. They were tethered, but they could be a distraction. He felt around for a rock about the size of a crab apple and threw it as hard as he could in the direction of the horses, returning instantly to his previous hands together, knees drawn up like a body in a burial pot. The rock might have hit one or just scared them both, but either way, one of them neighed loudly and then whinnied again. Petroc sat up suddenly.

"What the fuck? What's with the horses? Jesus, what's that smell? Is something on fire? I'd better check." Glancing at the immobile boy, all curled up safely, Petroc got to his feet and staggered off to calm the horses. Nectan barely stirred and continued snoring. Dilectus cautiously got to his feet, grabbed hold of his stick and gripped it like a spear he'd been trained to throw. But this wasn't a spear and he'd only ever thrown them at a bag stuffed with straw. He stared down at Nectan and thought of the three times he'd hit him so hard on the head. Maybe only a boy, but Dilectus was strong, and he was angry. He plunged his pointed stick, still smouldering at the end, as hard as he could right into Nectan's eye. And then he ran as though Satan himself was chasing him, stumbling over rocks, scratched by branches and thorns, tripping twice and once falling flat on his face. Easier to run downhill, but planfully this time, he ran for higher ground. As he ran, his heart pounding, his stomach retching and his bowels turning to water, he continued to hear the unearthly screaming of a man covering his bleeding face with his hands.

By daybreak, he could run no more. He found a small cave, and hoping it wasn't the home of a bear, he curled up inside and pulled mounds of bracken partially over his exhausted body. His sleep was fitful, and his wrists hurt more than anything else he could remember. There was no bear, and as he watched the setting sun, he decided that was the direction he should go. The scumbags had talked about going to the forest. The only forest he had ever heard of was to the east of Garn Goch, so heading west seemed like his best option. But night-time travel was hard going; he stumbled frequently and got badly scratched by wild brambles with big thorns.

For days – how many he'd lost count – he'd been wandering through woods and copses, skulking past farmland, and wading knee-deep in bogs. Crouching in thickets at the slightest noise, always careful not to leave footprints, and in the morning, always messing up the piles of leaves or bracken he'd pulled together to sleep on, not that he got much sleep, especially when it rained, which it did aplenty. Even when he took a dump, he piled moss and rocks over it. Severus had told him how a scout, sleuthing around an enemy camp, had to be careful to leave no tell-tale signs. There were wee burns and prattling streams, so water was no problem, but it was hard to find anything to eat. He picked a handful of glossy berries, but they were bitter and made him sick. When faced with a choice, he chose higher ground. Another thing Severus had told him when he was six years old and always following Severus around like a puppy. Severus had looked him sternly in the face and said in his most serious voice, "If you are going to have a pitched battle, always go for the higher ground. Remember that Dilectus." The six-year-old had slapped his right fist to his left chest, the way he'd seen soldiers do on the parade ground. Severus, laughing heartily, returned the salute. That's how you learn principles you never forget.

After how many days he'd completely lost count, he saw mountains that looked like they might be the ones near home. The next encouragement came from a small square fort with timber buildings atop earth ramparts. It was clearly Roman and evidently abandoned long ago. He prowled through it, hoping something useful, even edible, might have been left behind, but it was scarily empty and provided no suitable cover for a hiding place. There were roads leading out of the entrance facing the sunrise and another to what must be the southerly direction. Both stretches of road were overgrown and in bad repair – people had probably removed paving stones for other uses. But maybe one of the roads was still used as a farm track. Creeping along the ditch at the side of the road was easier than struggling through the uncleared ground of gorse and blackthorn with its long, sharp thorns. And it led to habitation.

He climbed a beech tree with thick foliage so he wouldn't be spotted and carefully surveyed the place in front of him. It was a fine-looking farmhouse surrounded by smaller buildings and outhouses. A large stable and a number of parked bullock carts suggested it was a prosperous settlement of some importance. But there were few people around and happily no sign of dogs. He selected the most distant of the sheds and crept inside. It was full of old farm implements, with piles of straw to disappear under if necessary. It looked like a safe place to hide for a few days, but he was too tired to care one way or the other. In the early mornings of the next days, he'd raided the hen house and taken a few warm eggs, but after some enjoyment, they had been making him queasy and he'd been more careless about tossing the shells away. His first mistake.

Dilectus jerked awake at the same moment. Strong hands had his arm in a powerful grip and was twisting it hard behind his back. The sun was streaming in through the loose slats in the barn, which dazzled him. An angry voice shouted in his ear, "Gotcha now, boy."

Chapter 8: Brother Molio Goes to See the Bishop

Long before the rolling English drunkard had any hand in making the rolling English roads, the Romans had built one of the long straight roads they were so proud of, all the way from the walled town of Isca Dumnoniorum on the southwest coast of Britannia up towards Lindum Colonia and the great northern city of Eboracum. With a foundation of sand and crushed rock, it was topped with lime-based mortar and huge paving stones quarried from wherever was close and convenient, all nicely cambered for good drainage. They called the first part of the road the *Fossa* because it followed an earlier ditch that had been dug as the western frontier before the tribes of Cymru had been brought under control. About halfway along the Fossa, they had built a fort, but the local tribe, the Dobunni, were sufficiently friendly that it quickly evolved into a walled market town called Corinium, with an imposing forum and basilica. After AD 323, a bishopric was established, with the diocese extending all the way to Villa Arcadius.

Lady Galeria had made a priority of supporting the bishop. Bishop Julius, in particular, had become her friend and confidant. The hospitality at Villa Arcadius was so sumptuous that Julius tended to visit there more often than to any other of the more distant communities of his flock. Galeria made generous donations to the diocese, and Julius, without doubting her pious motivation, staunchly protected her rights as the undisputed head of the villa's estates, something not always guaranteed to women in Roman tradition and law. Julius had approved her plans for a magnificent new mosaic and reassured her that using her wealth for the Glory of God was not a contradiction of Jesus's obvious ascetic values. Unfortunately, on his way back from a synod in Treverorum on the nature of the Trinity, Bishop Julius took ill and died.

When the news reached Corinium, all the clergy of the diocese got together and quickly wrote a letter to Siricius, the recently elected Bishop of Rome, requesting the immediate appointment of a new bishop. They emphasised the size and importance of the diocese, how its centre, the market town itself, had a thriving wool industry, the availability of a converted basilica built on the abandoned Roman army fort on the Fossa, a suitably grand episcopal palace thanks to their beloved and Godly Julius, and how the tribal area of the Dobunni also included the remarkable baths of Aquae Sulis, whose popularity brought large crowds ripe to hear the gospel, despite its pagan associations. The letter failed to mention that the diocese extended across the Sabrina Estuary and incorporated Castra Legionis, the town of Venta Silurum, and the richest villa in the region. They were concerned that if they sounded too grand, they might get some big-name bishop who would be bossy and difficult.

They also failed to mention that the Dobunni people, known for their dark hair, courtesy of their origins in the Iberian Peninsula, spoke a language different from the Celtic tongue of the fair-haired people to the west, in Cymru. This made it possible only to preach and conduct services strictly in Latin, which made the conversion to Christianity yet more challenging. Even more problematic, and thus not mentioned, was the presence in the same area of another even more mysterious community group scattered around the upper reaches of the Sabrina River. Their spiritual connection with witchcraft and the cult of the mother goddess Cuda had predisposed them to stories from the Christian gospels, but whether they could be described as Christians, well, that was rather a matter of opinion.

Julius, in his wisdom, had been perfectly happy, allowing the ordinary folk to blend their ancient beliefs, rites and customs into Christian practices. If they wanted to link the popular Cuda with her baby and her cauldron to the Virgin Mary, the most Holy Mother of Jesus, so be it. Lady Galeria had told him years before that winning over women folk would ensure far greater church membership than any other approach. Having women to admire and look up to was important for suffering little children to come unto the activities of the church, just as Jesus Himself had commanded.

Despite these more subtle elements of local custom being omitted from the request to the Pope, the diocese received his written answer in record time of only five months. Everyone was excited. He had appointed an outstanding young priest from Rome by the name of Exuperius, who had most recently been active in Burdigala. He was very knowledgeable about the Sacred Scriptures. His ship would sail as far as possible up the Sabrina

River towards Glevum. Could a welcoming party meet him there and arrange final transport to Corinium? The only detail that the papal secretary had himself failed to mention in the letter of appointment – perhaps, he was unaware of it – was that Exuperius had been doing all he could to be appointed to the Episcopal See of Tolosa, writing letters to the priests and religious orders urging them to nominate him. This was, after all, the richest city in Transalpine Gaul, with all the delights of Roman civilisation, aqueducts, a circus, five theatres, baths and stout walls. To be sent instead to the most barbaric and distant outpost of the Empire, with its wet climate and constant tribal agitation, regardless of its prosperous wool trade, was a bitter disappointment.

Molio knew none of these things. He only knew that after a long wait, the diocese had a new bishop who'd been ordained a priest in Rome itself and was probably from Gaul. That might explain how he was able to tell the papal secretary about the most convenient way to get to Corinium.

Molio, who had not written and had come unannounced, was beginning to regret his impulsive decision to visit the new bishop. After declaring who he was and where he was from to a boy in a crisp white tunic, he'd been kept waiting for what seemed like hours on a cold marble bench in the forecourt of the episcopal palace. He'd almost decided to slip away when the bronze hinges of the ornately carved door squeaked open, and he was summoned inside. He knelt at the feet of a well-dressed younger man and kissed the ring on his extended hand. It was a large, shiny, deep purple stone set in an ornate gold mount.

Without looking up, Molio muttered, "Thank you for seeing me, Your Grace."

"Welcome, Frater Molio," Exuperius responded, using the Latin word for brother as more of a title than of kinship. Yet he sounded sincere, especially when he added, "My earnest apologies for keeping you waiting so long," followed by the faintest hint of criticism, "but I had no letter or other warning of your visit. Please sit here next to me. Can I get you something warm for your shoulders? Everyone told me how finely Bishop Julius, God rest his soul, had furnished this palace, but I confess I find it a touch draughty." And without waiting for the affirmative answer Molio would have liked to have given, continued, "What brings you so far from the lands of the Silures? You don't seem to be, as I've been repeatedly warned, a wild, swarthy warrior with curly black hair, so I suspect you are not native to those parts. That's if the learned Tacitus is to be believed," he added with a wink. "I've been preparing, you know, in order to understand my new flock."

Worried that this talkative new bishop would take control of the meeting, Molio offered no witty rejoinder nor statement of his tribal affiliations. He reached into the leather satchel he was carrying and pulled out various sheets of paper and of velum. He thrust them towards Bishop Exuperius.

"I am employed as a scribe in the library of the Villa Arcadius in your diocese and have come, Your Grace, to bring you evidence of pernicious thoughts being promoted by powerful persons highly influential in the land of the Silures, specifically at the Villa by Domina Galeria Arcadiae. The evidence is contained in these letters."

Without taking the collection of documents, Exuperius sat back in his grand chair, looking puzzled. "Pernicious is a strong word, Frater Molio, *perniciosus,*" he repeated, emphasising each syllable, "linking us to death and destruction. A very strong word indeed."

He sat back, staring at Molio, who dropped his gaze to the ground in discomfort.

"I've heard only positive things about the Domina Arcadiae, especially that many of the finer furnishings of this penitential house were generously donated by her over the years."

"If Your Grace would just look at the materials I have brought, I am sure that."

"Where did you say you were educated, my dear Frater?"

"I was sent to study theology in the college set up by Bishop Viventius in Viroconium – it was arranged by the priest at Villa Arcadius."

"Excellent, excellent, but where did you first learn to read and write and to speak smooth Latin, good Brother Molio?"

"A school was established at the Villa, and my parents, who lived far away to the west, had sent me there."

"And who established that school, do you know?"

"I believe it was Domina Arcadiae."

"*Hmm.* Indeed. That is what I had heard as well. So now you have brought me incriminating letters, private correspondence perhaps?"

Molio was smart enough to know exactly where this was drifting. He became defensive.

"Your Worship, please do not think for one moment that I enjoy bringing you tales or of seeming to speak ill of the lady whose house provides me with protection and a livelihood. However, I believe that when you peruse these materials I have brought, you will agree that this is evidence of an offence before God.

"I've marked those passages that are especially troublesome. Listen to this, your holiness. It is from Pelagius to Lady Galeria: 'Dear Galeria, most illustrious child of God, blah, blah, blah…' Let me get to the key points; he can be rather long-winded. Good. Here he says, 'Please read the holy scriptures with the attention they deserve, never forgetting they are the words of God… blah, blah, blah… thank you again for your most perceptive and deeply profound questions regarding God's grace and how it supports our actions. When I emphasise the importance of having free will to do both good and evil, I mean the original possibility of natural, free will derives from God and that God has given us the law to instruct us and gave us Jesus as an example to follow. Your intelligent observation that Jesus Himself often talked about heaven but rarely about hell has caused me to ponder the issue and it is my opinion that if we look carefully at the Greek and Hebrew texts, when He mentioned hell in his sermon on the mountainside, He uttered the word *Gehenna*, as a place of punishment. I believe translating this word as *hell* is a mistake. *Gehenna* is, I have heard, a real place – a valley outside Jerusalem, an unclean place of horror for Jews where all sorts of trash and dead bodies were burnt. Thus, it is my conclusion that Jesus's vivid descriptions of the joy of heaven were to encourage His followers to choose, of their own free will, the path of righteousness by promising them later rewards rather than threatening them with eternal damnation'.

"Your Holiness, if that is not blasphemy, I don't know what is. I know the Bishop of Hippo has written sternly against such ideas and has repeatedly explained that God's Grace is the union of the Creator with human creatures, the favour whereby we may share God's nature."

"But, dear Frater, these are matters of theological interpretation and have been and will be discussed for many years to come." Exuperius was quite unused to high-brow discussion of this sort. He was already worried enough about which books and holy works actually belonged to the proper canon of sacred scripture. One obscure Hebrew word was surely trivial.

"I disagree, Your Holiness, the great presbyter Augustine, a man of God, has made definite pronouncements on this matter, which surely have been accepted as doctrine by the Roman Church. These contradictory positions of Pelagius and Lady Galeria surely merit excommunication if you were to take the matter up with the Pope in Rome."

"I suppose so, but that is not strong evidence. Maybe you need to retrieve more of the correspondence, perhaps find material that is more sinful."

"Trust me, Your Excellency, I have indeed such material in which the lady has been expressing ideas that even Pelagius cannot stomach. Listen to his rebuke; here, let me find it. Yes, here it is. This is Pelagius writing: 'I cannot fully agree with your position, dear lady, that now Christianity is the legal religion of the Empire that there can be no more martyrs to sanctify. Or that in place of being fed to the lions, suffering by means of extreme but voluntary deprivation of food and water is insufficient evidence of one's godliness. It seems you are implying that the motives of extreme ascetics, or even the holy martyrs, are suspect, that one's actions are designed to seek salvation rather than being practised with all humility of mind. I believe asceticism is a holy lifestyle and one that prepares a person for a life of sacrifice and penitence, and I have been writing advice on such matters to a number of noble women in Rome who seek my guidance on spiritual matters. Recently, however, I have been influenced by your concerns and have indeed been advising young women that moderation is best in everything, and the body has to be controlled, not broken. I urge that those with earthly treasure should use it to feed the hungry, clothe the naked and visit the sick. You, dear lady, have been the inspiration for these clarifications of Christian life."

"If I may interrupt you there, Brother Molio, I salute your diligence in searching for signs of blasphemy. Yet what you just read suggests that the lady of Villa Arcadius influenced Pelagius rather than the other way around. If she, a lay person and worse yet, a woman, is encouraging heresy, that is indeed a grievous matter that must be addressed."

"Well, let me tell you, Your Excellency, it is far worse than that when she speaks in vulgar tones and tries to influence Pelagius against the most holy doctor of our church, Jerome of Stridon, who has been strongly advocating the importance of celibacy and virginity. Let me read you this passage, which is a draft of a letter she sent to Pelagius. It is quite long, but I must read it all since it is so inappropriate and most unladylike and is, in my opinion, sure grounds for excommunication.

"It begins: 'I need to emphasise, dear Brother Pelagius, that I believe you slightly misremembered our conversation during your visit to the villa many years ago. You have written that I was your inspiration for advocating, along with other theologians, the virtue of virginity and your belief that widowhood is a more exalted state than remarriage. And I understand from copies of other letters from you that have been widely shared among my friends in Rome that you are encouraging young girls to remain virgins and widows not to remarry. I first heard of such notions when I read a treatise from Jerome, which I felt was truly misguided. What I think all of you men of the cloth fail to realise is that unless a woman who is widowed has her own source of wealth, which is rare, she will have no means whereby she can support herself and thus must remarry or she will end up begging on the streets like so many women here in our town whose husbands have been killed in the endless strife of military campaigns and civil wars. What you are advocating as a blessed state in the eyes of the Lord neglects the social and financial realities that women face.

'Arguing that your position was influenced by my decision not to remarry after the early tragic death of my husband, Arcadius, is unfortunate. My decision – taken with free will, I am glad to say – was simply because I prayed to the Lord to take his soul and I offered myself as a penitent on his behalf by promising never again to lie with another man. I do not now believe one can strike a bargain with God, and, in fact, the state of celibacy is so unnatural to me that many times I have bitterly regretted my decision and have often craved the touch of a man and what so many church fathers are now calling the passions of the flesh, as though these were somehow undesirable. Perhaps as you yourself are celibate, you have little experience of the joys of carnal knowledge and are less able to understand that these passions are given to us by God as part of our nature. You are, I believe, so right in thinking that sexual desire and behaviour were not the sins that drove Adam and Eve from the Garden of Eden. There is nothing unholy in desiring the physical passion of intercourse with another human being.'"

"Stop right there!" Exuperius exploded. He appeared agitated. He had leapt up from his episcopal throne and was now pacing around the chamber. "These are very evil thoughts, but since they are not confessed to us by the person entertaining them, we are not truly privileged to hear them. You are right to think that these are blasphemous, even heretical thoughts. Please leave the material here for me to examine more closely, think about it, and see if there are any more confessions of this kind. If you will continue to be my eyes and ears in this diocese and you are able to come across any additional material that might be used for procedures of excommunication, please bring them to me. And if there can be ways of combatting the influence of this controversial monk, Pelagius, please dwell on them, including any possible role you could enact to mitigate the bad influence of this kind of open interchange of offensive material. Now go, with my thanks for bringing these matters to my attention. You will be in my prayers."

The bishop held out his hand for his ring to be kissed. The meeting was over. Molio was excited at the positive responses he had received after a chilly initial reception. He felt newly blessed as a soldier for Christ. He wondered if he could confide in anyone at the villa about this important meeting. The head of security at the villa was someone he'd had an eye on. He had seen the man in church frequently when mass was heard by the priest – Molio himself was not yet consecrated and usually sat quietly at the back. And he had also noticed him in Galeria's small chapel, usually alone, praying. There was no sign of a wife. Such a well-built, slim, handsome man he was. He'd often thought he'd love to get to know him as a friend. This experience with the bishop was something maybe to break the ice and start some conversations – not about celibacy, although that surely was only relevant to fornication between men and women, or virginity, which was surely only relevant to girls, like Mary the Mother of Christ – but maybe about the need to watch out for heretics like Pelagius.

Chapter 9: A New Search Party

When a week of sleepless nights turned to two, despite her constant self-assurance that Dilectus would soon be found, Elen realised something more needed to be done. Although she fully trusted Meirion and the Garn Goch guards and retainers to be as diligent as humanly possible in their search, she couldn't stop herself from thinking that Romans might be better at this kind of thing. Searching for bands of brigands, ambushing raiding parties and communicating across an extensive network of forts and watchtowers was all in a day's work for Roman troops. Severus was preoccupied with training new recruits down at Isca Dumnoniorum. Although the castra there had not been home to a legion for a long time, there were enough open spaces for drills and manoeuvres, functioning baths and eager merchants willing to supply Severus's men with food and other needs. So, Severus was away and was busy. Reluctantly, Elen knew she needed to approach Flavius.

Meirion, looking haggard and tense, was even more reluctant. "To be honest, Elen, I feel insulted. Don't you think we've been doing everything we can? I did send word to the villa. Of course, I did. They've more or less adopted Dilectus and my first thought was that if he escaped the kidnappers, that's where he'd go. But formally going like country yokels to beg help from Lord Supercilious seems very much like you've lost faith in my efforts and ability."

Elen had learned from marriage to Caradocus that even the best men in the world hate to be disrespected and are quick to perceive it even when it isn't happening. She understood her mistake immediately. 'Don't be so silly, I'm not suggesting any such thing', wasn't the right answer.

"Meirion dear," she pleaded, taking both his hands in hers, "you've been magnificent. Everyone says you've been superhuman, showing the strength of Hercules and the persistence of Sisyphus. All I want to suggest is that if we enlist Flavius's help, that's another search party over another stretch of countryside, and he's the sort of wealthy person always happy to bribe people for information."

"What a dreadful comparison! As I remember the story, Sisyphus never succeeded in his task and never got his stupid boulder to the top of the hill. But, OK, I'll do it. We've scoured every inch of ground around here and found bugger all. I'll go and visit the villa. I'll tell Flavius that you sent me to plead for help because I'm just an incompetent barbarian."

Elen shrugged. *Don't comment, just agree, at least he's going,* she told herself. She couldn't deal with someone so angry in such a passive way. She understood where it was coming from. Meirion still felt responsible for her son's abduction.

The next afternoon, Meirion gave a group of concerned household members at Villa Arcadius a detailed account of everything known about the kidnap. Flavius listened attentively without saying a word. Suddenly, he interrupted Meirion's cursing his own negligence for the tenth time.

"The farm boy said they were wearing hoods, right? *Cuculli?*"

"Yes, sir."

"But he also didn't know what a monk was and said the hoods were pointed? On top?"

"Right."

"Well," Flavius responded, "as the saying goes, *cucullus non facit monachum.*"

Everyone stared at him. Flavius paused for effect. "I understand your suspicions, Marianus; these two might have been the Priscillians posing as the holy men – the monks or deacons or whatever they were – who injured Caradocus and eventually poisoned him, thinking he was *the* Macsen Wledig, the man who'd been persecuting their sect so viciously. But have you ever seen a monk's cowl coming to a point *on top* unless it is pulled down over the head and face? Which it couldn't have been if they had been catching a feisty little cub like Dilectus. My hunch is they were actually members of another sect, hardly even a Christian one, a pagan cult, really, worshipping the old Celtic goddess of fertility, Cuda. They've been active around Corinium. As the mother goddess Cuda has been connected by some to Mother Mary. Totally absurd, but to avoid legal harassment, they need to pretend to be part of the official state religion and for all I know, some of them may well believe in Jesus and worship him as the Son of God. The cult – like all other groups uncritically following a charismatic leader – is a real curse, according to my sources. Cuda's so-called guardians, or *genii,* call themselves *cucullati*. They're nasty, coercive and even violent – more like goblins than monks or priests."

Flavius paused for the punchline. Showing off his knowledge was a small pretension of his.

"The *genii cucullati* wear unusual, pointed hoods." He paused again. "So, if I'm right, it gives us a place to look. I don't blame the Dubonnii in general. It's just there's a strong heritage of sorcerers and witches, mostly in rural areas of the upper reaches of the Sabrina River and those dark forests around there. Dear old Bishop Julius was always complaining about how impossible it was to deal with such people. But what would they want with our boy Dilectus?"

Flavius didn't want an answer. He was thinking out loud. "Of course, bad people can always be easily bought. Maybe they were working for someone else. And if they were acting as holy men, they could move around without anyone paying attention. Like those Priscillians who first turned up, snooping around at Garn Goch."

Flavius stopped there. He understood the implications only too well. Scoti slavers had become a menace, brazenly capturing strong-looking boys and whisking them off to Hibernia via the poorly controlled northwest coast of Cymru. But taking only one boy, a prince, and not the other, a strapping farmer's son, seemed to exclude that theory. The real villain was elsewhere.

"Marianus, please return to Garn Goch. I'll organise a search party from the villa to comb the forest areas north of us. There's an abandoned temple up there and a ruined bathhouse once used by mineworkers in the forest, I believe. Worth looking around there. On the other side of the river, there are two modest villas. I know them quite well and we can make enquiries about suspicious activities or Cuda cultists. They've been unsettled by the news from Gaul, so I expect they're ultra-vigilant right now. Tell Elen we'll not stop till we find the boy. When Severus hears about this, he'll be *apoplectic* – any kidnappers better watch out."

Flavius picked Lestinus to lead the search party. Originally just a house servant at the villa, he had distinguished himself by organising a small group of civilians to provide a modicum of protection for Lady Galeria when Flavius and Severus had been away from the compound for a long time. He had grown up in the area, but like so many employed in the villa, he could read and he spoke enough Latin to get by. Flavius briefed him on what they were looking for. Five men on the villa's best mounts, well equipped with arms and rations, set out early the next day. They decided not to take any hounds with them as there were not enough of Dilectus's personal items around to allow them to pick up a scent. And in any case, where they were exploring was where Flavius assumed the kidnappers might be taking the boy, not where he'd originally been nabbed. Meirion had already convinced Flavius the Garn Goch search party had been intensive and had not come up with a single trace. The only hope was to second guess a destination. Meirion mentioned one of King Conanus's ideas: that knowing Dilectus was his grandson, the kidnappers would soon be demanding a huge ransom. Flavius was doubtful. But recognising that money could loosen reluctant tongues he supplied Lestinus with a bag of silver siliqua to dispense in exchange for useful information.

Days later, the search party returned, tired and dispirited. Lestinus found Flavius alone in the library and gave him his report. They'd travelled northeast, following the Sabrina estuary on the main road from Isca Silurum to Glevum. By nightfall, they had reached the Roman Camp Flavius had mentioned, progress being slowed by stopping to ask everyone on the road if they had seen two hooded monks with a young boy. The fort, on a small hill, had been abandoned, and without a Roman army contingent to patrol the road, it likely explained why everyone they questioned was so guarded and unwilling to talk. They spent the night in a small chapel they discovered at the site. When they saw a mosaic and Lestinus read out the inscription, the other men all decided to sleep outside. The little temple was dedicated to the god Nodens. "I am a true and devout believer, but their Christian faith seemed rather shaky," Lestinus commented, and Flavius nodded. There were signs people had recently been making offerings, Lestinus confirmed, but no signs of a little boy.

From there, they'd headed north, passing isolated small settlements and farms. Somewhere – Lestinus wasn't sure where – they came to a busy area with several prosperous-looking farms. They started to talk to one old fellow who warned them to be careful of the lord up north. As though on cue, a group of men rode up to meet them and they were told they were entering Cornovii territory and were not welcome. So, being outnumbered, they turned back, crossed the Afon Gwy and headed east towards the dark forest. Following a track through the woods with signs of ironworks and coal mining all around, they came to a small shrine. It was deserted, but there were signs that people had been there. It was so eerie the other men insisted they leave.

Flavius was surprised when Lestinus started to laugh. "We had one funny incident, though, Dominus. We decided on our way back to check out the Sabrina crossings because you had thought that captors might have used the river to get away. We got close to Glevum, where there are fords, at least at low tide on the estuary, and then moved downriver to where there are boats and ferrymen. We watched a few boats and were then excited to see two *portitores* in the distance rowing a man dressed like a monk. He was coming towards our side, so we hid in the reeds, watched him pay, and then, as he set off with a leather bag, we jumped out, grabbed him and threw him to the ground. Imagine our surprise when we had him restrained and pulled his hood back; we recognised him! It was one of your scribes. Of course, he didn't know who *we* were at first, so he was screaming and yelling and using the Lord's name in vain shouting that his dominus would cut off our cocks and feed them to the pigs if we hurt one hair on his head. My men were laughing that he didn't have much hair anyway, so we'd be perfectly safe. After we found out he was Brother Molio, who we know is working for you, we offered to give him a ride back. Anyway, he turned us down and said he had his own transport waiting – goodness knows what. But I hope he's back safely. He's actually a nice guy. Always smiles at me in the chapel."

"I haven't seen him, come to think of it. Did he say where he'd come from?"

"No. But I asked him since it felt unusual. He said he was on official Villa Arcadius business, and it was none of ours. Anyway, this was irrelevant to our mission, Dominus. I'm sorry it was such a failure. And I had no idea people have turned so unfriendly and suspicious. Society is going right down the latrine. People are scared. For as long as I've been around, they've grumbled about the presence of the army, and now the troops are being steadily withdrawn; they're grumbling about civil disorder."

"Seneca would argue that if we destroy basic human fellowship, we will be no better than animals no matter how clever our thinking is. In principle, Christian fellowship should be able to replace the legions. That's what my mother thinks. She believes if we could convert the Picts to our local Celtic form of Christianity, their constant annoying raids would end."

"I'm a very devout believer. I listen to the bible stories during services, and I try to read the short Latin texts you've had copies made and placed in the chapel, but it's hard going."

"Better than trying to read them in the original Greek! What we have has been copied into everyday Latin by the very man you tackled to the ground! I hope you didn't break his right hand or arm!"

"I'm afraid I've no idea who this chap Seneca is – is he a friend of yours?"

"I wish. But if he were, it would make him three hundred and ninety years old. He killed himself a long time ago."

"Maybe he needed good friends."

"Maybe he did, Lestinus, and maybe needed to be rid of one very bad one."

"I wish I had the time and learning to be able to read about those ancient Romans in all the fine books you have."

"I'm glad you're interested. But you are a young man. Maybe one day you'll find the time. And since we're talking about this, there is one thing I'd like you to promise me: if things do get worse and the villa is ever threatened, you will protect your family first and foremost, but you will also do what you can to save some of those books. Grab what you can and keep them for your children's children."

"You're putting too much trust in a servant who couldn't even find the boy, Dilectus. Do you think he'll ever be found? Somebody must know something. I think one of the farmers up north wanted to tell us something more before we were chased off by the Cornovii."

"I'm sure they were not regular tribal men, Lestinus. They've always been a rather peaceful farming tribe up there. I'd wager those men were thugs hired by someone maybe rich, maybe powerful, maybe both, who doesn't like too many questions. Will Dilectus ever be found? My mother says it is up to the Will of God. We've done all we can to help God out. Now it's up to Dilectus. He's young, but he's a clever boy. I'm not really a betting man, but I'd wager on Dilectus over a couple of sneaky men in hoods any day! But let's get word to Garn Goch. Waiting is hard, but that's all that is possible right now."

Chapter 10: Tension at Home

It was early evening when a young man on horseback clattered into the cobblestone courtyard of Y Gaer Fawr at Garn Goch unchallenged.

"I'm looking for Marianus. I have an urgent message from Villa Arcadius," he shouted. One man grabbed the horse's bridle and offered it a leather pail of water; another ran to the main residence. Seconds later, Meirion appeared.

"I'm Meirion, *um*... Marianus. What do you want?"

"I have a letter from Dominus Flavius, but I can tell you what it says. He wants me to advise you that after an extensive one-week search, they have been unable to trace the missing boy. They have offered a large reward for information. They found a pagan shrine in the forest with indications of men and horses having been there. But no other signs. He says from the evidence, there is no indication he was taken by Priscillian monks, but possibly by some other kind. Sorry, forgotten their name, but it's in the letter. He says if he's right, they are being paid by someone, which means he will be kept alive as a hostage or for ransom, which he says is encouraging news. Scoti slavers would have taken both boys. He says to tell you to keep searching and making enquiries but to expect to be contacted by the abductors soon."

Yelling at a servant to take proper care of the messenger and his horse, Meirion dashed into the royal quarters to find Elen. She was in her chamber, embroidering a cushion cover. It was getting dark, and she had lit two candles, but she was still straining to see her work. Perhaps she had been crying. Without any formalities or niceties, he relayed Flavius's message word for word, waving the folded parchment note for emphasis here and there. He stumbled over the words and sounded agitated and desperate. Elen sat listening without comment or expression.

"You're taking this quite calmly," Meirion accused her.

"Don't be ridiculous. I'm doing everything in my power to control myself. My stomach is churning, and I want to throw up. I still think it can only be the survivor of those Priscillians, the one who poisoned his father, seeking revenge. Nothing else makes sense to me. I'm having nightmares of his tortured body showing up on a road near here. Come and sit here and comfort me. Bolt the door."

Meirion sat rigidly next to her on the wide sofa, a gift to Elen's mother, Brangwen, when Conanus was still courting her. Elen put her arms around him. He started to sob.

"It's all my fault. I'm so sorry, Elen. I should never have left him after our riding lesson. I should have waited until I saw him rub down the horse and go inside. The instant he vanished I should have ridden out looking for tracks. I promised you I'd find him. I've failed. I'm a total failure. You must hate me."

Elen put her hand over his mouth. "Shut up, for God's sake. No one's to blame and feeling sorry for yourself is unhelpful. Apologising for something you're not responsible for doesn't make me feel better. Self-pity is unattractive. You might as well blame me for raising a wilful child who ran off to play when he knew that was wrong. I've only once in my life been this stressed or feeling so hopeless. Be strong. Be a comfort. Put your arms around me before I tear out my hair like the pagan Greeks."

Gingerly, Meirion put one arm around her shoulders. He had never touched her before. He had always wanted to. Elen teased him.

"Come on, I'm not your frail grandmother. Give me a proper hug."

Meirion changed position and put both arms around her. She buried her face into his shoulder, then let her composure fall away like a bandage suddenly stripped off an open wound. "I'm so terribly scared," she sobbed, "what are they doing with my darling son? He'll be terrified and praying for me to rescue him like I always did when he was a toddler. What if he's in pain? What if they hurt him? What if they kill him?" Each staccato comment was accompanied by Elen hammering her clenched fists against Meirion's back and he pulled her closer to him. He freed one arm, stroked her long hair and gently massaged the back of her neck the way a lover would.

"We're going to find him. He's clever. He's strong. He's your son. He has a destiny awaiting him. Severus has been teaching him survival tactics and how to fight."

"You're right," Elen whispered, stretched up and kissed him hard on the mouth. When she broke away, he moved his hand to the back of her head, pulled her closer and kissed her very gently.

They were now in that moment between a man and woman in which they both feel desire, both long for a touch, both physically aroused, both desperately needy for companionship, support and reassurance, both wanting to escape possible realities. But it was also a moment of intense awkwardness, fear that feelings would not be reciprocated, terrified of being rejected, worried about the embarrassment and shame of misjudging the other's intentions.

The problem for Elen and Meirion was they shared an intimate but nevertheless platonic past. Between them was the spectre of a courageous and principled Celtic officer of the Roman army. For Elen, the thought of sleeping with another man seemed to sully her romantic memories of her dead husband, filling her with the guilt of her life continuing while he lay under a nameless marble slab. For Meirion, thoughts that he was betraying a man he admired above all others – who had rescued him, employed him, trusted him and entrusted him – were matched by an uncharacteristic lack of self-confidence. He was of low rank, a person who had risen in prominence not by breeding but by his own efforts. Some would think that a positive attribute, but among the wealthy and those conscious of rank and breeding, it rendered one forever inferior in their minds. Elen had none of those pretensions or elitist feelings, but what about those around her, a princess, a figure of fable and admiration? He could hear his own sister, a friend of Elen's, heaping scorn on him for not knowing his place. And he was younger than Elen; that was a disadvantage.

The problem with such a constellation of doubtful feelings, indecision and worry is that hesitation means loss. If you stop and approach the situation rationally, both knew the answer to their physical needs was simple: 'Stop right now. Back off. Be tender but not passionate. Kiss like old friends – no tongues'. But Elen remembered how carefully Caradocus had asked her, 'Do you want to do this, Elen?' a question that could yield only one answer at the moment in which physical intimacy had already occurred – it was the question for the next level of activity. Elen posed a new question, one harder to answer:

"What do you want, Meirion?"

His answer was instantaneous and honest. "I want you. I love you. I always have."

Elen didn't answer, which was also honest. She'd actually never thought of loving Meirion because she loved only one man. But she liked him and trusted him, and he was good with Dilectus. The choice was easy. She pulled up his tunic; he raised his arms, and she slipped it easily over his head. Then, she pulled down her dress and pressed her breasts against his chest. He groaned appreciatively and rubbed his hands over her bare back. "God, you're beautiful," he said. She broke away from him and stood up, dropping her dress and her underskirt to the floor. "Get your kit off, young man, and come lie with me before I get goose pimples. It's cold in here."

Meirion stripped off the rest of his clothes, his heart beating so hard and fast he feared his prick wouldn't rise to the occasion, but Elen reached out and touched it gently with her fingertips and it obligingly sprang into life. He lay on top of her, foreplay unnecessary – it had been verbal, imaginary and shortened by need. He entered her easily and, for a moment, lay immobile on top of her, then kissed her on the mouth, which delighted her.

Now, for the first time, Elen became aware of new sensations. Caradocus was muscular and swarthy, barrel-chested – Hippocrates would have called him a mesomorph in Greek. He was a gentle and considerate lover, not a charging bull, but he was, matter-of-fact, concerned about her pleasure but focused on the task, directive but not demanding, usually silent except for appreciative moaning towards the end, always grateful afterwards but not cuddly. Caradocus was the only lover she had ever had, and it hadn't really occurred to her before that every man felt a little different and made love in uniquely different ways. Meirion was lissom, graceful, thin without a trace of fat, flexible; if he were dancing, you would call him light on his feet. Somehow, he was able to employ his hands magically, now cupping a breast and then tickling the crack of her bottom – but not in a studied way designed for her delight but rather relishing her magnificent attributes. His eyes were always open, looking at her, and he felt different inside, too, maybe because of the way he moved or the angle and tempo of his thrusts. She hadn't wanted to make comparisons, but the contrasts were so great she was forced to notice them without judgment. Meirion wasn't a better lover, just different.

Meirion, too, was desperately trying to keep Caradocus out of his mind. His doubts about loyalty to his friend and mentor, his consciousness of station and feelings of unworthiness to be a lover of the most beautiful woman in all the inhabited world and a nagging sense he might be exploiting her sadness and worry over her missing son, were all combining to distract him. Only Elen's responsiveness and enthusiastic movements, like wrapping her long legs around him to pull him closer to her, allowed him to relax and indulge himself. Meirion had had other women, not many, but all girls in whom he had been interested, if never actually in love. And consequently, he had a fairly good sense of female sexuality, not structurally speaking since there were no anatomical guides, but a clear understanding that women could experience as much pleasure as a man, despite every young woman being told it was her duty so just put up with it, and every priest reiterating some version of Bishop Augustine's words that taking pleasure in sexual intercourse is a sin of lust.

When it was over, Elen nestled up close to Meirion with her head on his chest and her one free hand fondling him gently. His left arm was around her and his right hand had mysteriously found her left breast. He wasn't thinking about the possibility of babies; Elen was but didn't care. Her future had just been altered.

"Are you..." Meirion began to say, but Elen took her hand off his softening cock and placed a finger firmly over his lips.

"*Shush,*" she whispered. "Don't say a word. You said such lovely erotic ones while you were inside me. Say any more and you will spoil the mood."

Meirion tried to bite her finger the way a puppy would when you play with it. They both smiled and snuggled closer still. They fell asleep. In the middle of the night, Meirion got up to pee. He found the lidded pot in the corner of the room and tinkled as quietly as he could. He tiptoed back to the bed and stared down at Elen, her hair tousled around her face and her bottom exposed to the elements. He pulled the soft sheepskin kaross over her and lay down quietly beside her. His last thought before he fell asleep was, 'I want to marry this woman if she'll have me'.

Chapter 11: Dilectus Discovered

"Gotcha, you little fox cub. Egg thief. Ooh – stinky poo."

Dilectus struggled, but one arm was already being forcibly twisted behind his back. He'd badly injured one of his captors and now they would surely torture and then kill him. He tried to wriggle free, but the more he squirmed, the harder the twisting and the more it hurt. Too dispirited to fight back, he scrunched up his eyes against the sunrise and stared at his captor. Not too terrifying. A red-headed boy, a bit bigger than himself, stared back.

"What's your name?" the boy demanded.

"Dilectus."

"You're a Roman?"

"No, I'm a Celt."

"Dilectus sounds Roman. What's it mean?"

"Beloved. What's yours?"

"Patricius."

"That's Roman, for sure. And I know what it means. Nobleman. You don't look noble. You're just a kid."

"I bet I'm older than you. I'm bigger than you. But I'm a Celt, too. My parents call me Padrig. Why did you steal our eggs and throw the shells around?"

"I was hungry."

"That explains why you ate them, not why you stole them. Ever heard of asking politely?"

Dilectus didn't reply. He sounded like an ordinary boy trying to be a smart arse. But could he be trusted? He'd thought the numerous rats and mice would carry the eggshells off, but obviously, they hadn't. Now, he was caught, held in a wrestling grip by a miniature Milo of Croton.

"Ouch! You're hurting me," Dilectus whined.

Padrig immediately loosened his grip. "You don't scare me. You stink, but you don't look like a killer. Everybody's looking for one."

"How do you know? How old are you?"

"I'm twelve. I listen when grown-ups talk. I go to school. I've learned to read. My dad's important. He travels a lot. He works for a lord. He went away yesterday. He left me in charge."

"What does he do, your dad?"

"He's a *curialis*."

"Jesus!" Dilectus exclaimed. "My uncle Severus says tax collectors are scum."

Padrig went red in the face to match his hair. "That's stupid," he said indignantly, "and you shouldn't blaspheme. Are you a pagan? My dad's honest. He helps people if they can't pay their taxes. He used to work for the Roman magistrate, but the fellow scarpered. Now, Dad works for the lord. He has to. But he's good. Dad's a *decurion* and plans entertainment for the public and he volunteers in our church. My *tadcu* is a priest. He's retired now – he's majorly old. He's called Potitus, after the martyr the lions wouldn't eat."

This was too much information for Dilectus. "Lions? Are there lions here? Where am I? And who's looking for me? I've been hiding for days. You'd better not give me away."

"We're in Banwen. The land around here is near the Silurians but owned by the Vitalis family up north. That's who Dad works for. The men can't be looking for you. They're looking for a boy they say's a prince and a murderer." Padrig eyed Dilectus's muddy face, matted hair full of twigs and bits of straw, legs covered in scratches and deep red sores around his wrists. "You're no prince. Who's *your* father?"

Dilectus hesitated. 'If you're caught when you're a scout,' Severus told him when he was six, '*never* give away too much information; tell 'em your rank and your cohort but nothing else.'

"My father's dead."

"Oh! I'm sorry." Padrig sounded so genuine that Dilectus began to warm to him.

"Who's looking for this prince?"

"Everyone!" Padrig said excitedly. "My dad is. He said there was a big reward for finding him. So's two holy men. The one who's nearly dead said the prince is tall and strong and super dangerous and, another of the lord's officers, more senior than my dad but does the same kind of work, he's paying for information as well and is also looking everywhere for the holy men because he wants to protect the prince, which my dad says is probably cowpoo..."

"Hold up, I can't follow any of this. Have *you* seen the two holy men?"

"No, but I heard one of them is dying from a bad wound, so they want to catch this killer prince and cut his heart out."

It was at that moment that Dilectus finally lost any bravado he had left.

"Then, I'll never see my ma again," he wailed.

Padrig was finally the big brother. He'd let things go too far and he knew it. "Come on, squirt, stop being such a woolly sheep and tell me what's going on." His tone was gentle and encouraging.

Dilectus wiped his nose with the back of his hand and sniffed. "Do you believe in God?" he demanded.

"Sort of."

"All right, swear by God you won't tell anyone who I am?"

"I swear," said Padrig, making a quick sign of the cross over his heart. "Who the hell are you? Are you the Messiah?"

"Don't be stupid. But I'm sort of like a prince. My mum is Princess Elen, daughter of the King of the Silures and the Demetae. I was grabbed by two horrid men. Then I escaped when I stuck a burning stick into one of them's eyes. Now I don't know who is chasing after me or why and who I can trust."

"You can trust my dad, if he was here, or my mum."

"I can't. Those horrid men said something about a *curialis*. One of them is called Neck or Nic or something. They thought I couldn't hear them whispering. My friend Severus told me in a tight spot act stupid, but listen carefully."

There was a long pause before Padrig spoke. "You're right. You can't trust anyone. We can't even trust my dad. You should have seen him get excited when he was telling me of the reward being offered. Said it would be enough for him to quit work and get back to farming and pay for my education. We have to keep you hidden until we can figure out what to do. I'm going to go inside and sneak out some bread and some milk. No one will notice. I'll wet a rag at the pump, and you can wipe your face. You look like crap. Don't poke out any more eyes while I'm gone."

Padrig slipped out of the shed. And with his parting words, Dilectus knew he had found a true friend. But unless Severus or his mum or Lady

Galeria were to show up in person, he knew he dared not show his face. And where the hell was Banwen? He'd never heard of the place. Don't trust anyone. *Shit, Padrig didn't even trust his own dad. What if Meirion wanted me out of the way? The way he looks at Mum, I can tell he wants her. And why didn't they take Doggy? Maybe Caradog's pa set it up for money. Could Severus be sick of coaching my sword work? And Flavius, he's a wily fox full of big talk. Maybe he wants me dead.* Dilectus covered himself with more straw and sobbed silently.

Padrig was back with half a loaf of bread and a clay pitcher of milk. "Hey, I got bread but not five loaves and no fishes either. Jesus, I'm not. Shit kid, where've you gone?" He grabbed a wooden hay fork and poked about.

"Ouch," Dilectus emerged, with giveaway streaks down his dirty face.

"Here's a wet rag, Silly Dilly. Shit, what's wrong with your wrists?"

Dilectus told him the story of his escape between gulps of warm milk, and Padrig was impressed.

"Wow, you're gutsy little Dilectus. But those need treatment. Burns don't heal easily. Our cook keeps telling me. I'm going to go find a ditch and get some dock weeds. There's a wise woman in the area who showed me how to get the oil, the jelly, from the centre of the plant. The leaf doesn't help much; it's the gooey stuff that works." Padrig was enjoying equally his vastly superior knowledge and his bossy caregiving.

After smoothing the dock gel on Dilectus's wounds with his finger while Dilectus scrunched up his face with pain but didn't cry out, Spartan that he was, Padrig said, "I've got to go. School. I'll get into trouble, and they'll wonder where I am. But I'll come back later, so don't move from here whatever you do. But don't crap in the hay, either."

Late that afternoon, the two boys cemented their friendship. Not in so many words. Dilectus boasted he could ride a horse and jump it over a hedge as high as he was. Padrig boasted he knew all about girls. Dilectus was immensely curious. He demanded to know more.

"I am a sinner," Padrig admitted woefully. "I'm going to hell. I paid one of the serving girls to have sex with me."

"True's god?" Dilectus's eyes widened.

"Sort of," Padrig admitted. "She said she didn't want to have a baby, even for two siliquae, so she let me touch her, you know, the front bum, between her legs. She showed me how."

"What did it feel like? Someone told me it has teeth and can bite you."

"That's crap. It felt soft, and when I poked a finger inside, it was wet and slippery. I got a hard-on. When she saw that, she kissed it and sucked me till I squirted. I'm going to hell."

"Doesn't sound like a bad sin. No one got hurt. I rub myself against a pillow; it feels good. It feels even better when I squirt. The first time it happened a few months ago, I was so surprised I thought I must have some sort of disease."

"People say that enjoyment of such things *is* a sin. One of the monks around here is always talking about the evils of the flesh. Yeah, I didn't force her or anything, but I bribed her because I've got more money than she has, I took advantage of her. That's not right. That's a sin."

"Does she feel guilty like you do?"

"Don't think so. She winks at me in the kitchen. Hope nobody notices. I think she's teasing me. Maybe she'll tell someone."

"More likely you'll get it for free next time." Dilectus hoped a bit of humour and a bit of wishful thinking would get Padrig's mind off the sinful angle, and he hoped his new friend wouldn't notice his own boner, which had been emerging along with his vivid visualising of the whole event.

But Padrig did notice. "Looks like we both need to find some willing girls, otherwise it is just going to be you and me!"

Dilectus jumped on him in a mock wrestling match, both boys giggling. Hands groped under clothes and all thoughts of sin were quickly dispelled.

"Where's the damp rag you brought?" Dilectus asked cheerfully. "And how're we going to let my mum know I'm safe? Who else can I trust? Maybe the scary Lady Galeria. But where's my villa from here, d'you know?"

Padrig shook his head. "I've heard of it, but the only villa I've ever seen is my dad's boss' place, the Villa Vitalis. It's a long way north, but maybe we could go there? What do you think?"

"Shit, no. That's a crap idea. You're the only person I can trust. Can I stay here until I can tell my mum I'm safe and she can come and get me? Alone."

"OK, let's talk tomorrow. You're safe here. But you're only safe if you're not found. We gotta be super careful."

Padrig had slipped out of his house a woven woollen blanket, some more bread and cheese, and three prunes, a newly imported Roman delicacy that Dilectus had never had before. As *Curialis*, Padrig's dad, Calpurnius, was obviously doing well. So that night, Dilectus slept better than he had for days. Even so, he startled easily. When a horse had whinnied in the farm stables, he'd sat bolt upwards, shaking and grabbing the hayfork that Padrig had poked him with and was now a defensive weapon. But for the next two days, Padrig wasn't able to come to the shed. The boy had household chores that he couldn't escape. When he finally did, he was full of joviality and excitement – he hadn't had so much fun and responsibility and feelings of heroism and rescue imagery ever before. It was in stark contrast to Dilectus's state. He was again jittery, frustrated, lonely and scared. He'd been aching to talk again to his new friend and terrified that something had happened to him, or worse still, Padrig had decided not to bother to come and see him any more.

"I'm thinking Satan might be who captured you," Padrig said confidently. "Those two were devils. You can't kill a devil. That's why the one whose eye you poked out is still out there looking for you, just feeling a bit unwell and angry as a viper."

"That sounds like horse poo." Dilectus snapped at him. "Anyway, there were two of them."

"That's what I'm sayin'. Satan employs swarms of little devils, demons and hobgoblins. Everyone around here knows that."

"Not Christian folk who go to church." Dilectus was getting upset. "Do *you* believe in Satan?"

"I certainly do. So did Jesus. He even called Peter 'Satan' once. It's Satan who temps us and makes us do evil things. Like I did."

"Lady Galeria was telling me and my friend Claudia – hey, I've just remembered Claudia is another person who'd like to get rid of me. No, not for real. She calls me a nuisance, but I'm sure she likes me; I like her – anyway, Domina said that her friend Pellicanus preached that we do good things and bad things because we choose to. We can't blame someone else; we need to take responsibility."

"I blame you for grabbing my cock yesterday!" Padrig said.

"Me? Crap. You started it with all that talk about girls. You must be Satan!"

Padrig grabbed Dilectus by the ear and gave it a twist. "Take that back and say you're sorry!"

Dilectus easily pushed him away. They were both laughing so hard they failed to notice the shed's door had been quietly pushed open and a large demonic figure was standing there, staring at them.

Chapter 12: A Mother Always Knows

"You know that small fort the army built where the Afon Taf merges with our estuary?"

"More of a watchtower, really," Flavius interjected. "It was part of the Castra Augusta's defensive network originally, but we abandoned it ages ago once the Silures settled down. Even the good harbour there, Tamium, on the Sabrina, is hardly ever used these days. Please continue."

"Dear." Galeria sighed patiently, recognising that knowing things others didn't was one of her son's modus operandi. "If you would stop interrupting, I'd be able to. I'm not interested in some old fort; I was just trying to give directions since I haven't been around there for so long. What I was going to say is if you take the military road past the fort – all right, watchtower – and keep on for a few miles, you come to a settlement, nestled a little back from the sea, probably so's not to draw attention from raiders. There's a villa there which has been destroyed and rebuilt a number of times. I've never met the family, but it was they who put me on to the Italian tilers who did my gorgeous mosaic for me.

"Let me get right to the point. Despite the high cliffs, there are some good landing spots, apparently, and even Saxon pirates have been spotted hanging around there, which is a worry. According to my sources."

"*Aha!* You've got spies, too!"

"I fell into that, didn't I? But keeping up with news of local people's welfare and needs is hardly spying. A decent son would recognise his mother's empathy! The truth is that the family are sick of the constant threat of raids, so they've decided to go back to Armorica. They came from there originally. They'd built a small chapel with a lovely stone altar. I hear they're also constructing a church nearby, and although, it is well outside his diocese, Bishop Exuperius wrote to me about it. He's worried the whole place would be despoiled when they leave – the majority of Silurians are still pagan, and it's too far south from chief – woops, king – Conanus's fortress for him to be able to exert any control. I could show you the location on a map – you've got the Antonine Itinerary for Britannia in the library, don't you?"

"I do, but I lent it to Severus for his campaign plans. I know the rough area – remember we rode around all of the Silurian lands pretending to look for Elen! But getting to the point?"

"The bishop asked me for advice about the villa, and I've got an idea. I wanted to see what you thought of it."

"Does it have a name, this villa?"

"Probably, but I don't remember it. They're Celts, of course, continental, not from Britannia. Romanised for generations. They're Christians, and they're wealthy – originally from the tin, copper and lead mines around there, but more recently, something about supplying beef and mutton to the legion here at Isca – or used to be here. They don't want money for the place and will donate it all to the Church."

"They must be serious sinners, looking for redemption! So, what's your idea?"

"To use the chapel and the church and the villa and any surrounding sheds and barns to set up a centre of learning. The Church desperately needs more young men to become scholarly. Not quite like a monastery, but the same sort of idea – a centre for study, reflection, bible study, prayer, reading... and we could name it to honour the late emperor in recognition of his staunch support of the Nicene Creed in 381. We'd call it *Schola Theodosii*, Cor Tewdws in Celtic. What do you think?"

"About the name or the idea?"

"Both."

"I think they're both brilliant. The name because you could then certainly beg for funding from the emperor's family. And the idea because... well, because it's a wonderful idea, it would be just like Plato's Academy or Aristotle's Lyceum!"

Flavius sounded so enthused by the comparison that his mother couldn't tell whether he was being genuine or sarcastic. The answer came in his next breath:

"With the emphasis on the *idea*, since I can't imagine where you would find a single Christian scholar in this province learned enough to teach there, especially if it is so threatened by pirates."

"Well, as a Christian centre, we'd just put our trust in God to defend it."

"*Hmm,* yes, well, Mama dear, you know my thoughts. I'm a believer, but I've never once seen a prayer answered by the Lord. We've got to be realistic. What *I'd* trust are a few good Roman *onagers* with a large stock of inflammable missiles all along the cliffs."

"You're such a blasphemer! But I'll grant you one thing. God can't attack Saxon pirates directly without relying on the bravery of Christian defenders on the cliffs. He gave us the brains to use our superior weaponry for just and holy causes."

"Oh no! Don't you believe in miracles any more, not to mention Jesus's sermon that it's the meek who will inherit the earth? You've been reading Pelagius again. You call me the blasphemer! Maybe you should invite Pelagius to come back to be the master of your new *schola.*"

"Now I know you're just making fun of me! Anyway, I've got someone else in mind, a learned British priest called Ninian. He's just returned from Rome. On his way home, he met up with Bishop Martinus in Civitas Turonum, who organised stone masons to come back with him so he could build a church here."

"That's a bit odd, you must admit," Flavius wrinkled his forehead. "We've got perfectly good masons here – for a while, at least. But now I realise exactly who you're talking about, and I'm afraid you've missed your chance. That ship has sailed. My intelligence sources told me a Celtic bishop had gone north early this very year to the Novantae tribal lands to convert the Picts up there by order of Pope Siricius. And yes, he's got men building a church using beautiful candida stone. I couldn't imagine the Picts able to construct anything other than a grass shack or a dry-stone dyke, so I was sceptical about the information, but now it makes perfect sense. Except for one thing."

"What's that?"

"He has absolutely no chance of ever converting the Picts to anything. There are Scoti living up there as well – he might have better luck with them. But it's awfully bad timing – just after General Stilicho declared a Pictish war and sent Sev to conduct it. That's why we've been gathering relevant information."

"More spying!" Lady Galeria exclaimed in mock horror.

"For sure. But this sort of information is vital. The Picts and the Scoti aren't really the problem. They're lawless and vicious, but apart from some bad slavers, they're mainly after food. They aren't good farmers, and their homeland is rugged and unsuitable for most crops. They live on milk and meat, so stealing cattle is mostly what they're after on their raids. But despite their viciousness, they're Celts like us and speak a similar language – well, maybe the Caledonians, less so the more northerly Painted People. The Germanic Saxons, however, are a totally different kettle of fish. They're losing territory to the Huns, and they want to take our land, just like the Romans once did, but they at least brought civilisation to these islands; the pagan Angles and Saxons bring only mayhem. They are the ones we must unite against. Are you ready for a glass of wine? I got a new shipment in this morning, all the way from Tuscia."

As though psychic, a manservant appeared in the doorway at that moment. Before Flavius could order any wine, the servant spoke up.

"Excuse me for interrupting Domina, but there is a woman I do not know in the foyer who is insisting on talking to you. Alone," he added, looking towards Flavius.

"Is she begging? You could ask her kindly to go to the back, and Jodocus will take care of her."

"I don't think she's a beggar, my lady; she looks most respectable and has an escort of two armed men. She said she has to talk to you privately."

"I'll see her. Did she give a name?"

"No."

"All right. Show her in and then leave. Maybe wait outside at a discrete distance. Flavius, could you please get Lestinus to take the men around to the rear courtyard and give them refreshments? He knows to ask them to surrender any weapons first. I hate it, but I've become suspicious ever since Dilectus's abduction."

The tall, matronly woman who was soon seated next to Galeria was not what she had expected. She was well dressed, wore a fashionable bonnet and was more confident than any of the usual collection of distressed, often desperate women from the town who knew of the domina's inability to turn away anyone in need. She also spoke fluent Latin.

"My name is Conchessa, originally from Gaul. My husband is a decurion. He works for the civitas of the Cornovii, which is now under the control of the Vitalis family, whom I know you know. My father is a priest, Father Potitus, now recently retired; he lives with us."

"I have heard of him. I am a friend of the bishop in your diocese of Corinium."

"Thank you, dear lady. I just wish to establish my credentials. My matter is complex. For days now, I have been worried about my son, Patricius. He's been acting strange and secretive. I thought he was ill. He appeared to be stealing food from the kitchen. We have a modest farm and there is never a shortage. I questioned him, and he denied there was anything the matter, but a mother always knows. I waited, hoping he'd come to me with the truth. Then, a few mornings ago, when he neglected his jobs around the house and sneaked furtively outside, I followed him."

Conchessa paused. She was still doubtful that Galeria was the right person to tell.

"I couldn't believe my eyes. There was my son, in earnest conversation and a bit of roughhousing with another boy about his size. It turns out that he has been harbouring a younger boy in one of our farm sheds. This boy is the one who has been missing for weeks."

"Praise be to God, good lady. You're saying this boy is the missing prince, Dilectus? And he's safe, but being held captive by your son somewhere?"

Padrig's mother looked alarmed. "Being looked after, not held against his will. He is in hiding because, between the two boys and their limited understanding of the world, they have worked out that he's still in grave danger. The boy is fine. A little dirty and he has real bad sores on his wrists. But he's fearful and suspicious. They both are. They're both convinced that people are out to kill him."

"Well, Heaven be praised. Alleluia! Our prayers have been answered. I know Dilectus very well. We must tell his mother immediately. I can't imagine what she has been going through."

"That was my initial reaction, too, believe me. His mother is Princess Elen of the Silures. Everyone knows who she is. And there have been at least two groups of armed men who have come to our estate in Banwen, making enquiries. The boy – Dilectus – escaped from his kidnappers, and he and my son are convinced that these search parties are out to recapture him. And to do him harm because when he escaped, he seriously injured one of them. Dear Lady Galeria, you must believe me when I say I questioned them closely, at first telling them that such fears were groundless. But I changed my mind when they explained their thinking, even though I am certain most of it is twisted.

"I became convinced their suspicions are not wholly irrational when my son said immediately that he didn't trust my husband, his father, not to turn his new friend over to dangerous people because of the size of the reward being offered for his 'discovery' and possible recapture. That really took me aback. His own father! I've heard other men, possibly from your villa, were also offering a reward, and Dilectus said that his mentor who was teaching him martial arts seemed to have lost interest in him because he has been away for many weeks; and your son might be trying to destroy his friendship with Claudia – is that your granddaughter's name? That one sounded even more far-fetched than all their other conspiratorial ideas, but he's clearly scared of Dominus Flavius.

"Dilectus also told me, with tears in his eyes, that his mother had always said she and he were all the family she ever wanted now his father was dead and that the two of them were a team, together for always. But now he's sensed she's interested in remarrying, probably the man who's been teaching Dilectus to ride, as he would then also want the young prince out of the way because he'd want his own children to inherit the Silurian Kingdom. Sorry, my lady. I'm babbling, but after listening to them, I was becoming equally suspicious, especially as my husband has said on a number of occasions that his counterpart, another decurion employed by the Vitalis family, had expressed an unusual amount of interest in the case and was offering a huge reward for the capture or execution of two monks, whom everyone says were the ones who kidnapped Dilectus."

"Some of this sounds like childish imagination, like being scared of ghosts and witches or goblins hiding in their bed-chambers," Galeria finally got a word in. "We do have to let Elen know he's safe as quickly as possible. And who is keeping an eye on them while you are here?"

"The one person *I* can trust. My father. The boys don't know, but my father will simply make sure no one goes near the hiding place – the shed – or questions Padrig's taking food or disappearing for hours. And, of course, we must tell the princess. My two manservants and I will ride to Garn Gogh after I have rested here for a while if I may be so bold as to request your hospitality. No one else can be trusted at this time."

"You trusted me!"

"Dilectus told my son, and then me, that you were the only person in the whole world he could really trust absolutely."

"That has to be one the finest compliments anyone has ever paid me," Galeria said slowly. After a pause, she recovered her practical self: "Yes, you should go. You must go. Elen needs to hear as soon as humanly possible. I'll ask one of my best guards to provide further escort. Lestinus is a devout man who knows the area better than most. It was he who led our own villa search for Dilectus. He can come back here, and Elen can pick the escort for you and she to return to your home, retrieve the boy and reward your son. I think once we two and Elen go public together and announce his return, that alone ensures his safety, at least for a while. And then I will also enlist the help of one other man who is untouchable, and that is my friend, the new *magister militum,* General Severus. He's been coaching Dilectus in military skills, and they are genuinely close. They're usually inseparable. But he has indeed been away; he has a campaign to organise. Maybe Dilectus can't appreciate some grown-up's responsibilities and feels a bit abandoned. Severus will give us guidance about what to do next."

"That's excellent, my lady. Dear God, thank you, and you, Domina, have given me great relief. Can I be allowed to raise one other matter that is only tangentially related? Are you planning on attending the wedding celebration of the young Vitalis boy, Vitalinus, who is calling himself Vortigern? I hear that you had a major influence in finding him a suitable wife?"

"That is true, Conchessa, but I wasn't actually planning on going."

"Please do go. I hear Sevira is deeply unhappy. Vortigern is a selfish man, interested only in his own advancement. Don't ask me how I know this, but I have a sixth sense about these things. As a mother, I have three daughters as well as my son, Patricius! Flavia Sevira is deeply unhappy. All the servants gossip as they do. Vortigern is abusive, cruel and insulting. He screams at her that the only thing he ever wanted was to be married to Princess Elen. Can you see, dear lady, how easily a web of evil can be spun, with male ambition, jealousy, lies and innuendo all adding suspicion and distrust? It is not confined to the two boys. Our Christian world still struggles with the Devil."

Chapter 13: Stilicho's Pictish War, AD 398

The discovery of Dilectus brought enormous relief to some people and a great deal of carefully masked angry frustration to others. For no one was there a proper sense of closure. No one knew who the kidnappers were, or what they wanted, or who might have been paying them. They seemed to have disappeared.

This generated considerable suspicion across the region, especially as the whole story was told over and over by word of mouth, many of the mouths' owners not being entirely sober or in possession of any actual facts. Dilectus's own paranoid thoughts were easily replicated in whispered conversations at the market, after church, in dining halls, and in servant quarters by well-meaning folk deeply curious about what it all meant. A local crisis event like this was far more worthy of speculation than the occasional story of political chaos on the continent. And in any case, for a while there was a period of relative peace and calm. An army was being formed, Stilicho was coming, the raids from the north would end, recent skirmishes with Saxons had seen them driven off – people were beginning to feel safer. All except Dilectus. Whomever wanted him gone was still out there, and a badly injured make-believe monk who was known to be violent had another score to settle. After a conversation with Dilectus and Galeria, Severus thought he might be able to help a little with the tension at Garn Goch by getting Meirion out of the picture for a while. He was superb as master of horse – not a cavalry office per se, but certainly no-one would question him being appointed as Severus's lieutenant and being given the temporary title of *magister equitum.*

Severus's planning for the arrival of Stilicho and the promised imperial troops had taken more time and cost more money than he had anticipated. "It's always the way," he'd told Senica, when she grumbled she hardly ever saw him these days.

"It's always your way," she replied, "you're such a perfectionist."

"More like old age is slowing me down," he retorted, jokingly, but for the first time in his life he was feeling the physical and mental strain of command under almost impossible circumstances.

He knew he should ask Senica to leave the villa complex and move back into town. It was closer to his hastily refurbished headquarters in Isca Silurum, the name he now preferred to Castra Augusta. He agreed with Flavius that if they wanted to have an equal partnership with the locals, they had to start giving them proper recognition. Being the officially appointed military commander for the whole of Britain had given him great opportunities without having to ask anyone for permission. One of his best decisions was to allow King Conanus to initiate a project of rebuilding and strengthening the fortifications of Garn Goch, especially the two towers protecting the main entrance gate. The Romans had partially torn these down two centuries earlier. It was the ideal policy for the transfer of control from Rome to the local chieftains, but had unintended consequences. The most immediate of these, though not immediately recognized, was in the neighbouring tribal region to the north: Vortigern was furious that the Silures were getting special favours. When Severus sent word demanding he supply a contingent of fighting men, he replied he lacked the resources, something no tribal chief would ever have dared to say when the Emperor in Mediolanum was firmly in control.

It was the same damn story across the south of Britain, where people were less impacted by Pictish raiders and more threatened by the Saxons. Providing troops for the Roman army was one of the obligations of all the subjected tribes and landowners, but they had learned a long time ago the strategies they could use to avoid such responsibilities. Wealthy villas offered money instead, which was fine in principle, but the shortage was of trained soldiers and money wasn't the issue after Stilicho had sent boatloads of equipment – weapons and uniforms – which included considerable amounts of coin. Severus could now pay soldiers, but recruiting was hampered by one simple fact, obvious to all. A campaign against the northern Picts would produce little in the way of loot. The Picts had nothing. It was widely known they were savages whose wealth was counted in cattle, and even their shaggy little cows yielded only the toughest meat.

A great organizer, Severus was the kind of leader who knew the value of giving considerable responsibility to competent lower-level officers wanting to make a name for themselves. Their family background was irrelevant; loyalty to him and agreement with the mission were critical. He sent out a group of smart young men with authority to select the fittest soldiers from among the garrison troops, offering them a bonus and taking only unmarried men without a family. Desertion had been a chronic problem the past few years, despite the severe penalties if caught – severe as in being cudgelled to death by their own comrades. Deserters were thus prone to form bands of violent brigands. Weakening the garrisons by fifty percent was extremely unpopular with local leaders and their people, so Severus's advance recruiters tried appealing to the tribal loyalties of young men in the towns and hamlets, urging them to uphold the honour of the Iceni or the Trinovantes or the Parisi. The first time for a few hundred years a Roman army commander had appealed to tribal loyalties. And as for the regular Roman army troops, the difficulty motivating them was that beating up the Picts, who were just irritatingly mysterious, didn't seem as glorious as following the beloved Caesar into battle at Pharsalus.

It was, therefore, a motley collection of Roman army veterans (few of them Roman or even Italian), tribal warriors and inexperienced recruits looking for adventure, who'd been gathered together at Eboracum. Severus had selected this important city as the best staging point for the campaign. Eboracum had spiritual significance for those men who were both Christians and concerned about doctrinal niceties – the first Bishop of York had been present at the Council of Nicaea. And among those with any loyalty towards the Empire, it would be known that the great Constantine was proclaimed Emperor in that same city after his father had suddenly died there in AD 306. Proclaiming emperors had become something of an army tradition in Britannia. Best of all, it was a wealthy city and Severus's advance party of eager new officers were persuasive. They encouraged the townsfolk to donate quality provisions to the gathering troops as part of their civic duty to reward the young men willing to die just to protect them from future raids.

The parade ground of the army fortress at Eboracum was used to accommodating seven thousand men, so squeezing in the nearly nine thousand who had been collected up was no problem. Severus arrived to address them with severe trepidation. He had a commanding parade-ground voice, and, although fluent in Latin, he was able to slip into the Vulgar Latin patois the troops used to communicate with each other, a kind of pidgin, full of slang terms, Gallic curse words, mispronounced Latin, even smatterings of Greek. But he wasn't sure how they would take the critical items of news he had to relay.

"Friends, soldiers, loyal men of the four mighty provinces of Britannia and proud conscripts and *foederati* from across the waters: greetings. And may whatever god you worship be by your side from now on. You are here by command of the most pious and blessed Honorius, Augustus of the Western Empire, *imperator et pater patriae* and of General…" here Severus paused slightly, this was the hard part coming, "Flavius Stilicho, *Magister Militum* of the Empire. Our esteemed general had hoped to lead this important campaign; however, he is unable to come. Instead, he has appointed me, Severus, the Comes Brittaniarum, to lead you on this important mission…"

At that moment a resounding cheer went up, a huge noise as men banged their swords against their shields, shouting '*barritus!*' and his nickname '*Fortis in perpetuum*'. Relieved, delighted, but stony-faced, Severus raised both hands for silence.

"Don't get too enthusiastic. This is not a traditional campaign. Our enemy is on their own land. They know it well. Some call them demons because they can sneak up on you, attack and then disappear in the continual mists of this bleak place. I was a young officer under Comes Theodosius in the campaign of 368. It took us a full year to get things under control. I don't have a year and neither do you. So, here's the plan. We go in hard and fast. Use cavalry when we can. We kill anyone who defies us, and we confiscate all weaponry and anything that looks like it has been stolen from raids. You'll be able to tell. They don't make much themselves, but they trade in honest barter with Greeks and Phoenicians, so if some item looks fancy, it's probably theirs. There will be no raping of women. Keep your cocks in your hands – I mean your pants. [Scattered laughter.] No killing of children, even if they're attacking you. If you burn a settlement as punishment for resistance, make sure the people get out first. Only kill farm animals you plan to eat. Remember, *they* are the savages, not us. This will be strictly enforced. Understood?"

This time, there was no cheering or laughing. Only a general murmur of disgruntlement. Severus raised his hand again.

"All right. Listen. What I said may not be popular. But think of this. We have been retaliating against those painted people for years and years. Has it ever stopped the raids or the burning and killing here in Britannia? No. Retaliatory raids [here Severus had to use the phrase '*lex talionis*'; he couldn't think of a simpler expression] have never worked to keep us safer. We're going to try something different. My military adviser, a profoundly wise man indeed, said our real enemies are the Germanic peoples, the men from faraway places you have never heard of, like Iutum and Angeln, in addition to Saxonia. Let this campaign show all our enemies how determined we are.

"Now, here is the next bit of bad news. Half of you here will be selected by your commanders to advance into Caledonia. The emphasis will be on safety first. The Picts avoid a pitched battle. So will we. They like sneaky raids and ambushes. So will we. Our casualties will be minimal. The other half of you will be working on improving defences in this region. We are going to build new forts all along the east coast and equip them with guards trained for the purpose. We all know if Saxon ships are sighted early, meeting the boats coming ashore gives us a huge tactical advantage. Once they gain a beachhead, they are harder to deal with – look how well the Britons kept the great Julius Caesar from taking over this island the first time. It's no disgrace being selected for this work detail and your pay will be increased to match those of you riding or marching north. There will be two weeks for selection and then a month of further training, and then we get down to business. Unit commanders, dismiss your men."

When the time came to cross the Wall and venture beyond the Antonine boundary, now just an unmanned turf embankment rather than a defensive line, the situation was much as Severus had predicted. Settlements they came to were mostly empty, with any portable possessions, farm tools, clay crockery and iron pots all removed. There wasn't any booty worth plundering. When lightning attacks with arrows and javelins occurred, the troops burnt down the huts in the nearest settlement and helped themselves to scrawny, black-faced sheep and chickens. When they were able to catch someone, one of the elderlies who wasn't quite fast enough to escape, they were extensively questioned, one might say grilled, for information on the whereabouts of important people or chiefs who could be taken as hostages. But few answers were forthcoming. Mostly, those being interrogated acted as though they were deaf or simple-minded. Severus watched a couple of the attempted interviews and came away convinced they were neither deaf nor daft but undoubtedly canny.

When ordinary people were in their usual work clothes, knitted woollen skirts and other garments, often dyed in different colours and patterns, they came across as surprisingly ordinary and not especially savage. They only painted their bodies when they were going into battle. They didn't seem that different from the three more southern tribes, the Novantae, the Selgovae and the Votadini, who'd been coexisting with the Empire north of the Wall in a state of mutual disregard. Like those tribes, the Picts had a few inhabited hillforts, and in the abundant lochs, Severus saw large groups of crannogs, artificial islands of huts built on stilts over the water. He would have liked to talk to the people living there, but to his regret, he had not thought to bring any boats with the expedition.

As he said to Meirion one evening when they were drinking wine together: "You know it's a crying shame we didn't try to approach these people by sending ambassadors bearing gifts and getting a bit of serious intelligence as to what they want, how they live, what their issues are. We have such superior technology and war equipment, and training one of my best cohorts could wide out their entire army – if they have one – in a pitched battle. Christ, even the name 'Roman Army' scares the shit out of most foreigners. But this buzzing at us like clegs on a summer day just makes us look ineffectual and weak. Even my no-reprisals strategy probably won't have any effect. I think they raid because it is in their nature like a drunkard drinks wine. But if we understood them better, maybe we could civilise them."

Meirion nodded in agreement, then chuckled: "Imagine if we brought a few of their prominent young people, you know, like sons of chiefs, to come and stay at Villa Arcadius. Lady Galeria is always going on about being charitable to the less fortunate among us. Think of the wonder of eating her oranges shipped in from her estates in Hispania and then going for a proper bath with warm water, then a cold scrub. I swear they'd never leave!"

"We'd have to toss them in the river first to get all that blue dye off their bodies. And Galeria wouldn't give them an orange until they said grace first to thank the Lord for the bounty from her garden! But you do have a point – Caesar spouted the same about the barbarians in Gaul. Once they were exposed to the luxuries of civilisation, they were dead keen to become peaceful citizens of Rome. It seems like in four hundred years, we haven't learned anything about taming savages. I think we need to go home. We're just wasting our time here. Our casualties have been minimal, but our influence even less."

"What will you tell Stilicho?" Meirion asked.

"I'll write a report, and that idiot court poet can whip off a panegyric full of exaggerations about the success of his mission. In fact, I could give him helpful cues by writing how the Picts were wild painted savages who bowed and cowed and knelt at the very name of General Stilicho, or better still, Honorius. I should mention the forts we're working on as well since Stilicho or maybe the Emperor paid for them. I can say we now have the watchtowers that will alert us to the approaching Saxons. And that's probably how Stilicho's Pictish War will go down in history and how the Picts will be remembered. But I'm also going to praise the troops. The training was hard, but they pulled it together. And they seem to trust me. If I can get them all home alive with only blisters to complain about, I'd rate this mission as a success. In the report anyway."

Meirion smiled. He was lucky to be there and even luckier to be taken into the confidence of the Comes Brittaniarum. Severus had suggested he come along as an aide de camp. Meirion wasn't a combat soldier but was just superb with horses. So good that Severus asked him to put together an elite cavalry unit, a *palatini*, and gave him an acting commission in a special *vexillatio* detachment. It was designed not so much as protection for Severus but to be able to give chase when the Picts rode off after a brief surprise attack of spear-throwing horsemen. Severus's respect for Meirion had grown even stronger than when he had first made use of him as a scout and messenger – a literate, working-class lad with a gift for horses. Perhaps it was the wine they were drinking or the fact that Severus was talking to him in such an unguarded way that Meirion suddenly broke into Severus's train of thought.

"Can I ask you something, Severus?"

"Sure."

"It's rather personal. Private."

"Have you committed a crime?"

"No. I'm in love."

"With Elen," Severus completed his sentence.

"What? Why would you say that?"

"Aren't I right?"

"Well, yes, but how could you guess? I've not told anyone."

"Guess? It was no guess. Everyone knows. It's the way you look at her. It's the way you bring her into conversations when her name is entirely irrelevant. It's the way you fuss over Dilectus even though he's being a brat and ignoring you. We all know. I did have to tell Flavius – he hadn't noticed – but Galeria and I have been joking about it for months. And you are not alone. Elen is still utterly gorgeous. Dear god, even I'm in love with her – but strictly from afar, no need to panic, although I'm richer than you are and better looking."

"Cowshit! You're short and getting fat and you are old enough to be her grandfather. I'm not threatened. But I seriously wanted to ask your advice. You know about women, rank, status and stuff. Would she just laugh at me if I told her my feelings? She knows I like her and am incredibly attracted to her. But does that mean I can ask her for her hand in marriage?"

"*Like*? *Like*? Where's your passion, boy? What about adore, worship, dote on? You're wrong about my understanding of women. I've been faithful to Senica our whole married life. Flavius claims it is out of fear, but he's mistaken. I know a good thing when I see it, and she's all I've ever wanted, and I tell her so. As to telling Elen, I'm the Shah of Persia if she doesn't know already."

"If she knows, why doesn't she say something?"

"And risk being wrong and humiliating herself? Elen has more class than that. If you don't have the guts to tell her honestly what you feel, you don't deserve her, that's for sure. Why are you holding back? Why are you talking to me, not her?"

Meirion hesitated for a moment. "Well, shit, I ask myself the same question. I'm of much lower rank. She's going to be queen one day, very soon, in fact. Conanus isn't well. I'm just the stable boy. Her father would have me executed if he thought I had designs on his daughter. And I'm younger than she is, and we have a history, as you know so well, especially with her dead husband whom she worshipped. Why would she want me?"

"Good god, boy," Severus said, shaking his head, "who said anything about marriage? You're a long way from there if you haven't even courted her or composed her a love song. You Celts from Cymru are supposed to be good at that."

"Thanks, Severus, useless advice. If I sang to her, that would be the end of it."

"Whatever you think she might like, stupid. My point is you have to court her. Give her a gift. Heavens above, your sister is her best friend – why don't you ask her?"

"I sort of mentioned it to Sioned, and she just laughed at me, saying Elen wouldn't look twice at an upstart puppy like me."

"That's big sisters for you, my friend. She's probably a little jealous, and the thought of you and Elen together probably freaks her out."

"You do seem to know about women after all. But you haven't addressed my original question."

"Which was what?" Severus looked puzzled.

"The status thing. Elen could have any man she chooses, and I'm sure she wants a rich one with vast estates."

"I'll be honest with you, Meirion; that is perfectly possible. Women in her position don't usually get to choose who they marry. But when Conanus dies, Elen will be rich with large estates. I'm sure old Conanus fantasises a powerful land-owning son-in-law who will double the size of the kingdom."

"Now I know you are quite wrong. If you think Elen would do anything because some man told her to, you don't know her as well as I do. She had Caradocus wrapped around her little finger and old Chief Conanus as well. And Sioned has told me that she has already rejected Vortigern of the Vitalis family."

"Did she indeed? That's interesting. Did he proposition her or something?"

"I don't know for certain. I think he came on to her in a very aggressive way."

Severus didn't respond but he became quieter. It seemed that the information had interrupted the jovial mood. His next remark sounded like he wanted to end the discussion.

"Look, Meirion, stop being a sheep waiting for a dog to show you where to go. Stop with the worry and the shit about status. Stop thinking you might be rejected. You might be. You need to act and take the risk. And you shouldn't waste any time: *'fugit inreparabile tempus'*. Virgil."

"Never heard of him!" Meirion exclaimed.

"You're just an ignorant Celtic stable boy!" Severus replied, recovering his humour. "When we get back to Eboracum and demob the troops, I give you permission to take the Silurians and the villa men back home as quickly as you can, and you ride into Garn Goch like a man, demanding to see the princess at once, and then you pour your heart out. It's an order. And no singing!"

Chapter 14: All Duck and no Drake

Naturally, it was Elen who obeyed Severus's order despite never having heard it. "Meirion dear, I've got something important to discuss with you. Why haven't you yet asked me to marry you? We can't just keep on sneaking around and ducking our responsibilities. We're carrying on like rabbits, and any minute now, I'm going to get pregnant. I don't want people to think we were forced into holy matrimony."

It was Elen's directness that intimidated Meirion, who wasn't normally intimidated by much. Or maybe he was. Cocky was how people described him. It was so complicated. Having been around Elen as a young man and as a married woman, her incredible looks he'd more or less taken for granted. Now, they were lovers; he had become aware of something profoundly unsettling. She was so attractive to men that men, without exception, showed desire for her. Even an old guy like Severus had commented on her desirability, and Elen had told him about the way that awful Vortigern up north had courted her, arrogantly assuming she would want him and being aggressive when she told him bluntly, she did not. He had almost raped her there and then, and Meirion couldn't get that thought out of his mind either.

Was he going to spend his entire life feeling jealousy, if that was the word, towards all the other men in the world who gave Elen longing looks, mentally undressing her and wondering why this stable boy should be the one to have her? It just made the status difference so much greater. He'd thought about nothing more than wanting to marry her ever since their first moments of intimacy made it seem that such a possibility was a possibility. So why hadn't he asked her? Because he knew what men would say behind his back – how could a little squirt like him, who wasn't a warrior or rich, get a woman like Elen? So undeserved! On top of that, she was taking charge of the situation in a totally unromantic way. It was too matter-of-fact. Perhaps, his delays had frustrated her to the point she was now asking him, but even so, that wasn't the way it was supposed to be.

He stormed out of the room. The heavy oak door clanged behind him.

Oh god, Elen thought. I didn't handle it well. But what's got into him? Why the reluctance? If he wouldn't talk to her about his apparent hesitancy, surely it was up to her to make the first move like this and just bluntly deal with it. But maybe that challenged his masculinity in some way. He'd never lost control like that before, although he'd occasionally expressed intense frustration about some problem before trying to solve it, and she knew he had a tauter bowstring to his soul than Caradocus, who had been a more placid, self-contained kind of person, or his older sister, green-eyed, red-haired Sioned, who like all true Celts had warrior blood and felt at one with nature. Meirion was tainted by spending too much time pleasing Romans. He must be feeling inadequate.

When he returned, somewhat contrite and knowingly foolish, he told Elen what the problem was.

"Look, Elen; I know what your father will say, just like all the other important men around here: 'What the shit's wrong with Princess Elen, getting herself involved with the son of a cook?' They're all so status-conscious, those fat old noblemen in their plaid trousers who are all terrified of Rome but call me a Roman lapdog because I'm respected by Severus. Severus, who gave me a chance in life when even your husband looked down on me." He didn't raise his primary discomfort: that every ogling man in Cymru wanted her physically.

Elen listened patiently. She knew this was an important moment in their relationship. Her first marriage had been madcap, impulsive, reckless and passionate. Thirteen years later, things were very different. Her older sisters, her only siblings, were both dead. Her husband was dead. She was the heir to an even younger unified tribal kingdom – if she could keep it. Stability, as her father had stressed, was essential. Her world had been defined by the Roman Empire, like it or not. Now, without a bloody revolt or protracted rebellion or guerilla warfare, her people had independence – not granted voluntarily nor taken by force, simply emerged by reason of neglect. The fraying farthest western edge of an empire unravelling was the first to reveal the decay. These were dangerous times. Meirion offered stability if not passion. The sex was good. He was kind and usually considerate. He was patient with her son, although recently... *Ugh.* She couldn't ruin this moment, this opportunity.

"I love you, dear. More than you can possibly know. And I need you. Dilectus needs you. He needs brothers. Since when have the Celts worried about status and nobility? That's Roman cow dung. When the Roman Empire was under pressure from the outside, noblemen and slaves, all looked and acted the same – I heard that somewhere. We don't have either here. Do I put on airs because people call me a princess? Your birthright is just as important as mine and neither of them are important at all. We're not horses. Bloodlines don't matter. Jesus, you can't even cook like your mother, so I don't know what you've inherited from her except warmth and decency."

In important moments, humour can be risky. Meirion wasn't smiling, so Elen hurried on. "Let me put this another way. You say my father won't accept you. It just shows how silly you can be. He's been nagging me to marry you for years. It was his damn idea. He knows the old Celtic ways in which it's fine for the woman to ask the man first. You're nice in bed; you've obviously lost your hang-up about my darling Caradocus, whom you revered, I know. So here we are – don't you want to be regent to the Queen of the Silures one day?"

"No! I certainly don't. But I do want to marry you if you will have me, just as I am. And we'll make beautiful babies for old Chief Conanus to have more grandkids. So that's that. You'd better send the servants out to look for bog myrtle in the mountains."

Chapter 15: All Politics is Local – and Personal

King Conanus, chief of the Silures and, on a good day, the Demetae, thoroughly approved of the marriage between Elen and Meirion, especially when Elen admitted to him she was probably pregnant. He asked Meirion to come and talk to him, man to man. It was the last thing Meirion wanted to do, but he knew he had to.

"Listen here, young man," Conanus began. "I like you. I didn't like her first husband, but then I only met him once and we didn't talk – it was the night he ran away with my beautiful third daughter. She's always sworn he was a great husband and certainly young Dilectus is a good fellow. But I do know you, and you please me even though no father *ever* considers his son-in-law good enough for his daughter."

He gave a loud guffaw, which quickly turned into long bout of coughing and Meirion saw for the first time how frail he now was.

"Anyway, I'm happy to welcome you into this family," Conanus eventually continued. "It won't surprise you to know I'm dying. I've felt it for quite a while and it's a miracle I've lasted this long – must be because I'm such a good Christian, God is looking after me. Or maybe He doesn't want to see me hanging around heaven and wants to delay my arrival." He chuckled again, this time pulling the sheepskin rug up to his mouth to stifle another coughing spell. "It's good you're getting married. I've ordered the kitchen staff to prepare a feast and my *bajulus*, as the Romans call my liegeman, to make the arrangements for a great reception as well as for a coronation.

"On this matter, I've got serious issues I need to tell you about. First, you won't be king. You'll be a regent, another Roman idea – god almighty; when I think how the bloody Romans infiltrated every aspect of Celtic society, I cringe because now they're losing their grip on their empire, and they haven't told us how to be a free people again. Sorry, I'm getting distracted.

"Just remember it was Flavius Arcadius who set up the idea for me to be king, and he and Elen's first husband, a Demetae, negotiated an alliance between that tribe and us. Be sure to remember that to keep peace and avoid power struggles, you have to nurture that alliance. And we can do that by not making you king. Elen will be accepted by both tribes as Queen – she's got the looks, the education, the smarts and the boldness to give them all fantasies of Boudica when the Celtic people were proud and strong. We have to maintain that legend and the image if you like. Mint coins with her face on them. Flavius is always nagging me to set up a mint. You can do it. You're young, and it won't seem to you such a bloody fool imperial idea. Where was I?

"Yes. Flavius. You know him well. That's a help. Consult him, but don't be too quick to accept his advice. He's got his own problems. How long do d'you think he can keep such a fancy villa going with no Roman army to provide the ring of shields? He thinks we should keep following Roman law. But with no one to enforce it, I think we should return to the laws of our ancestors. This makes succession tricky. If Elen and you have a boy, he'll be next in line. If you don't, keep trying 'till you do. But babies and mothers die awfully easily; to be blunt, it's more than likely that Dilectus will be king after Elen. Now, there's an additional problem. You used to be close to Dilectus. Ever since his abduction, he's been avoiding you – no, don't deny it, I'm old but not stupid. I don't know why, but you need to patch it up for the sake of the tribe. He's smart, Dilectus is, but the buggers in the villa have Romanised him more than I like.

"Well, there you have it; that's my homily. Better than any, you'll hear from the Garn Goch priest. I'm disappointed in him. I hate to think what he's going to say about me at my funeral. Now piss off, I'm tired. And Meirion – good luck, you're a decent man."

When Elen asked Meirion what her father had told him, Meirion was hesitant.

"It was a bit of a ramble through the blackberry bushes, in fact. The key blackberries I took away from it seem to be, one; I shouldn't try to be king; two, the Romans are on their way out, but three, instead of relief, that might be very bad. Also, we need to have a son and heir, and I need to try to win Dilectus around, although god knows I've tried. Your father's anticipating the final end of Roman colonial rule and doesn't know what all of us long-suppressed tribal people will do. Oh, and he thinks he's dying."

"Can't you be a bit more forthcoming than that? He spoke to you for the best part of an hour."

"To be honest with you, Elen, it was all rather annoying. I never wanted to be a king, so telling me I can't be one really rubbed me the wrong way. You know I'm totally supportive of you and will do everything I can to help you, but I don't seem to be getting any respect. I have no authority, and everyone still keeps talking about Caradocus and how wonderful Dilectus is, although he's being a real pain and does nothing but hang out with his friend Padrig or spend all his other time at the villa. I can't get through to him when he's never here."

Meirion could not put his finger on what was eating him, but feeling powerless was perhaps a good summary. He was about to get married, but as husbands go, he was the second best. As a younger man, he had seen intimately how Caradocus, respectful always to his wife, was undoubtedly head of the household. Meirion felt head of nothing, and he couldn't even get respect from his future stepson.

Chief Conanus's death made it worse. The king is dead; long live the queen. Stupid phrase, Meirion thought, how could Elen, who had once defied her father and the Romans, slip so easily into the assumptions of hereditary succession? The old Celtic ways would at least have required the assent of the tribal elders. And there were too many mixed-up ceremonies coming on top of each other – the funeral, Celtic; the marriage, Roman Catholic; and the coronation... shit, no one knew what it was, a pig's breakfast of ancient rites and contrived symbolism. Flavius had suggested, given the other warlords like the tribal chief of the Demetae and Vortigern, lording it around the place, Meirion should focus everything on getting the allegiance of the tribal landowners, all the clergy, the common people and the townsfolk of Venta Silurum. 'In the end, power comes from the people,' he'd said, but whether this was only his fantasy of the Republic of more than four hundred years ago, Meirion wasn't sure.

And then the baby came, a girl, and Elen was totally preoccupied. As one would expect, Meirion reassured himself. But then all the weight of tribal business and issues fell on his shoulders despite having no fuckin' authority. For the first time ever, he started to dislike his marriage. And

Elen, seeing his withdrawal, his constant snapping at the servants, his crass insistence on making love when she had barely recovered from the delivery and her breasts were tender and she was tired all the time, decided he just wasn't the man she thought he was. Marriage can be challenging under the best of circumstances, but the combined effect of so many changes was making this one rockier than most.

Black thoughts Meirion, too, couldn't get out of his head. Everybody loved Dilectus, even though he was being a perfect prick and acting resentful about his new baby stepsister. Lady Galeria fawned over him; Severus was thinking of taking him on as a junior officer. He'd given the eulogy at his grandfather's funeral in both Celtic and fluent Latin, the little show-off. Elen should have asked him, Meirion, to say the final Celtic prayers. Life would be easier if Dilectus's kidnappers had succeeded. No one had figured out who they were. Maybe another group could try something, with any luck.

Realising these ruminations were unhelpful, Meirion resolved to talk to Severus again when he got the opportunity. Growing up without a father and then finding Severus was the man who trusted him and gave him a job and a purpose, which meant Severus had truly become a substitute father for him. He'd already given him wonderful advice about how to approach Elen – pity she had turned out to be so difficult as a wife. That wasn't Severus' fault. The time he'd spent with Severus on the Pictish campaign had been about the only time in the past few years he'd been truly happy. He would need to go and see him again. Bugger the daily administrative headaches of the tribe.

Chapter 16: A New Century – Old Problems

The first year of the new century was widely thought to be the time the Messiah would return to Earth in triumph, surrounded by apostles and restful martyrs arising in bright array. It was well past the promised time. Fortunately, not many people were following Bishop Augustine's advice to prepare for the second coming by *'from now on let those who have wives live as though they had none'*. And the advice hadn't gone down at all well with the wives. Around Garn Goch, the only sign of a triumphal entry into the world was the presence of the new child. And it couldn't be the messiah, as Elen had given birth to such a beautiful baby girl. Sioned, serving as the trusted nanny, had a no-nonsense style, warm but demanding. It was exactly what Elen needed. And to everyone's relief, the baby had come early on a Thursday evening. To be born on a Friday is bad luck, as that's fairies' day. Fairies can get up to all sorts of nefarious antics, even change the weather if they want, which they often do in Cymru, and not only on Fridays.

The only sad thing was that a girl was no use as a backup for Dilectus in the line of succession that Conanus had hoped for, or even an alternative, as Meirion had been quietly hoping for. Dilectus was becoming more and more the heir apparent, and the title 'prince' was being slipped in ever more frequently. He had returned from his ordeal as a local celebrity and was growing up fast. His education was guaranteed by his virtual adoption into Galeria's household at the villa. His skills as a warrior were becoming increasingly apparent. When the time came, he could be a strong leader in these troubled times.

Elen couldn't understand why Meirion had become so disgruntled and petulant. Everything was going his way. Sure, her marriage to him had raised some older matrons' eyebrows on account of Meirion's lowly status, but the majority of people were delighted. Lots of folks agreed: He was popular. The princess needed a man. He was a good one. His mother was only a cook, but she was queen of her kitchen, and she brought her son up well. Meirion's red-headed sister, on the other hand, was a bit odd. Too blunt for a woman. Said what she thought. Didn't seem to be looking for a man. But as for a widow marrying again, well, that was fine. Why not? The Celts of Britannia were adopting Christianity in their own way. This meant the new trend among educated and wealthy families in Rome towards renunciation of sex and of marriage, which threatened family as the foundational unit of society, did not touch Roman Celtic culture one little bit. The notion that widowhood was somehow more blessed in the eyes of God than remarriage had fortunately not caught on.

Dilectus wasn't interested in anything to do with church doctrine, but in these awkward teen years he found himself resenting his mother's remarriage. It wasn't that he disliked Meirion. Quite the opposite. Meirion had trained him to ride, handle horses and had initiated the first country-wide search after his mysterious disappearance. But at that age one doesn't always feel gratitude with so many things just taken for granted – and in any case the search had been a failure. Why was that? He couldn't even verbalize his feelings about their marriage, except that when Elen had first told him of their engagement, he had blurted out, 'But you always told me you could never love another man like you did my father!'

Trying to be patient, she had sat him down and explained her feelings for Caradocus had never faded but that it was easy to love another good man somewhat differently. She was now a different stage of her life and things like stability and security and the chance to have another child were important elements of a new relationship. Her love for Caradocus could never be superseded – she was speaking in Celtic but used the Latin *accipere locum* to emphasise her point – but now she had a new and different love.

Dilectus stomped out of the room. Elen let him go as she had once done so with his stepfather. It takes time to adjust to stepfathers and they to stepsons, but her advantage was Dilectus didn't remember his own father and everything he knew about him he had learned from her endless heroic stories. And Meirion had been part of those stories. A minor player in the drama. Now Elen could write a new act. Family history is different from political history. With families, it is those who remember their history who are bound to repeat it. What Elen didn't know, couldn't possibly know, is that a boy's affection for his mother is something more complex at the reflexive emotional level, below rational awareness and understanding.

Meirion, at that level, was a rival. The little green worm of jealousy for a mother's love had an erotic component to it, not recognised consciously. None of the great Greek philosophers Flavius admired so much had ever offered such an interpretation, but Sophocles understood it. Why else would his best play, Oedipus the King, have been so popular? And still be popular nearly eight hundred years later?

Jealousy, suspicion and a long history of admiring and loving Meirion as a mentor and a teacher combined in a confusing way. And to deal with the confusion, Dilectus, with his mother's permission and Galeria's agreement, took two of the stable's best horses, packed up his limited possessions and got himself over to the villa. Severus offered him a room. His duties as supreme army commander meant he was hardly ever at home. Senica would enjoy a bit of company, he said.

Flavius was happy to drag Dilectus into the library whenever he could find him and make him read out loud from the latest dispatches. 'Great practice,' Flavius asserted, 'the more you read, the better you are at it and then the more you enjoy it. If reading itself is effortless, you can forget the words on the page and enter into the story or engage in the arguments being presented.' He'd often encourage Claudia to join them. Dilectus liked that. He felt very comfortable with her. He could see how much smarter she was, and he no longer tried to show off or tease her. And she in turn respected his confidence and somewhat greater worldliness. While her knowledge of geography greatly exceeded his, he knew his way around the surrounding countryside far better than she did.

Occasionally, she suggested they go into town together. Venta Silurum was no longer the sleepy little market town that was going into decline after Maximus had taken the legion to Gaul. There was a new general in town, the numbers in the castra were swelling and the men needed feeding. It wasn't quite as prosperous as it had been in the heydays of a few years ago when Severus needed new weapons, boots, leather jerkins, ox waggons, bridles and horse feed, all sorts of bits of armour which hadn't been sent by Stilicho as promised. But there was still enough activity at the Isca Silurum to make shopkeepers happy and the skilled craftsmen busy all day. Local *cervisia* brewers were making handsome profits. Even the children had money to spend after successfully gathering shellfish off the rocks at low tide. Bigger kids with good shovels did well digging in the muddy sand for clams. The town's streets were bustling.

With crowds, however, came danger, and Dilectus was hypervigilant after his experiences. When they went into town, Dilectus carried both a dagger and a sword. His sword was a smaller version of the classic Roman army issue of long ago, the *gladius*. The infantry was no longer using that type and had moved on to longer swords. But the gladius, with its triangular point and sharp edges on both sides, was manageable by a strong boy. And this time Dilectus did show off.

"Uncle Severus has been training me with this sword for years. Its name comes from us Celts, you know – we call it a *kladimos*. You thrust with it, Claudie, you stab your enemy right through the heart. Well, not directly because you might hit the bone and then it won't go in. What you do is go below the heart. Below the ribcage. And you point it up and push it upwards as hard as you can. The neat thing is before you pull it out you give it a good twist, which cuts the tubes going to the heart and then the guy dies right away. Bang. Dead at your feet!"

Claudia was interested. "What if he's wearing armour, Dil? The soldiers at the castra, even the guards at the villa, have a sort of shiny breastplate protecting their rib cage. What then?"

Dilectus didn't know and decided humour was better than ignorance. "Then you ask him oh so politely to lift up his breastplate and bare his floppy fat guts and then you stab him to death."

They both laughed. "Maybe I could come up behind him with my sharp bone embroidery needle and poke him in the bottom, and that would make him jump and then you could go for the heart. Girls have dangerous weapons too." She grabbed his hand and ran off down the street, both shrieking like goblins. For the first time, he noticed how enticingly her breasts moved as she ran.

When they got back to the villa, they found Severus and Flavius standing in the courtyard in earnest conversation.

"What have you two been up to?" Flavius asked. "I thought you were going to read the latest book I ordered. It came last week. It's got pictures. It must have been produced by workshops at Mons Vaticanus. It cost a fortune, but I knew your grandmother would like it, Claudia, and you could read it to your children one day. It tells the story of Aeneas fleeing Troy and coming to Rome."

When the two teenagers disappeared to look for it – pictures made a nice change – Flavius continued bringing Severus up to date with the latest news.

"Bad things are happening in the East. The new prefect there has stripped Alaric of his title, *magister militum* for Illyria."

"Shouldn't have been given it in the first place." Severus grunted. "My relatives there were incensed. *He's* been stripping the province of any damn thing he wants."

"Maybe, Sev, but the anti-Alaric feeling is now so bad that rioters in Constantinople have been randomly killing enlisted Goth soldiers there – by the hundreds. I predict Alaric will turn his attention again to the West. Mark my words."

Back in the library, there was silly giggling going on, much to the irritation of the scribes who were trying to work. Dilectus and Claudia had found striking illustrations in the new book.

"Look, Dil, this is Dido on her deathbed. She's half naked. Look at her breasts. They're smaller than mine."

"I don't think so. That's wishful thinking. You'll have to show me to prove it."

"*That's* wishful thinking, you little puppy. Put your tongue back in your mouth!"

"Come on, Claudie, be a good sport and give me just a quick look!"

She started to tug down the top of her dress, smiling provocatively, then stopped abruptly. "Never," she said, running out of the library with Dilectus giving chase, shouting, "teaser, teaser, teaser – come on, Dido, why don't we go to the bathhouse?"

Flavius cornered them in the courtyard. "Stop it, you two. I don't know what you're up to, but you're disturbing the peace. I thought you were both more mature. Dilectus, you were calling Claudia 'Dido'. I don't want to know what that's about, but both of you can now sit in the library, get some parchment from Brother Molio, and each of you write me a short essay on whether Dido killing herself for love is a sign of a noble passion, which the Greeks would argue, or a sign of personal weakness which us Romans think. And you can think about whether killing yourself is a sin for Christians. Get it written before dinner tonight, or there'll be none."

Deciding Galeria would quickly override any threatened punishment from Flavius, the two rebels continued talking in the library.

"Dil, I need to meet older boys and young men. Can you introduce me to your new friend Padrig or Patricius or whatever his real name is? You've been rattling on about him for months. Can't you ask my grandma to invite him to the villa? She told me she's met his mother, who's a sweetheart."

"Why not come hunting with us one day? You're a good rider and quite good with a bow and arrow."

"You know I'd never get permission. Girls are supposed to focus on weaving and stuff."

"That's silly," Dilectus said. "Galeria has often told me girls can do anything boys can do, and the only problem is that boys make the rules. I'm sure she'd let you go. Autumn's here, and the deer are out mating, so it's a good time for hunting. Flavius would probably forgive us if we brought home some nice venison. But I don't know about meeting Padrig. He's a nice chap and good-looking, though he's not as tall as me now. I don't want you to fall in love with Padrig. If he went away somewhere, you'd have to end up killing yourself, and I wouldn't like that."

"Hey, Dil, that's the second nicest thing you've ever said to me," Claudia was serious for a moment, and Dilectus looked embarrassed. "Come on, we got to write something down, or we won't get any supper. Let's just say killing yourself is a sin because God gave you life and only God can take it away."

"Do you believe that? Why did God take away my father when I was a baby?"

"I think our priest here would reply we can never know God's purpose, which seems like a convenient answer to me and can never be disproved. But maybe God sent Padrig to find you in the barn before those kidnappers did."

"If you heard what Padrig says about God, you'd be as sure as I am; he wouldn't have picked Padrig for any such task."

Claudia poked him teasingly with her foot and he grabbed her ankle and tried to take her shoe off. "Blasphemer!" he said.

"Pagan!" she replied. They were children again.

Chapter 17: One Got Away

It wasn't until May the following year Flavius's predictions proved to be correct, and if God were in any way involved in any deaths of any kind, His purpose would be even more opaque than usual. With Stilicho distracted by trying to combat an invasion of Vandals and Alans in Raetia and Noricum, Alaric took full advantage. He marched his people into Italy. It had serious repercussions for Severus and what was left of his standing army in Britain. Learning of Alaric's movements, Stilicho ordered Severus to take his troops to the continent as quickly as possible to help protect Italy.

"Alaric and his Visigoths are threatening Italia again, and Stilicho is demanding a withdrawal of our best troops from here to go help him," Severus grumbled to Flavius. "Damned unwise, really. He's pulling troops off the Rhine border as well because the fuckin' Vandals and Alans are swarming all over Raetia. He can't campaign on so many fronts at once. He needs to make deals with some of them. Probably Alaric; he's at least a Christian and literate. He can be paid off. I'm so tired of all this back-and-forth swill. The Empire has a problem. The fuckin' Goths are bad, but they're basically a bunch of exiles and would-be immigrants. Alaric probably wants his title back and a place to settle down. Why not give him that instead of letting him surround Mediolanum? And we have to see the disgrace of our pathetic emperor scuttling off to the swamps around Ravenna. I know why he's there. Honorius is shit scared and reckons he's safe hiding in the marshes."

Flavius nodded in agreement, to be supportive, but he added carefully: "One of his problems is the wealthy powermongers around him will resist any financial deals like that. They're not the ones freezing their arses off in the Alpine foothills."

"Wait till they have barbarians looting their luxurious mansions. Then they'll sing a different tune."

"Well, that's not going to happen. Mediolanum is possibly a bit vulnerable, but Rome is indestructible. Can you even imagine what a wall fifty feet high and ten feet thick looks like to someone on the outside wanting in? But right or wrong, Stilicho is your commander-in-chief. What are you going to do?"

"I've got to follow orders, even stupid ones. But I'm reluctant. I'll have to go along with the troops myself. And to be mobile, we can't take along the usual riffraff of hangers-on. I'll try to leave men with families here, but it is going to set back our plans for protecting Britannia. The campaign against the Picts three years ago wasn't very successful, but my strategy of not wreaking havoc on their villages and so-called farms has, I think, paid off. Tribes are like neighbours. When two groups in close proximity have chronic ongoing conflict and hatred, countermeasures by one side just result in retribution from the other. That tit-for-tat nonsense just goes on and on until they've forgotten what they are actually fighting about. I learned this from you. But if it's known we're once again removing troops, they'd be tempted to take advantage.

"I'm going to train the garrison troops to be more prepared to ride out on strong patrols – again, your idea for our villa and the *civitas* defence when Maximus left eighteen years ago. So, I'll promote the few competent junior officers and leave them behind – actually, your nephews have proved themselves. Young Marcus, in particular, will get a big promotion. I think he's popular with the men. He needs to stay here. But Rufus Lucius will have to come with me. I'll make him a tribune but assign him to my staff as a liaison, which should keep him out of harm's way. That'll please your mother. I'm short of senior commanders. There is a chap called Gerontius. He's from Cantium. He impresses everyone, and he's a natural leader, although I worry he's a bit impulsive. Ambition can make an effective soldier but not a good follower."

The bonds between the two friends were so strong that any possible flaws in these plans were easily overlooked. Severus respected Flavius's strategic skills. Flavius respected Severus's organisational and planning ability, knowing how expertly Severus could lead an expeditionary force to the continent. But neither of them was a soothsayer, and neither of them could have possibly foreseen the practical consequences of publicly mobilising Roman army units. And for every action, there is a counterreaction. In this case, it wasn't the Picts. It was Scoti raiding parties engaging in the extremely profitable business of capturing innocent Britons and selling them off in Hibernia as slaves.

While the two friends were having this discussion in the old command headquarters of Isca Silurum, fifty miles away, near where the River Neath enters the broad Tawe Bay, two other friends were enjoying a furtive hunting trip. At first light, Dilectus had brought over to Padrig's estate two of the best horses in Meirion's precious stables. Padrig had sneaked out of his house a bag of crushed oatcakes, a small copper flask of beef broth and two wooden bowls.

"I brought breakfast. We'll need to light a fire. Damn, I forgot spoons."

Dilectus just laughed. "I've got fingers. Did you bring extra arrows? I know you're a lousy shot; you'll need plenty."

Padrig made a face at him, and they rode off happily, heading south on the Sarn y Leng, the military road running past his father's farm. Roads were hardly used these days except for supplies coming up from the coast. But Dilectus was still cautious. He wanted to follow the river instead. The countryside was gorgeous – a cold April had meant the spring daffodils were still in flower, but hawthorn hedges were bursting into life with masses of creamy-white blossoms. Where the soil became drier and sandier further from the river, large stands of silver birch were intermingled with small hazel trees and their long yellow catkins.

The appearance of a huge, wily hare led them through thick brush and wasted four arrows. Four misses made them both more determined to catch it, with Padrig now convinced it was possessed of an evil spirit, most probably a *cyhyraeth*. Dilectus, spending so much time among Romans, was more practical, and he thought only of his stomach. He just loved the way his new step-grandmother, Rhonwen at Garn Goch, cooked a skinned hare in a sealed clay pot sitting in a cauldron of boiling water, with as much of its blood as could be saved. Unfortunately, Padrig's interpretation was clearly correct, as after a frustrating hour, the hare was still very alive and Padrig very grumpy.

A red deer was an easier target, but it, too, got away after a wild chase. By the time they turned their attention to breakfast, it was already well past lunchtime, and the sun was now quite low when they came to a clearing that looked like a good spot to rest the horses and, more importantly, eat their brewis. Like all good Celts, the older teenager knew every tree and every plant had its own soul, so when they saw an inviting hill at the other side of the clearing, Padrig was delighted.

"This is perfect. Look at that clump of rowan trees up there. They'll keep us safe!"

"From what?" said Dilectus, looking around in alarm.

"From witches, of course!"

They tethered the horses and clambered up to the top of a small hill, picking up dry kindling for their fire as they went. But at the other side of the hill, they were startled to see in the near distance a group of five or six burly men with their hair tied in large knots on top of their heads. Unsheathed swords dangled from their belts and behind them, a larger group of women and children. But they weren't the wives and offspring of the armed men. They were all bound by their wrists with heavy rope.

"Dear Christ," Padrig whispered, "they're Scoti slavers. We've got to get out of here."

"We should attack them and free those poor people."

"Are you mad, boy? We left our bows with the horses. Oh shit, now they've seen us, they're pointing at us. You run for the horses and get away. Two of them are coming up fast. I'm going to distract them. The old plover trick. Go on, get the fuck out of here."

Dilectus hesitated. Padrig gave him a hard shove. "Go!" He snarled and then stood up, shouting loudly, "Christ save me!" and, limping badly and pretending to stagger, he made off slowly in the opposite direction. It was a great idea, but Christ, according to later pious commentators, had a better one, not involving escape. A third Scoti appeared from behind a thick gorse bush and tackled him to the ground before he could stop pretending and dash for cover in the forest, just like the hare. Padrig struggled, but the man was larger and stronger. When one of the other two arrived at the scene, they bound his arms and then, without a word, frog marched him back to the rest of the group.

The slavers had seen two youths on the hill and quickly realised they'd been tricked. The third man ran surprisingly swiftly for a fellow of his build. But Dilectus had made it to the horses, untied both, mounted his and was feeling for his bow behind the saddle when a stone whizzed past his head. Startled, he dropped his bow on the ground. Turning, he saw the man, closer than ever, put another stone in his sling. Reflexively, Dilectus put his head down, hands around the horse's neck.

"Rhedwch!" he yelled in its ear and kicked his heels hard into its flanks.

Abandoning any paved roads for the shortest direct path, he raced as fast as he could for Garn Goch. He arrived scratched and scruffy, his horse stressed, nostrils flared. When Meirion appeared to find out what all the yelling was about, Dilectus's speech was garbled.

"We gotta get your best men. I need another bow. Where's Caradog? He'll help. They're armed, but there aren't many of them. Padrig saved me. Now, we have to rescue him and the others. They're in chains. They must be heading to the harbour. We can head them off. Is there anyone at Nidum? They must have a boat. I'm a coward; I should have attacked the bastards. If I could have got my hands on a sword, they'd all be dead. I should have rescued him. I was too scared. I'm so sorry. Now we have to go – before these devils reach the coast. Call out the men, Meirion. Right now. Please. We got to do something."

"For God's sake, shut up and tell me what you're carrying on about. Start from the beginning. You've ridden your horse too hard – that's irresponsible. And where's the other one they tell me you took this morning?"

By the time Merion was able to make sense of Dilectus's blethering and calculate the time and the distances involved, it was too late to launch a rescue party.

"In case they haven't left the area, I'll get a patrol out first thing tomorrow. We'll scour the countryside, I promise. We'll get reports of who else might have been captured. There will be many desperate families out there and maybe dead men if anyone tried to resist. The people in the small settlements are at the mercy of this kind of wickedness. Your mother is going to be terribly upset. She is going to demand better protection for the ordinary people. But what you have to do now – and I'll send a couple of chaps with you – is you have to ride right now, tonight, following open roads, to get to Padrig's parent's house and tell them what happened. I don't know those people because they work for the Vitalis estate on property granted to them by a Roman governor a long time ago. I don't hold that against them; you tell me they're good people, and I believe you. Are you too exhausted to get there? You're always scarpering off there – how far is it? Ask if you can stay overnight once you get there and come back tomorrow. Then you can join in the search."

Dilectus gave Meirion a rare, quick hug. Both of them had the same image in their minds: Padrig, lying bound and scared in the hull of a Scoti boat, with others crying, moaning and terrified people – joined by the cyhyraeth, most likely. Hardly able to understand their strange language but aware they were destined for Hibernia in a ship rolling around as it left the protection of the channel for the wider Irish Sea and an unknown future of servitude. Would he ever see his family again? Would he even survive? If there was a god, why did he let such a catastrophe happen?

Late that night, Dilectus asked Padrig's father, Calpurnius, the same question. Both of the parents were utterly distraught. They had come home from work-related travel that afternoon to find the Scoti slaver gang had appeared shortly after Padrig and Dilectus had left for their hunting trip. The household was in chaos, with two sheds burnt to the ground, food and jewellery stolen, but no one young or fit enough to be taken for slaves. The younger servants had been pushed down into the cellar by quick thinking but terrified older servants. Miraculously, Padrig's grandpa, Father Potitus, had been away from the household, helping a fellow priest in another parish prepare his church for Gaudy Day, a Celtic favourite – who wouldn't rejoice over the ascension of Christ to Heaven? Potitus was too old to be seized as a slave, but had he tried to resist the Scoti would have killed him without hesitation.

Dilectus and the two men from Garn Goch helped put out some still smouldering and charred timbers. Dilectus ruefully noted that one shed had once been his hiding place. Now, no longer fearing Calpurnius, he poured out the story of Padrig's capture and Meirion's promise to launch a rescue party as soon as it was light.

With Conchessa in tears, Deacon Calpurnius thanked Dilectus for bringing the news. "In answer to your question, young man, we cannot know God's purpose. But I am confident He has one. Padrig is a good lad, but he is not as devout as I would wish and often neglects his prayers. From the story you told, he made a brave decision. God may have given him the courage. He could have died there and then. And that assures me God will keep him safe and has a purpose for him in the future. You should understand that Prince Dilectus, for it will give you peace. Brother Pelagius preaches that we make our own choices, but I believe, as I think he does, that being in God's favour – having God's grace – helps us make brave choices so our fears can be mastered. My son Patricius saved you; is that not God's will? I am sure God will ultimately save him, too. One day," he added, hugging his wife close to him, "our son will walk back into this house, knowing the mercy of the Lord."

Dilectus wondered if Brother Pelagius was the preacher Galeria always quoted. It certainly sounded like him, with everyone having free will and being responsible for their own actions. He liked that idea. It reassured him that his friend, who had now saved his skin twice in his short life, had made his own decision to protect him from harm. Without putting it into words, this insight calmed him. If Padrig had made a willing sacrifice out of love and friendship, it was up to the beneficiary not to feel guilty about surviving the attack but to use the opportunity well. If God had a purpose for Padrig, could God have a purpose for him, too?

That night, sleeping in the guest house of the Calpurnius family, guilt swept over him again. Why should he be lying on a springy mattress stuffed with dried rushes, supported by leather thongs stretched across a polished oak frame, when his best friend in the world was wallowing in the vomit of his seasick fellow prisoners? It wasn't fair. But he thought again of what Calpurnius had said and the words of this mysterious monk, Pelagius. He had the freedom to make his own choices. At that moment, he decided to be a better person. To stop feeling resentful that his mother had married a commoner and ruined their own relationship. And to think about finding his own love, someone just for him and he for her. He thought about Claudia.

At first light, the next morning, Meirion, true to his word, personally led a party of his best riders to scour the area that Dilectus had described. They all knew the quest was near hopeless. They did find the Garn Goch horse that Padrig had been riding, which was something. But the capture took place so close to the coast that the slavers would be long gone. Although the raids had been worsening, they were so inevitable that they had become accepted as one of the dangers of life never to be talked about. Instead, parents invented fantastical stories of ogres, giants, or dragons who, every year, would demand one or more strong, healthy children from the scattered settlements. Getting eaten was a more comfortable ending than a lifetime of slavery, and the threat of being selected was a useful disciplinary tactic.

Chapter 18: Repentance and Retribution

Ever since he had been consecrated as a priest in Burdigala, Exuperius had been using his contacts and friends in Rome to obtain a position in Tolosa. Beautifully situated on the River Garumna in the south of Gaul, near the border with Hispania, Tolosa, with its pleasant climate, was the fourth largest city in the Western Empire. Surrounded by a strong wall, with straight streets, baths, theatres, aqueducts and the latest sewage system, it was undoubtedly one of the most desirable places to live, especially with its new basilica due to open soon. Everyone who knew him was well aware of his bitter disappointment at receiving his first diocese at Corinium. It was incredibly remote, cold and damp, and the winter days were depressingly short. Travel was difficult around the episcopal see, and his congregation had strange, almost pagan beliefs – they seemed to be from another era. The only excitement was the intrigue regarding the flourishing Pelagian heresy at the distant Villa Arcadius. But that had its own challenges.

Then his luck changed, or was the good Lord finally listening to his prayers despite their being on the self-serving side? Late in the year AD 401, the sitting pope died and was succeeded three days before Christmas by Innocentius, a reasonable and generally tolerant man who immediately offered Exuperius the bishopric he craved. Finally, Exuperius said it was the best Christmas present he'd ever received. He packed his bags in a hurry.

Brother Molio had become a nuisance. It was another reason he was relieved to be going. He sent no messages to Molio that he was leaving, and although it was overly cautious, he decided to travel by carriage on roads leading in the opposite direction to Villa Arcadius. He could cross over to Gaul from Dubris just as easily as leaving by the Sabrina estuary harbours, he told himself. Before departing, he took the box of Galeria's private correspondence he had accumulated and ordered it burnt. It had been interesting, certainly. Being privy to something as personal and as private as the interactions between a wealthy noblewoman and her father confessor, the controversial monk Pelagius, was intriguing. He'd never been convinced there was enough material to bring a charge of sinfulness that could lead to excommunication or add to the mounting evidence of Pelagius's views being so contrary to orthodox church doctrine. He wasn't totally convinced the verbal overflow of those prolific writers, Augustine and Jerome, should be considered to represent the Word of God. But it had been fascinating in a voyeuristic way, and the intimacy of reading a woman's deepest thoughts was novel to him, erotic, in fact. He felt nagging guilt he had strung Molio along in this way, and their conspiratorial connection was also now a serious threat to him. If anyone found out…

Guilt and anxiety combined are powerful negative emotions. There were two solutions. To deal with the anxiety, he needed to place full responsibility on Brother Molio and, if possible, ruin his future – he did, after all, deserve some degree of punishment. Maybe a lot of punishment since it was he who first stole the letters and insisted it was the bishop's duty to peruse them and look for beliefs and notions that would lead ordinary people astray. To deal with the guilt, Exuperius used the new antidote of the Roman Christian Church: confession and penance.

There was, however, no formal process in place for confessing one's sins either in public or to a priest in private. A smattering of devout individuals had started the idea of making confessions at the beginning of Lent, but it wasn't a prescribed practice. For Exuperius, it was sufficient to acknowledge in his prayers that he had sinned, although he always put it as having been led astray, like Adam, by a snake in monk's clothing. His penance was his own idea. He had been quite struck in Galeria's correspondence with Brother Pelagius as to how she reconciled the need to live a more abstemious way with her obvious wealth and high standard of living. Simply giving alms to the poor was not truly a sufficient action. Galeria frequently stressed that she tried to distribute her wealth by encouraging the village community to acquire the skills and the resources to raise their own standards so no one would go hungry or be in desperate need. She didn't specifically mention the worn adage of how teaching a man to fish was better than giving him a fish, but she made frequent references to the sharing of resources. Two good oxen could plough several fields if shared, and education allowed anyone to draw on the Romans' obvious technical superiority in building and agriculture.

Exuperius was impressed by these ideas, and he resolved to follow her example. But as a man of the cloth, he had none of Galeria's practical skills and know-how to share. He would, however, inherit in his new diocese a large collection of valuable altar vessels, the silver chalices and gold platters on which sweet wine and unleavened bread would be carried to the congregation receiving the holy sacraments. *Surely, woven reed baskets would do just as well for the host, and glass goblets would be adequate for the wine?* He reasoned. A new resolution evolved: to humble his religious trappings and sell the precious vessels, using the proceeds to support monasteries in need – in Libya, Egypt and Palestine. And that would also be in keeping with the polemics of Father Vigilantius, who was becoming annoyingly critical of all common church practices, especially pseudo-asceticism, hypocritical continence and the growing extravagant veneration of the relics of past martyrs and holy men.

It was a modest plan but compelling and Exuperius felt good about it. A short letter to Galeria and then he'd be off to his ideal sinecure. But it proved to be ideal for only a short while. What he could not have predicted, indeed nobody could have, even Flavius, was that a mere five years later, the Vandals would cross the frozen Danube, sweep across Gaul and besiege the lovely city of Tolosa before moving on to Africa.

Meanwhile, however, back in the present time at the Villa Arcadius, Lady Galeria had received a short but troubling letter. It was delivered by a special messenger wearing a handsome green uniform bearing the insignia of the Episcopal Diocese of Corinium – a mitre and a crosier on a shield background. Not having had any personal interaction with Exuperius since his arrival, apart from a few formal letters, Galeria was rather taken aback. She summoned Flavius to meet with her before she opened the letter with its red seal and green ribbon. She asked a housemaid to take the page to the kitchen for refreshments in case an answer was required.

"Did you know that Exuperius was into all this heraldic nonsense?" she asked Flavius. "So different from old Julius in the past."

"No, I didn't," Flavius admitted. "Look at that ever-so-fancy ribbon under the seal – green for a bishop, how trite! Well, go ahead and open it and see what he wants. I'm sure it means he's going to pay us a visit at long last."

Galeria tore open the folded parchment and started to read:

"*To the esteemed and blessed Daughter of the Lord, Lady Cecelia Galeria Arcadiae, I offer sincere greetings tempered by the recognition that I, your humble servant Exuperius, have as of yet not had the opportunity or relief from my parochial duties to call upon you since my arrival, and for which I offer my heartfelt apologies. I have, however, received nothing but the most favourable descriptions of your good works and your important contributions to this humble diocese of Corinium Dobunnorum, as well as your work with the church college.*"

"*Yuk!* How pompous. He's worse than me, and that's saying something." Flavius smirked. Galeria waved her hand at him dismissively and continued reading, squinting at the document. Her eyes weren't as good as they used to be.

"*It is with great sadness, therefore, that my first official communication with you should be a matter of prodigious seriousness. However, I believe it is my duty to report to you that you have in your household a monk by the name of B^{ro} Molio who has betrayed the trust you doubtless placed upon him and which he has repaid by theft and deception of the most heinous kind. He has brought to me, over an extended period of time, either originals or copies of correspondence between yourself and B^{ro} Pelagius in Rome that he contended contain blasphemous material and abhorrent doctrines and polemics that undermine the fundamental beliefs of the Holy Roman Christian Church. I am sure you will agree it was my sacred duty to consider any such charges. However, I failed to see the veracity of any of the claims he was making, and I urged him to return all the documents to you at once. I would, under normal circumstances, come down to Venta Silurum, despite its great distance and the harshness of travel, and together, we could have confronted Molio and subjected him to detailed questioning. It was my impression he had not come by these documents in an honest manner agreed upon by your good self. Unfortunately, however, I have been summoned by Pope Innocentius to appear immediately in Tolosa and to be anointed as bishop of that episcopal see. Thus, I am compelled by circumstances beyond my control to pass the issue of this criminality and malfeasance on to you to decide in your great wisdom as to the appropriate judicial consequence.*

May the Peace of God remain with you always, your most humble and devoted servant, Exuperius."

Galeria held up the parchment from one corner by her thumb and forefinger and waved it derisively in front of Flavius's face. "Well, there you have it! What on earth do you make of that?"

"God help any congregation having to sit through a sermon from this man," Flavius replied in obvious disgust. "Quite apart from his tedious style and run-on sentences, it smells highly duplicitous to me. Disingenuous."

"But what does it even mean? He's saying all the correspondence that has been missing for months was stolen by Molio and taken to him, and only now is he letting us know?"

"That's what it sounds like. We must confront Molio immediately and listen to his side of the case." Flavius clapped his hands loudly and a servant appeared. "Run and get hold of that messenger that came from Corinium, and ask Brother Molio to come here immediately. Make it sound urgent but not threatening."

A few minutes later, the pageboy in the fancy uniform was standing before them both, shivering like a dog about to be beaten.

"When did Bishop Exuperius give you this letter?" Flavius demanded. "We will almost certainly need you to take back a reply, perhaps tomorrow when we have composed one."

"He gave it to me four days ago and told me to deliver it today. I can't take back a reply, sir; he's left Corinium in three horse-drawn carriages. I'm no longer in his employ. He paid my wages until the end of this year and dismissed me from his service. He'll be in Dubris by now, sire."

"Did he not leave any other documents or letters for us?"

"No, my lord, just this one letter. Nothing else."

"Who is in charge in the episcopal palace?"

"I don't know. I was told to return my uniform when I got back, after which my services were no longer required. There is a deacon there who normally manages things. I don't know his name. We just always called him 'deacon'."

Flavius snorted in exasperation.

"All right, young man," Galeria interrupted, her voice trembling, "you did what you were told, and we are grateful. Thank you. We are just surprised at this turn of events. Did the bishop, by any chance, tell you about the contents of this letter?"

"No, Milady, he did not."

"Well, so be it. We are taken aback. And concerned, but it is not your worry. Go back and finish your refreshments. I'll arrange for you to spend the night here and you can return in the morning."

The page bowed and backed out of the room. The villa servant reappeared.

"Sir and lady, there is no sign of Molio. No one knows where he is."

"I want him found. Urgently. Keep looking wherever you might think him to be. Ask everyone in the library, any of the scribes. Check the chapel. Ask Father Potitus. Does Molio have any friends anyone knows of? Alert all the guards. If you find him, I want him arrested and held, with no chance of escape, got it?" Flavius's voice was harsh, and the words were forced out through clenched teeth. The servant nodded furiously and scampered away.

Flavius turned to his mother. "So, a man of God, a bishop no less, a link in the apostolic succession, was so guilty about what he had done – or probably not done in this case – he scampered off like a rat running from a terrier."

"Now, son, take a breath. I know it's troubling and I'm deeply disturbed. But the bishop is reputed to be a very holy man. Until we hear the full story from Molio, we must reserve judgment and not come to any hasty conclusions. I just want my private papers returned. The bishop implied Molio has them. I think in the wrong hands they could damage me and certainly Brother Pelagius, who has opened his heart and mind to me in a most soul-searching and deeply private way."

Flavius grunted. "I don't know how you can keep so calm. We've been betrayed, of which I am confident. When I find Molio, I'll listen to his excuses and explanations, whatever they are, and then I will ruin him. If I cannot arrest him and punish him, I'll destroy his miserable life."

Molio had disappeared. Soon, everyone in or near the villa knew he was being hunted; they just didn't know why. And now he'd gone to ground without a trace. But a week later, at midnight, when Lestinus, carrying a bronze oil lamp, was doing his rounds checking on villa security, he heard a low: "Psst!"

"Who's there?" Lestinus barked, holding his lamp high above his head but seeing no one.

"It's me. I'm in the bushes. You have to help me."

"Of course, I will." Lestinus placed his lamp on a wall and walked over to the darkness of the shrubbery. He put his arms around Molio and embraced him. "Dearest Molio, thank God you're safe. I've been so worried about you. We've got to be careful. They're accusing you of theft, which can't be true. Oh goodness! You're growing a beard!"

"My disguise. I've taken refuge with the *genii cucullate*. They have a very private monastery in the forest."

"I thought you hated them? They're a mystical cult," Lestinus whispered.

"Yes, but they believe Cuda is the Virgin Mary, and they hate the villa people and heretical Christians and rich Romans. *Amicus meus, inimicus inimici mei*. They'll look after me. I am ruined, Lestinus. I am totally ruined."

"Do you need funds?"

"Not yet, I've been saving. I need your support and your love. I think a time will come when we can get our revenge and strike a blow for the true Christian faith and belief in God's Grace, by which all human actions are accomplished. I am defending the truth of God against the vilest heresies. When this is understood, it will allow me to be redeemed in this life as well as the one to follow. I need you, darling Lestinus, in the flesh and in the spirit."

"I'll do anything you ask. Anything you want. I love you, Molio."

"And I love you." They kissed again. "Now I must go. You will hear from me. Christ be with you and within you."

Chapter 19: Behavioural Activation

Dilectus was impatient and grouchy. It wasn't just the typical mood of a fifteen-year-old. He was back at Garn Goch and his presence was needed, but he was still so unsettled that Elen had suggested he ask Flavius if he could talk to the villa physician. There had always been a Greek doctor at Isca Silurum to treat the men's frequent injuries. But with the Roman army under Severus and by order of Stilicho somewhere on the march in the middle of Gaul, the only doctor left was an elderly physician for whom Flavius had managed to find a stipend and comfortable accommodation in town. He listened to Dilectus's complaints. They were mostly about the people around him rather than any aches or pains. The old man gave him a concoction of herbs from Galeria's herb garden, mixed with wine and honey and told him to eat a daily clove of raw garlic, which Claudia later complained about. None of these remedies made him feel any better.

But griping to the old man about his life had been weirdly helpful. It clarified the things he'd been upset by but hadn't wanted to admit to himself or anyone else. He'd become quite used to being able to wander into the villa library when bored and find something interesting to read. There were no books at Garn Goch. Hunting trips had been restricted ever since the tragedy of the previous year, and in any case, with his best friend Padrig gone, there was no one to go hunting with. Caradog was in full-time employment on the family farm and Meirion was being awfully boring, fussing around Elen and the new baby. Everyone was busy. This should have told him something.

Dilectus had played with his half-sister occasionally, but the truth was he resented her and all the attention she was getting from his mother. It was quite sickening the way everyone oohed and aahed over her, saying how much she looked like their gorgeous mother, even though she was an ugly little thing that peed all over his arm when he'd picked her up and bounced her around.

No one had managed to discover who had wanted him kidnapped or killed and his deep suspicion towards Meirion had not gone away. There was the further distinct possibility someone had tipped off the Scoti slave party. It just seemed too much of a coincidence. He'd taken two horses with Meirion's consent over to Padrig's house near Banwen on that fateful day last year. No one else knew where he was going or the area he had planned to hunt in once he'd collected Padrig.

Disliking these feelings and continuing to feel guilt at his escape to Padrig's cost, he tried spending time over at the family's farm. He liked talking to Padrig's grandfather, the old priest Potitus. He was a practical, down-to-earth man, who, when he gave a sermon, which was rare these days, always managed to blend in stories the local people would be quite familiar with, the old gods like Nodens and the Celtic giants who threw rocks at each other across the Hibernian Sea, and the goblins and fairies who inhabited the woods and forests. 'When you walk through the woods,' he'd tell his congregation, 'listen for rustling sounds. They are not the rustling of leaves but the sounds of God's wood nymphs who will protect you. All things possessed a spirit – he claimed – you can see the spirit of the air if you look towards the mountains on a clear morning before the sun is up. The white vapours you see rising from the stream is the breath of the river god of that area.' Potitus was a firm believer in the great Chain of Being, with God at the top, with Jesus on his right hand (no discussion whatever of same or similar substance), followed by the archangels, then the angels, down to people and on to animals, insects, plants and rocks. He did place men one rung higher than women. When Dilectus reported this fact to Flavius, he just laughed sardonically, saying, 'Well, when you are created out of a man's rib, how can you expect to be his equal? But I like the sound of your old priest, and we need a new one here at the villa; I'm going to see if he will accept a part-time job.'

"Why are you spending all that time talking to him, anyway?" Flavius added.

"My mother told me to get help as she can't stand me moping around Garn Goch. And your old doctor guy was no use. His potion just gave me a guts' ache."

"Your trouble is simple, Dilectus. You don't have enough to do. You're mad because Severus refused to take you with the army to fight with

Stilicho. I think he was being a bit overprotective, myself, but he knew what my mother and your mother would think about you galivanting around the continent. Military campaigns are not the fun and games survivors make them out to be when they come home alive. You're mostly shitting in your undies, freezing your arse off, or digging graves for guys you once knew. It's not glamorous. Find something to do. Find something constructive here at the villa if you like. You're just in the way at Garn Goch. I'm short of a scribe, but your writing is still only one step up from Egyptian hieroglyphics. See if Mother has jobs for you. Or find Claudia; she's also a pest around here, a veritable grain beetle. Maybe you share the same sickness," Flavius added with a smirk.

Claudia was not in a good mood. "So, finally, you have deigned to pay me a visit! I suppose now your big buddy Padrig is gone you don't have anyone else to play with."

"Lovely to see you too, Claudie. Flavius warned me you'd be your usual charming self."

"Go away, Dil. I need a man. I need a husband. I don't need a child to come and bother me."

Dilectus was prepared. "If you come with me up to the hill on the other side of the herb garden, I've got something to show you. From the dark arts."

Shaking her head, Claudia reluctantly followed him through the herb garden, out of the gate, and up the small path leading to a guard post. Usually, this would have been occupied by two or three well-armed men, but Severus had taken the best of the guards with him to northern Italy. They hiked a little higher up the hillside, over a wooden bridge across a brook, and into a clearing where they had a good view of the villa, the recent extra fortifications, and the cluster of farms between there and Venta Silurum in the distance. Dilectus stared into the deeper rock pools of the small stream, hoping to catch a glimpse of a trout.

"We should come up here with nets and a spear and try a spot of fishing, Claudie. Wouldn't that be fun?"

"Is that your idea of the dark arts?"

"Oh, no. Sit down; I'll show you what I brought." They both sat on a moss-covered wall, perhaps a holding pen for sheep long ago. He took an apple out of his pocket.

"This tiny apple! I bet it's super sour. Can't you do better than that?"

"*Shush!* I'm going to show you something." From a sheath at the side of his belt, he took out a small dagger. It was well made with a bone handle and swirling patterned steel, glinting in the sunlight. He carefully cut the apple in half, width ways, muttering, 'I hope this works'.

He held up one of the halves and showed it to Claudia. "What do you see?"

"I see half an apple and a few pips."

"Count the pips."

"There are five of them in a circle. So?"

"Look carefully, Claudie. It is not just a circle. The pips are arranged in a pentagram, and there is a faint circle from the core around it. To pagans, this is highly sacred. My people in the old days knew this was a symbol of life and healing. Look, if I hold it this way, one of the pips represents the great spirit, and the others point to the directions – north, south, east and west. The five elements of the pentagram represent the five elements of existence – earth, air, fire, water and spirit."

"Which is it? Directions or the elements?"

Dilectus looked at her to make sure she wasn't making fun of him and said, "Both, really, you can make it anything you want it to be. The circle around them is the great circle of life, of wholeness, of the eternity of nature. Pagans believe this protects you from evil."

"Half an apple?"

"No, silly." This time, he knew she was joking, but she touched the pentagram with her fingertips and Dilectus was happy, especially when she placed the same fingers on his lips.

"There, I've protected you from evil!"

"You have, but I can go one better." From another pocket, he took out a small package wrapped in soft leather. "I've made something for you. Not exactly me. I took the gold and silver coins Flavius gave to us when we were children. I went to a craftsman in town and asked him to melt them down and make an amulet like a pentagram for you. I made a drawing with a piece of chalk of what I wanted, so it's my design, even though I don't know how to work metal like that."

Claudia blushed when she opened the leather pouch, took out the gold amulet with the five silver apple pips inlaid and held it in her hand. A fine silver chain dangled from a tiny eyelet attached to the rim of the amulet.

"It's beautiful," was all she could say.

Clutching the necklace in her hand, she stood up and sat on Dilectus's knee, putting her arms around his neck and kissing him on the mouth.

"Do you know how to make love to a girl?" she demanded when she stopped for air.

"Sure," he said, but it didn't sound convincing. "How about you?"

"I'm not going to ask how you know *if* you know. I don't want to know – how you know. *I* only know from what the kitchen maids and serving girls at the villa have told me. They make it sound horrible, but judging from all those love poems by Ovid that Granny used to read to us without hesitation, I think they're wrong. But Jesus, Dilectus, let's face it. Most girls my age are married with three children by now, and here I am, a maiden, just like one of the Vestal Virgins. I'm going to be old and withered like a dried plum, and no man will want me..."

"I want you, Claudie," Dilectus answered with such seriousness and intensity that Claudia started to giggle.

"You're just a boy, half my age, but you are very good-looking."

"Well then." Dilectus was warming to the entire conversational drift. "Let's do it here and now!"

"That doesn't sound romantic to me. I can feel you're eager. That was one of the things the scullery girl told me – men are ready and willing at any time, but when the crucial moment comes, they get so excited they can't always perform. Seriously, though, now isn't a good time. We've got to wait until a critical period of the month when I won't have a baby. And I have to be in the mood. And you have to have taken a nice long bath. I want the first time to be perfect, with no worries and no pressure."

"I do know how to touch you – down there. Padrig told me all about it."

"Oh, I can just imagine two nasty little boys giggling about it all. Touching is no problem; I can do that myself perfectly well. But some of the other things I'm not so sure about. That's why we have to plan for the perfect time and place. Night-time, with just a few candles and a warm fluffy sheepskin blanket – *after* a bath, and at a certain time of the month that I will specify."

"You're very precise," Dilectus said, sounding disappointed and let down. "Where's the wild spontaneous passion? Ovid had a line about being 'dragged along by a strange new force'."

"Yeah, but he followed it by saying, 'Desire and reason are pulling in different directions'. That's precisely what is happening. It won't be a perfect experience if I'm worried and you are over-excited. Deryn – that's the maid who's told me the most – says some men get so excited they squirt their seed before they even get started and get all embarrassed. You don't want that, little Dilectus, now, do you? Come on, it's time to get back. I'll work out the details and let you know. You'd better move into the villa. Uncle Flavius told me he had invited you often enough. You're almost family."

****

Nine hundred miles away, near a town called Pollentia, a very different conversation was taking place.

"You did well to get here. I heard you were reluctant to leave Britannia to join our efforts to defend the motherland. Here, have some more wine." Flavius Stilicho, supreme commander of the Western Roman army, poured Severus a large glass from a silver pitcher. He was a tall, thin, distinguished-looking man, dressed in an immaculate Roman uniform, clean-shaven with close-cut hair that had once been blonde from his Vandal father's ethnic background but was now prematurely grey. At fifty-three, he was a year younger than Severus. They had met before. They had both served under Theodosius as junior officers, except that Stilicho was a cadet in the elite imperial guard.

"I don't know how you heard that, sir; I just needed more time to train my troops."

"I've got spies everywhere. I'm sure you do, too! But never mind. You got here quickly."

"Thank you, sir. We left Britannia in November. The channel crossing was easy, but my chaps don't know Gaul at all, and it was slow progress, finding supplies in the winter. I've got one second in command, who's good, and in my general staff, I have fine young men, all handpicked. We commandeered provisions as usual, but I didn't want to antagonise the people, so there was no looting. I heard you were in Raetia dealing with a Vandal rebellion, and the Visigoths were approaching Milan, so we picked up the pace to get here."

"Yeah." Stilicho shook his head. "I was sure all these north Italia rivers would slow the bastard down, but it's been a dry winter. I told the Emperor to stay put in Milan, but he didn't listen. Knowing I was coming and hearing you were on your way thankfully made Alaric give up chasing Honorius and retreat west to meet us. So here we are, Severus. With your troops, we've got about thirty thousand men. I can't get accurate intelligence to estimate Alaric's force, but it is at least as large as ours. It's hard to tell because they've got family members and camp followers like you wouldn't believe. But I'm confident we can beat the hell out of them, but I never underestimate an enemy's strength or determination."

"Well, sir, that's what I came to talk to you about. We Britons have never faced Visigoths before. And although I trust my guys' bravery, I feel we need some sort of advantage. They may have their backs to the river, but we don't even have higher ground to give us an edge."

"I think you're too worried, Severus. Your men respect you. You're a fine general, and I have complete faith in you. Look how well you did against the Picts. Anyway, do you have a plan?"

"The Picts never met us in a pitched battle. It was all hit and run and us chasing them. The Goths are warriors. I respect them, and Alaric has had his successes. So, yes, I have a plan. My proposition is we surprise them and attack them on Sunday. Easter Sunday. They're Christians. They will be celebrating and feasting."

"But so are we, general. I'm a Nicene Christian, thanks to my noble mother rather than my father. I'm surprised that you are suggesting this. Don't you respect the most holy days of Christianity?"

"I do, sir, but I respect the lives of my men a lot more. In a straight clash, we will sustain huge casualties. We might not even be able to force a clear victory – huge losses with no definitive outcome. But they won't suspect an Easter attack for one moment, and if we can win the initial engagement, he will retreat, maybe even leave behind all the spoils he's collected across northern Italia. And we'll have enough men surviving to march by your side the rest of this year, perhaps trapping him in a place where we do have a real advantage. We don't here."

"I don't know… I don't like it. The Roman elite are always criticising me even though I've saved their arses over and over again. Don't know how much you understand of palace politics, but I've got almost as many enemies at the court as I do out there. This will give the Christian senators another cudgel to beat me with. And I've got my own principles, too. My wife would kill me if she heard about it, which she will. It would be a bad look. *Hmm.* Easter Sunday, you're saying – just three days from now? It's a violation of Christian principles."

"So is killing hundreds of good men, with all respect, general. The element of surprise will force them to retreat early."

"Let me think about it. I heard you were brave; I didn't hear you were devious as well."

"But, sir." Severus started to remonstrate.

"It's all right. Don't say anything. If we do it, what would be the time frame?"

"On Saturday night, they'll be keeping the usual vigil and fasting. On Sunday morning, at first light, they will hold the celebratory Eucharist. So, we attack at sunrise. They'll be tired and hungry and totally distracted."

"What about our men? They'll want to keep vigil too."

"I don't know about yours, but my Celtic Britons aren't into fasting and praying. They're more into feasting and partying. On Easter Sunday, they love a good feast – hunks of roast lamb with leeks and parsnips and honey cakes. They can't have a good feast if they're all dead."

"You are devious. You have it all worked out. I'm going to regret it, but I think I'm going to do it. I'm not usually known for sticking to conventions, anyway. Lights out at midnight on Saturday, no trumpets. *Vigilare* next morning will mean an attack. I'll confer with my commanders, but we must keep this absolutely quiet. The slightest leak and the surprise element is gone, and then all we have is a violation of our faith and endless berating from the Pope safely in Rome."

Chapter 20: Ergo Propter Hoc

"Greetings, dear friend. Christ, you look a wreck! But it's good to have you back. I bet you have lots to tell us."

"Too much, Flavius, I'm so sorry. I have very, very bad news, and I'll just spit it out. Your nephew, Rufus Lucius, was killed on the field of battle. It's tragic, and I feel responsible. I did not send word because I wanted to tell your mother and his parents in person. That's the right thing to do. And in any case, I am back here about as quick as a letter these days."

"That is terribly sad news indeed. Stop apologising and tell me what happened. We haven't heard from his parents, Lucius and Aurelia in Londinium for a long time. They didn't come back to the villa for Christmas, so we're all a bit worried. But let's get Mother in here so you can tell her. She'll want to hear all the details. She'll be upset, of course, but she didn't have the same kind of relationship with those two grandsons as she does with Claudia. Come on, sit. I'll get her."

When Galeria had joined them, Severus gave a quick summary of all that had occurred.

"I've had an unwelcome dose of statecraft," Severus explained after the initial tears for his breaking news. "Stilicho is a complicated man. He's like a general's general. He had a Latin translation of the memoir of Scipio Africanus on his bedside table in his field tent. He kept quoting Sulla admiringly, but actually, he's the least bloodthirsty Roman, well, half-Roman, I've encountered. He's a thinker like you, Flavius. I know he has a reputation for being politically ambitious, but my sense is he genuinely wants to save the Empire."

"I don't know if reading the exploits of generals from five or six hundred years ago, counts as being a thinker. Why don't people like him embrace modern times? The world is changing," Flavius interjected, but Severus just ignored him.

"We surprised the Visigoths at Pollentia and beat them fair and square. They took heavy losses; we, mercifully, had rather few. Alaric moved his people eastwards, but we learned *he* was claiming the battle was a draw, which is kind of cheeky coming from someone in full retreat. Meantime, the Emperor was so shit-scared of him that he left Mediolanum and scurried off to Ravenna. I've been there long ago because it's across the sea from Illyria. It's got nothing but swamp and marshes all around it, created by a canal draining into the River Po. There's an artificial causeway connecting it to the mainland. Easily defended, so he feels safer there. Did you know the harbour can accommodate two hundred and fifty warships? Then Stilicho heard that Alaric, undeterred, thought he might head off to Gaul across the mountain passes. That was more than our general could handle, so we moved quickly and passed the southern end of the big lake there, Benacus, they call it; it's beautiful. We set up a sort of ambush north of Colonia Verona Augusta, and Alaric walked right into it.

"It was one hell of a battle. We thought we had him totally licked, but he and his best troops fought like tigers and managed to take a nearby hill and erect his standard. I was the closest unit and Stilicho ordered a full-scale attack. I had to lead it, of course, and I'm really too old for that sort of shit – excuse me, Galeria – and my whole general command staff had to join me. Up till then, I'd managed to keep young Rufus Lucius out of any fighting but couldn't this time. He fought courageously before being felled by a Goth cavalryman with a lance. It was quick. He didn't have a chance. I'm sure he didn't suffer. He'd have been dead before he hit the ground."

Severus's comforting words only made Galeria cry some more. He kept going, still less helpfully.

"We failed to take the hill, by the way. We were all exhausted. But despite that I rather feel Stilicho let Alaric escape. He fled with what was left of his troops across the foothills towards Illyricum. He's going to cause trouble again, but right now, the emperor is claiming a great victory. They invited me to be in the parade in Rome, but the thought of Honorius at the head of a triumph when he had done nothing turned my stomach. I decided it was time to come home and face my own disgrace."

They sat in silence for a while. Finally, Galeria spoke.

"Severus, you brought so many of your troops back; you're a hero to them. And to us. It's tragic about my grandson, but you're not responsible in any way. He knew the risks when he enlisted. I have this strange feeling, like a premonition, that somehow our family's fate is intertwined with this

King of the Goths. I first heard the name Alaric the year Emperor Theodosius died. Flavius, you reported that at least half of all the Goths who fought for Theodosius at the Frigidus River in '94 died in the battle. Their leader, this Alaric person, was commended and given the rank of *comes*, but when Theodosius died, he was kicked out of the army."

"Well, to be fair," Flavius interrupted, "I think he resigned his commission in the Roman army. But sure, they were ingrates and treated him badly. And so, what happens? At that point, the Goths elected him King, although I don't think they'd ever had someone with that title before – like Conanus!" He chuckled.

"Anyway, by being disrespected, he's become an adversary. But it *is* uncanny how it has impacted us as a family, with Sev having to leave Britannia and fight and now poor Rufus Lucius being killed by the Goths. Alaric's been a puppet in the power struggles between Eastern and Western emperors – the East gave him the title of *magister militum per Illyricum,* which he abused shockingly, which is why Sev hates him, isn't it Sev? And then they took it away from him and murdered hundreds of Goth soldiers and their kin in Constantinople. As I understand it, that's why Alaric turned his attention to Italia and why Severus and his troops were needed so badly. But I'm sure this is the last we'll hear of him. My informants tell me Stilicho plans to contain him by reinstating the title and bribing him to stay in one place. If that's what he wants, he'll give up the struggle against the power of Rome and Stilicho. I don't think he'll intersect with this family again."

"Severus, did you actually see Alaric?" Galeria asked.

"I did. At a distance. Twice."

"Was he dressed in animal skins, the way that awful poet Claudian always described the Goths?"

"Not at all. He was dressed like a Roman officer with a bright red cape leading a beautiful black horse. Claudian is so full of bullshit propaganda and he's a total bigot. That's what happens when your only purpose in life is to flatter the powerful leeches at the court. But Alaric stood out. He's tall, and he wore no helmet and carried no shield, although he had shield bearers around him. His standard was simple. I couldn't make out the symbols, but it had a lot of gold, and two large men shared the task of carrying it. He had a presence, all right – bareheaded like that, with long wavy hair. For battle, his men tie up their long hair in a topknot and they usually have beards and often droopy moustaches. He was clean-shaven."

Galeria listened attentively. She did not explain that she'd had dreams about Alaric. In one of them they were in a boat together going to Hippo in Africa to talk to Augustine – what about wasn't clear in the dream. In another, he was asking her for a cup of water as he lay dying – naked in exactly the pose of the sculpture of the Dying Gaul. Everyone had seen copies of the famous sculpture Nero had brought from Greece and displayed in his palace. The villa even had a copy in bronze, but Galeria and her young husband Arcadius had had it moved to a storage area. In her dream, the dying warrior, after she gave him a drink of water, had taken the torc off his neck and given it to her, saying, 'Keep this for the wife of a barbarian'. The dream had totally unconnected elements as dreams usually have, but the naked warrior's body had strength and a powerful masculine element to it, and the torc was clearly connected to her gift to Sevira.

She changed the subject. "You said you wanted to go personally to tell my daughter and son-in-law about Rufus Lucius's death? I thank you for thinking that, Severus. Organise whatever escort from the villa you need and have Flavius cover all your expenses for horses and carriages. Is it safe enough for Senica to accompany you? Would she like to go? Surely you could visit your sons there as well? When's the last time you saw them?"

"Too long ago to remember but thank you, Galeria. I'll make arrangements."

When Severus and Senica got to London, they were shocked by what they saw. The Roman walls were still standing, but they were not being manned by sentries or guards. Many shops and houses were boarded up, their owners having left for places thought to be less subjected to Saxon raids. Some of the signs nailed to the boarded front doors stated the occupants had left for Armorica, where they had family. The wharfs along the river were still standing, but most of them needed repairs and there were only a few merchant ships tied up alongside. People were saying Victorinus had been appointed governor, but without a military force to maintain law and order, if he was around, no one had seen him or his wife recently – although she was reputed to be a classy dresser with gorgeous silk dresses with gold thread. Their villa was empty.

Severus and Senica's sons were thrilled to see them, apologising repeatedly for not writing home often enough and fulsome in their praise for their father's military successes, although they were hazy on the details. But they explained they had no intention of ever returning to Venta Silurum where they had grown up, or indeed anywhere in Cymru. They had both been working for the town administration, the Roman comptroller in charge of finances for the diocese, the *rationalis summarum*, but that post had been vacant for some years. They were not drawing regular salaries and, as a result, were engaging in various private financial activities and transactions, using their previous contacts and business know-how. Neither Severus nor Senica could imagine what these sorts of activities might be, but they began to doubt they were entirely legal.

What the young men did explain to them was that when Londinium was the capital of the Britannia provinces, huge amounts of money could be made in trade and getting supplies to the Roman army. However, once the army was in such a precarious financial situation, with on-again-off-again military missions, regular supplies were no longer needed. They did say that when Severus had organised over six thousand troops to go to Italia, it had been a boom opportunity. But since then, everything had dried up. The army was not providing any kind of law enforcement or security – if anything, soldiers in the area were the most lawless of all local inhabitants. People were leaving as best they could, and a diverse collection of migrants, drifters, opportunists, beggars and prostitutes from all over the empire had gradually been moving in, many of them squatting in rough camps outside the walls. Sometimes, they just broke into abandoned houses and took them over.

The two sons of Senica and Severus were clearly doing well. They were well dressed, and they had servants who were able to make decent meals for their parents' visit. But they complained bitterly at not being able to find suitable wives. It did seem to Severus, although he didn't challenge them, at least two of the young serving girls were also serving as concubines. They spoke no Latin or Celtic, and Severus was told they were Belgae orphans. They were being treated well. However, the general state of decline and the collapse of civil society was shocking. Their two sons had ideas of going to the continent where there was still some stability. They had selected Treverorum, and Severus shook his head. "Your best bet," he argued, "is to go to a city with a prominent bishop – that was where some degree of safety's to be found." The future was so uncertain, however, that when Severus and Senica left, they knew the goodbyes were the last there would ever be. They promised to write, and Severus promised to get more orders their way once all the troops that had returned with him from Stilicho's campaign were settled again in forts and garrisons. It would take time, but orders and payments would be coming through. "Don't leave in haste," was his parting advice, but there was little confidence behind it.

Senica, who was a practical woman with no formal education, made a comment Severus repeated to Flavius the next time they talked. "She's really perceptive, Flavius. What she said was, 'The Empire is like a huge cloak that has covered us and protected us and enfolded many different peoples. But it is old, and its seams are coming apart. Moths have attacked it and there is mould from water damage. And we here in Britannia are at the very edge of the cloak and it is fraying here first, and the tassels are breaking off. And the weakest of the tassels are the towns because they are full of people who can only have food if they buy it. And the money just isn't there'."

Severus's own despondency increased further after all efforts to contact Lucius and Aurelia had failed. A house, really a small villa he had been directed to upon enquiries, had been abandoned and squatters were living there in squalid conditions. A warehouse on the river where some surly merchants had told them the couple conducted a trading operation was still standing but showed signs of a recent fire. "A warehouse on the Tems will only survive if you have it surrounded night and day by armed guards," someone told him.

"And half the time, it will be the armed guards who rob you blind and disappear," added his obviously tipsy companion. So, what on earth had happened to Flavius's sister and her husband? This was not the news he'd hoped to take back to the Villa Arcadius. Through long interconnected chains of cause and effect, catastrophic events far away on the continent were triggering lethal ripples across Britannia.

The journey home was a bleak one, with long reflective silences and many tears. The Arcadius family of Galeria had been decimated and their own children disconnected. For the first time in his life, Severus thought about the nature of society. As people stopped producing their own food and making their own possessions, took up specialised skills and made single-item consumer goods, they became disconnected from the true necessities of life. The entire system of civilisation demanded civic order and stability; mutually agreed conventions of behaviour and lifestyles didn't need to be policed. Urban societies also required a monetary system, and coins were now being hoarded, clipped or counterfeited. The famous Londinium mint Flavius had once spoken so proudly of was now closed. People were back to bartering. Back home in southern Cymru, Villa Arcadius and its external resources and productive farms, the town with a reliable market provided by the presence of a legionary headquarters and with a strong tribal chieftain, all interconnected, they had been protected, despite the pressure of brigands and pillagers, from the obvious reality Londinium thrust in his face: The empire was coming to an end. Maybe civilisation itself.

Chapter 21: Savagery in the Woods

"What are we going to do with Dilectus?" Severus asked his friend.

"What d'you mean?"

"Surely you've noticed he's a total mess. He's spending his whole time here, he hasn't got a meaningful job, he mopes around Claudia like a lovesick puppy, and he talks all the time about how worried he is about his mate Padrig. He says he can't stand the atmosphere around Garn Goch because now his mother has had a baby girl, they're all disappointed and acting weird, and he's still suspicious Meirion had something to do with either his first abduction or the second attempt to capture him as a slave. As you'd expect, their relationship has totally broken down. I'm sure Meirion hasn't the faintest idea why Dilectus is avoiding him with such disdain. They used to be so close. And it's all thanks to Meirion that Dilectus is now such a good horseman."

"We never did manage to solve the mystery of that first kidnapping," Flavius admitted. "D'you think it's just possible Meirion was involved? Planned all along to marry Elen and then his own sons would become heirs – not expecting them to be a girl?"

"So, you're suspicious, too?"

"Not really, Sev, but anything is possible. I've always argued since the other boy wasn't taken too, they weren't slavers, and as there were no demands for ransom, they weren't just common criminals."

"But the second incident was clearly slavers."

"Yeah, but who told them where the two boys were going hunting? It couldn't have been anyone on Patricius's estate 'cos he got captured, and Dilectus got away. We've been very suspicious those mysterious monks years ago were in someone's pay and that someone wanted Dilectus out of the way as a rival. Someone with ambition."

"Yes," said Severus slowly, "someone like Vortigern Vitalis."

"Goodness! Why him?"

"Because Meirion told me on our Caledonia campaign he'd learnt Vortigern once made a move on Elen. A very aggressive one. He tried to force her to marry him despite being betrothed to Magnus's daughter – as your mother was arranging."

Flavius remained silent. Yes, it was possible. It was the sort of devious jockeying for power that four hundred years of colonial domination by the Roman Empire had taught to the indigenous conquered peoples they called barbarians. Assassinations, poisonings, incestuous marriage, 'legal' executions – they were all an integral part of the history of imperial succession. And would most probably continue to be an element of politics for the next four hundred years of Roman control of the known world – however much it might be fraying at the edges. Power struggles were built into human nature, like gold being heavier than silver. Or just maybe, now Christianity was the accepted religion, Jesus's teachings on Mount Eremos would inspire the faithful to strive to be meek, to be peacemakers, to be merciful, and to hunger and thirst for righteousness.

"You're at a bit of a loose end right now, Sev. You've got the army settled into their barracks. Why don't you and Dilectus go on a serious investigation based on the few facts we have – like you and I did in the old days when we searched for his mother and father?"

"Not very successfully! But it's a good idea. You relied on Lestinus leading the original search, but they didn't come up with much. It would be good for both of us. We'll check out the so-called monks of Cuda – your suspicion they were involved I've always considered to be correct. And that Cuda shrine deep in the forest they found showed signs of activity and you were never able to follow up on that place. I'll get Lestinus to repeat all the places he went to and get Dilectus to describe where he might have been taken before he got away. He remembers certain things, I know, but not all the details. Recounting horrific experiences *after* they're all over and one is safe helps terrifying images to flood back into memory where you can rethink them and work on them constructively in your mind. When they just sit as vivid experiences in the back of your mind and you don't let yourself think about them, that's when they can make strong, brave men go crazy. I've seen enough good soldiers unable to deal with dreadful events to know what I'm talking about."

Dilectus loved the idea. Being questioned right after he came out of hiding had just increased his anxiety and made him more likely to block out the most terrifying moments. But now, almost nine years later, he could think calmly about the details and doing so seemed almost therapeutic. Severus was impressed at how much of the experience he could now recall and re-examine more objectively. The arrangements were great as well: two of the best horses from the villa and a sturdy little pony to carry all the necessary comforts, like extra blankets, a waxed cotton sheet that was waterproof, bread, meat, wine and utensils. With money jingling in their pockets, they knew they could easily buy additional supplies.

They even started by going back to the exact spot below Garn Goch where Dilectus and Caradog had been playing with the coracle, and then following a possible route from there, avoiding main roads, and going generally in the direction of the mysterious people that so many folks thought to be witches. Lestinus had reported suspicious activity around an abandoned temple, and they made that a likely third night's stop, hoping something familiar would jump out for Dilectus. The temple that had impressed Lestinus was perched on a hill that once hosted a tribal fort. It had a commanding view across the River Sabrina at exactly the limit of the tidal bore from the estuary, which made fording the river easier and safer.

They could see why Lestinus's squad had been perturbed. The square temple had been defaced. A marble bust of what had once been Nodens had been smashed repeatedly with a hammer. Probably the work of early Christians once their legitimacy allowed them to despoil sacred pagan sites and they hadn't quite internalised the idea of turning the other cheek.

Various signs of recent habitation were scattered around – eating utensils, some lamb chop bones, signs of a fire and an empty wineskin, even the skeleton of what looked like a dog, perhaps sacrificial? But nothing about it resembled anything Dilectus could remember. He kept telling Severus when he'd escaped, he was on a hillside, and there were a lot of trees.

Next day, riding north towards higher ground they soon came to the edge of the gloomy forest the locals called Coedwig o Daneg. On the way they found niches here and there holding crude images of the goddess Cuda, including one carving in which she was surrounded by figures with pointed hoods. Dilectus gasped.

"That's what I was trying to describe. Remember Caradog and I both said they wore those funny pointed hoods attached to their capes? This must be the area they came from."

Thinking they were close to the shrine Lestinus had reported, they rode a short way into the woods, frequently looking over their shoulders and stopping at the slightest noise. There were ruts in the ground that looked like they might have been made by loaded waggons, but a long time ago. Following one of these trails, they came to another shrine, smaller than the elaborate temple setting on the cliffs overlooking the Sabrina. This shrine was a square edifice; it must be the one Lestinus had found. But it was not as he had described. Right in the middle of it was a grizzly sight. A thick stake had been set firmly into the ground. And on top of the stake was the head of a man, barely distinguishable as such, given the maggots, bird droppings and strips of dried skin. Although it must have been there for years, there was still an unpleasant stench.

Dilectus started to gag, turn and ran out of the shrine. Severus, who had been a soldier all his life and seen every imaginable horror, was also covering his nose, but he moved a little closer to inspect the severed head.

When he found Dilectus outside, he said: "Well, boy, I think we can conclude two things. One is that this was one of your kidnappers. The other is that this is a warning – a warning to maybe the other one regarding the price of failure to capture you and a warning to you that your escape is not forgotten or dismissed. Poking out of the head's eye socket, which you may not have noticed, is a short stick."

Trying to absorb the meaning or symbolism of this horrid scene, the two stood in silence for a while. Finally, Severus offered a comment.

"You want to know my guess? Once the two who grabbed you had failed, the plot might easily be exposed. And if they were being paid, they weren't going to collect any money. So, I think both would have been hunted with the intention of silencing them. Maybe this was the original rendezvous spot where they were supposed to deliver you. But maybe only one of them showed up, the one you managed to injure. He was killed, his head was put on the stake and the stick in the eye was a warning to the other man regarding a failed mission."

"Sounds plausible, Severus, but that's a heap of maybes. It's also possible the two men showed up to admit failure. They had an argument, and the shorter one could have killed the injured one, who was near death anyway. Padrig told me the story that a man with a badly disfigured face was out there looking for me. Perhaps he lived for a bit but might have become such a nuisance to the other one that he had to be killed. Or he died from the injury and the other one cut off his head – actually that makes no sense. Your theory seems better."

"We'll never know for sure, but let's say this is a rendezvous spot to which they were heading with you. And you said you ran west towards the sunset as best you could judge. And they would have tried to follow you. I say we now move west where there are communities and farms. North of here is just a deeper forest. Let's get going. This place is giving me the creeps. And you look like you are going to throw up any minute."

They rode on. Neither of them knew the area. They were obliged to stick with tracks and to follow roads when they came to them. There was little sign of habitation. A few hovels indicated the level of subsistence was rock bottom. Enquiries of frightened children and suspicious women, even when silver coins were being flashed around, produced puzzled heads shaking. "No, we've never seen any monks or soldiers or strangers anywhere around here." All of a sudden, this was a region where there was never ever a visitor – "Until you two, sirs, came." Severus suggested they go north towards Viriconium, where Dilectus was born, and then swing back via Banwen to hear if there was any news of Padrig and end up back at Garn Goch. Severus looked forward to paying his respects to Queen Elen. He'd never forgotten the sight when he first saw her as a young girl and nearly fell out of his chair.

They were riding along a well-used path, with trees on either ride, completely relaxed but a bit dispirited, when an arrow whooshed inches past Severus's head and thumped loudly into a tree trunk in front of him.

"Fucking hell," Severus shouted as both men, crouching low to the horses' necks, turned and looked behind them. Five horsemen were riding rapidly towards them, one already lifting his bow again. Mortal danger requires a rapid response drawn from learned experience and instinctive reflexes. Severus was already fumbling behind him to loosen the pony trotting along behind them.

"Crouch down and ride like hell!" he yelled at Dilectus, who dug his heel hard into his horse's flanks. "Get to higher ground when you can," Severus yelled again.

Assuming Severus was right behind him, Dilectus continued galloping between the trees, searching desperately for higher ground where they could gain advantage over a superior number of well-armed men intent on killing them. This was not a gang of highwaymen whose boldness was an increasing threat without the Roman military presence nor legitimate patrols by the militias of local authorities. Robbery was clearly not their motive, nor was it to deter trespassers. Dilectus turned to see how far behind Severus was, the man being heavier and not such a good rider. He was nowhere to be seen.

"Oh fuck, you bloody fool," Dilectus screamed aloud. Dilectus wheeled around but did not retrace his steps exactly. Keeping to whatever slightly higher ground he could, he rode back on a parallel path, hoping to come across the intruders from behind, if not above. When he came to a clearing, he gasped in horror at the scene in front of him.

Severus, with two arrows sticking into him, was on his hands and knees, his right hand still gripping his sword, which was flat on the ground. Towering over him was one of the men, bleeding from his left arm but taunting Severus with his sword. Lying on the ground were three of the other men, dead or dying, and behind the man about to kill Severus was the fifth man shouting: "Kill this mad bastard; we got to get the other one."

Screaming, Dilectus charged forward from the woods, surprising the fifth man, who stared at him just in time to see Dilectus's swinging sword. He dropped to the ground, head lolling awkwardly backwards from his half-severed neck. The man guarding Severus turned. A mistake. Staggering to his feet, clutching his sword with both hands, Severus lunged his whole body forward and thrust his sword with what was left of his strength into the man's belly, then rolled over onto his back. The assailant was screaming in fear and clutching uselessly at the blood gushing from his gut. Dilectus leapt from his horse, ran over and shouted into his face, "Shut up!" and plunged his bloody sword into his throat, grunting. "That should help you."

Kneeling beside Severus, he cradled his head in the crook of his arm. "Jesus Christ, Severus, why did you turn back? You're a bloody idiot." Tears were rolling down Dilectus's face. Severus coughed and blood spewed out of his mouth. Dilectus wiped his face with his sleeve. "Just lie still," he said, "I'm gonna get you home."

A faint smile crossed Severus's face. "I've seen many men die from battle wounds. I know what it looks like. Now I know what it feels like."

"Don't be silly. And stop talking. I'm going to take care of you. You saved my life."

"Live it well – that's an order." Severus's voice was weak and raspy. "If I saved your life, it's to right a wrong. I owed this to your father, who was a true friend. And I owe this to your mother, whom I initially wronged and hunted rather than protecting her as I should have." He coughed up more blood. "Water," was all he said.

Dilectus ran to his horse and grabbed his leather water bottle. He put it gently to Severus's lips. "Tell Senica not to cry; I was always true to her. Tell Galeria if I go to heaven, I will see her there; tell Flavius if I go to hell, I'll await his arrival. Search the bodies for clues… where they're from. The leader is a *curialis*. There'll be… evidence. Be careful how you use it. Disrespect their bodies… give a warning… a warning like in the shrine…" His face was turning white as the blood from the deep arrow wounds pooled inside him. His voice was getting fainter and fainter. Severus reached up and pulled Dilectus's face closer to his own, and he whispered: "I've watched you grow from a baby. I've taught you what I can. You'll be a king one day. Be a good one."

Dilectus hugged his body. It was already lifeless. 'Give a warning, give a warning, give a warning'. The words were pounding through his head. He tethered his horse and found Severus's. The pony was nowhere to be seen. The attackers' five mounts were clustered in a group the way horses trained for battle would do. In his fury, Dilectus wanted to kill them all by systematically and painlessly slashing the jugular veins of each horse. But Meirion's voice stopped him, '*Horses are noble creatures, respect them always*'. They weren't to blame; they followed orders. He stripped them of their bits and bridles, saddles and panniers. Good horses would find their way back to their stable. Choosing the largest stallion, he led it to the front, stepped aside and whacked it on its rump. "Go free," he yelled, "Untacked. Carry a warning."

He rifled through the clothes and possessions of the leading assailant. He found what he wanted and felt an enormous sense of relief. Then, using their own swords, he savagely but methodically decapitated each man. 'Give a warning'. He had no stakes, and none of the attackers had spears or javelins. If he left the heads on the ground, wild animals would soon carry them off. 'Give a warning'. He found in one of the saddlebags a long but thin plaited rope made of horsehair. All five men's hair was long enough to knot it in with some twists of this long rope. 'Give a warning'. Dilectus climbed a tree that had a branch partially overhanging the path. He slung the rope over the branch and climbed down. He hauled on the rope and knotted it around the trunk; 'give a warning'.

With one last effort and still wiping tears from his face, Dilectus heaved Severus's body onto the back of his horse, then mounted his own. As he rode off with Severus's horse beside him, he turned back. It was a macabre sight. Five severed heads dangling from a tree and five mutilated bodies blocking the path, their weapons broken in disgrace. He'd given a warning.

Chapter 22: Mortal Dominoes

Throughout history, there have always been events that, while considered important in their own way at the time, are only recognised as profoundly consequential sometime later. Severus's death was one such event.

At the most personal level, Severus's loss hit Flavius harder than he had imagined possible. Galeria mourned his death because she had genuinely loved Severus for all sorts of reasons. But for Flavius, Severus had constantly been a powerful, steadying influence, someone he could rely on, who was practical, a strategic thinker based on realities, not the theories and historical precedents that addicted Flavius. But he was also Flavius's only friend, male or female, the person for whom there was no need to pretend or posture, to please or protect. And after Dilectus told him the whole story of what happened, Flavius went into a deep depression.

At the funeral, which was attended by hundreds of ordinary people as well as dignitaries, Galeria made special arrangements to support Senica. Her two sons had already left for the continent and were not able to attend. Galeria personally contacted all the people Senica mentioned as her female friends and gave them a special place at the cemetery. The cemetery was the military graveyard outside Isca Silurum, and the procedure was strictly according to Roman custom, with echoes of the old Celtic burial traditions. There was no open casket, but people were encouraged to approach the coffin and make an offering of some kind – could be a coin or a flower, a written message, or a piece of jewellery. The carved marble memorial stone was not yet ready but had been ordered. A deacon from the diocese gave a blessing and recited the necessary prayers. A military band sounded trumpets. A small group played a dirge on a local instrument, a reed pipe ending in a cow horn. It produced a harmonious but melancholy tone. Because the people of the area loved to sing, a choir sang a number of psalms and one elderly woman no one had ever met before performed a long chant, ancient, mystical words no one understood. After that, Galeria announced everyone should walk back to the villa grounds, where refreshments were being prepared. For the old people, a number of carriages and wagons were at the ready.

Dilectus had been invited to sit with Galeria and Flavius, but when his mother, heavily pregnant, arrived from Garn Goch with Meirion, their young daughter Brangwen, and Meirion's sister Sioned, he immediately excused himself and ran over to join them. Finally, knowing his enemy enabled Dilectus to embrace – figuratively as well as literally – Meirion and Elen. Galeria, observing everything, thought how strange it was that it took a tragedy like Severus's death to bring people together and bond in shared grief. She did not know Dilectus's paranoid feelings had finally been dispelled. Neither did Flavius because Dilectus had made no mention of what he had discovered about the identity of Severus's murderers. Dilectus understood risk.

Flavius had asked Senica if he could deliver the eulogy. He wasn't sure what he would have done if she'd said no because he had been writing it non-stop for the past few days. He delivered most of it in Latin but stopped every now and then and explained in Celtic what he had just said. He was dressed in fashionable and expensive trousers and coat and did not wear the toga he usually wore around the villa. He didn't want to come across looking too Roman. He was, after all, a true Briton – on his father's side, the Roman bloodline had been enhanced by endless marriages of both Celtic and Gallic women, and his own mother, originally Hispanic, had fully embraced the Celtic culture and language of the region. Being a Christian was what defined her and everyone else, regardless of clan, tribe, or nation. Nevertheless, at that moment, it was difficult for Flavius not to think of Marcus Antonius delivering the funeral oration for the murdered Julius Caesar in the Forum of Rome, even taking some lines from the reported speech.

"Dear friends, citizens and proud people of this blessed region, I welcome you with a heavy heart to this ceremony and entreat you to remember with joy the blessings my dearest friend Severus has brought to us all. I would like to quote the great historian, Appian of Alexandria, who three hundred years ago was able to record from many reports and witnesses what Marcus Antonius said in his funeral tribute to Julius Caesar. He said, 'It is not right for the funeral oration praising such a great man to be delivered by me, a single individual, instead of by his whole country'. I, too, am humbled by the fact Severus was admired and respected throughout Cymru and Britannia generally, and therefore, I feel I do say my few words on behalf of not only those present but of the country as a whole. I, too, could list his many accomplishments in his military service and enumerate the many battles he has fought and won. I can also repeat the words that most quickly come to mind when Severus's name is mentioned: honest, loyal, brave, inspiring, dutiful, a leader of men and a model for aspiring youth. I, too, could also read some items from his will. Although men who work for the public good are rarely able to enjoy large financial rewards for their dedicated services, Severus left some generous bequests to improve the health services for the retired and wounded soldiers at Glevum; for Cor Tewdws, the academy that Lady Galeria has funded to bring literacy to this region; and because he is a practical man who spent, or should I say misspent his youth at the castra here he has set aside funds for a fountain to be constructed in the centre of Venta Silurum so that children can always find fresh water to drink on the only two hot days we have each year."

There was muffled applause and some laughter for each of the items in the will as people were not totally confident someone as austere as Lady Galeria would approve of clapping at a funeral. When Flavius listed some of Severus's military successes, there was again respectful cheering but respectful silence when Flavius continued:

"Now, good people of Britannia, whether Celt or Roman, native or visitor, Christian or follower of the old gods, I wish to end with a brief comment on what Severus meant to me as a friend. You know he was born in Illyricum, where his family hailed from, but his father, a high-ranking officer in the Roman army, was posted here with the legion in Isca Silurum. So, we grew up here as boys together, sharing many good times. He was a loyal and faithful friend who often protected me bravely when needed. He was tough, brave and a fair fighter for just causes. When he was attacked, he single-handedly killed four of the five brigands, and thanks to brave young Prince Dilectus, all of the five have met the just end they so richly deserve.

"Some of you will know my mother is a pious Christian woman who tried hard to encourage Severus in his Christian faith. As may be true for many of you, he struggled to fulfil all the commandments of Christ's teaching and the devotional duties that our good deacons and priests, presbyters, monks and bishops exhort us to follow. But Severus was nevertheless, to his core, a good man, not without sin – who can say they are? – but the kind of man whom I firmly believe will be welcomed into the Kingdom of Heaven. I say this based on the teachings of that fine Briton, Brother Pelagius, now preaching in Rome. If we strive to live good lives and exercise our free will to resist evil as best, we can in the circumstances in which we find ourselves; we will achieve salvation regardless of our exact adherence to any one faith. May God, whomever He may be, receive this good man's soul. On your behalf, dear friends, I bid him farewell."

This time, there were shouts of joy and cheers, right fists thumped against left chests and lots of tears and some wailing and sobbing. Dilectus, still fighting his feelings of guilt, cheered loudly, convinced that Flavius had said it right: Severus was dead, but his soul was in heaven. He hugged his mother, who was in floods of tears and clasped hands with Meirion, who said, "Flavius's genius is frightening. Elen, my love, you're crying so hard?"

"I'm crying for Severus, who saved me in the end from Flavius. And I'm crying in terror and in pain, dear. My waters have just broken and I'm going into labour. Can you get Sioned and me to the villa immediately? Dilectus, take your baby sister, find Galeria and tell her we are borrowing a chamber in her house."

The birth of Elen's third child was not in any way a consequence of Severus's funeral, though perhaps it was hastened by the emotion of the moment. Meirion blamed Elen for insisting on travelling to Severus's funeral when she should have been confined for the last months of her pregnancy. Thanks to Sioned's calm skills as a midwife – the third time she had supported Elen through a delivery – the baby was born in the comforts of the villa with no complications. Everyone praised Elen for the third live birth with no other failures, which was quite surprising given her very advanced years. There was less happiness about the baby being another girl – if you thought lines of succession were truly important, it just further increased the status of Dilectus, who'd already used up three of his nine lives, if cats and humans shared the same risk factors.

The baby was named Rhonwen in honour of Meirion's mother. The christening took place in the villa chapel, using the beautiful font Galeria was so proud of. Elen and Meirion just accepted infant baptism as a thing that was done, and anyway, they were right there where it was convenient. Sioned was asked to be a godmother, and Dilectus was the godfather. Flavius joked to his mother that he was shocked the parents hadn't asked *him* to be the baby's godfather as he would have liked to have had an opportunity to give them a lecture on Pelagian ideas on original sin. Galeria retorted that was exactly why he hadn't been invited.

The loss of their commanding general, however, led to dire consequences for the men who had served under him. News of his death spread rapidly among the soldiers he had recently led, both to Caledonia, with minimal casualties but few results, and to join Stilicho on the continent, with considerable casualties but achieving victory for Honorius and honour and glory for the wild army from Britannia. His demise was keenly felt among the troops, who not only admired and respected Severus but knew there was no other leader of his calibre to command them effectively. If you're an undisciplined soldier, you know others are likely to be the same and thus not comrades to be relied upon in dangerous times. Severus had commanded the army to disperse to the key forts around the country, with orders, inspired by conversations with Flavius, to train for patrols to confront threats like raiding parties and not to skulk behind the castra walls, getting fat and lazy and waiting for trouble to come to them. Some of the key forts had fallen into disrepair, with so little imperial money being spent in the province as retaliation for not receiving adequate taxes. Isca Silurum and Isca Dumnoniorum were in good nick, thanks to Severus having leaned on the local chiefs, but Deva Victrix and even Eboracum were run down. Uncomfortable quarters make grumpy soldiers, especially when edgy to begin with.

There was also a lot of talk across the whole country that neighbouring Gaul was becoming increasingly destabilised. Saxon raiders were bad, but they at least had to come across the sea to Britannia. The restless Germanic tribes, Vandals, Sueves, Alans and god knows who else, however, were massing right on the Rhine frontier. Some of them, like the Goths and the Franks, were already being settled as *foederati* inside the empire. To those who thought themselves true Romans, it was a detested policy. The popular opinion among the well-to-do citizens was that it weakened the army. In fact, the vaunted Roman army would have been pathetic without them, even though their loyalty could never be taken for granted.

Then, to the Britons, it looked like the Emperor and Stilicho were focused only on protecting Italia. If these bloodthirsty tribes overran Gaul, Britannia would be next – everyone said so. The Celts had long-standing antagonism towards the Germanic tribes. In that atmosphere, the loss of their general was deeply frightening. So, they did what they had done in the past: they elected a new commander. A *magister militum* could only be appointed by the commander-in-chief and the Emperor. Sure, but why wait? Marcus's name was mentioned favourably in the mess halls and parade grounds (not that anyone was parading, but they were gossiping). Marcus – yes, young, definitely a patrician. Appointed to an elite squad by Severus himself. A good-looking, intelligent young man, highly educated. And the nephew of a very rich man, Flavius of the Villa Arcadius, a legate who had once campaigned with Theodosius in the good old days. Marcus, flattered, was elected by acclaim.

Immediately, he was pressured by all the senior officers to proclaim himself emperor and lead the army to Gaul, the way Magnus Maximus had done in 383. As is often the case, they were completely ignoring what had happened five years later. Marcus contacted Uncle Flavius for advice. *He* hadn't forgotten. Flavius immediately told him it was a crazy idea and utterly pointless. Marcus lacked the leadership experience; the troops were needed for defence at home, and another army stomping around Gaul and threatening the Emperor would be chaotic – civil war and ultimately as big a failure as Maximus had been. Marcus agreed they should wait. He told the officers of his high command the time was not ripe. They all disagreed. This wasn't what they'd elected him for. So, exactly two months after being elected, Marcus was arrested and executed.

At the most personal level, it hit Flavius like a javelin to the gut. His young nephew was the second of Galeria's grandsons to die, and he was partly responsible. He'd given him good advice, but he'd not anticipated the reaction of the men around him. Galeria would be devastated, not to mention Marcus's sister Claudia, who had always looked up to her brothers. Rufus Lucius had died honourably in battle; Marcus was put down like a rabid dog. The family was fading away. Once Galeria passed on, Claudia would be the sole heir to the villa after Flavius's death.

For the army and for the island of Britannia as a whole, the easy end of Marcus was a terrible precedent. 'Now we just have to pick another candidate, one more compliant to the will of the majority and not bounded by silly ideas of risk, legality, oaths of allegiance to the Emperor, or inhabited world implications'. Their next pick was, however, another unlikely choice. Gratian was a civilian, an urbanite Briton, who had some irrelevant experience as a town councillor and an ordinary municipal official. But he was someone who offended none of the competing interests and factions. They dressed him up in purple robes, gave him an impressive-looking imperial crown and provided a bodyguard. Four months later, the gloss had worn off. The bodyguard became an execution squad.

The army's third pick, early in the next year, AD 407, was more sensible, although he may have been chosen simply for his name: Flavius Claudius Constantinus. Constantine the Great was a legend and had himself been declared emperor by Britannic troops up in Eboracum a hundred years earlier. And at least this Constantine was a soldier; he didn't need to ask anyone for advice. Knowing the fate of his two predecessors – predeceased, one might say – he wasted no time in taking the entire army of Britannia to Gaul.

Conditions in Gaul were complicated. On the last day of the previous year, AD 406, swarms of barbarian tribes crossed the Rhine, made easier, the story goes, because it was frozen over that winter. They surged across Gaul and as far as Hispania. But these tribal groups, the Vandals and the Alans and the Franks, had all been fighting each other, so the dreaded 'invasion' caused misery with looting and, as one might have guessed, vandalism, but not the dreaded take-over. Constantine and his second in command, Gerontius, were initially quite successful in crossing Gaul unopposed by imperial troops. This was sufficient success for him to declare himself Emperor Constantine III, much to Honorius's annoyance. There were sure to be repercussions – what sort of traitorous scum would just go around claiming to be an emperor in the real emperor's backyard? There would be consequences.

Chapter 23: Eternity Beach

The tragedy of Severus's murder had another series of consequences, suggesting fate was not some random perturbation of the stars. Context is a powerful determiner of human events. To his mother's concern, Dilectus had, for the past few years, been avoiding family conflict at Garn Goch and spending most of his time at the villa. His activities there were divided between military training under Severus's direct tutelage and scholarly study under Flavius's eye. After the funeral, Flavius felt he needed to talk to Dilectus as a substitute father figure. Despite never having been one, he thought he might be more useful than his stepfather Meirion, despite the recent melting of their icy relationship.

He found Dilectus hanging out with Galeria's chief gardener, a burly, red-headed man who had once worked in Cantium on one of the large fruit tree farms.

"What are you up to, Dilectus?"

"Oh, greetings, Flavius. Did I tell you that was a great funeral oration for the general? Severus would have loved it, teasing you for sure about all the big words you used and trying to outdo Cicero! I'm bothering Magnis here. He's showing me how, by a combination of what he calls grafting and pruning, you can create those flat, wall-hugging apple trees Lady Galeria loves so much. I should become a gardener."

"Well, there are worse things in life than that, aren't there Magnis? But I'd rather you focus on politics and your future role. So, come walk with me." When out of earshot of anyone, he added, "I notice, by the way, you seem to have resolved your issues with Meirion."

"I have. I have proof now he's totally innocent."

"Oh, good! Excellent, in fact. So, you've discovered who is guilty of trying to harm you?"

"I have Flavius, but Severus, as one of the last things he said to me, was not to tell anyone."

"Why on earth would he say that? Don't you want justice? Don't you want to feel safe again?"

"I think I understand why. And knowing the nature of the threat makes me feel safe enough. And there can't be justice unless I could prove it, which would be difficult. Accusations have consequences, even if true."

"All right. I trust you and Severus even more, God rest his soul. But I feel we need to be focusing more on your scholarship. Why don't you visit the college my mother has been working to establish? It's in your future kingdom. I've been supplying them with books, but I don't have a good feel for what they're doing with them. Christians have a bad habit, in my opinion, of only reading material that's straight from the bible. Why don't you take Claudia along? She's also at a loose end. Take one of her friends as a chaperone, so there's no gossip. They've got accommodation in what used to be the villa there. It won't be too comfortable, but it should be sufficient. I'd love to get your report on what you find, how many students they have and what they're teaching them. The staff are monks – don't flinch! You said you were over all that! – but they haven't established a formal monastic order, not like Ninian has up at the White House."

Dilectus reluctantly agreed. It sounded like Flavius was finding him busywork. But when Claudia enthusiastically supported the idea, his attitude changed immediately.

"Forget that stuff about a chaperone for me. Uncle Flavius is so old-fashioned. Anyway, I don't bloody well have any female friends – everyone I know my age is managing a household and looking after a brood of kids. A ride there would be fine, I'm sure. Grandma is shocked I'm practising with a bow and arrow – and I'm pretty good, though I do say so myself. She says I should be doing embroidery, but I can tell she's actually pleased I'm doing something men do. And when we get there, I'm sure they'll have separate rooms – out in a barn for girls if it's run by monks. Or we could just ask to share a room." She gave Dilectus a leery, coquettish look before prodding him with a finger and adding, "You wish. In your dreams, young lad."

Dilectus laughed to cover his blush. He knew she was joking. But the mere fact she mentioned something so intimate as sharing a room, even if negating it right away, told him something important: The basic idea of it was not horrifying to her. It was time for him to stop being so shy and so easily embarrassed.

As it turned out, the man who introduced himself as the guestmaster had different ideas. Claudia was the granddaughter of their principal benefactor. "I have a lovely room for you, good lady." Dilectus, on the other hand, was a nobody as far as the college was concerned. He seemed to be just another Silurian from Garn Goch. His notoriety in town (everyone in Venta Silurum knew who he was) had not penetrated an academic institution which felt above the day-to-day goings on in the country, as opposed to studying the gospels and occasionally the classics. "You're the son of Lady who of Garn Goch, you say?" the guestmaster asked. "Elen? Well, how nice. It was so good to meet you. The abbot will no doubt ask you more questions, but in the meantime, I have accommodation in the men's dormitory between the refectory and the stables. It's quite comfy and there's plenty of water in the nearby well you can use for washing." He was about to explain where the men's latrine was located but decided it wasn't delicate to raise in front of a lady from the Villa Arcadius.

The next morning, a distinctly grumpy Dilectus joined Claudia in the refectory for a hearty bowl of porridge. He'd drunk a little too much mead the evening before. "I didn't sleep a wink." He grumbled. "I don't know who those fellows are, but they snore like hogs. I suppose you had a wonderful night in silk sheets and bathed in a tub filled with warm water and rose petals."

"Not quite," Claudia whispered – there was no rule requiring silence after the benediction, but no one else was talking – "this place is creepy. Let's try to meet the abbot, give him the books Uncle Flavius made us bring, get a quick guided tour and then ask for a picnic lunch and go for a ride along the cliffs. I'll bring my bow and with any luck, we'll see the Scoti who captured your friend or a boatload of the Saxons we're always being warned about."

The abbot was delighted with the books and willingly arranged for a packed lunch of pickled herring in cream, brown bread, thinly sliced leeks and imported mustard from Gaul, a recent Roman addition to the typical Celtic fare. He apologised for the absence of wine – 'the trade routes are dreadful right now' – but said that although they were not, in fact, a monastery, the staff were skilled in making ale and a bottle of their best brew would be provided. Claudia boasted she was so good with the bow that if they came across any pheasants or hares, she'd bring something home for the abbot's dinner. He deflated her by saying he didn't eat meat.

It was a gorgeous day. The wind was brisk but not cold. Looking across the sea from the high cliffs, they could look south to the clear shores of the Dumnonii tribe and to the west to the vast expanse of the open ocean. A small stream cascaded down to a pebbly beach. They tethered the horses and fetched them water from the stream. Dilectus organised the picnic while Claudia ran along the beach, stopping to pick up shells. She collected them by lifting up the hem of her skirt and making a little basket. When she came back, Dilectus noticed her bare legs and how shapely they were – strictly appreciation of beauty, he said to himself, but he noticed from the sensations in his groin that his body wasn't focused on aesthetics.

"Look at my shells, Dil!" she said excitedly, "the rocks over there are just covered in big mussels. D'you think the abbot considers mussels to be meat? We could gather some for our hosts. Where's that knife you're always practising trying to throw at tree trunks and barn doors?"

Dilectus stared at her, smiling down at him. Her cheeks were flushed from running in the sand, and her long blonde hair was tousled wildly around her face.

"Sweet Jesus, I can't stand it, Claudie. Come down here and kiss me, or I swear I'll run into the ocean until Neptune drags me under, never to be seen again…"

"What? Kissing *before* the pickled herring? Good thinking. But I'd quite like to see Father Neptune rise from the waters to claim you, so if you run first, I'll just sit quietly here and eat the bread… Now move your bum over and give me a space to sit on the rug."

Claudia lay back and hitched up her skirt. "I'm sorry you couldn't find us a nice sandy beach. These pebbles are killing me." She reached for the cloak she'd been wearing while riding and bunched it into a bundle under her head. "That's better. Lie next to me. Do you think there's anybody around? I don't want them to see us. Here, help me pull down my underpants. They're tight. I dressed for swimming."

"I didn't know you could swim," Dilectus interrupted.

"I can't. Can you?"

"No. Claudie, you seem distracted. Are you nervous?"

"Of course, I am. Aren't you?"

"No," he lied, "we're best friends. No more talking, please."

Dilectus gasped with delight when he saw Claudia's blonde bush, and he ripped off his tunic and undid his loincloth, his *subligaculum,* which all young men wore neatly folded around their junk, allowing his cock to spring free, upright and hard. Claudia put her hand around it. "Holy Moses!" she exclaimed, "is that going to go inside me?"

"I'll be gentle. You help me." He clambered over her, supporting his weight on his elbows and knees. "Grab hold of it and put it in."

What had seemed an implausibility turned out to be easy. Both his and her parts were perfectly designed for just this very activity and nicely lubricated as well. And it was so much more friendly, being face to face, than the way they had seen male dogs, cattle, sheep and horses so often roughly mount the female from behind. Dilectus was gentle, but Claudia was pushing up her hips hard to meet his thrusts, loving the grinding against her pubis more than the sensations inside, which had a certain strangeness about them. She pulled his head down towards her and kissed him. Dilectus was desperate to feel her breasts, but she had a tight *strophium* on under the upper part of her dress and he didn't know how to take it off. Next time, he was definitely going to ask her to get rid of that first.

After a short while, Claudia suspected that Dilectus's little groans of appreciation and rapidly pushing movements meant something was going to happen, and not having the inclination to go into any calculations as to the exact time of the month for her, she demanded, "Pull out before you squirt, Dil, please."

He didn't answer, but her timing was perfect. "It's coming." He groaned and pulled back, rising to his knees and grabbing his cock with his hands, and as he grunted, Claudia could feel a splash of something warm on her bare tummy and then again and then once more.

"Goodness." She giggled. "What a little fountain you are, my boy!" Dilectus just grunted his satisfaction and flopped onto his back next to her. She rubbed her tummy. "Sticky," she said, "nobody told me that!"

"We can wash up a little in the sea," Dilectus replied, "and since neither of us can swim, we'd better not go in too deep." He tried not to sound dominating. It was Claudia who liked to be in charge, to tease a little bit and act the big sister, although thank god she really acted like the horny harlot next door rather than a sister, which in any case she was not.

"That was amazing. You're amazing. It was so perfect I don't see how it can be sinful."

"Whoever said it was sinful?" Claudia replied.

"Every cleric connected to Villa Arcadius, as you well know, talks endlessly about 'the lusts of the flesh' and the 'evil sin of fornication' even for married people unless they specifically are trying to create a baby, and we specifically were trying the exact opposite. They all yak on about the glory of virginity – the priest, Brother Molio, the bishop. Everyone. Except for Padrig's grandpa. You must have heard them."

"I did, but I just ignored them. As Granny said to me once, the 'poor dears' are just men and most of them have never loved a woman or tried to understand them but are more than happy to tell us what we should do and what we should feel. None of which came out of the mouth of Jesus."

"She's one smart lady, that domina. D'you know she wants to take me to Rome?"

"You'd better not go without me, young lad, that's all I say. Why haven't you opened the ale? I'm very thirsty."

Chapter 24: Early June, AD 408. A Fateful Decision

"A good morning to you, Mother," Flavius said cheerfully as he strode into the dining hall. A serving girl rushed to the kitchen to get him a plate of the smoked fish he loved. A fat, filleted brown trout, netted in the Sabrina River and cold smoked high over smouldering oak chips – superb. Also, it was a good sign the increase in Scoti raiding parties up the estuary was not deterring the daily efforts of the local fishermen. One sometimes forgets everyday life can go on, even in times of national crisis.

"You're in a good mood, dear," Galeria replied. "Rare these days, if you don't mind me saying so."

"Ah! That's because I've got good news and bad news – or the good news might be bad and the bad news good, depending on how you look at it."

"Tell me the good news first."

Flavius hesitated. "Our Britannic soldier and would-be the third emperor of that name, Constantine, has managed to capture Arelate in Gaul. He's made it his headquarters. Even installed a bishop as a sort of backup security and to give him legitimacy. And he's dragged his oldest son, Constans, out of the monastery where he was training to be a monk and is planning on promoting him as a commander. Hate to think to what actual rank. Probably Caesar, knowing how brazen he is. I still can't decide if he's a traitor, a tyrant, or a hero. Either way, Honorius won't be pleased, facing a usurper's army, Goths still a threat, his wife Maria dead, and detractors grumbling about Stilicho."

"Constans? Surely that isn't his son's name?"

"No, it wasn't until last week. Constantine has renamed him after Constantine the Great's son. I think he's trying to impress people he is of high rank rather than a common soldier, and he's surely trying to create a link in people's minds between him and the emperor who legalised Christianity. Our local Constantine is brilliant at impression management.

But from being a low-ranking officer to an army general, he's done amazingly well – although there are rumours he's a heavy drinker."

"Flavius! You're always accusing me of wandering off track! What's the bad news other than the death of our Empress?"

"The bad news is this means if you still wish to travel to Rome, it can be done with some safety now. You take a vessel from right here and travel around Hispania to."

"Are you serious? Are you encouraging me to go? Oh, what great fun. Hispania too! I might drop in on my relatives, whom I've not seen for literally ages. That'll break up the journey."

"For my sins, yes. I'm just too saddened and frustrated by the world to argue with you or anyone any longer. And for the first time, the trip seems possible or at least not outright lunacy. In fact, going by sea and stopping in Hispania and seeing your kinfolk is a great idea. That's the ideal route. From there, you would pass through the Pillars of Heracles and then directly to Arelate, where the Rodonos enter the sea. If you make the visit public and can see Constantine, you will surely be welcomed as it gives him legitimacy. I am not sure we should, but it will enhance your safety. From there you again travel by sea to Portus. We can try to advise the procurator there of your arrival and he can arrange road transport to Rome itself – it's just a few miles. Or by the river, I'll have to make further enquiries. This is the first time I feel there is an opportunity for your trip to be something other than completely foolhardy. Who will be in your retinue?"

"Well, Dilectus, of course."

"You'll have to ask Elen."

"Not at all. You always refer to him as your clever boy, but he's a man in his early twenties now. I'll be asking him and him alone. He can get his mother's blessing if he wishes. But come to think of it, Elen's closest friend and advisor, Sioned, would be a good support for me. I've met her a few times, and she's a real toughie. She helped deliver Dilectus, so I'm sure she'll be over-protective, which is what you want. And just think how it will help Romanize a wild red-headed Celtic Silurian to actually see Rome. I trust Lestinus, captain of our guard, to round out the group if you think the villa can spare him."

"Don't ask me to make that sort of judgment. The villa can't spare any of you. But Lestinus is solid and a group of four won't attract unwanted attention. Dress plainly and carry lots of gold, not in your purses but sewn into the hems of your cloaks – you're going to need thick ones for an ocean voyage even at this time of year."

Galeria gave him a despairing look. "*Aquilam volare doces!*"

"*Hmm,*" Flavius replied, "OK, Minerva, you've made your point. You should have taught me to be less pompous a long time ago!"

"At least you recognise it! That's a step ahead." She stood up and kissed her son on his forehead. "That's from Minerva – God forgive me for repeating her name! But I hear Rome herself is vulnerable. How safe is it going to be? I'm not reckless, whatever you think of me. Haven't the Goths been threatening the city?"

"It will be safe as long as Stilicho is in control. He's managed the situation brilliantly. He's in favour of paying off the Goths and giving their leader a title. It's not popular with the Senate, but then nothing sensible is with conservatives. I've just received reports his wife has arranged to marry their second daughter, Thermantia, to the Emperor. That should further ensure his position for now."

Once the decision had been made, the villa was in a flutter of excitement that hadn't been seen for years. Galeria sent a fast rider to find Dilectus and deliver the invitation, ostensibly to ask him to agree and to seek his mother's consent. But Galeria's note simply read, 'It is on. June 23rd'. Lestinus, who was unmarried, eagerly accepted the job of bodyguard. Flavius had sat him down and explained the multiple risks of the venture. Flavius promised to double his regular pay and to pay a significant bonus on the safe return of the party. If he were killed, God forbid, the sum would be paid to his elderly and most pious parents, who lived in town.

Three days after signing the agreement, Lestinus quietly went to the stables, selected a horse and rode, as casually as he could, north to the valley of the River Vaga. He dared not enter the great forest, but he knew this was near the mysterious temple and so-called monastery, which was the meeting place designated by Molio. On this occasion, their rendezvous was very different. After waiting impatiently for some hours Molio appeared but with another man dressed in an unusual type of monk's garb.

Molio was stiff and acting formal, which confused and disappointed Lestinus. "This is Brother Petroc, also in hiding. He is being hunted by a lord who once offered him blood money but reneged after his friend died from injuries caused by the vicious whelp, your Dilectus. That young man is a murderer. We were thrilled to get your message. By God's design, you are the official bodyguard. So now you have an additional charge if you still wish to help me: two sanctified executions in the name of the Virgin Mother of Christ."

Chapter 25: The Departure

It required meticulous planning, not to mention serious financial resources, to arrange for Galeria and her party to get to Rome by sea. It was undoubtedly the method least fraught with surprise attacks, road congestion and endless bribing of local officials to move from one district to another. But a sea voyage was subject to pirate attacks. There were even tales of smaller craft being attacked by huge black and white creatures, whales from hell, they were called, *Orcinus orca*. Flavius insisted there be at least one escort vessel carrying volunteer militiamen from among the trustworthy retired legionnaires from the Colonia at Glevum.

For the passengers, he managed to contract a Phoenician merchant ship, as they were the most reliable and knew the route well, but it cost him a fortune, he grumbled. He assumed, correctly, his mother would be visiting for a while, and he had tried to negotiate a return trip fare, at which suggestion the *navicularis* agent for both captains had simply laughed out loud, saying once – or indeed, *if* – the party reached Rome, there would be no coming back. Flavius chose not to ask whether that was because Rome would be so enticing or so deadly. He was reconciled to the possibility his mother wouldn't return, but he desperately needed Dilectus to come back. Elen had given birth to another baby girl. Miracle from God as it was at her age, a living male heir, especially one as smart as Dilectus, was essential to prevent old Chief Conanus's prophetic worries about the future from becoming reality.

Flavius kept repeating to himself, 'If only Sev were still with us, he could have arranged all this travel in a flash'. Then, feeling nostalgic as well as a bit guilty for neglecting her recently, he sent word to Senica, inviting her to the big farewell picnic planned for his mother's departure. He also remembered to invite Jodocus Demetarius and his wife, Cornelia. They were Dilectus's grandparents on his father's side, after all, and following Caradocus's murder, Galeria had made the elderly couple part of her initiative to bring a sense of extended family to the villa community. She had offered Jodocus, who was an experienced administrator in the now-defunct Roman government of Venta Silurum, a job as *bajulus* of the villa's surrounding lands.

The farewell garden party was to be held under the four great oak trees on the villa estate. That was comforting for all the guests. Oak trees were magical. Flavius made every effort to make the event a joyful occasion despite his feelings of dread and the catastrophic images he couldn't get out of his head. Galeria was giddy at the thought of seeing Rome for the first time, and even Dilectus had asked Flavius for a list of the most important edifices he should be sure to visit, forgetting for a moment Flavius himself had never been to Rome. The departure date was to be June the 23rd, so the picnic was ordered for one day earlier, Midsummer's Day. The carvery corner had three new lambs and a heifer turning on spits. The wine cellar at Villa Arcadius had been emptied. All the children of the kitchen staff had been offered a bronze *nummus* for every basket of bilberries they could collect in the wild. It was early in the season, but a shiny coin from the villa treasury encouraged tenacious searching of all sunny locations. Wild strawberries, which didn't require any extra honey, were a reasonable substitute for the younger children to gather, as these could be found closer by. A dairy farmer had supplied bowls full of the thick clotted cream that the people over towards Corinium were famous for. Cockles and oysters were available in large buckets of seawater to keep them fresh; all they needed was a dash of vinegar and then they could be piled on a nice slice of dark bread. A mountain of large black mussels had been gathered from the rocks where the crystal-clear waters of the Sabrina turned salty. They needed to be boiled in white wine with sliced leeks and dandelion leaves to open the shells, and then they were ready to put in a bowl with their liquid. The queue of people waiting with their wooden bowls wound halfway across the meadow.

Most of the women had made headdresses of wildflowers – marsh orchids, poppies and wild roses. The children had strung garlands of the more plentiful foxgloves, yellow irises, buttercups and vetch. Someone was playing the syrinx well enough for the older children to be dancing and cavorting around the traditional summer solstice bonfire. An outside observer could have been excused for thinking the entire picnic felt a lot more like a traditional Celtic feast than a party for the departure of a grand

Roman lady known for her Christian devotion. But apart from murmuring just a little at the excess of the event and mentioning 'conspicuous consumption' twice to Flavius, Galeria, deep inside, revelled in the fact ordinary people were getting a chance to live for a day like the Emperor himself – or the Pope, as Flavius remarked with a touch of cynicism.

Elen and Meirion and their two young daughters had arrived in a waggon with trenchers loaded with Silurian delicacies: cooked ox tongue in aspic, blood sausages and boiled puddings made of boar and venison livers mixed with oatmeal and pepper and the white part of leeks. But their enthusiasm for the event was restrained. They were deeply worried about Dilectus's safety, but he was worried about nothing. He'd obviously started too early on the wine. Perhaps that was a sign of worry.

The time came for a proper Christian blessing, and to Dilectus's delight, old Potitus from Banwen provided it. Even though he could only occasionally help out in Galeria's chapel, he was badly needed – there was still no permanent priest in the position, and as for a bishop, Exuperius's replacement had not yet arrived. Father Potitus, never having been on a boat in his life, provided some non-liturgical flourishes of his own creation, calling on God to protect them from the fire-breathing sea monsters of *Oceanus*. Most people thought the Scoti were a more likely threat.

Feeling a little worse for wear, Dilectus solemnly asked Claudia to walk with him away from the party, which had become boisterous and noisy. When he'd first seen her arrive, accompanied by her friends, with a flower wreath in her hair and a gold necklace Galeria had just given her, he knew he had to tell her that day. And the fact that her white Egyptian cotton dress, which accented the curves of her body, had flooded him with desire made him even more determined to seize the day, the way Ovid told young lovers in his distinctly erotic poems Galeria often read to the older children without a blush – *'pluck the bloom. For if you don't, it meets a wasted doom...'*

Claudia had been a little restrained all afternoon. She was sulky; she hadn't been allowed to go on this trip – her language skills were far better than Dilectus's and she had read a great deal more history of Rome. She was also worried, so she accepted Dilectus's invitation without hesitating. She excused herself from her friends, who immediately started giggling as the couple walked away. They, too, were suffering from the desperate shortage of young men. Constant fighting, from minor skirmishes and brief raids to major battles and long campaigns, had taken its toll on the population of eligible bachelors in Cymru. It was sadly one of those moments in history when intelligent, educated young women could be drawn, preternaturally, to monastic opportunities.

They found a spot out of the wind with low spreading bell heather to sit on. Dilectus had snatched one of the tablecloths, which had only a few wine stains and three grease spots, and ceremoniously laid it out on the ground. They sat in silence, just holding hands, the way Dilectus's parents, Caradocus and Elen, had once sat on a hillside outside the walls of Viroconium Cornoviorum on the day of their wedding. Caradocus, calling himself Macsen Wledig, had tried to make a garland of dog violets and honeysuckle, but it was late in the year, and he had to keep apologising for their tired look. Bell heather can't be easily plucked, and, Dilectus, who had heard the romantic hillside story from his mother many times, made no effort to recreate the carefree times of twenty-two years ago. The Molossians of war had been unleashed, and nothing would be the same again.

It was in this sombre mood that Dilectus finally spoke.

"Will you marry me?"

"As long as you don't 'see Rome and die'! I don't want to be a widow, with all the crap you Christians are spouting about the blessedness of widowhood."

"You're more a Christian than I am. You know what I think of those attitudes. But I'm not going to die, so you're stuck with me if this really is a 'yes', and you're not put off by my youth."

Claudia gave him a gentle shove. "Fiddlesticks, boy, a few years is no difference at all, although my five in emotional maturity could be a consideration."

"Be serious, Claudie. I love you. I desire you. I want to make you happy."

"Seriously, then, this is bad timing for me, my dearest. My parents are missing and presumed dead; both my brothers are known to be dead. And anyway, I'll have to ask permission from Uncle Flavius – he's head of the household."

"You don't have to ask anyone's permission. You have free will. I've heard about it from Padrig. And Flavius agrees with it."

Claudia smirked: "Well then, neither of them recognises what us women have to put up with. You *men* might have free will. We're just slaves. I'll have to ask Galeria – she's an inspiration, and she's the real head of the household."

"Good, that's fine with me. She's already agreed."

"You lie! *She* accepted your lukewarm proposal on my behalf?"

Dilectus pursed his lips. "Well, not exactly. She once said to me it must be your choice, but if you wanted me, she'd be as happy as an oyster."

"Sounds more like her. But why an oyster? I didn't know oysters were happy."

"Look, love, my Latin isn't that good. I *thought* that's what she said, but as I generally understood the sentiment, I wasn't going to ask any challenging questions."

"All right! Fine! We're in agreement. You've got yourself a wife, and I've got a barbarian who promises to come back alive from his holiday jaunt to Rome – without taking me."

"You do seem quite matter-of-fact about it all! I'm totally thrilled, delirious." He hugged her wildly, with kisses all over.

"I was expecting it," Claudia said when she broke away from his embrace. "All my friends told me this would happen based on the soppy way you always look at me. But you're the only living creature who knows I'm not a virgin and there can't be another man in the whole world who is such a crazy lover as you are. Let's do it – I don't mean that, I mean let's find the priest, he's right here."

"Dear old Potitus was looking a little worse for wear the last time I saw him. If we can sober him up, what else do we need? I don't have a ring…"

"Bad start," Claudia said, enjoying Dilectus's crestfallen look. She then fished deep into the pocket of her dress. "I hope you're better prepared for survival on your trip. I've got two here. The 'Happy Oyster' gave them to me this morning. They're hers."

"Jesus, everyone in the world seemed to know we were going to get married except me. Did you ask her for them?"

"Of course not. Grandma Galeria offered them to me. I'm not sure why, but she was crying when she did so. I hoped they were tears of joy. She gave me this gold crucifix, too, and said, 'Villa Arcadius is yours when Flavius is gone'. I didn't know he was going anywhere."

Dilectus grabbed her again, pressing his face against her breasts so hard it hurt. She didn't pull away. Silently, she prayed, 'Dear Lord Jesus, protect this man'. But she wasn't absolutely sure someone who had not yet confessed, and never would, to fornicating outside of marriage would actually have Jesus's ear. So, she threw Branwen and Venus into the mix of her prayer. Surely it was good to spread the protection task to more than one deity? Dilectus, at that moment, was thinking of Padrig and their early explorations, which had taught him something of the art of giving and receiving pleasure. Openly expressing needs and wants and ensuring they were reciprocated in a mutual fashion was the key to good lovemaking. He was certain it meant Padrig was still alive. They both had free will, and Dilectus was determined to use it wisely.

Chapter 26: The Ocean Voyage

The June weather was pleasant. Not too hot but strong sunshine and the days long. There was a gentle wind, which was ideal. Their boat departed from the small natural harbour the Romans had built on the mouth of the River Isca, which was only a few miles from Isca Silurum and the villa. Being right on the Sabrina estuary, it was easy to set sail from there for the west coast of Hispania. The oak-planked, carvel-built merchantman was only about sixty feet long, with one mainsail and a small spirit sail fore and the external rudder aft. Their quarters were tiny and ablutions primitive, but the four passengers from the villa were all delighted to be at sea – a novelty for all of them, including Galeria, who, as a bride, had crossed Gaul to reach Britannia and barely remembered the brief crossing of the Channel.

Once in the open sea, they sighted a merchant vessel coming from Hibernia, heading to Gaul. There was some anxiety at first – Scoti pirates? – but their captain identified it as a trading vessel. He said it was one he had seen a number of times before, and he knew it was carrying a cargo of dogs to the continent. "Dogs?" Dilectus asked incredulously. "Yes," the captain replied. "Celtic hounds, Hibernian Wolf Hounds specifically, are highly valued by the wealthy in both Gaul and Italia. It's about the only valuable commodity the Scoti and other pagan tribes there have to offer," he added somewhat contemptuously. Dilectus had the strangest feeling as he watched the other vessel disappear over the horizon. It was making him think of Padrig and his clash with Scoti slavers six years earlier. *'Dogs, huh? Our own wolf hounds are great hunters, but the Hibernian breeds might be better. I'll have to remember that'.*

Once they moved into the open waters of *Oceanus* and the land became just a distant smudge on the horizon, the large swells began to lift the boat and send it hurtling down again in a steady rhythm. The little boat pitched and rolled mercilessly. Dilectus was enjoying himself watching how the sailors managed the shaft of the huge tiller and how they nimbly adjusted the running rigging to keep the mainsail taught. Galeria was not enjoying herself in any way. She stopped one of her frequent prayers and said, "This is as bad as riding a camel!"

Dilectus laughed. "Have you ever ridden a camel, Lady Galeria?"

"No," she admitted, "but I've read lots of stories about camels. I used to be interested in a comment Jesus once made about camels fitting through small spaces, which made me curious."

"Do you believe in Jesus, Lady Galeria? Uncle Flavius told me Jesus lived so long ago we can't be sure about what he actually said because it depended on people who didn't really know him very well writing it all down from memory."

"My son Flavius should not be filling a young man's head with doubt," Galeria replied a little sharply.

"But he said it was good to doubt and to seek the truth by good observation and rational thought."

"Well then, let me make one good observation. Our knowledge of Jesus's life comes from four different people who wrote the gospels, and they often tell much the same story, which suggests some degree of reliability, doesn't it?"

Dilectus decided he didn't really want to get into this sort of discussion with someone as important as Lady Galeria. And it would have appeared argumentative to add that Flavius had observed there were huge discrepancies between the four gospels. He decided to shift focus.

"Will God look out for us on this voyage?"

"I'm sure of it. Think about your life, Dilectus. You have had three narrow escapes already. The first one might have been due to your bravery, but bravery comes from the Grace of God. The others required huge sacrifices by someone else. Patricius has probably become a slave, and Severus died in his attempt to save you."

Galeria saw the dark look cross Dilectus's face and realised she had made a mistake. The guilt of being a survivor when others have died or suffered can be intense. She knew the first disciple, Peter, had carried just such a burden all his life. Dilectus must be feeling keenly the sacrifice others had made on his behalf.

"I think these incidents mean two things, Dilectus. One, you were loved so greatly by two good people. The other is that God must have a purpose for you and maybe Patricius as well. As for Severus, if there is a heaven, he is in it now. He liked to talk about his low opinion of the church and its teaching, but if ever there was a man free of sin, it was he. And since he didn't believe in much, we cannot assume *his* goodness came from God's Grace. You're going to have to meet Pelagius when we get to Rome. When we get back, especially when you are king, you might be able to influence other Celtic people to see these are important ideas. I'm not so impressed by his ideas on asceticism, however. But thanks to me, I think he's been shifting to the idea of using our skills and our good fortune to help others, which is good, and away from a focus on personal self-sacrifice and deprivation, which doesn't help anyone. You might meet some of these people in Rome. But the biggest mistake I feel is thinking about physical passion, and the desire to share that passion with someone else comes from the Devil. Giving and receiving pleasure is a beautiful thing."

Dilectus blushed furiously. No one had ever spoken to him like that. Even when he'd first told his mother long ago, he'd kissed Claudia on the lips, there had been no mention of pleasure. And not even a hint of arousal. Elen's only question was to make sure he had not forced himself on her. 'That,' she had said, '*would* be a bad sin.'

Seeing his discomfort, Galeria decided to drop the conversation. Even so, the words of Augustine of Hippo, she had once read in a book borrowed from her bishop seven years ago, had deeply disturbed her: 'Nothing is as powerful for pulling a man's spirit down as the caresses of a woman'. Or words to that effect. Just because he had been promiscuous in his youth, it was quite wrong of him to claim that 'the joining of bodies' was inherently sinful and the bad but necessary part of marriage. She knew many theologians were beginning more and more to interpret Eve as the cause of Adam's – in other words, man's – downfall. There was what she saw as a dangerous new trend in the Christian faith. Siricius and his push for priestly celibacy was quite contrary to the importance of women and female celebrants in the early days of Christianity. Thankfully, the current pope wasn't as adamant. This was important, as Innocentius was claiming universal power over all of Christendom. But even so, the trends were leaning towards significant deterioration in the rights women enjoyed under Roman law and custom. Rights she herself had been able to exercise in the management of Villa Arcadius.

Only when she turned around suddenly as the boat heaved unexpectedly, did she realise Lestinus had been listening attentively to the conversation? He immediately looked away and pulled on a rope as though he had been checking on the sails, which seemed suspicious. Surely, he wasn't interested in theology – or sailing? Although she had noticed he was more pious than she'd ever realised, such as genuflecting with the sign of the cross when she said grace at mealtimes. *Well,* she said to herself, *good for him; devout young men were going to be needed. Maybe after seeing Rome and all its glory, maybe even meeting famous theologians, he might be tempted to enter the priesthood on his return. He could read and write well, and his Latin was coming along. Far better than Sioned's.* Poor Sioned. Whatever languages she could or could not speak was entirely irrelevant at that moment. The only sound coming from her was harsh retching as she leaned over the side of the boat and vomited for the umpteenth time over the side. *Thank the Lord she was sensible enough to do it over the leeward side,* Galeria thought to herself.

Chapter 27: The Eternal City, Late Summer, AD 408

The guest house of Villa Anicia was considerably more sumptuous than Villa Arcadius, which told Dilectus something about the main residence, to which he had not yet been formally invited. He could tell his presence with Lady Galeria had caused a degree of consternation among the host family. Galeria was happy to lie about his background. 'His father was a Roman officer, a centurion, attached by a special commission to my son Flavius, who was a legate. He gave his life defending the Empire'. This was a major exaggeration given that he died from poisoning by religious zealots, Priscillians, while ASP from the Roman army. But no one questioned him or her further. Galeria decided not to push credibility by saying his mother was a princess – they'd all be far too curious about bloodlines. There was always the risk they'd try to trace a fake connection to one of the noble families they were in conflict with. Long-standing feuds and family vendettas going back generations were *pro forma* among the Roman nobility.

During the long, rough sea voyage, Galeria had taken Dilectus to the quieter bow of the boat and spent some time preparing him for Roman high society. After carefully cutting his hair with scissors she had brought and trimming his beard to a neat point, she gave him some basic lessons in manners.

"Dilectus, dear, they will know instantly you are what they call a barbarian because your Latin is still pretty bad. I'm sure none of them could tell a Goth from a Vandal, but you will find there are many Goths living in Rome as citizens – retired from the army, freed slaves, who knows. And I'm sure the fine ladies of the Palatine Hill are terrified of all of them. Your advantage is you are young, tall, good-looking and, most importantly, you are a man. Men are in charge in Rome still, but your nice physique will have all these old ladies in a twitter – not that they'd ever admit it, even to themselves. So, if you're polite, keep your mouth shut, bow but not too low, take lots of baths and wear the tunics I'll buy as soon as we arrive; I'm quite sure you will get a room in the guest house. Lestinus, however, will have to sleep in the servants' quarters. I'm not sure yet what they'll say about your Aunty Sioned. I've prepared her for this already and she was gracious and understanding. It's her hair. Bright red hair will remind them of tales they must have heard in school about how the warrior Boudica nearly wiped out the Spanish Legion hundreds of years ago. Romans don't like defeats. Well, who does? But Sioned will at least be accepted as my lady in waiting, so she'll certainly be near me in the guest house."

Dilectus was impressed at the arrangements Galeria had managed to make from far away Britannia. The mansion they were staying at on the Palatine Hill belonged to the elderly Anicia Faltonia Proba. Galeria mentioned she was the descendant of a Roman Christian poet, but the significance of that was lost on Dilectus. Of more interest was that their hostess was a widow, and the other family members in the house were her daughter-in-law, Anicia Juliana, and Proba's granddaughter Demetrias. Juliana's husband was nowhere around and as a former consul, he might have been up in Ravenna with the Emperor. But Juliana was fully in charge of the household, which Dilectus noted with interest. As time went by and the guests from Britannia were more established, he also noted how Juliana kept her daughter well out of the way of the visitors. Even though Demetrias could only have been ten or eleven, there was clearly an effort not to expose her to any young men, especially a looker like Dilectus.

During the first few weeks of their arrival, the little group from Britannia had spent days wandering the city, staring with fascination at the great monuments of the Empire, like tourists from the countryside in a large city for the first time. It wasn't just the fine buildings and triumphal arches; it was the throngs of people they weren't used to. A city of eight hundred thousand had swelled to close to a million, with recent arrivals all talking nervously of undefined threats. Both Dilectus and Lestinus wore their swords at first but, after a few days, stopped bothering. The crowds were so thick they could never have drawn them from the scabbards hanging from their belts if an assassin or a mugger had suddenly appeared. More germanely, the crowds were not overtly hostile, being completely disinterested, or seemingly self-preoccupied. Dilectus saw one scruffy, monkish-looking man holding a huge sign in Greek. He asked Galeria what it said, and she replied, without smiling or further comment, "REPENT,

THE END OF THE WORLD IS AT HAND." A swarthy, heavily tattooed man in gladiatorial garb was walking around shouting in Latin, 'Damn Telemachus to Hades'. Everyone ignored him or hastily moved out of his way. And on every corner, there were beggars covered in filthy bandages and half-naked, emaciated women holding hollow-eyed children or clutching babies to their shrivelled breasts. The visitors were shocked. Dilectus just couldn't get his head around the sheer number of people in the street – a hundred people at the Saturday morning market in Venta Silurum was considered a large crowd. And the stench was pretty bad, too, although Galeria always held a small silk handkerchief doused in lavender oil up to her face when they strolled around the major sights with their mouths agape. 'Just like hicks from the Iron Age,' Sioned kept remarking.

After the first few days, Galeria planned the sightseeing visits better, staying closer to the wealthier areas and venturing into the Forum only when there was a speaker she hoped to hear. Even there, a toothless beggar with a suppurating eye tried to snatch at her hairnet, sensibly the only jewellery she was wearing. She loved visiting Hadrian's rebuilt Pantheon and grumbled that it should be a Christian church. Acting as a tour guide to the other three, she also insisted they visit the Baths of Caracalla. The one place she refused to enter was the Flavian Amphitheatre. The thought of what had happened to so many Christian martyrs filled her with horror. The deaths of thousands of slaves forced to be gladiators made her wonder about the nature of humankind and exactly what the Romans meant by civilisation.

If even Christians could be so bloodthirsty perhaps her son Flavius was right to think of the great Greek scholars as being a better source of moral behaviour than the teachings of her church. She wondered about the nature of sin. The pessimistic African bishop in Hippo was beginning to write pamphlets challenging Pelagius's sound ideas that no human was innately sinful any more than they were innately good. So many learned bishops were willing to scare people into conformity with their notions of right and wrong by threatening them with hellfire and torment for eternity. But Jesus was more likely to talk of the rewards in heaven for leading a life like He modelled. He often said how lovely heaven was; he hardly ever mentioned hell. She was sure the people Christ judged as good were those who enjoyed life, took care of children, respected the natural world God had created, loved their neighbours and helped and took care of the less fortunate. And Pelagius was insisting we could choose to do these things – with God's help. But even without it.

Galeria had originally wanted to talk to Siricius, the Bishop of Rome, about such things, but he was now long since deceased. The current pope was Innocentius and Galeria was thrilled her request for an audience, sent via Bishop Exuperius who was still feeling guilty, had been granted. *All the financial support she had given the diocese back in Britannia had paid off,* she thought, but what she couldn't know was that Exuperius was very much in the Pope's favour by this time.

It was early September, and she had only been in Rome for a few days when she borrowed Proba's carriage to get to the magnificent Lateran Palace. When Innocentius, a youngish man in his early thirties, finally appeared, he was full of excuses.

"My apologies, dear lady, but I am unable to meet with you today. We must postpone your visit to a more opportune time. This morning, I received some terrible news. A few days ago, in Ravenna, General Stilicho, who had led Roman armies to many great victories, was executed by decapitation. It was carried out under the orders of Olympius, but the Emperor must have approved it. Olympius is a wicked man, insatiably ambitious and always jealous of Stilicho's success. He was against Stilicho's dealings with the Goths, but somehow, we must come to terms with these people if there is ever to be any peace. If I can overlook the fact that they are Arians, so can the Emperor.

"Good lady, I am sure you know nothing of worldly politics or of military matters, but I can assure you this is a great loss for the Empire and a crisis for us here in Rome. I must meet with my advisers and dignitaries of the Church. I must dictate letters and organise my formal position on the matter without incurring the wrath of Honorius. It is a difficult time. If the self-anointed King of the Goths understands the power gap this creates, he will surely exploit it, and I would not blame him. The Senate has been unwilling to meet his requests for payment and a designated homeland. He is an Arian. I have no love for the man. But we must have peace and stability for the sake of all. If he sees a weakness, the Goth will be at our gates before the year's end. May the blessings of the Lord be with you, good lady. We will talk another time."

Chapter 28: Starvation and Death – the First Siege

Galeria was the first citizen in Rome to hear the news that not only had Stilicho been executed but had been declared *damnatio memoriae*. But as the word spread, chaos erupted. Galeria wrote to Flavius 'depending on what happens next we may be trapped here for a while'. The one thing Galeria, like the Pope, was certain of was that the Goths would immediately take advantage of the execution of Stilicho. Her letter arrived at the Villa Arcadius in late October, by which time Alaric and his army were very much at the gates. It was something he had wanted to do for a long time, and this was the perfect opportunity. He took control of Ostia and Portus, the twin harbours where hundreds of ships delivered daily all the food supplies from the Empire's 'granary' in North Africa to the city. And he halted all river traffic up the Tiber. His first siege of Rome had begun. Food supplies were drastically reduced. The grain ration was cut by half and then by two thirds. But that wasn't the worst aspect of the situation. Because Stilicho had recruited Goths to his army, many of their family members were living in Italian cities. Across the country, but especially in Rome, anger against these migrants erupted in violence. Hundreds were slaughtered. Prejudice against all barbarians had always been present, but a combination of Goth brazenness, such as marching into Italia and their relative success on the battleground, had escalated Roman antagonism and fear. Revered Christian theologian Jerome, whose writings were so prolific, regularly called the Goths 'savages'.

Conditions for the travellers from Britannia could hardly have been worse. Starvation and disease spread rapidly throughout the city. Dead bodies piled up the streets. The wealthy families of Rome were able to release some stored food supplies, but a city this size needed tons of grain from Africa every single day. Fighting over handouts and other scraps made the streets too dangerous for travel. On the Palatine Hill, however, private security forces created something of an oasis in the chaos. And the residents continued to meet and talk and hold discussions and entertain intellectuals and theologians as though nothing were happing.

What amazed Dilectus, hovering in the background of the discussions, was the intensity with which Galeria's friends and distant relatives discussed what he considered totally meaningless and frivolous issues concerning religion. The debates were intense, sometime involved reading letters or pamphlets written by highly regarded clergymen – monks and bishops, and sometime hosting these same men as speakers. While Dilectus failed to see the significance of exactly how poorly Origen had translated parts of the Hebrew Bible, or why living by yourself for years in the Egyptian desert qualified you for sanctification, the one thing that amazed him the most was how these people, living in the greatest luxury imaginable, could so willingly discuss the virtues of the simple life, of asceticism and charity.

It was clear they were all doing – as Galeria was known for back home – some acts of generosity to the poor. Food was being sent out, and sometimes medicines and even alms. But it was obvious to Dilectus these great families of Rome had carefully amassed extra food supplies while people were beginning to starve from the shortages. They weren't exactly divvying up all they had to everyone in need – they were simply feeling virtuous by sharing something whose loss they would hardly notice. And anyway, there were still desperate people begging in the streets. Were the folk receiving the help those respectable poor who attended church regularly and doffed their hats to carriages passing by? And who was feeding those fine horses rather than feeding the horses to the starving masses? The Celtic way, the way of his Silurian tribe, was that during good times and good harvests everyone shared the bounty of the land, and during hard times, everyone starved together. It wasn't entirely true of his grandfather King Conanus, but his excuse was how excessive taxation by the Roman authorities had forced more Roman ways of hoarding and controlling community resources, which privileged the strong and promoted tribal conflict just to survive. Dilectus had first seen the evidence of amassing wealth when Flavius had shown the young boy the vast hoards of gold and silver riches that maintained the villa – and in the process the difference between the families with the villas and the peasants without them.

If you were a pagan in Rome, the reason for the widespread misery was obvious. The gods were angry. The Christians had managed to banish underground all the sacred rites and rituals, and now the city was paying the price. There was a push to reintroduce traditional sacrifices to appease the gods and save the city. Pope Innocentius reluctantly agreed to allow these, but only if they were conducted in private. That would be pointless, the high priests argued; sacrifices needed to be visible and should take place in the Forum for all to witness. So that led nowhere, and the gods remained angry and did not come to Rome's defence.

A more pragmatic idea was to negotiate with Alaric. Rome's needs were clear. People were dying in such large numbers there was nowhere to bury them. Rotting corpses lay in the streets. And the slaves inside the city, many of them Goths themselves, were getting restless. In the first negotiation, Alaric, in full control of food supplies coming up the River Tiber, held most of the *latrunculi* 'dogs'. But now food shipments from Africa weren't coming up the Tiber to him either. Making his first demand, he started at the high end. He wanted all the gold and silver in the city, all valuable household goods, freeing the slaves, a Roman military title and a place for him and his people to live. One of the most interesting elements of these demands was that they indicated how Alaric and the Goths, who had been suffering as a nation pushing and being pushed around the empire, wanted to settle somewhere in an alliance with the Emperor and be potential citizens. But the Senate, whose members would be giving up their gold, and the Emperor Honorius, whose advisers saw any alliance as a threat to their own power, both baulked.

Not being in a desperate hurry, Alaric kept the negotiations going with the envoys from the Senate and eventually lowered his demands. The final agreement was no military title but for the city to give the Goths, among other things, five thousand pounds of gold, thirty thousand pounds of silver, four thousand silk tunics, three thousand hides dyed scarlet – the Goths loved the colour red – and three thousand pounds of pepper. Wealthy Romans were skilled at tax evasion. When the city government couldn't squeeze out of the elite all the gold and silver needed, they were forced to melt down sacred pagan ornaments and statues. The payments were sufficient for Alaric to accept the terms, making him seem more reasonable. He didn't let on that he, too, was running short of food. He withdrew his forces to central Italy – pity the residents there – and the siege was lifted. Slaves in the city fled to join Alaric – there could be some nasty moments for their previous owners if ever they were to come back.

Nobody was happy with the outcome. Jerome, sounding off as usual, blamed the disastrous situation on the recently beheaded Stilicho, writing to a friend the next year in a letter widely copied and distributed that *'Rome has to fight within her own borders, not for glory but for bare life. And she doesn't even fight but buys the right to exist by giving gold and sacrificing all her substance'*. He went on to say: *'This humiliation has been brought upon her not by the fault of her Emperors, who are both religious men, but by the crime of a half barbarian traitor who, with our money, has armed our foes against us'*. Stilicho's mother was a Roman, but his father was a Vandal cavalry officer in the Roman army – hence the little racist dig. But traitor he was not. As for Honorius in the West and Arcadius in the East (now recently deceased) – religious men they may have been in word, but not in deed.

In the middle of the drama of the siege, the suffering and the constant recriminations and blame game, Galeria was aroused late at night by a loud pounding on her door.

"Who's there?" she called out.

"It's me, my lady, Lestinus. It's urgent."

Galeria aroused Sioned in the adjacent chamber, found their dressing gowns, and the two of them faced Lestinus.

"I've contained a visitor in the anteroom. She's asking to see Lady Galeria. Says she's a relative. Says it's a matter of life and death."

"Did she give her name, Lestinus?"

"Yes. She claims to be Serena. The widow of General Stilicho. Can we believe her?"

"Whether we do or not, we need to speak with this person. Bring her in, for goodness' sake. Where's Dilectus?"

"Asleep, I imagine. I was on guard duty this evening."

"Go and arouse him, please. This sounds serious."

When the mysterious visitor was seated with Galeria and Sioned, she begged them, "Have your security guard lock all the doors and close shutters so no light can be seen. I may have been followed. Dear Cecelia Galeria Arcadiae, I am Serena, wife now widow of General Stilicho and cousin of Emperor Honorius of the family Theodosius in Hispania. I was the adopted niece of the great Theodosius, so I am not related to you by blood, but legally, we are cousins of sorts. My daughter Maria was married to Honorius for nine years and tragically died two years ago."

"These things I know," Galeria interrupted, "I read Claudian's description of Maria's great beauty, and I believe you are indeed Serena. So, a great and joyful welcome to you. But did Honorius not then marry your second daughter, so why are you here and why are you afraid?"

"I was the one who encouraged Honorius to marry my daughter Thermantia, but now he has pushed her away, divorced her as a virgin, he claims. Olympius has poisoned the Emperor's mind. The villain conceals under the disguise of the Christian religion the most atrocious designs in his heart. I fear for my life. My son Eucherius, who was on his way here to Rome, has just been murdered. I will be next. I beg you to give me sanctuary."

Galeria didn't hesitate for one moment but instantly recognised the risks. Serena had a controversial reputation. "Of course, dear lady, you are welcome to stay here until there can be proper protection arranged, but we are guests of the noble lady Proba, of whose reputation you will know, and I'd have to ask her permission in the morning."

"I just hope her mind hasn't been twisted by the false rumours and vicious gossip with which I've been slandered. Senators, damned cowards, think *I* encouraged Alaric to besiege Rome. Blaming me and my poor husband for their own greed and unwillingness to negotiate and compromise."

Serena was fighting tears. "Galeria, is this not how civilisation ends? Condemning good people on the basis of whispering, gossip and the hateful words of jealous, inferior people?"

While Galeria and Sioned were settling the distraught Serena down and bringing her some simple refreshments, not daring to summon any of the servants to assist, Lestinus was off finding Dilectus. After a day of guard duty and handing over the duty roster to Lestinus, he had not gone back to the main living quarters of the house but had bunked down in the guardroom near the main entrance. Lestinus, hurrying to find him, glanced over a wall down the street. In the faint light of the moon and the stars, he saw four armed men carrying torches, obviously searching in dark areas. He ran to where Dilectus was sleeping and shook him by the shoulder.

"Wake up, Dilectus. Lady Galeria needs you. Men are approaching the house, and you have to guard the entrance. Don't let a soul in, Galeria says. We have a visitor who's being hunted. It's vital to stop anyone trying to enter the house. That's what she said. Use whatever force is necessary. Under no circumstances allow anyone to pass through. It's a matter of life and death. I'll go to the back of the compound and check nobody's trying to get in there and stand guard there. You go to the front. Take your sword. Be quick."

As Lestinus disappeared in the darkness, Dilectus pulled on a crumpled tunic lying at the foot of his bed. The entire guest house had a smooth marble floor; he didn't need to put on sandals. He hastily strapped his sword belt around his waist and hurried to the main entrance. Dilectus was not one to panic. But when he got to the inner door of the house, he saw the main entrance had already been breached. Why it was open at all, he didn't know. But coming towards him across the forecourt were four soldiers in uniform, carrying spears and swords, and three of them, behind the leader, holding burning torches. Dilectus drew his sword.

"Step aside, young man. Put your sword on the ground. Don't do anything fucking stupid," the lead man commanded.

"Stop where you are!" Dilectus demanded. "Don't come any closer. Who are you, and what do you want?" He whirled his sword as a display of casual contempt Severus had taught him years ago.

"None of your fucking business. But I'll tell you we're from the Praetorian Guard, and we have orders from the city prefect to arrest a traitor to the Empire who we believe is hiding in this house. Now, stand back before we kill you for interfering with a lawful arrest."

The lead soldier made a half-hearted shooing-away jab at Dilectus with his spear. That was a mistake. One of Severus's favourite moves had been what he called the bull-fighter's duck and weave. As quick as a striking cobra, Dilectus side-stepped the tip of the spear, transferred his sword to his left hand and with his right hand, grasped the wooden shaft of the spear and yanked it hard out of the surprised soldier's hand and threw it on the ground. With two quick closer steps, he put his sword unerringly to the man's throat. He'd grown up knowing he was left-handed, but as it was so unlucky, he had trained himself to use the right, for writing, for caressing, for drawing back a bowstring, for throwing a javelin. But he never stopped practising with the more natural left, and it surprised most opponents in practice duals.

It surprised the praetorian guardsman. The man stepped back half a pace and calmly raised both his hands. "Whoa there, you young idiot. Look around. Behind me are three men. No shields. We don't need them. Swords and spears. And there you are, barefooted, half-dressed, tousle-headed like you've been disturbed buggering a goat. Good for you – someone has taught you tricks. But the moment I drop my hands and back away, these three guards behind me will chop you into small pieces before you take your next and last breath. We kill robbers and thieves and drunken barbarian scum like you every night of the week."

Dilectus looked at his situation. It wasn't good. It didn't really matter if he managed to kill one of them. These men were used to being obeyed, being in control and being violent. Resisting arrest was a ticket to Hades. But if he stepped back and lowered his sword, they were certain to kill him anyway. They knew he was a barbarian. They could have been from any part of the vast empire themselves, but in Rome, they were Romans, which meant they felt innately superior in every way. Dilectus's clever little move was a death sentence briefly delayed, regardless of what he did next. The absolute certainty of the outcome gave him a calm fatalism. "I love you, Claudia," he muttered and dropped his sword to the ground.

Chapter 29: Claudia and Vortigern

At Villa Arcadius, Claudia was bored. It was the middle of October, over three months since Dilectus had left on Galeria's jaunt to Rome, of all bloody daft ideas, and she missed him more than she expected. She should be feeling positive. It was a lovely time of the year. There was a chill in the air, making a good hot soak in the baths even more inviting. There was a good harvest, and the pantry of the great villa kitchen was stocked with provisions needing to be preserved and sealed in pickling jars, but she was becoming oddly fastidious in her choices of food. It was hunting season for wild game birds, and the workmen of the villa were out every day bringing back impressive bags of pheasants, geese and swans. With Galeria's absence, however, Claudia knew she should be supervising their preparation in the kitchen and sending someone over to the bishop's palace in Corininium to keep the clerics there happy, even though there was, as of yet, no new bishop. In other words, there were plenty of chores for her to do, and the more there were, the more she was putting them off and the more bored she was becoming.

She wandered into the library to find her uncle.

"I'd no idea how much Grandma did behind the scenes in this villa. I can't manage it all, Uncle Flavius. I'm behind with some of the essential tasks before winter. Dilectus had promised they'd be home about now, and I won't have finished all the jobs I'm supposed to be doing."

"Which ones have you started, my dear?"

"Well, none of them yet. I'm trying to decide on priorities," Claudia admitted.

Flavius sighed softly. "There's your difficulty, I think. You need to pick one of the tasks, one that can be done fairly easily, and as soon as it is finished, you reward yourself with a lovely walk on the grounds or up the hill to the four sacred oak trees, or I'll find you something interesting to read, which I know you love. You can't wait till you're motivated; you have to start with something and then give yourself a reward. Eventually, getting a difficult task finished becomes its own reward. Brother Pelagius calls it exercising free will, but I call it self-improvement. And you'd better get prepared for a longer stay before your husband-in-waiting gets back – the more recent news is not too good. I'm sure there will be delays."

With his last comment Flavius saw how Claudia was bracing herself to fight back tears. She hated to cry, especially in front of her unflappable uncle.

"Look here," Flavius said quickly, "you need a distraction. Pining is bad for the humours – you will get too much black bile. God help me; I know only too well. Why don't you forget about the duties and write a cheerful letter to Dilectus? Wish him a Merry Christmas, as it will be Yuletide before he gets it."

This time Claudia did burst into tears. "You're no help!" she shouted, and Flavius realized honesty was not tactful in this situation. Even so she seemed a little more emotional than usual. But he had an idea.

"Lisen Claudia. We both need to take action. Let's follow my advice and do something constructive. The leading chieftains of Britannia have called for a major council of war. That devious bugger – excuse me – Vortigern has organised it. You know his family has lands and a villa north of here in Viroconium, but they also own some estates around the town of Ratae, which is where we're meeting – it's a bit far from here, but three main roads converge there, including the Fosse and Via Devana. So, it's handy for all. I'm going and I'm representing this region. With Chief Conanus's passing, Elen, your new mother-in-law, has her hands full, coping with two tribes and two babies. But if you came along with me, you could represent them – Dilectus is the next male heir, and you're his wife. If you'd be interested. You'd need to bring a lady's maid, and I'll organise an escort of our most trusted household guards from the villa…"

Flavius's suggestion was interrupted by Claudia throwing her arms around his neck and kissing him. "Yes, yes and yes!" she spluttered. "Exactly what I need. When do we leave? I'll start packing."

All the tribal leaders and local strongmen, eagerly planning on replacing the hated Roman administration in faraway Ravenna, were sufficiently responsive to the growing Saxon menace they had willingly responded to Vortigern's call for a serious meeting at Ratae Corieltauvorum. The bishop of Viroconium, where the Vitalis family hailed from, had helped spread the word of a meeting. Not that clerics were being invited, but these days they had the most effective communication network and many of them, sympathetic to the teachings of Pelagius – as was Vortigern himself – were beginning to cosy up to the more powerful chiefs of Celtic Britannia as the best hope of resistance against the pagan invaders.

Ratae was a smaller town than Venta Silurum, but had a few solid stone houses able to accommodate the assembled dignitaries. The house assigned to Flavius had a beautiful mosaic floor depicting a deer being killed, which Flavius told Claudia was the story of Cyparissus. Around the walls were charming decorative friezes of birds, cupids and flowers, which made Flavius sad. This must have once been the residence of a comfortably off official with exceptional taste, now abandoned like so many others. The meeting itself was convened in the town's public basilica next to the forum – another irony that struck Flavius: Celtic and Britannic chiefs meeting in a classic Roman building to discuss the self-defence of an all but abandoned Roman province, once a jewel in the diadem of the emperors.

Before the meeting in the great hall of the basilica started, Flavius sensed there was muttering about his bringing a woman into the meeting room, although she carefully sat behind him in a smaller chair. People were staring at her, shaking their heads. Eventually, one man, whom Flavius didn't recognise, stood up, pointed to her and said loudly, "Women are not permitted in this chamber. You must leave. It's disgraceful you've been brought here. Who's your chieftain?"

Flavius rose to reply, but Claudia was quicker. She wasn't Galeria's granddaughter for nothing. Even though she was trembling with fright, she placed her hand on Flavius's shoulder and gently pushed him back to his seat.

"Thank you, Lord Gaius Flavius Arcadius," she said in Latin, "for rising to defend me. But since this impetuous person has questioned my existence without even the courtesy of introducing himself, allow me to defend myself and make my own introduction as is the protocol of my people, the Silurians."

Claudia then switched to Celtic in which she was fluent, but she specifically over-emphasised the accent of the common people around Venta Silurum. Flavius smiled broadly; this was pure theatre. There wasn't a man in the room, including himself, who was smarter than this young woman. He thought of Boudica in her prime. He pitied the man who'd objected.

"First," Claudia said, "I request permission from the convenor of this council, Lord Vortigern, to address the group."

Surprised, Vortigern just shrugged and nodded his head.

"Thank you, my lord. Let me next acknowledge the lands of the peaceful Corieltauvi people where we assemble today. I give them my respects. I also acknowledge the ultimate sovereignty of our Lord Jesus Christ. *Masterstroke* thought Flavius, *I've never heard her utter Christ's name before,* then he remembered she often wore a small crucifix on a chain around her neck Galeria had recently given her.] My name is Gwladus, granddaughter of the Lady Galeria Arcadiae, and the wife of Dilectus, son of Queen Elen and the heir to her dominion of the combined Silurian and Demetae peoples of southern Cymru. I thus come as a joint representative of my people together with Lord Flavius and have as much right to attend such a council meeting as that of the impolite person who objected to my presence. I will not leave this chamber as he demanded. However, it is my intention to listen rather than to speak since my companion, Lord Flavius, is, as you all know, highly skilled in all aspects of statecraft and military policy, and I defer to his prominence in this regard. He will speak for both of us. Thank you for your attention. God protect *lady* Britannia!"

She sat down in the astonished silence of the room. Then, one or two of the chiefs started rapping on the table with their closed right hands, and soon, everyone was doing so. Only Vortigern did not do so. He was scowling. *If I hear that name Dilectus one more time, I'm going to fucking scream,* he said to himself. Then he raised his hand for silence and said: "Let us proceed before we get any other interference from…" he desperately wanted to add 'that cheeky bitch' but continued "… the floor. The Saxon menace is what we are here to discuss. But I suppose we should have a round of introductions, which, as this young woman has so forcefully reminded us, is appropriate."

With introductions over, long discussion ensued, which were largely moans and gripes about the Saxons, the Romans, Constantine, pirates, Picts, *bacaudae*, Honorius, the Saxons, bishops, the merchants in Londinium and the Saxons. The reality was that Saxon pirate raids had become more audacious that summer, attacking merchant shipping destined for

Londinium. In one month alone, three sailing ships coming from the mouth of the Rhine and bringing valuable glassware, tiles and pottery had been looted and sunk. The Roman navy for the region, and responsible for communication with Britannia provinces, was based in the port at the mouth of the Bononia river, but all of the ships had been commandeered by Constantine to get his troops across the Channel from Dubris and had never returned. Even though the navy was mostly for transportation purposes rather than a true protective fleet, its sudden absence had emboldened the Saxons so that the merchant shipping interests and what was left of the commercial enterprises in Londinium were agitating for 'something to be done'. The business community longed for the days of Roman military control; their usual complaints about high taxes, price regulations and currency manipulation by the administration were now forgotten.

Vortigern finally tried to direct the conversation towards an idea he had had that might be a solution to a number of related problems.

"If we let the Saxons settle on the north shore of the Tamesis estuary," Vortigern said assertively, using the Roman name of the River Tems, "just where the estuary widens and the river water turns salty, we can keep an eye on them. They'd be between two of the old shoreline forts: Othona to the north, Regulbium on the great Cantium headland to the south. There's a villa on the estuary shore with good farmland around, I've been told. There's a wharf they can use for coming and going and trading and lots of good fishing. And in return, the usual deal – they supply fighting men who can help control the Picts and the Scoti raiders."

Few liked to challenge Vortigern. It could prove unhealthy. Flavius rose to his feet and to the occasion. Like Claudia, he spoke in Celtic but threw in a lot of Latin words for emphasis.

"Lord Vortigern, if I may be so bold as to make a comment, this is an audacious and indeed creative idea. I commend your willingness to be thinking laterally on this matter. I'm not sure, however, whether you have access to the latest intelligence. I have the advantage of my mother keeping me informed on social matters, and of course, in the past, the much-lamented General Severus always kept me conversant with military affairs. I thus know, for example, that the villa there has, like so many others, been abandoned for at least five years. The family got tired of the constant raids, packed up and joined their relatives in Armorica, not called Little Britannia now for nothing, although whether they've jumped out of the kettle into the cauldron remains to be seen. Of course, an abandoned villa could still be useful to the Saxons, although I believe they build their houses halfway into the ground. Being unoccupied does save us from having to expel any legal residents when transferring ownership to Saxon immigrants.

"But the two forts you mention, although very serviceable, have no garrisons at present. For the last thirty years, they've been manned by loyal auxiliaries; we all rightfully call them *numerus fortensium*. But thinking tactically, it is my belief the Empire's days of relying on strongly defended fortifications are long over. Our watchtowers in the north – set up, I remind you, by Severus when he led the campaign for Stilicho – have been so often overrun by Picts that they are now mostly in ruins. And our defensive forts on the continent have proved useless in stopping large tribal groups from invading Gaul, Illyricum and even Italia. Think about poor Gratian, chosen by the army themselves. He was cautious and recommended a defensive strategy, and look what happened to him. The army knew you have to take the fight to the enemy, not wait for them to come to you. And that's exactly what Constantine has done. Personally, I think it is too late for a usurper to have any real influence, but if he is accepted as a co-emperor or a Caesar and can control Gaul, then we will be safer here, even though no Roman army will ever return.

"Severus was doing what he could to keep troops in the places you mentioned. He found funding to pay them and encouraged local volunteers to support them. But after he was tragically killed, what could still be called the Roman army fell apart, and you all know how well that worked out for my nephew Marcus, poor man. Now, third time lucky, they found themselves a competent commander and a real soldier, but they underestimated Constantine's ambition. Now, all of the Roman forces have left us, just like Magnus Maximus did. But we're not weakened. Every chieftain here has good men under his command. If we work *together*, we can repel the Saxons, but the Saxon raids are so quick and sneaky most of the local men prefer to go home and defend their families – which is short-sighted thinking in my view, as a strong mobile force would be a deterrent to any raiding party, whereas one or two men defending a farm or even a fort seems more like an invitation."

Flavius sat down. He knew he tended to be long-winded, and he could see Vortigern and the other chiefs were getting twitchy. Vortigern spoke:

"Well, Gaius Flavius Arcadius, it's you Romans who have left us in this mess. My strategy is to invite just one group of Saxons who have shown a willingness to come and settle in the area, subject, of course, to local customs and laws and to provide auxiliaries which can help defend the whole coastline from raiders, including other Saxons. We make a formal treaty – *foederati* is the most Roman concept I can think of. We grant them land; they pay tribute to our chiefs. If they can't afford that, they offer fighting men to defend a common homeland. Win-win, I say."

Men around the table were muttering their approval and nodding to each other. Some banged the table lightly with clenched fists. Flavius bowed his head, shaking it from side to side. Suddenly, he rose again to his feet, his hands shaking slightly. He struggled to control his desperation. He knew he was about to make the most important speech of his life, but his own hopelessness was weakening him.

"I urge you, nay I beg you, not to implement this plan. Don't get me wrong. I'm all for trying negotiations. But Stilicho's strategy of paying the Goths to go away has failed – partly, I admit because the Senate always resisted the expenditure. So, offering the Saxon's money, contingent on the raids stopping, I just can't imagine working. The real problem you have to understand is that they don't come for gold. Actually, I've heard they prefer silver, but in any case, treasure is not what they're after. We know many are violent, they rape women, seize children as slaves, plunder and loot, but that isn't their main purpose. Put most simply [and here Flavius resisted adding 'for you semi-literate knuckleheads']; they come for the food – the rich produce of our green and fertile island of Britannia. They come to steal cattle and corn and fruit. They are not good farmers, and they are short of land. They're being squeezed from behind by steady barbarian encroachment, people even more aggressive than they are. The Angles and the Saxons are pagans; they cannot swear an oath in the name of the one true God; they cannot be trusted.

"Chieftains here, many of you Christian, are men of honour. Your word means something. However, the one thing we have learned from the recent *foederati* incursion on the continent is that barbarians will break a treaty without hesitation. You may not have liked the Roman occupation and paying taxes to the emperors, but as a true Briton, albeit a Roman Briton, I believe that while we have endured foreign laws and loss of autonomy, we have benefitted from a degree of peace and security which has allowed us to flourish, you men to enjoy luxuries, hot baths and running water and good roads. And your tribes have grown fat and prospered. Stilicho has done his best to pay off Alaric the Goth to stay in one place and to allow settlement. But it hasn't worked. The Germanic tribes, including the Saxons and the Angles, are all under pressure from the far more ferocious and brutal Huns, so they need more living room. Gold or silver is useless when your people are starving. Yes, we have been badly harassed by marauding Picts and Scoti. The Scoti were always willing to settle north of the Wall, which is fine. There's nothing much there; the Picts just want to steal things because their lands are too wet and cold and barren for easy farming. Neither group pursued raids because they wanted to settle in our parts of Britannia – they never tried to do so. They just steal and pillage. It's a nuisance, but it is not a threat to our entire existence. Some are even being converted to the true faith. I know. My mother is funding a missionary up there who is quite successful. It is completely different to what is happening on the north-eastern frontier of the Empire. Only two large rivers are the boundary, and as we have seen, easily crossed. Even more easily when they have already been allowed to settle on the Empire's side.

"We, my friends, have one major advantage. We're an island. That is our defence. The Mare Friscum and our own Oceanus Britannicus are truly narrow seas, but not nearly as narrow as the Rhenus or the Danubius. Our only hope is to collaborate, unite our native Celtic tribes and chiefdoms as Christian communities, and keep everyone else at bay. Look, my friends, I'm willing to organise an effort among the wealthiest of us to pay the Saxons to stay away. Stilicho is trying this with the Western Goths, those they call Visigoths, I believe. But they can't eat gold or use it to keep Huns off their backs in Magna Germania. We should build some ships or commandeer trading vessels and attack the raiding parties out at sea and drown them like rats before they even set foot on our shores. If we fail in this, we usher in a long and violent dark age in which we Celtic Britons, should we survive at all, will be driven to the rocky edges of Cymru and Dumnonia to join the Hibernian monks and holy men living in caves on rocky islands – good literate Christians all, but not what you would call productive family men, raising children and crops, on the success of which our survival depends. Please don't open even a crack the one solid door we have. You can settle a hundred Saxons who might be good neighbours, but every one of them will have four family members back on the continent whom they might have over for dinner, and every one of them has another four relatives who hear good reports of what we offer, and the trickle will become a flood, and we Celts will be swept away, unable to contain them. And by the way, Lord Vortigern, my informants tell me the Saxons aren't nautical and they don't like fish. They are meat eaters. So, whose cattle will get eaten when the first settlers arrive?"

The moment Flavius uttered these last three sentences, trying to be funny at Vortigern's expense, he realised he'd made a big mistake. Until then, his passion and his logic had made an impression. But once he was trying to be sarcastic and snide, he sounded insincere. The warlords around the table who had been nodding were now shaking their heads.

"We're in agreement then, *most* of us," Vortigern took control. "Flavius, your warning is duly noted, but my plan is sound. Instead of preaching doom and gloom, you could make yourself, your connections and your fortune all quite useful by seeing if we can indeed recruit men to garrison the two nearby forts once again. They offer reasonable protection. Surely there are Frisians up north, maybe not guarding the Wall any longer, but willing to serve again if we pay them enough?"

"I'm not one for prayer, Vortigern, but I pray to the Lord you are right, and I am wrong. I will find some funds, but I will also be helping my neighbours, the Silures and the Demetae, to defend themselves with trained mobile fighters and cavalry. Yes, we will strengthen the walls of their civitas and try to keep hold of the now abandoned fort, the Castra of the Legions. Almost twenty years ago, I strengthened our villa's defences and built new walls, *lilia*, and observation posts, but without the army in the Castra, what would be the point of a fortified villa? Today, my family lives in fear and when our good friend Chief Conanus was alive, he was barely able to control looters, slavers and brigands, although his son-in-law has now trained some competent cavalry troops. You lords of the eastern provinces will have to find in yourselves the bravery of Boudica. You will be the first to feel the pressure. We in the west can hold out for a while, just as long as Stilicho contains Alaric and negotiates with our Constantine so they can face a common foe. But if that fails, even my fine villa and the few other Roman-Briton landowners still left will disappear forever. Pray, my friends, pray."

Flavius called for their horses and, with Claudia and his retinue, rode swiftly away. The night was cold and dark, but the road was good and clear of the usual traffic. It was safer to leave. No one could be trusted, least of all Vortigern. The man was a born tyrant. Interestingly, he had the semblance of a rational plan, despite its obvious flaws. Vortigern was not the man to lead the Britannic tribes against the barbarian hordes from Germanic Barbaricum. Perhaps he could lead the other Britannic tribes in a pitched battle or two, but in the end, if he'd allowed the Saxons to settle, he'd be pissing against a *procella*. Flavius was a good reader of character. Everything about Vortigern shouted ruthlessness and ambition. But there was no way that he could be aware of the extent of the self-interest of this son-in-law of the deceased Emperor Magnus Maximus, whose abused wife defiantly wore a beautiful golden torc of exquisite Celtic craftsmanship.

Chapter 30: The Politics of Revenge and Appeasement

It was a much warmer night on the Palatine Hill, even at one o'clock in the morning.

The command "Stop!" rang out in the darkness. "Stop this instant. Let that brave young man go. This is not his fight. I am Serena, wife of Stilicho, the finest general Rome has ever seen, and niece of the great Theodosius. It is I whom you are seeking; I know not why. Leave him alone. State your business."

"We've got a warrant for your arrest," said the captain of the guard, picking up his spear and pushing Dilectus aside in an attempt to regain his dignity.

"On whose authority?" Serena demanded.

"By order of the Senate of Rome, signed by a representative of the Emperor, his sister Lady Galla Placidia."

Serena's laughter sounded almost hysterical. "Placid, she is not! Galla Placidia is my stepdaughter, you dope; she was raised by me and Stilicho in our own household. I hate to think what pressure you cruel people put on her to sign my death warrant."

"It's only an arrest warrant, madam. We are to take you to a private place for security purposes."

"And there you will kill me. Quickly, I hope, rapidly with the *laqueus*. I have nothing left to live for."

Galeria was weeping silently. Sioned glared at the men, with only one thought going through her mind: 'I hate these civilised people'. Dilectus was trembling. He had a deep pain in both sides of the small of his back. He wanted to vomit. Suddenly, as they were leading Serena away, he grabbed her arm. And half garbled, half-whispered, not knowing exactly what he was saying, he blurted out:

"I've never met you, but I know you in my heart. My mentor, Severus, fought alongside your husband. He told many tales about him and his noble wife. You're the bravest of the brave. If there's a heaven, you and Stilicho will soon meet there."

Serena managed what might have been a smile across her terrified face. She lifted a heavy jewelled necklace from her neck and slipped it over Dilectus's head. "Thank you," she whispered and kissed his cheek before the guards grabbed both her arms and hustled her away. No other words were spoken, the only sound was the harsh tread of four pairs of boots marching in step down the granite paving of the street.

The next moment was darkly comic. Looking agitated and sounding breathless, Lestinus suddenly appeared from around the back of the courtyard. "Nothing to see back there. No danger, Dilectus. All clear. Oh, dear Lord, what's everyone doing out here? What have you got around your neck, Dilectus?"

Only Sioned was composed enough to answer. "Fuck off, Lestinus. Go back to the guardhouse. The three of us might tell you in the morning, but right now, we are going inside and I, for one, need a jug of wine. Now piss off."

Although Galeria and her companions talked endlessly about the incident and its significance, Dilectus never repeated exactly what Lestinus had said to him. But he knew what it meant, and from that moment on, but trying hard never to show it, he treated Lestinus with the deepest suspicion. And, a few days later the word spread rapidly: Serena, Stilicho's widow, had been executed for treason and for conspiring with the Goths.

"Why did Serena seek refuge here? Was it because you're related?" Dilectus asked Galeria, still struggling emotionally with the events of that fraught night.

"Probably, although we're only second cousins by marriage. She has… had… much more powerful and elite relations than me. Everyone always said she elevated Stilicho's status, not the other way around. Of course, his brilliance as a general was most important, but he could never escape being half a Vandal – think about how Jerome and others always talked about him in derogatory terms. Serena was the queen of matchmakers in the imperial court – she found the court poet Claudian a wife, and look how she managed to marry two of her daughters to Emperor Honorius! That takes some doing."

"Severus told me on our tragic expedition that Stilicho worried about her ambitious plotting not always being in line with his diplomatic and policy initiatives. Severus wondered if, as a couple, they were trying to manipulate their son to become emperor of both the West and the East."

"It's always possible, Dilectus, mothers and fathers dream of what their children might become or achieve, but I doubt it. Those were the kinds of whispered rumours that resulted in all three of them being dead. Serena was a headstrong and dominant woman. The necklace she gave you she took off a statue of Rhea Silvia in the Temple of Vesta. Flagrant! None of us respect pagan symbols, but Rhea Silvia! Wow! That takes nerve. You know who Rhea Silvia was?"

"*Uhm... er...* no."

"I'm shocked!" Galeria smiled. "She was the mother of Romulus and Remus, a Vestal Virgin raped by the god Mars! Maybe I never told you children that story – you were too young. Anyway, it's yours now, the necklace, I mean. But going back to their relationship, marriage is tricky when both husband and wife are important or powerful in their own totally different way, with different needs and different vulnerabilities. You might want to think about that."

As for the Goths, they were packing up their gold and their scarlet hides and their pepper and moving away. Everyone said the execution of Serena must have been their endpoint. It was obvious now, people muttered, that she was Alaric's close friend; she might have been able to let them into the city. But now that she was dead, Alaric would have to have realised there was no one else who would collaborate; that's what helped make up his mind to depart. Galeria, who hated rumours and speculation, kept telling herself it must have been true that Serena was conspiring with Alaric; otherwise, Galla Placidia could never have done such a vile thing to her stepmother. Galeria had met Placidia a number of times and liked her. She was barely nineteen and clever, highly educated and very well-read. She reminded her of her granddaughter, Claudia. She just couldn't bring herself to believe Placidia could be so evil. Perhaps the Senators had forced her hand; perhaps they'd given her hard evidence of Serena's treason. It was the only thing making any sense.

While the group from Britannia continued to feel quite traumatised by the whole ordeal, there was enormous relief among Galeria's circle of aristocratic friends, who brought back out their well-hidden stashes of valuables. They lamented the inevitable new shortage of pepper, but being such good Christians felt nothing about losing the treasures of the pagan temples. Dilectus's astonishment at the speed with which the ultra-wealthy were able to return to normal life led to more than one deep conversation with Galeria. Her affection for Dilectus, now her grandson-in-law, had intensified as her admiration for his survival skills and practical capabilities had grown. More and more, he was reminiscent of Severus in his youth.

"I talk to people in the streets who seem important and are willing to gossip with a nice young barbarian who is, 'Thank God, not one of those Goths'," Dilectus told Galeria. "And they all assure me King Alaric has simply withdrawn for now. Yes, he's lifted the siege. But he's still negotiating with the Emperor. He wants a military command and a place for his people to settle. Apparently, the Pope is advocating on his behalf. But if there's resistance from the big guys, there's nothing stopping him from coming back and besieging the city again. I can't understand how calmly all your important friends are taking the situation. It seems to me it's still awfully shaky."

"I think you are right, dear; precarious it is. But let's face it: wealthy people are squeamishly reluctant to give up any of their riches, and the Emperor is loath to give up any of his power. He sees agreeing to Alaric's terms as a sign of weakness and surrender. But you've said, quite wisely, I think, even the devout people who are hosting us, including the church leaders, can be terribly hypocritical. They talk enthusiastically about giving alms to the poor as proof of living a charitable Christian life, but not at a level like the wonderful old lady Marcella. She truly lives in poverty. She is exceedingly pious. But even she isn't going to starve. She owns a huge palace on the Aventine Hill – we're going to visit it as soon as things settle down.

"Do you understand, Dilectus, that these people's wealth comes, like mine once did, from family holdings and vast estates across the empire many miles from Rome? This is how they receive their income, get special food supplies, travel with ease in private ships. They don't fully realise that while they are indeed enormously generous in helping the poor and the church and doling out charity, they still remain in complete control of the source of wealth. One day in the future, the common people and the peasants will catch on to this, and there could be serious rebellions against aristocracies. I've heard there are already peasant revolts, the *bacaudae*, back in Hispania and even close to Britannia.

"This is why when we go back home, we need to stop thinking we can live behind the walls of a defended villa when people outside are suffering. Flavius has been telling me this ever since Severus was killed – and of course, his attempts at an alliance with your people, the Silures, were part of trying to sustain Roman values and civilised ideals while surrendering power to good rulers like your Grandfather Conanus. I think your mother, now that she is queen, understands this well. Which means there will be enormous responsibility on your shoulders one day. Just remember these noble thoughts of yours right now when, in the future, you're faced with important policy decisions and threats from neighbouring tyrants."

Dilectus just sat there nodding. It was easy to call other people hypocrites, but what had he ever done to help common folk? He stood up and went over to Galeria and hugged her in a way no man had dared to do since Magnus Maximus had left Britannia to take over the empire. Galeria knew what he was feeling. At that moment, like every young man facing the future, he needed a mother. It was a huge burden of responsibility she had just laid on him. He surely had skills. Goodness, he had even, in the height of the siege, found a way to sneak out of Rome at night, mingle with the Goths outside and return with a basket full of precious food supplies. Here was a man one could depend on. But did he yet have the wisdom? Conceivably, together with her granddaughter Claudia, he did. She resolved to show him, when they all returned, how to access the treasure of the villa that was under her stewardship – better still, tell him now. He and Claudia nicknamed Augusta for her feistiness, might still be able to salvage some of her vision for the villa and the surrounding *vicus* or village community. But no one can foresee the future or know what will happen next.

Galeria now felt she had a special obligation to get Dilectus safely back to Britannia, so she wrote to Flavius, seeking his advice on the timing of their return. However, the usually reliable imperial postal system was not doing well, given the general turmoil, and the letter took two months to reach Flavius. He knew little about the political intrigues at Ravenna, but he knew a great deal about the increased Saxon activity in Britain. He replied to her letter, suggesting that she wait just a little bit longer in Rome until the sea voyage would be safer. By the time his reply reached her, Galeria was already stuck. Alaric was besieging Rome for a second time.

Everyone important knew exactly how this had come about and this time they weren't immediately putting all the blame on Alaric. Most people thought his request for land, an annual payment in gold and a supply of food, was not unreasonable.

One of the problems of despotic rulers, however, is that the men they surround themselves with tend to be either sycophants or secretly ambitious rivals. Honorius, stuck in Ravenna, exemplified this truth. He no longer felt like a god, as emperors had always claimed to be. The Eastern Empire was a constant challenge. He bitterly regretted agreeing to Stilicho's execution. And his recent decision to allow slaves to join the army now looked foolhardy. Worse still, the man who replaced Stilicho (and had engineered his fall) was no soldier and soon lost another battle, this one at Pisa, and fled into self-imposed exile. The British usurper Constantine was insisting on being recognised as co-emperor, despite his son Constans having now been defeated in Hispania. And to add insult to injury, the Britannic provinces were in open revolt – no taxes were forthcoming, Roman administrators were being thrown out, and to top it off, some of the city notables had been pestering him for help in fighting off increasingly threatening raids. Fat chance of that. He ignored their letter. He had much bigger worries.

Alaric's demands were taken to Honorius by his new praetorian prefect of all Italia, who privately suggested adding another plum to the offer: Honorius was lacking competent generals, so why not make Alaric *magister utriusque militiae* – supreme military commander, the same rank as Stilicho held? Even the Pope thought it a good idea, but it was too much for Honorius. His decision was read out in public in front of Alaric and his troops: the request for grain and gold was fine, but 'no honour or military command would *ever* be awarded to Alaric or any of his family'.

Insulted and feeling humiliated, Alaric once again set off for Rome. But after a few days, his common sense overrode his annoyance. On top of that, he heard Honorius was now going to recruit ten thousand Huns to join the Roman army to attack him. It is easy to assume when the history is being told, King Alaric could just march up and down Italy with impunity. But smart people in Rome knew that, in addition to his army, he also had with him more than thirty thousand civilians – all the families, wives, children, old people, camp followers and general hangers-on moving around with him in waggons with wicker frames covered in animal hides. Not comfortable. Not easily fed. So, he modified his demands and tried one more time. This time, his proposal was taken to Honorius by a small group of sympathetic Roman bishops. He simply asked for land rights to settle his people in Noricum as a homeland and as much grain as the Emperor thought reasonable. Honorius declined the offer. Did he not understand Alaric was only looking for a place within the Empire to settle down? They were, obviously, already inside the Empire as immigrants – the empire's borders were always essentially open. Now, they wanted to be accepted and settled, as many other groups had recently done. It wasn't an unreasonable request, but anti-Goth sentiments were too powerful. With this last effort rejected, Alaric, predictably, marched once again to Rome and besieged the city for the second time.

It was late in the year, and for those trapped inside Rome, guaranteeing their food supply was still not possible. This time, the circle of important aristocratic women Galería was now a part of decided to take some action. They met for a luncheon in Proba's magnificent dining hall. Young, shrewd Galla Placidia, born just a few years before her father, Emperor Theodosius, died, was there. Proba's daughter Juliana was there, along with her friend, the ageing widow Marcella, who was a dedicated supporter and associate of Jerome. Galeria did not care for Jerome's teachings, probably influenced by Flavius's intense dislike of Jerome's admonitions against reading and appreciating the greats of Greek and Roman literature just because they were pagans. 'It wasn't a dream Jerome had,' Flavius once quipped, 'it was a nightmare! What sort of idiot wouldn't appreciate the writings of Cicero?' But often bitter conflicts among the dynastic *domūs* of Rome were set aside at this time of crisis.

Two of the women who attended were just visiting Rome from Sicily and had found themselves, like Galeria, inadvertently trapped in Rome. One of them, Caelonia Albina, was the daughter-in-law of a remarkable, if zealous, woman who truly did donate her wealth to religious causes – the indomitable Valeria Melania. The other was Albina's daughter, known by everyone as Melania the Younger, to avoid confusion with her grandmother. She and her husband were visiting from Sicily and had found themselves trapped by the siege. Pelagius had once told Galeria that he found it difficult to keep all these posh Roman families and their marriages and devotees clear in his mind. He was distrustful of the elder Melania because she was so strongly supported by the Bishop of Hippo, Augustine. He also rejected the extreme asceticism of Melania, who had spent time with monks in the Egyptian desert and founded monastic institutions in Jerusalem. But Pelagius admired Albina and her daughter, who were being attacked by Jerome, who was even more antagonistic to Pelagian ideas than Augustine.

The idea that the dignitaries at the luncheon came up with was to persuade the Senate to elect one of their numbers to be a rival emperor, who could then appoint Alaric to the military command he was after *magister utriusque militiae*. His brother-in-law Ataulf could get a title as well: *comes domesticorum equitum*. Alaric thought it a great idea. An elderly senator, Priscus Attalus, volunteered to be Honorius's rival and happily set up his own imperial court in Rome. For his part, Alaric liked his new title, and he lifted his siege in late 409. Galeria, who heard of the negotiations only from the other wives and mothers, was feeling quite overwhelmed. Rome, instead of the shining city on the seven hills, had become a disaster. When the siege ended, she started to make urgent plans for the four of them to return to Britannia. But there was further fighting between Italy and Africa. The Mediterranean, '*Our* sea', as the Romans called it, was again dangerous. The voyage was postponed until July of the following year. Galeria relaxed. Things were falling into place and somewhat under her control. Now, she could focus her few remaining months on spending more time with Pelagius and trying to better understand the beliefs of the powerful women with whom she was now closely associated. It would be important for the survival of her villa to be able to imitate the ways of the pagans and read the entrails of the sacrificial goat.

Chapter 31: Deus Ex Machina

Far from the glamour and glory of Rome's great basilicas, the marble and majesty of her triumphal arches, the fountains and finery of her public parks, a stocky, sandy-haired young man reined in his horse awkwardly and turned to his mother.

"Isn't Cymru a paradise? It's God's garden, the original Eden – except for the horrid sheep. This must be the most beautiful country in the entire world."

Together, they gazed at the rolling green hills unfolding to the craggy mountains far to the north, the tops of their highest peaks already iced with late autumn snow. To the south could be seen the silvery sparkle of the sea. Ahead of them was a high hill, all reddish in the soft afternoon sunlight, topped by a jumbled collection of ill-matched buildings. The surrounding meadows were dotted with blue and gold – cornflowers mingled with the cowslips and Cymru poppies.

As they approached the stone bulwarks at the top of the hill, they could see signs of unfinished repair work, a partially collapsed wooden scaffolding, and stonemasons' tools lying around. No one was working. They rode in unchallenged.

"We have visitors in the forecourt, my Queen," a servant announced casually.

"Show them up," Elen replied, "Rhonnie, pick up your toys, please, sweetheart." She helped push aside a collection of small clay animals and started smoothing her daughters' hair with the palm of her hands, then doing the same to her own. As the visitors were ushered in, she broke into a warm smile.

"Conchessa! What a lovely surprise!" Elen ran forward, grabbing the woman's hands to interrupt her formal curtsy. "None of that in this house, madam! I'm sorry everything is such a mess. We've been trying to get the walls of the main gate fixed for months, but you can't get competent masons any more. Sit, sit. Just throw the toys off. Brangwen, dearie, run and ask the kitchen for refreshments. Rhonwen, pick that cushion off the floor right now... and who is this fine young man with you?"

Conchessa, smiling at the usually imperturbable Elen being so flustered, replied solemnly:

"He is a gift from the Lord. This is your son's dear friend, my own Patricius, returned to us."

Padrig was standing back, humbly, staring at Elen, whose famous beauty he had only observed a few times from the distance, long ago. She was still stunning, but her face showed signs of strain and gray strands peppered her famous strawberry-blonde hair. She looked tired.

"I've come to see Dilectus and to thank Meirion for his efforts to find me," he said as Elen came to him and kissed both cheeks, her arms around his hard, wiry frame.

"Sweet Jesus, am I dreaming? Is it truly you, Padrig? My husband is off somewhere; I'm not sure exactly where he is looking for new bloodlines for his horses. And Dilectus is still trapped in Rome, according to the latest news, which only comes to me from Dominus Flavius at the Villa Arcadius. When Dilectus learns of this, he'll be absolutely overjoyed. You're home! I can scarcely believe it – I want to poke my fingers into you like Thomas did to Jesus!"

When the visitors were settled, with mugs of hot dandelion tea, Elen demanded to hear his story and Padrig lapsed into his native Celtic, but with an odd accent she had never heard before.

"With your little girls listening, I'll not dwell on the horrors of crossing the Hibernian sea in chains or being marched under the whip to the remote farm to which I was sold. My work was to tend sheep in the freezing cold and isolated hills. If any went missing, I was beaten, and once, when I tried to escape, I was caught and locked in an iron cage without food for a week. That was when I finally started praying in earnest, hundreds of times a day, even in the snow and icy rain. My faith grew, admittedly for the first time, and my love of God and my awe of Him became intense. I begged for guidance, not for rescue, and one night, in a dream, it came. A voice told me I would return home and that a ship was ready for me. Well, the coast was countless miles away, but despite my terror of being caught, I just finally walked away, not even knowing where I was going. I was certain God's strength was guiding me.

"So as not to bore you, good Queen, let me just say I was somehow led to a ship, a merchant vessel – traders exporting a large pack of the much-admired wolfhounds of Hibernia for sale on the continent. At first, the captain refused to take me; he probably guessed I was a runaway slave. But I prayed hard, and he relented. I refused to prostrate myself before them as they were pagans. Instead, I promised them one day, they, too, would come to have faith in Jesus Christ. And so, we sailed for Gaul. It was midsummer's day or the day after, over a year ago.

"It has taken me so long to get back to my dear family because things didn't go well. I escaped Sodom for Gomorrah. The merchant who was supposed to buy the dogs did not show up, and the area of the rendezvous had been stripped of all food supplies: first, we heard, by the army of a general called Constantine, and then by marauding peasants, those they name the *bacaudae*. It was a desert. We were starving, the dogs too, and the sailors were teasing me, telling me to pray to Jesus for food. Of course, it's not right to ask for specific things only to be shown how to find them, and soon we were. We stumbled on an abandoned farm. It had been stripped bare, but some of their pigs had survived and were running around free. Easy to catch, so we feasted well, and the dogs got meaty bones to gnaw on. The men were impressed, and at that moment, I knew I had to return to the country of my enslavement and with God's grace, convert them to Christianity. It's my calling; I heard His voice. But first, I must be trained as a priest like my grandfather and taught to be a missionary, and I have arranged to leave early next year to attend a learned monastery in Gaul, in the town of Autissiodorum."

Elen was transfixed by his story, and the girls loved hearing about the dogs and imagining them on the ship, running around barking and yapping and trying not to fall overboard. But now, for the first time, Elen interrupted Padrig and asked:

"Couldn't you attend a monastery or college in Brittania? Lady Galeria has established a centre of learning right here in my kingdom, and Dilectus has even visited and taken books from the villa's library. And I've heard great things about a Father Ninian who's working with the Picts up north."

"Yes, indeed, Your Highness, my grandfather tried to persuade me to consider those options, but because I couldn't finish my schooling my education is seriously lacking, my Latin is weak, and I must restart my studies at the very beginning. I've been in touch with Bishop Garmon, newly appointed to the see of Autissiodorum, who's offered me the tutoring I will need. I'm not clever. I'm a weak student, as Dilectus knows. I hope he'll be back before I leave in the spring of next year."

"Oh, dear God, I hope so too," exclaimed Elen.

"In case he's delayed, I'd like to leave a message for him. And for Dominus Meirion too. Do you have a scribe, my lady, who could take down my words? Even my writing is as rusty and useless as an old bent nail."

With Padrig off to another part of the residence with the hastily summoned scribe, Elen and Conchessa huddled together. Ever since she'd personally brought the news of Dilectus's safety to Garn Goch, she and Elen had shared a special bond despite not seeing each other very often. And with the prospect of their respective sons being linked again and extending their childhood friendship, all barriers to the expression of deep and honest feelings were lifted.

"Dilectus is going to be so thrilled – not just because Padrig is alive and has a worthy mission, but because he felt guilty that Padrig had sacrificed himself to save him. That guilt warped aspects of his mind, I think. And it will be healing that Padrig recognises that Meirion not only rode out early the next morning to find the slavers but spent weeks and weeks after that chasing down every lead while Dilectus isolated himself at the villa, nurturing bad feelings. Lady Galeria's granddaughter pulled him out of it to some extent."

"More than some! Remember, it was my father who married them before Dilectus left! I'm not sure my dad was fully sober at the time, but it was legal and proper in the eyes of God. But you, dear Elen, you look exhausted, although your two sweet little girls are obviously happy."

"I think I'm overwhelmed. I never realised how much I depended, practically and emotionally, on my sister-in-law, Sioned. And Galeria spirited her away to Rome. I should have objected. I need to worry about my people as well as the Demetae, who are equally part of my domain. My father died before his promised abdication, and I suddenly became queen without any support. Meirion tried his best, but he was so uncomfortable in his subordinate role. I think he fell in love with the *idea* of me, only to find I have flaws like anyone else. And although he loves them dearly, he was disappointed our two children are both girls – not that he'd ever admit it even to himself. I expected him to be an ideal stepfather to Dilectus, but my son changed after his ordeal and before Padrig rescued him – twice, come to think of it. Meirion became quite bitter about it, and he and I have, I hate to say it, grown apart."

Elen paused, her voice choking up.

"Meirion took the death of Comes Severus extremely hard. He'd been his advocate from the beginning. My plan is to step down as queen when Dilectus returns and let him take the crown; I've never felt comfortable with it. Sioned can manage the household. And through his marriage, Dilectus will bring us all the best Roman resources of the thriving villa, the intellectual guidance of Dominus Flavius, and the wisdom and empathy of Lady Galeria."

Conchessa nodded with a knowing smile. "I know some of what you're talking about," she agreed. "With Padrig's return, my husband has finally retired. Not soon enough. He's not well. He gave up the role of *curialis* once the other decurion in the employ of the Vitalis family disappeared under mysterious circumstances. And in any case, their heir, young Vortigern, no longer resides in the family villa in Viroconium. He's moved the entire household to somewhere like Ratae; it's central, and he's trying to consolidate his power with other tribes. His poor wife Sevira has died in childbirth; recently, maybe you heard? I shouldn't say this, but it was a relief. She was desperately unhappy. The baby lived. A boy. Just think of it, Elen: The Emperor Macsen Wledig's grandson! What will he grow up to become? The family villa is completely run down, and so is the town. You'd be shocked at the state of Viroconium – it's not the thriving community you remember. My husband's a Cornovii, and he says the tribal people are struggling. Without the Roman army bases and trade through Deva Victrix and Segontium, the local economy collapsed. The bishop is still there… but for how long, I wonder?"

Elen put her arm around her shoulders.

"We have our sons, my dear friend. And for that, we can surely thank the Lord God."

Chapter 32: The Early Summer of AD 410

It's all very well to have a plan and an agreement between two parties, but when there are other equally powerful parties involved who haven't agreed to anything, you can't expect your plan to go smoothly. Senator, now Emperor (in name only) Attalus, recently baptised as a Christian, and King Alaric, now *magister utruisque militiae* (in name only), were getting on fine. But a third power broker wasn't cooperating. Heraclianus, one of Honorius's toadies, had recently been rewarded for his role in the assassination of Stilicho by being appointed as the new governor of the African provinces. He stood by Honorius, quietly panicking in Ravenna, and refused to send the usual grain shipments to Rome. Trying to make up new rules and new positions as you go along was a convincing sign the Empire was in trouble. Alaric was starting to realise what so many before him had come to recognise: when it came to the game of devious, manipulative power politics, no one played it as well as the Romans.

Alaric told Attalus *he* would take a cohort to Africa and force Governor Heraclianus to resume the shipments of food on which the city eternally depended. But that terrified Attalus – having the Goths in charge of central Italia was bad enough, but if they got their nasty barbarian hands-on Africa, it would be the Gothic Empire, not the Roman Empire of the West. So, as Emperor (in name only), he ordered Alaric to hold off and said he'd send his own man with a small Roman escort and lots of cash to use as bribes, and they'd seize control of the African food supply. Unfortunately, the escort was too small. Heraclianus's African troops simply killed them and forwarded the bribe money to Honorius. Now, the food supplies were well and truly cut. Shortages in Rome became acute again, especially as many merchants hid their stocks of food, waiting for prices to rise astronomically and reap handsome profits. Alaric again said he'd go over there and take control, but Attalus refused to sanction such a move. Fed up, Alaric summoned Attalus to Ariminum, where he'd been spending the spring.

There, he stripped Attalus of his title and imperial regalia and decided to have one more stab at negotiating with Honorius.

Communication in times of trouble is always challenging. Flavius, with his small network of informers, actually had better information about all these goings on than did Galeria in Rome itself. And it worried him greatly. He wrote another letter urging Galeria to get out of Rome immediately. But getting the mail across Gaul was a slow process. Constantine, the usurper from Britannia, had done well gaining control of Gaul, and his son Constans had had some initial success in Hispania, surprising for a man who had been training to become a monk just a few months earlier. But after Constantine's other general, Gerontius, rebelled, conditions in the entire region deteriorated into seesaw clashes between the forces of Constans and Gerontius and between the forces of Constantine and Honorius. Flavius's letter reached Galeria far too late to have any value. She desperately wanted to leave, but it was not possible. Alaric was once more outside the city walls.

Alaric's new round of negotiations had not gone well. The cause was one of those immensely complicated circumstances, which, as Flavius said when he learnt about its months later, 'if it were made into the plot of a Greek play, audiences would reject it as too implausible'. The circumstances required the involvement of another Goth general, one Sarus. He'd been passed over in the tribal election, giving Alaric the kingship of the Goths in 395, and with no fury like a Visigoth scorned, he was now the bitter enemy of Alaric and his brother-in-law. However, he was an excellent soldier, and Honorius was happy to use his services as a general. He had some initial success against Constantine III of Britannia but eventually was forced back to Italy. But when Alaric was waiting outside Ravenna to meet personally, by invitation, with Honorius, Sarus – whether on Honorius's order or not – took a small troop of Roman soldiers and attacked his encampment. Alaric narrowly escaped but was finally at the end of his patience. "Enough is enough, for Christ's sake," he screamed to the sky as he rode away from the swamp that was Ravenna, "Rome itself will be ours before the autumn equinox."

So there the Goths were, outside the walls of Rome for the third time in two years, but let's admit it: no foreign invader had breached those walls for eight hundred years and they weren't likely to do so now. The Attalus 'fake emperor' manoeuvre may have failed, but the city had earned a short respite. Prices were still high, but good imported foods – pork, olive oil, honey and grain – were once again available. Galeria had sent Sioned out shopping with some of Proba's house servants, and they'd come back with wine, fresh sausages, mushrooms, asparagus and artichokes. Sioned had also bought some cabbages and leeks, which she passed on to the servants, along with a large jar of honey – most of them had children who would appreciate it.

Galeria's group of noblewomen in Rome, feeling invulnerable as they always had been, were now meeting quite regularly in Marcella's palace. Galeria found the old woman to be intensely interesting. After only seven months of marriage, her husband had died. Her story was similar to Galeria's own, but her decision to turn to asceticism was very different and differently motivated. Her convictions were so fervent, in Galeria's opinion, that she felt the woman had come under the spell of Pelagius's nemesis, Jerome. He had written many long letters to Marcella; Jerome only kept writing to (in his words) 'the weaker sex' because men never asked him questions. She, with his consent, had shared these letters widely, which had given Jerome a huge audience – precisely what he wanted. She had certainly become the major influence on this group of women, although none of them acted quite as willing to go to Marcella's extremes.

Galeria admired her for being ready to give up all wine and the eating of meat, which, since Marcella had reached eighty-four years of age, didn't seem to have done her much harm. Galeria respected the fact she wore simple brown cotton dresses, read extensively, spent many hours in prayer and used her resources to travel widely in the footsteps of Jesus, visiting churches and monasteries from Judea to Egypt. Jerome had stayed at her house for three years back in the 380ies, and it was during this time he'd started his huge project of translating the bible into understandable Vulgar Latin. Marcella and her good friend Paula were so erudite they were able to help Jerome with some tricky translation problems since Jerome was fluent in Greek but not Hebrew. And surely it was just malicious gossip that Jerome had a bit of a thing for Paula. *All well and good,* Galeria thought. But why did she insist her chastity extended to never being able to spend time alone in the company of a man? What was all that about? Galeria could just hear her cynical son saying, 'Oh, Mother, what is she scared of? Being attacked by a man or attacking one?'

Despite these thoughts there was no doubt the meetings in her enormous but plain house were intensely interesting. After some months Galeria decided she was accepted enough and respected enough she could suggest inviting Pelagius to meet with the group one time and to explain his theological positions, which only some of them had heard first hand.

It was a pleasant day early in June, and the summer heat that could be quite oppressive in Rome was still a month away. Galeria told Dilectus of her plans and made a request.

"Brother Pelagius has been invited to speak to our women's group at Marcella's palace tomorrow afternoon. It may be our last chance to see him if Alaric gets hungrier than us and leaves, allowing everything to fall into place for our departing Rome in a month or so. I'd like you to come with me to the meeting. We'll take a carriage as always, but you should be armed. You won't be able to sit in on the meeting as it is women only, of course."

"With the obvious exception of Brother Pelagius!" Dilectus smirked.

"I'm afraid he outranks you in their eyes, although if some of these fine ladies saw you, they might prefer you to Pelagius – God forgive me for saying such vile remarks," she said, smiling broadly. "Anyhow, you will have to wait outside if that's all right with you."

"For sure. How did you get Pelagius to agree? The other times we've seen him and listened to him, he was always surrounded by a throng of admirers. I think his ideas are getting a lot of attention in the Forum and the streets, maybe not so much on the Aventine Hill."

"I think Pelagius sees the meeting to be a good chance to defend himself against the constant criticisms of Jerome and especially the Bishop of Hippo, that African Augustine. But actually, Lestinus gave me the idea. He mentioned how much better it would be for people to hear him when he was not surrounded by noisy crowds. So, it's all go. Please keep tomorrow afternoon and evening free to be my escort; Lestinus should come along as well. You're welcome to hang about in the outer grounds of the palace, which are elegant, but don't expect any refreshments – that's the price of being entertained by ascetics. You'd better not ever quote me, Dilectus!" Galeria chuckled.

Chapter 33: Prudent Security or Unrestrained Suspicion?

'Lestinus suggested it' or words to that effect. Strange. Galeria was a smart woman. Much smarter than he was, Dilectus would be the first to admit. Couldn't she see something curious in her security guard suggesting anything at all regarding religion, far less having an opinion of the kinds of locale where it might be possible to interact with a man like Pelagius without the throng of adoring crowds? What the hell was all this about? Then, there was the strange incident in which it seemed like Lestinus had given him a false or at least misleading version of what Galeria had asked him to do. She surely hadn't ever suggested that Dilectus, barefooted and half asleep, bar the way of four heavily armed experienced soldiers of the Praetorian Guard? That was an obvious suicide mission. Was it, in fact, a murder mission? Lestinus would know that where Pelagius was talking to a small select group, there Dilectus would be – honour-bound to defend him should an attack of some kind be launched. And this next time, facing unfair odds, Dilectus wouldn't be so lucky. But why would anyone still want to kill him? Who?

Vortigern. The lord who employed the father of Padrig, his childhood friend. Padrig's father was a *curialis*. A despised occupation by many, but it could be carried out decently if the official was a benevolent man. Even Padrig's father was not above suspicion – Padrig had grudgingly agreed the reward monies being offered for Dilectus's capture would tempt anyone, even a good man. But Padrig had also told him, casually, that Vortigern employed two men to serve the curial role of gathering taxes, and the other one was considered harsh and ruthless. The leader of the five men who had killed Severus was impeccably groomed and very well-dressed. He wasn't a common criminal. He was someone important. After hacking off his head, Dilectus had gone through his pockets and through the soft leather purse hanging from his belt, and he had found something incriminating. A ring. A signet ring. One the man had obviously taken off his finger and hidden before the attack. Dilectus had pocketed it himself, and when home, he'd dug up some sealing wax, melted it with a candle and dropped a blob onto a piece of clean white papyrus and pressed the ring into it. The impression was clear: two capital letters, V and V, above a Latin word for leader: *Vortigern Vitalis, Dux*. Vortigern's seal. This man worked officially for Vortigern.

That was why Severus warned him not to reveal anything he might find out. Flavius and Meirion both loved Severus so intensely that they would have combined their not-inconsiderable forces and launched a major attack on the heir and chief military commander of the neighbouring tribe. Perhaps if Vortigern were isolated or unknown, such a foray would have been both just and successful. But Vortigern had already united tribes right across Britannia through both wealth and reputation for ruthlessness. Perhaps something that had been said during the short, intense fight when Severus dispatched three of the five men had given him a clue or a flash of insight that Vortigern was behind the attack. That it had been an opportunity to remove the heir of a neighbouring tribal conglomerate and to punish his mother, the woman who had summarily rejected his amorous approaches. Proud, conceited men didn't take rejection by a surely desperate widow like Elen lying down. Severus would have sensed it was crucial to avoid a civil war solely in the name of justice or retaliation. It wasn't going to bring him back to life.

It was now obvious to Dilectus. Lestinus had been bought. Vortigern had the deep coffers to do it. A lifetime of easy riches could tempt any man. It only took thirty pieces of silver to tempt Judas. If Lestinus was going to try to isolate Dilectus in some narrow alleyway and kill him, he needed to be on his guard. He was confident he could beat Lestinus in a straight swordfight, but what if he had hired others? He thought avoidance of any opportunity to be attacked was the best and safest way to proceed. He would suggest to Galeria he stay close to her during the important meeting, with its sermon, to be followed by the all-important question and answer period. Lestinus could be assigned to provide an escort for Pelagius. That would avoid what was obviously a plot to find Dilectus alone, isolated and vulnerable.

Without offering any specific reasoning behind his plan, Dilectus put his suggestions to Galeria as to how they should handle security for the important meeting. Pelagius might need someone to offer protection, given he was now quite a controversial figure, although among this particular small group, he was admired, so the risks were minimal. He, Dilectus, would stay close to Galeria and her companions, and since men were not invited, the security would be in effect until everyone trooped inside the meeting hall to hear Pelagius's words of wisdom.

Galeria listened politely. The whole concept sounded unnecessarily complicated. It was only out in the streets of the rougher districts that any form of security was needed at all. Dilectus appeared to be slightly paranoid. Could the recent experience of nearly being killed to prevent a tragic but lawful arrest be eating away at his confidence more than she realised? But something else troubled her. Lestinus was utterly trustworthy, and yet, he had an odd fascination with Pelagius ever since she'd noticed him eavesdropping on the ship. Was it admiration or antagonism, she wondered? *Ah,* well, it wasn't important.

"Brother Pelagius is a big boy, Dilectus! He can look after himself. He's a man of God and greatly loved in this city. He doesn't need protection. But we will just play it by ear; thanks for your thoughts. He told me he was going to make his own way to the meeting, and all anyone had to do was to admit him to the conference room and introduce him with a few remarks. I told him I'd be honoured to fill that role. It will be the privilege of a lifetime."

Marcella, a native of Rome, had inherited a palace that was one of the largest on the Aventine Hill. Her simple lifestyle and frequent donations to the poor meant that the palace was very uncomfortable, and many of the female intelligentsia who gathered around her preferred to meet in one of the other grand houses. However, Marcella's constant companion and favourite student, Sister Principia, helped organise a sufficient number of reasonably comfortable chairs to accommodate the expected crowd. And knowing Pelagius's reputation for having a hearty appetite, Principia quietly arranged ample simple refreshments. Galeria's predictions were happily not correct.

Marcella's fame and reputation meant that everyone of importance was sure to come to the salon to be both entertained and educated. Proba was going with her daughter Juliana and her granddaughter Demetrias – they invited Galeria to go in their carriage, but she had to decline as she had

Lestinus and Dilectus in tow. She said she'd meet them there. Some of the attendees would be there because they were close to Jerome and wanted to listen and report back. This was the motive for Agenuchia, who had fled Gaul the year before for the safety of Rome. Galla Placidia was there, of course, but decidedly less interested in theology than showing her face, and she came dressed to impress. Others in the audience were particularly interested in Brother Pelagius's likely theme: Augustine's erroneous views on predestination. Pelagius was appalled by the idea that no one could be good without God's assistance or that humans were irrevocably tainted by Adam's fall. There were also a few women from Eclanum in southern Italia who'd been trapped by the current Gothic siege. They wanted to ask questions about the highly controversial ideas of their deacon, Julian, who was asserting that the sexual impulse, the sixth of the senses as he called it, was ordained by God and was morally neutral if carefully balanced between 'rational thinking and animal feelings'. It promised to be a very stimulating and intellectually inspiring afternoon. Everyone was excited.

As the participants were ushered into the meeting chamber, Lestinus and Dilectus waited outside with Galeria, who was designated to lead Pelagius into the hall and make a formal introduction. Certain that Lestinus would not attack him while Galeria and some of her friends were standing around in the reception group, Dilectus was mildly distracted by the elegance and glamour of the star-studded occasion. When he next looked around the marble hall, he suddenly panicked. Lestinus was nowhere to be seen.

"What the fuck?" he muttered as he dashed to the gallery opposite the grand staircase, with its alternating rises of alabaster and pink Travertine marble. Pelagius, simply dressed in a brown cassock with his neatly trimmed, squared-off beard and flowing hair down to his shoulders, was nearing the top of the stairs. At the top, he stopped, looked towards the welcoming group a hundred feet or so down the frescoed hallway, raised his right hand and made the sign of the cross as a blessing in front of his face. As he stepped forward, a man appeared from a decorative niche of the wall, right behind the famous preacher, the darling of Roman high society. It was Lestinus. His sword was raised in both hands high above his head.

In moments like this, it is the unexpected that often slows reaction times. But Dilectus's realisation was faster than could be put into words:

'He's not after *me*; he intends to kill *Pelagius*'. To run around the balustrade of the gallery would have taken far too long. Lestinus was poised to strike Pelagius with full force – a death blow between the shoulder blades. Instinctively, Dilectus pulled out the dagger that his mother had given him years ago. He had practised and become quite good at throwing it. To do so effectively, however, you needed to estimate the distance from the target. In this case, three and a half rotations of the knife would be essential. Success depended on the grip – by the handle for the half rotation – the force of the throw and the flick of the wrist to ensure a stable spin. Anything other than the point of the dagger being driven hard into the target would just be like a bump, a tap on the shoulder, a distracting clatter as the small knife fell harmlessly to the floor.

It did not. What determined success? Luck, practice, skill, God's will? All of them combined, Pelagius himself might have argued. He turned in surprise to see an unknown man right behind him drop a sword and fall to his knees, groaning, while a second man raced around the gallery and elderly ladies were running shrieking towards him.

Dilectus was about to deliver a finishing blow to Lestinus, but Pelagius stopped him. "There is still civil order in this city, young man," he said surprisingly calmly. "You saved my life, I believe. Do not take another. Let the lawful authorities take up the matter. Ask Domina Marcella to send her retainers to fetch the civic guard to take this man away."

"Ah, Lady Galeria, your young friend protected me. Perhaps with God's assistance," he added with a definite wink, "only God can send a dagger straight and true across a wide space. All I can say is how sad some men cannot stand the thought of ideas contrary to theirs. Can they not see the mysteries of the Lord God are too profound for us mortals to claim we understand God's purpose, or indeed the essence of the natural world? It will be a woeful day in Christendom when enquiry and curiosity are banished by dogma posing as the authoritative truth. Now, Lady Galeria, lead me to your good daughters in Christ that I may encourage robust debate."

Chapter 34: Shortly Before Midnight, August 23rd, AD 410

Dilectus was ready to leave Rome. Galeria insisted on him going by himself. There were lots of good reasons for taking any chance to escape. Alaric was in no mood for further negotiations. An attempted meeting face-to-face with Honorius outside Ravenna had collapsed, thanks to the usual duplicity by the Emperor's allies and associates. Alaric had escaped the surprise attack on his party and returned to Rome. Now, his army of Goths and their families and children surrounded the city walls for the third time and were increasingly disenchanted and desperate. Food for them on the outside was again in short supply. Inside, after the hunger of the siege the previous winter in which Alaric had been so successful in stopping the flow of rations to the city, Romans had made sure they were well stocked with provisions to last for months. The massive walls of the city could easily withstand an attack, and most of the citizens were complacent and in a festive mood throughout the holiday month of August. But to Galeria, it was obvious that considerable danger was festering outside. Alaric, King of the Visigoths, had had it with broken Roman promises and futile, bad-faith negotiations.

Galeria was not worried about herself and Sioned. She had powerful friends. But she knew a well-trained, even if inexperienced fighter like Dilectus would be instantly conscripted by the city's Prefect, in charge of all security. On top of this was the fact that Dilectus had put the point of his sword to the throat of a low-ranked officer of the Praetorian Guard. Such men hate being shown up in front of subordinates. They had left the villa guest house with their captive, but that didn't mean they couldn't return with some easily trumped-up charge of resisting an arrest. And now, wounding a member of her own party with possibly contestable motives and no clear evidence of the guilt of the victim was precisely the kind of trumped-up charge they might think of. If there was any chance at all of his getting away, now was the time.

In his letter of the previous year, Flavius had made suggestions as to a possible overland route for them all to take back home if, for any reason, a large ship could not be found at either of the two ports for Rome. Flavius tended to show off his wide-ranging knowledge, and he did so in the letter. 'I've been asking around and consulting Ptolemy's map of Gaul, and I think your best bet is to go to Ostia and find a vessel heading to Massilia. From there, a good road leads to Tolosa, where I am sure Bishop Exuperius would fall over himself to give you accommodation and any other help you might need. The military road extends to Burdigala. From there, it looks like the going gets a bit tougher, but the objective would be to reach Armorica, being especially wary there as peasant rebellions are going on. I'd recommend a fishing town there with a wonderful little harbour I've been to, called Binica. You'll be able to understand their Celtic and fishing boats cross the channel regularly to Tamium on our own Sebrina estuary and then you'll be home'.

"He makes it sound so easy, Dilectus, like a doddle in the park, but I do think it's the best route for you to get back."

"Do we still have enough money to pay for all that travel, Galeria? We've been here so much longer than anticipated."

"Don't you worry your sweet head about such matters; they're my concern. I have raised extra funds by selling most of my family estates in Hispania. I've signed over the title for good hard coin. It's truly the end of an era for me, but it's a sensible move. Things there are so risky. Constantine's son initially took control of the province, but since then his general rebelled and now everyone is fighting everyone else. And the *bacaudae* are in revolt again. Giving up a major source of our wealth won't be good for the villa's finances, but we have to change direction anyway – the world is not going to be the same."

"I'm so sorry. But I'm just glad you are resourceful. I hate leaving you and Sioned here without a bodyguard, but I agree I'm at risk, even though I've cheated Dis yet again! I've told you of my plan for leaving the city without being caught – by either side."

It's hard for any besieging army to get into a city completely surrounded by huge walls; it's almost equally hard for someone to get out.

Rome's fortifications were especially impressive: double walls joined above by ramparts zigzagged through the city at odd angles, giving wide visibility to the intermittent watchtowers. A few years earlier, the citizens had become so alarmed at the thought of Goths advancing through Italy that they'd organised their own work parties to strengthen areas of the walls in need of repair and general maintenance.

The only possible weak spots were the sixteen city gates. Some of them, the large dramatic entry and exit points, with their majestic marble arches and iron portcullises, were heavily guarded. Some smaller entrances were solid stone archways just wide enough for a carriage, with easily guarded heavy gates. But one, the Salt Road gate, the *Porta Salaria*, was a brick-lined passageway between two circular stone towers with overhead embrasures. There was a sturdy single wooden door with solid hinges secured by two heavy iron bolts from the inside. It was guarded night and day, of course, but once the bolts had been slid closed, the guards could be careless, sometimes drank too much and often dozed off.

Dilectus had discovered the Salt Gate after their party had arrived in Rome two years earlier. Thanks to Alaric's previous blockades of the ports of Rome, the sporadic food shortages justified a daring but risky move. Dilectus had successfully sneaked out of the gate and gone foraging for food items that were very hard to come by in town, particularly fish from the Mediterranean. Ditching his tunic and dressed in rough work clothes, he could easily slip out at night. Some of the market stalls supplying the Goth army housewives and children stayed open late, and for prices that were criminal, they often had some of the more special items. He had even discovered that an old cloth soaked in olive oil was a terrific way to silence the hinges and stop the rusty iron bolts from squeaking as he opened them. Returning was the greatest moment of tension. If any of the guards had noticed the bolts weren't in place, he wouldn't have been able to get back in at all and he would most likely be killed by archers on the ramparts. But after a few successful efforts, he'd become more confident. The guards remained completely unsuspecting until the morning when the relief guard yelled at the night watch for being so fuckin' careless.

What Dilectus did not know was that Alaric, a thorough and highly intelligent commander with considerable warfare experience, had stationed watchmen in hiding outside all the gates. Looking for vulnerabilities, they noted times of guard changes at night on the ramparts, rules regarding passwords, and any special times traffic was permitted to enter the great gates. These scouts had reported to one of Alaric's deputies – they were too scared to approach the great man himself – that at the smallest gate, they had noted a lean, athletic-looking young man, apparently a tribal person like themselves, who had sometimes slipped out at night. But of special significance was the fact he would return the same night and simply, but very carefully, push open the gate a crack and slip back in, clearly indicating that if he had unlocked the door to come out, no one was locking it again behind him.

When he got the report, Alaric was intrigued. Not quite like the wooden horse which brought down Troy, but a comparable carelessness on the part of the defenders of the Eternal City. He ordered a unit of his crack troops to be prepared for an urgent, last-minute order for a night offensive. He doubled the number of watchers at the small gate so they wouldn't miss an opportunity.

It was eleven in the evening of August, the 23rd, when two scouts ran as Pheidippides had done exactly nine hundred years earlier; this time, as the distance was less, these two did not collapse and die but arrived breathless, demanding to see the king himself.

"Tonight, my lord, the man we've been watching left the city. He acted like he was in a hurry. Instead of loitering around looking for food stalls, he is making his way to one of the roads west to Ostia. Should we arrest him? Two of our men are tailing him…"

"So, he doesn't seem to be coming back?" Alaric asked cautiously. "Maybe this time the door is locked behind him?"

"Maybe. But maybe not, sire. He was being quiet and cautious like he didn't want anyone to know he was leaving. Deserter, I reckon. There was no one up on the rampart to see him…"

"Except us, down below in our foxhole!" the second man said proudly.

"All right. Good information. You've done well." Turning to one of his top aides, Alaric demanded: "Get the special advance cohort together. Alert everyone – very quietly, and I mean it. We go in after midnight. If the man comes back, you will need to capture him; kill him if there is any risk he could raise the alarm. He could be a spy or a decoy. This is our opportunity, my friends, I feel it. Efforts to find someone sympathetic to our cause from the inside have failed miserably. This may be our lucky break at last – not planned, just enemy carelessness. A twist of fate. It's a sign some god is smiling on us right now. I'm sure Christ is on our side. Rome is a sinful and corrupt place, and tonight, my friends, we make history. Finally, we take it for ourselves."

Chapter 35: Hostages

The small group of patricians and church leaders of Rome – pagans and Christians for the first time not arguing with each other – sat awkwardly in the stateroom of the Palace of Domitian on the Palatine Hill. There were pitchers of water on the table and bowls of fruit, which must have been picked up off the floor somewhere else in the deserted palace. The group was undoubtedly one of the strangest sights of the past days when Visigoths were running wildly through the streets of the city. It was three days of more panic than actual mayhem, but it seemed like an eternity to the people gathered here. They whispered among themselves, some clinging to each other, while bored guards lounged against the walls. Despite the spears and lances in their hands and their wild hair and long beards, they didn't seem terribly threatening. Over what appeared to be their traditional fighting costume – surprisingly similar to Roman army issue – they had pulled on silk tunics, vests embroidered with gold thread and soft chamois leather jerkins, all recently looted. One even had a linen toga wrapped awkwardly around his body. The effect was comical, but no one was laughing. Three people were mopping their eyes with the ends of their linen kerchiefs.

Alaric, King of the Visigoths, strode into the room. The group of captives instantly knew who he was. So did their guards, who all dropped to one knee and bowed their heads. He looked tired. Yet his bearing and his demeanour shouted confidence: a man in command, a man claiming his destiny after years of struggle and attempts to negotiate, moving his people – men, women and children – from one country to another, seeking a place to settle, far from the vicious Huns who had destroyed their homeland. With him were two senior aides-de-camp, advisers, or interpreters perhaps, and a third man, who looked about the same age as Alaric, to whom Alaric turned.

"Well, well, well, what have we here, brother Ataulf?" he said, knowing the answer.

The captain of the guards stepped forward, eyes to the ground, and said, in his native language. "Great King, we were asked to round up hostages. These people, often disguised as common folk, were fleeing in the crowds, trying to reach the two basilicas you declared as sanctuaries. Some were bribing our own men with promises of riches if they would help them find a boat on the river to take them to the harbour. We asked the Roman mob, 'Who here is important and wealthy?' and they very happily pointed out all these people."

Alaric nodded and replied slowly in Latin, "So, you found enough Judases in the crowd to bring me the cream of Roman society. I believe one of you is the Lady Galla Placidia?"

An immaculately dressed woman – how could it be possible after three days of chaos? – rose to her feet.

"I am she."

"Come and kneel before me," Alaric ordered.

"I will not. I am the Emperor's sister. I am *Nobilissima Puella*, and I kneel to no one but God."

"*Hmm!* Isn't she Miss Self-Important," Alaric said to his aides in Gothic, and Ataulf nodded, smiling broadly. "Well and good," Alaric continued in Latin, "stand if you want to, but you're coming with me as a hostage. Your brother is as trustworthy as a viper, and you are responsible for the execution of the innocent Serena, whom I respected as the loving wife of the great Stilicho. Why you fool Romans execute your finest generals, I'll never understand. Who else is important in this crowd? You, big man at the back, a man of the cloth, who are you?"

"I am no one of importance, sire; I am a preacher, not a nobleman, a servant of God, not a politician, a soldier of Christ, not an earthly warrior. My name, sire, is Pelagius."

"Goodness! How about that! Even I've heard of you. Who hasn't? You're from Britannia and a fine preacher. I think your ideas are close to those of Arius, which my people follow."

"Good King," said Pelagius patiently, "I am too tired and far too hungry to discuss your erroneous beliefs, but I can assure you I don't share them. I was assisting my noble friend Lady Galeria and these other great ladies to reach the sanctuary of Peter's Basilica when your rough guards apprehended us and brought us here."

"Did they mistreat you? I gave orders there'd be no killing unless someone offered physical resistance. Maybe because you are as big as an ox, my men thought you were a soldier disguised as a monk."

"I would say ransacking private houses, looting anything that looked precious and ordering us to serve them wine fits the definition of mistreatment. But they did not physically harm us, nor, indeed, kill us, though my pious flock do not fear death and have faith in the promises Jesus made to mankind. We have, however, confirmation your soldiers beat Mother Marcella, an old woman of eighty-five, with cudgels because she wouldn't tell them where she kept her gold when, in fact, she had none, having given so much away to less fortunate people."

"You, Brother Pelagius, are a fine talker with big words. That was a bad incident, and I have punished those men. The old lady and her companion are indeed safe in the Basilica of Paul, where they should have gone in the first place. I honestly have no time for this kind of conversation. Guards, turn this windbag back out on the streets and let him fend for himself. The rest of you, if you can make the payments, we will escort safely to ships for Africa. That's where all your friends are fleeing as refugees, which is fine. We don't need you here. Rome is mine now."

Galeria, who had been sitting just behind Galla Placidia and patting her shoulder in an encouraging way, stood up.

"King Alaric, most noble of the Balti Dynasty, I am very familiar with your fame as a warrior. My name is Cecilia Galeria Arcadiae. I am of Hispanic ancestry, a distant cousin of the Dynasty of Theodosius, but I have lived with the great Celtic people of Britannia all my adult life. My son and his noble comrade Severus, who was appointed by Stilicho as Comes Britanniarum, have many influential friends in that province and in Gaul, and I am willing to trade places with the profoundly learned man of Christ, Brother Pelagius. Let him go as a refugee and take me as a hostage instead."

It was a sincere gesture, but the moment she saw the look of anger cross Alaric's face, she realised her mistake. Alaric took three strides towards her and scowled.

"Severus, you said? Severus the legate of the sloppy, undisciplined troops from Britannia? I was told it was his idea to tell Stilicho to attack me and my army on Sunday, the 6th of April, at Pollentia, when we were celebrating Easter. It put us at a disadvantage, although we recovered well. Sneaky bastard. I'm not taking *you* as a hostage."

Galeria, staring at his face, momentarily wondered if there was a hint of a knowing smile behind the apparent scowling anger. Was he trying to find an excuse to let her go? But rather than risk it, she replied:

"King Alaric, for any of us who are Christian, it sounds very sneaky indeed. Severus was a Christian and was baptised as a child in my own chapel along with my son. But in all honesty, he was one of the most irreverent Christians you are likely to find. He was also a very good man, as Brother Pelagius assures us is possible. I can almost guarantee he would not have known what day Easter was, and the fact it was a Sunday would have meant nothing to him. And if it is any comfort to you, he died four years ago, defending my grandson-in-law from brigands…"

Exhausted, stressed, struggling to remain polite and calm but defiant, Galeria fought to hold back tears, correctly feeling Alaric preferred strong gutsy women to craven ones.

Alaric's retort was only, "God's judgment on him, perhaps." He was getting impatient and quickly surveyed the rest of the group. His gaze settled on a younger woman who had taken Galeria's hand and was still holding it firmly.

"And who may you be? You're no Roman. I hope your disposition is not as fiery as your topknot! You aren't a noblewoman like the others here. Are you a slave? If so, I release you."

Sioned stepped forward without hesitation. "I am a Roman citizen and a barbarian just like you. I am a Celt and proud of it. My Silurian ancestors fought the Roman legions and never surrendered. This true lady, Galeria, is my friend and there have been no slaves at her Christian villa for a hundred years. I am her companion and where she goes, there I go. *Duw amddiffyn Cymru!*"

"Dear God, am I glad my wife is an honest Goth and not infected with pushy Roman manners. Guards get these wretched, annoying women out of here. Because I, too, am a Christian, I want no more bloodshed. Get them to the ships with the other refugees. I am going south to Consentia with the legitimate spoils of war, taking no more than what this Empire owes me and my people after years of broken promises, deception and treachery. I'm leaving you your lives, but I expect no gratitude. And you still seem amazingly capable of finding the funds needed for travel. I hear from so many others you all plan to 'escape' to Roman provinces in Africa – we'll see how joyful a reception you receive there – the governor's no friend of Rome. If I'd had my way, I'd have removed him, and we'd all have had food. Come on, Galla Placidia, you're coming with Ataulf and me."

Without another word of farewell or encouragement or criticism, he turned on his heels and strode off into fading light. The sunset caught the tips of so many shining marble buildings across this hill and the Temple of Jupiter on the Capitoline Hill – the true centre, the capital of the world. No more. He groaned, suddenly overwhelmed by the magnitude of the task of getting his army and his thousands of followers and family members into some sort of organised advance down the rest of Italy to Sicily, his next objective. And dealing with the flood of refugees as humanely as possible.

The two older aides stayed behind to instruct the guards, who had not been able to follow the conversation in Vulgar Latin, as to how and where they were to take the group, now hugging each other and talking excitedly as though all danger had passed and they'd all be going back to their normal lives. Pelagius rushed over to Galería and thanked her for her efforts on his behalf. He urged her, should they be given the opportunity, to accompany him to Africa. But Galeria said she wanted to go home. She had seen Rome in all its glory and its squalor, and she had seen it defeated and overrun but not destroyed. He blessed her, saying he understood. He'd write to her. Perhaps when things were settled, she would come to Jerusalem, where his friend Caelestius had already gone to preach and promote their ideas.

At Portus, after more horrible weeks of danger and delays, Galeria and Sioned were able to find a ship's captain, a *dominus navis,* headed for Britannia. He hailed from Cymru and knew the route well. A miracle. Sioned begged him for news of home, but he hadn't been back for years. Galeria was certain Christ was looking out for her, as so many other ships, especially merchant vessels, had already been commandeered by Alaric's officers for his planned assault on Sicily. She had no idea what had happened to Dilectus but prayed daily for his safety, feeling confident his love for her granddaughter would be favoured by God. While spending long hours waiting and worrying, she managed to write to Flavius, assuring him of her safety and imminent return. The ever-practical Sioned had scrounged paper and writing implements by bartering a few pieces of Galeria's jewellery with one of the Goths. Without looking inside, the soldier had seized an ebony box from a mansion he was ransacking and had been about to ditch it. He had no use for writing material. He agreed to throw in the box as well as its contents in return for the amethyst earrings he thought his woman would like.

When they finally boarded the vessel and could relax for the first time, the captain came to them with a worried look. They really should delay their departure, he said. There was a serious storm coming. Even Alaric's senior officers were making it known they would postpone the crossing to Sicily; the king was hunkering down in Consentia – he wasn't feeling well and had a fever. Should they still go, the captain asked. They would, of course, be going west to the Pillars of Heracles, nowhere near Sicily. What did her ladyship think? They could delay, but it would cost more in harbour fees.

Galeria was adamant: "I don't care about the cost, but I couldn't bear to wait any longer. I've seen Rome, goodness have I ever, and now I must go home. You too, Sioned."

They set sail early the next morning. By the afternoon, the sky was black with heavy storm clouds, and the wind had shifted due west. "We'll make good time with this wind," the captain said unconvincingly, with a worried look over his shoulder. There was a flash of lightning followed almost immediately by a deafening crash of thunder.

"Dylan, protect us all," were the captain's words before the squall pitched the boat violently forward into the swell. They were the last words spoken out loud by anyone on board.

Chapter 36: Ulysses Returns to Ithaca

Dilectus had never before welcomed the sight of the cliffs of Cymru as he did when the little fishing boat drew closer to the shores of Britannia and further from the coast of Armorica. It looked like home. It even smelled like home. The channel crossing was the easiest part of his entire journey. Initially, the fishermen were reluctant. 'That's not the direction we're going, absolutely not, not when the wind is coming from the east'. But when he said he needed to get to his wife, whom he hadn't seen for more than two years, they relented. They were romantics. Even though ethnically, many of them were Celts and even had relatives in Britannia, they had a certain Gallic love of life, which brimmed over when he stood them all to a cask of truly excellent wine. 'It's from Burdigala,' the innkeeper claimed in barely understandable Celtic, 'the endless coming and going of armies through Gaul has totally disrupted the usual supply chains to Italia, and the south – Arelate and Massilia – so they've been sending it up to us, not the usual vinegary piss we've had to put up with'.

The queasy sensation in Dilectus's stomach was not from the rolling and rocking of the fishing boat, which had never been designed for stability. He knew it was pure fear. Almost three years is a long time. He had changed. He had seen Rome in its glory and in its despair. His religious faith, such as it was, had been rocked off its wobbly foundations. The church was dominated by dogmatic old men making pronouncements about light, life and love when they were all celibate or recently reformed profligates who thought that confessing publicly to their riotous lives and abusive relationships somehow gave them license to pontificate on morality – which was ironic given the actual pontiff was considerably more tolerant and accepting than they were themselves. He now saw that what he used to consider Flavius's scepticism was simply a recognition that more truth could be found in the Greek philosophers than in the Psalms, letters and the canonical 'good news' in the bible.

Having changed so much thanks to travel, he wondered if Claudia would accept him as she found him. But ten times more worrying was how *she* might have changed. She was easily bored; he knew that. Surely, she would seek companionship, innocent to begin with, but where might it lead? How could he expect her to remain faithful for so long? He'd written but had no guarantee she'd received any of his tender letters. Flavius had better ways of getting correspondence to Rome, and in one letter to his mother, he had a sentence that Claudia sent her love, both to Grandma and to Dilectus. But putting the two of them together like that was too platonic for Dilectus's liking. Could she be hiding something? What if she had married someone else? By Celtic law, a marriage in which the husband had disappeared could easily be dissolved. His fears reminded him of something. What the fuck was it? Of course. It was Ulysses returning to Penelope. Would Claudia have turned away a hundred suitors? Probably not, there weren't even a hundred eligible bachelors in the district. But even three might have been tempting. He wasn't a great archer. He doubted he could shoot an arrow clean through arranged axe heads. Possibly, his knife-throwing tricks, recently so successful, could be offered as proof that he was the true prince if he disguised himself as a beggar. That's what he should do. Not show up and embarrass her if she had a new lover. Skulk around the villa in disguise, and if she was obviously happy with some guy there, he would nobly leave and join old lady Marcella's monastery in the Egyptian desert, eating locusts. He was getting a bit mawkish.

He paid the fishermen and set off on foot. Only a day's walk. On the way, he bought some pretty grungy clothes from a boy about his size who was tending sheep. When he arrived at the villa, looking indeed like one of the many disreputable beggars who were always taking advantage of Lady Galeria's munificent *caritas*, one of the old family retainers greeted him.

"Dilectus! Great to see you, sir!"

"Shut up. I'm in disguise. Where is Lady Claudia?"

"I'm not sure. I'll give her a call."

"Don't say it's me. Say there is a beggar needing food. But tell me. Is she married?"

"Yes, I believe so. Let me call her."

Dilectus's heart sank. He should leave this minute and head off to Egypt. Flavius would help him with the travel. "Is the Dominus home?"

"No, he's been gone for months. Up north somewhere. He took a load of books. Said he might be gone for a while. Let me call Lady Claudia."

Dilectus was stricken. Perhaps he shouldn't even see her. Too late. Claudia bustled into the courtyard.

"We can certainly give you food, but you should have come in the back entrance to the kitchen, my good man. Oh, dear God, it's you. Why are you dressed like that? Why didn't you ever write to me? Where's Granny?"

She threw her arms around him and hugged him fiercely. "You smell of fish. And sheep."

"The house boy said you were married," he demanded accusatorily.

"Well, of course I am, you dimwit. To you. Have you forgotten? I've got the ring and stuff. God, am I glad to see you. You know what's happened to Rome? No? Sacked by the Visigoths. Gone. Totally destroyed. They just danced their way in, apparently. Someone left the gate open; slaves are being blamed. Granny's missing and your aunt. I was so scared. Why weren't you with them? I thought you were their security?"

Feeling overwhelmed and dog-tired, Dilectus broke away from her embrace and her string of utterances he could barely process. He sat down on a bench, head in his hands, crying silently in relief, a feeling far greater than in any of the times he had had such narrow and lucky escapes with his life.

"Let me get washed up and find some respectable clothes. Then give me something strong to drink. Then, we can talk and tell each other what we know." Dilectus turned to the servant who had been standing there with his mouth open. "And you, you can help me by going to the tool shed and bringing back the biggest, strongest-looking *vectis* you can find – you know what I'm talking about? A crowbar."

After being fortified with some slices of cold meat and a large jug of posca, Dilectus, now smelling faintly of lavender oil and with his hair tied up neatly in a topknot, led Claudia to the little villa chapel, holding his iron bar.

"Uncle Flavius has bequeathed the villa to me as a belated wedding gift," she said. "Even if Grandma Galeria does come back, as we pray, she will, he says she will retire, and I will be domina. But he sounded as though he thought I should move. He wasn't sure it was safe. It was about four months ago that he left. He said he was withdrawing. He said it is all mine except for some treasure that was Grandma's, but he doesn't know where it is."

"Well, I do. I hope. Before I left Rome, Lady Galeria told me where she had hidden some money. 'Enough for you and Claudia to live on, even in hard times, and when I come back, I will suggest how we turn the villa into a community resource. I won't live much longer, and that has long been my dream. But you must use the treasure as you see fit – no conditions are placed upon it'. Then she told me where to find it."

Dilectus was now behind the altar in the chapel, covered by a richly embroidered linen corporal. He tossed aside a few boxes of chapel supplies that were stored back there. When a large flagstone was revealed on the floor, he searched with his fingertips for a crack. Finding one, he inserted the crowbar as hard as he could, and with both hands on the bar, he strained to lift the slab. It didn't budge.

"P'raps, this is the wrong stone." He grunted.

"Can I help?" Claudia asked, searching the area for something solid. She seized on a wooden block used as a doorstop. "Here. Step aside."

She placed the wooden block a short distance from the stone, reinserted the tip of the iron bar into the crack in front of the block, and gently pushed down on the other end of the bar. After a moment's resistance, the stone came free, enough for Dilectus to get his hand under its edge.

"Amazing!" he said.

"Not amazing. Archimedes. Didn't you pay *any* attention to that Persian teacher who taught us Greek mathematics? 'Give me a place to stand, and I can move the world!' Remember?"

But Dilectus was no longer listening. He'd heaved the stone aside. In the space below were two strong wooden chests, similar to one that Flavius had shown them both so long ago. Claudia gasped. Dilectus didn't try to open them. They were clearly undisturbed. They looked at each other and smiled. Dilectus lowered the stone and re-covered the area with the boxes of spare candles and flower vases.

"Safe there, for now, my love. Now I need to sleep. In the morning, we make decisions. Why are you making that face?"

"I'm afraid there is one decision already made. You're a father. You have a son. And I am happy to say he is now almost two years old. He keeps asking where his daddy is, and I tell him he has gone to Rome to save the city from the barbarians. I'll have to change the story and tell him that *he* is a barbarian, and as to the city…"

She could say no more. Dilectus was hugging her so hard and kissing her face that no words could escape.

The Final Chapter: Letter from Flavius to Dilectus, Christmastide, AD 410

To my dear friend and grandson, per honoris causa, Dilectus. Greetings and salutations. As it is just a few days before Holy Night, allow me to wish you a very Happy Christmas and to the family as well. You will enjoy your new-found son, little Caradocus, whom I probably know better than you do at this moment. But he will love Christmas with his father for the first time. Christmas and the story of the baby Jesus are always special times for children.

Thank you for your lengthy missive and the encouraging news of your connubial happiness. Allow me to commend you on your surprisingly fluid Latin prose, for which I am bold enough to take some measure of credit whenever I could wrest your attention away from the military training by Severus. May he rest in peace.

You asked me a series of most practical questions regarding the disbursement of the Villa Arcadius estate, and I will answer them frankly. I wish I could do so in person, but my health is not conducive to travel. I was able to move much of my library with me to the accommodation afforded me by Brother Ninian at Candida Casa. Unfortunately, it is cold and damp here when the wind blows off the sea, but to my delight, the days this past summer were long, allowing me extra reading time. Happily, Ninian permits me, as a layperson, not to participate in any of the rigours of monastic life and allows me comfortable accommodation in exchange for modest financial contributions to his missionary work. Alas, wine is hard to come by. However, the monks here brew a tolerable ale flavoured with elderflowers. I am convinced this offers many medicinal benefits.

You asked for advice on the disbursement of some funds to the *Schola Theodosii*, the Cor Tewdws, which my mother started. In her memory, I believe you should offer support, although, in all honesty, some military equipment on the cliff tops might be more useful. I am doubtful you could specify the funding must go to hiring a Greek or Persian scholar to teach at the college, but you could try. When obliged to hire teachers from the literate Christian community, the focus is on little other than endless arguments about what Paul the Apostle actually meant by a specific word. Already, we have long debates over Pelagius's sound ideas about free will and personal responsibility for one's own actions. If celibacy is pushed for no real reason other than the baseless idea that the desires of the flesh are inherently sinful, we will end up with an entire priesthood that's not interested in women, exposing them to even more temptations. As for not allowing women to be ordained, when did Jesus ever make such a commandment? His twelve disciples were all men, but only because they were the ones with worldly experience and the necessary self-confidence in the very restrictive Judaic community in Galilee. But Roman society has long recognised the rights of women and their value as leaders – look at my mother's example. And I think your beautiful mother, Elen, has proved her mettle, while your wife, my dear niece Claudia, is the smartest young person I have ever encountered. When we start persecuting Arians because they aren't sure Jesus was of the same substance as God the Father, we are in deep decay as a society since no human can possibly know the answer to the question of *homoousios to Patri*. As my mother so often advocated, when we determine how best to grow reliable crops and preserve food for periods of drought or flooding, societies will be able to stop raiding and fighting and will have the time, the peace, and the stability to focus on the creativity God gave us, in art, poetry, music, theatre and new inventions. As for denying yourself all the earthly pleasures of this life and living naked in a remote cave in the belief it will ensure you enjoy everlasting delights in the life hereafter – well, it is a risky gamble, in my view. And selfish as well, since how does such sacrifice help our fellow human beings? Surely, if there is to be a Judgment Day, living a life similar – *iousios,* note my humour – to the one Jesus modelled for us will be good enough.

But I digress, and my amanuensis is giving me quizzical looks. My apologies for this explosion of ideas in response to your simple question about whether my mother would have wanted you to make donations to the poor or to the Celtic Church. I may be biased and just fooling myself, but I have always thought my mother's form of asceticism was on target – the wealth that came to her by inheritance was not earned by her, but rather than simply giving it away she used it wisely to educate the local farmers in new techniques, hire teachers, support community projects in our *vicus*, build a church which encourages social cohesion. As you know, she admired her second cousin, Aelia Flavia Flaccilla, whose charity towards the poor, the crippled, the hungry and the orphaned earned her great respect. However, my mother always argued that teaching self-sufficiency was still more important. We have managed to save sufficient resources in gold and silver, but we don't wish to pay men for their fighting skills, as do the most ambitious warlords. We want men who are willing and able to fight, motivated by protecting their families and their homes. So, use our treasure for equipment, horses and training. But unless the tribes work together, such efforts will be little more than building sand forts on the seashore at low tide. Men's basest desires, lust, greed, ambition and cruelty emerge most rampant when we live in constant fear and terror – a self-perpetuating circle of inhumanity.

Let me be more explicit as to my suggestions for disposition of the villa. One by one our family of Arcadius has been depleted, such that Claudia, and you by marriage, are now the only surviving descendants and the heirs to the villa. But circumstances are such that I do not believe you can defend it as we face attacks from both foreign invaders and the tyrannical chieftains of the stronger tribes.

You should, therefore, take whatever contents of the villa appeal to you and relocate under the protection of your mother, the Queen, and Meirion, who is a good man. I know you will both miss many of the luxuries of the villa. If you are able to find the stone masons and other craftsmen who can build proper amenities at Garn Goch, you should do so to keep the skills extant. Not living in the villa will soon result in deterioration, but the land and the estates are more important, and you must do what you can to retain your rightful ownership. My mother's vision was to manage the lands in a fruitful way and to practice agricultural renewal, so no one goes hungry during challenging times. The ordinary people would work the land as tenants, with common ownership of resources such as ploughing oxen, a mill for grinding corn, collaboration in building a barn or gathering in the harvest. If not overused, the Sabrina River and estuary will, for many years, provide an abundance of fish and shellfish. They would thus enjoy prosperity and easily be able to afford taxes that could be used to sustain the church. After finishing school in the morning, children can help herd sheep and goats or feed the chickens and raise ducks. Young men would contribute a period of time as trainee warriors for the defence of the lands when needed. You could argue I am stating the obvious and I do not mean to preach to you, but you will see this as a Celtic form of management rather than a Roman one. The great Roman estates just had workers, usually slaves and overseers, with direct benefit to neither, only their owners. Cooperation and common ownership are also within the Christian spirit of helping one's neighbours. Why else did Christ tell the story of the good Samaritan?

Queen Elen and later you as king will be responsible for enforcing laws to protect the weak from the avarice of the strong. Roman laws can be modified by native Celtic traditions and custom, or, when reasonable, by Christian principles. But beware the aristocracy of the church fathers imposing backward ideas about how young women should lead their lives. To be a fair and just ruler you need to take advice and guidance from wise councillors representing a range of backgrounds and opinions across your realm.

In a most forward and inquisitional manner you ask whether I believe in the Lord Jesus Christ. I jest, but it is a complex question. I do; I believe he was a man, whether sent by God or created by God or just a humble carpenter with a vision, I know not. I believe we Romans nailed him to a cross, not knowing what we were doing. But I believe his purpose on Earth was to show how kindness, humility, tolerance, forgiveness and goodwill to all are the possibilities of human society. But Jesus the man was poorly educated and knew no Greek, so he didn't understand, perhaps, that reason, intellect, inventiveness and the pursuit of knowledge about our physical world are all equally important. His disciples and the followers whom we have sanctified were mostly uneducated, thus the potentially great minds of a Pelagius are now subordinated to trivial debates over the unresolvable hidden meanings of obscure words and texts. Fortunately, gospels record the best stories and parables, many of which Catholic Christians now ignore, especially the Ascetics – anyone who is famous for turning water into wine can hardly be considered to have held such values.

It is Christmastide but I feel no celebration for the birth of Our Saviour. Instead, I am reading Cicero, partly for his reminding us of the importance of Plato and partly because the disrespect the Church has created for our great Roman pagan writers and poets really troubles me. I fear, Dilectus, I have become just as irascible and grumpy as Jerome.

You further question me on how things could have gone so wrong within our mighty Empire in order, I hope, to learn from our history when you have the power of leadership. There are many factors. I hold that the decline began hundreds of years ago when we lost the Republic and the Greek ideals of democracy. Good men colluded in the ascendance of emperors, some of whom built magnificent public monuments, but only five of them have been good rulers. On the other hand, it has always seemed likely to me that Christianity as a faith and a way of life could never have survived without the absolute imperial power of the great Constantine, allowing him to order an immediate end to the persecutions and prohibitions, and without Theodosius's determination to make it the official state religion. But he did so with intolerance and destruction of pagan monuments and traditions. The Empire brought improved lives and some degree of peace to large parts of the world. It was not the conquered nations who chafed for freedom, especially once they enjoyed the privileges of citizenship. The pressure of major movements of unstable populations beyond our borders was something no one could have foreseen or controlled. There was a time when the disciplined Roman army was invincible, but once civil wars and divided loyalties pitted Roman soldiers against each other, the end was near, and the constant induction of foreigners to the army meant by the time of the great barbarian invasions it was difficult to tell the difference between the men in the army and the men they were ordered to fight. This I believe is a key lesson for the island of Britannia. Never be tempted to rely on mercenaries from elsewhere to fight your battles, especially the Saxons. They can never be trusted like the men you grew up with.

The big fresco, however, in my view, as to why the Roman Empire fell, is a societal force you too need to consider. Great wealth should never grant great power – the Greek city-states granted power to those willing to serve. Societies in which vast wealth is accumulated in the hands of a small and selfish segment of the population and not shared for the general good have not fared well. Especially when the benefits of the toil of many are enjoyed by the few, such as slave-owning societies. Think of the Egyptians under the Pharaohs. I was always so proud my grandfather ended slavery at the villa, and he wasn't even a Christian. Fortunately, Christianity will surely bring an end to slavery in the inhabited world. No true Christian can tolerate slavery.

As you can surely tell from reading this, Dilectus, I am overcome by a deep melancholia. I have too much black bile in my spleen, but whether that's the cause of my malaise or whether 'tis the result, I cannot tell. I have pervasive, despairing thoughts enough to turn my emotions sour. However, I face my demise with confidence that you and Claudia will flourish and live good and happy lives. Your father Caradocus was a man I confess I loved as a son, and your mother Elen, still the most beautiful woman in the world, rivals only my saintly mother in my admiration. Help her and Meirion be good rulers of the Silurian and Demetae lands and resist the tyrants who will seek their overthrow. Use the remaining treasure of the villa to defend the community – I have no need of it. Villa Arcadius itself is no longer sustainable, but the community it fostered is. Strengthen the walls of Venta Silurum, our *civitas*; guard the access to the Sabrina Estuary, our portal to the world; maintain good relationships with the Bishop and the Diocese of Corinium. Despite my cynicism regarding the Christian faith, the great Celtic Church is following Pelagius's more sensible ideas, with men like your dear friend Patricius who will become an important missionary one day, even in the wilds of Hibernia. The news of his return must have thrilled you and is a source of hopefulness and light even for me in the blackness of my mood. The structures and the power of faith will give some semblance of order and civilization with which you may resist the pagan Saxons, or perhaps in time, integrate with them, though it is my opinion that the rugged terrain of the Silurians, especially around your grandfather's stronghold of Garn Goch, will help provide you and the Celtic tribes some natural physical protection. I'm not a praying man, but this is indeed my fondest wish and hope.

This is my farewell forever, little Dilectus and clever Claudia – for that is how I remember you, as innocent children. Though I have many sins, I do not fear death, nor do I fear that when it is by my own hand, as it shall be soon, I will be forever damned. Death is oblivion, exactly the same end for us all; the afterlife exists in the memories and beneficence of those we leave behind. If any of our history and our family's story survives in the sanctity of upright people, I believe this climactic *Anno Domini* 410 will be recorded as something more than Alaric's sack of our beloved but certainly not eternal city – the beginning of a new and better civilized Romano-Britannic society is within your grasp. I would not have enough years ahead to see it and I would not wish to be alive if I am wrong.

Amor vincit omnia,
Your true friend, Gaius Flavius Arcadius

Epilogue:
Claudia, Dilectus and Caradocus Leave the Villa Arcadius

It was no small retinue leaving Villa Arcadius for the last time. Claudia had her son, Caradocus, named in honour of his grandfather, on her knee in a carriage that was far from comfortable. She was wearing, as she did always, two delicate necklaces, one a gold crucifix, the symbol of a powerful but still new faith, and the other a gold amulet inlaid with five silver apple pips, signifying the elements, and surrounded by a circle, the circle of life and the connection among all things. In her travel valise was a third necklace, studded with heavy sparkling jewels, which toddler Caradocus loved to play with. It had been given to her by her husband, Dilectus, on his return from Rome. He said it had come from the Temple of Vesta. He hadn't stolen it, he assured her; it had been given to him for a small act of courage by someone showing much greater fortitude. He told her he liked the symbolism – Vesta, like Brighid to the pagan Celts, was the virgin goddess of the hearth, home and family. His love, his Claudia, personified all those things – 'happily not the virgin bit', he'd added.

Two other waggons, and a number of mounted and armed men, including her husband, made up the convoy. It was Christmas Eve, and it reminded Claudia of what had always been her favourite bible story: how heavily pregnant Mary, a virgin, was riding on a donkey with her husband Joseph to find a place to give birth. The donkey was undoubtedly smoother than this carriage, but Claudia's travelling group lacked no resources. In one of the waggons were two padlocked strong boxes, containing more wealth than they could possibly use. Even so they were riding towards an uncertain future, leaving behind her family home, still in her nominal possession, and taking up residence in the tribal fortress of her mother-in-law, the celebrated Queen Elen, whose looks still made women like her gasp in amazement and filled the dreams and fantasies of men of every age.

The road they were on had been built more than three hundred years ago by Roman troops and slave labour to allow the army to conquer the Silures and the Demetae, to crush the druids on Mona Insula, and bring the Cornovii and the Ordivices to their knees. The last great hero of Celtic resistance, Caratacus, had been betrayed near to here and taken in chains to Rome. Now, she and her husband feared a new chieftain, more personally ambitious and tyrannical – Vortigern. The power balance had shifted dramatically. Where would this leave Dilectus and Caradocus, the heirs to this kingdom in southern Cymru?

The carriage kept bumping about – the road needed repairs. There were paving stones missing and weeds and bushes growing out of cracks in the cement. Claudia knew that Dilectus would be thinking about how they needed to get men out here to work on the road. He had Roman values, just like she did. Strange that. A pure-blooded Celt, he had been thoroughly Romanized exactly the way Agricola had hoped would happen so long ago. And she, of mixed Hispanic, Britannic and Roman heritage, spoke fluent Celtic and called herself a Roman Briton – just like her uncle, whose erudition had so shaped her education and thus her mind. Celts were good people, fun-loving, good singers, but they were messy and disorganised. They'd let the road deteriorate and hadn't bothered to fix it. Romans had their problems, but they liked order, neatness, organisation, laws, square courtyards, running water and carving their names and details on commemorative tablets. But in the end, it hadn't done them any good. She laughed to herself. She and Dilectus had the same values. Only God knew how they would fit into a new life in Garn Goch and the surrounding farms and settlements, which one day they would rule. But Claudia knew the end of one story was always just the beginning of the next. Nothing was meant to stay the same. Task number one: find a tutor for Caradocus. Teaching him to read and write and enjoy books was the first priority. The roads could wait.

****

Glossary
People (Fictional Characters in Italics)

Aelia Flavia Flaccilla: The first wife of Emperor Theodosius I, mother of Arcadius and Honorius, and a daughter, Pulcheria. She was of Hispanic origin, a staunch supporter of the Nicene Creed, and best known for her charitable works.

Agenuchia: She was a highborn lady from Gaul to whom Jerome had written in AD 409 his infamous letter on the 'Fate of Rome' in which he bemoans the fate of the empire in the hands of 'savage and hostile' barbarians.

Agricola: He was appointed Governor of Britannia in AD 77. He completed the conquest of northern England and Wales, was responsible for the massacre of druids in Anglesey and campaigned through Caledonia as far as the Orkney Islands.

Alaric (370–410): He was originally a commander in the Roman army, but with the death of Theodosius I in 395, he resigned and was elected leader of the western group of Goths, later known as the Visigoths. The Visigoths had initially been allowed to settle in Moesia (now Serbia and parts of Macedonia and Bulgaria).

Albina: From a very wealthy Roman family, she was married to the son of Melania the Elder. By this time an influential widow she had one daughter, Melania, known as 'the Younger' to avoid confusion. Albina had expressed interest in the teachings of Pelagius.

Anicia Faltonia Proba: An affluent Roman matron, the granddaughter of a famous poet; she lived with her daughter-in-law Anicia Juliana and her granddaughter Demetrias on the Palatine Hill; *Galeria's party were staying in her palace guesthouse.*

Arius: A priest born in Libya (AD 256–336), preached the doctrine of God the Father as central and Christ occupying a subordinate role in the

Trinity (of different substance). These ideas were not new; however, the general doctrine of Arianism has been named after him.

Ataulf (also Athaulf): Alaric's brother-in-law. After Alaric's death, he was elected King of the Visigoths and married the Roman noblewoman Galla Placidia.

Attalus: Priscus Attalus, a Greek member of the Roman Senate and a pagan, was selected to be a rival emperor to Honorius. In order to do so, he was hastily baptised as an Arian Christian.

Aurelia: Galeria's daughter and Claudia's mother.

Boudica (or Boadicea): She was the 'queen' of the Iceni tribe who led her people in an uprising against the invading Romans around AD 60. After destroying a detachment of the Ninth Hispanic Legion and burning two large towns, her rebellion was eventually defeated. Her name in Celtic means 'victorious woman'.

Brighid: Celtic goddess of the hearth.

Brangwen: Wife of Chief Conanus and deceased mother of Elen. Elen and Meirion called their first daughter after her.

Branwen: Welsh goddess of love and beauty.

Caelestius: He was a Briton practicing law in Rome where he met Pelagius, both of them shocked by the depravity and riches of the patrician class. He became a major follower and preached Pelagian doctrines, for which he was condemned by the Council of Carthage as a heretic.

Calpurnius: St Patrick's father, a decurion originally employed in the Roman civil service and a minor cleric (deacon?) in the local parish church.

Caradocus: A centurion in the Roman army who deserted and fled with Elen, whom he married, to live in hiding in Viroconium. A Celt (a Demetae), he is the father of Dilectus. He was murdered in the year AD 387 by Priscillians, falsely believing him to be the Macsen Wledig who had persecuted their sect.

Caradog: Dilectus's boyhood friend, the son of a local Silurian sheep farmer. The name is the Welsh Gaelic form of Caratacus.

Caratacus: A Briton and tribal chieftain in the first century AD who fought to resist the Roman invasion for ten years until he was betrayed by the queen of another tribe and sent to Rome in chains.

Ceredig: Elderly chief of the Demetae tribe, whose lands covered southwestern parts of Cymru and now in a formal alliance with the Silurians.

Claudia; Claudia, nicknamed Augusta by her family, is about twelve when this story begins. She is Galeria's granddaughter and living at Villa Arcadius, since her parents have moved to London. She needs to be married soon.

Comes Britanniarum: The most senior Roman military official in the four provinces of Roman Britain. The last person to hold this rank before *Severus's* appointment was Theodosius (the father of Emperor Theodosius), under whom both *Severus* and *Flavius* had served.

Conchessa: The mother of Padrig and daughter of Father Potitus. It is thought that St Patrick's mother was from Gaul and named Conchessa.

Constans: The eldest son of the usurper from Britain, Constantine III. Given the title of Caesar, he led part of the invading army to Spain, where he had some initial military success.

Cornelia: Wife of Jodocus, mother of Caradocus and paternal grandmother of Dilectus.

Cuda: A pagan Celtic goddess of fertility and the spiritual force behind the cult of the cucullate.

Cunomaglos: Scary mythical Celtic wolf lord.

Deryn: A well-informed house servant at Villa Arcadius.

Dis: Name given to the Roman god of death, similar to Pluto.

Dylan: A sea god in Welsh Celtic mythology.

Elen: Widow of Caradocus and mother of Dilectus, she is the daughter and heir of King Conanus of the Silures and the Demetae, Lord of Garn Goch. Her mother, Brangwen, is deceased.

Ennodius: The Proconsul Africae, married to Flacilia, one of Emperor Magnus Maximus's daughters.

Eucherius: The son of Stilicho and Serena; put to death in AD 408.

Flacilia: Eldest daughter of Emperor Magnus Maximus.

Flavia Sevira: See Sevira.

Flora: Roman goddess of spring.

Galla Placidia: She was a daughter of Emperor Theodosius and his second wife, thus half-sister to Honorius. She held one of the highest possible imperial ranks at the time, *Nobilissima Puella* (most noble girl), during her childhood. She was taken hostage by Alaric and after his death, Honorius married her to Athaulf, Alaric's brother-in-law.

Garmon: The Celtic name of Germanus, Bishop of Auxerre, who, ironically, was later sent by papal authority to Britain in AD 429 to counter the spread of Pelagianism.

Gerontius: The British-born general whom Constantine III promoted to lead the campaign in Spain. Later, however, he rebelled against Constantine.

Gratian: Emperor of the Western Roman Empire from AD 367 to 383. He rejected the title of Pontifex Maximus and was active against heresies, as well as abolishing public support for pagan priests and confiscating temple properties. He was defeated in battle by usurper Magnus Maximus.

Gratian: A Briton who was a member of the urban aristocracy and a minor administrative official, was elected head of the army in 406 after Marcus was executed; he, too, was soon killed by his troops.

Gwladus: The Welsh Celtic form of the name Claudia (modern form, Gladys).

Heraclianus: Appointed by Honorius as Comes Africae, governor of the 'granary' province of Africa, as a reward for his involvement in the execution of Stilicho. He opposed the efforts of Priscus Attalus to negotiate with Alaric.

Honorius (AD 384–423): He, born in Constantinople, was the younger son of Emperor Theodosius I and Aelia Flaccilla (who died two years later). His father named him co-emperor in 393, and when Theodosius died, he became Augustus of the Western Empire and his brother Arcadius emperor of the Eastern Empire. As Honorius was only ten years old, Stilicho was appointed Regent.

Innocentius: Now known as Pope Innocent I.

Jodocus Demetarius: The father of Caradocus and thus paternal grandfather of Dilectus. Originally a minor civil servant when Rome controlled Venta Silurum, he was by now employed at the Villa Arcadius as a bajalus.

Julian of Eclanum: At this time, Julian was a deacon, becoming a bishop in AD 417. He was deposed and exiled from Italy for refusing to sign a document condemning Pelagius. He strongly opposed the Augustinian concept that sexual desire is inherently sinful.

Lestinus: A Celtic servant in the villa, whose style had impressed Galeria, and she had elevated him to an important post as captain of the household guard, civilians who could be called on to defend the villa in times of need.

Lucan: Marcus Annaeus Lucanus, now generally known as Lucan, was a Roman epic poet during the first century AD (when Nero was Emperor).

Lucius: He was married to Galeria's daughter, Aurelia, and father of Claudia.

Macsen Wledig: The Celtic name for General Magnus Maximus. *Caradocus had adopted this name for himself as an act of whimsy, much to the confusion of later historians and chroniclers.*

Magnis: chief gardener at the Villa Arcadius.

Magnus Maximus: Commander of all Roman troops in Britain, with his headquarters in Isca Legionis *(near Villa Arcadius)*, he was elected Emperor by his troops, and after taking the Roman army out of Britain to the continent, established himself as Emperor of the Western Empire until defeated and executed in AD 388 by Theodosius. *He and Lady Galeria were strongly attracted to each other.*

Marcella (AD 325–410): From a rich aristocratic family in Rome, she was widowed at a young age and became one of the most famous of the ascetic noblewomen of the time. Her huge mansion became a centre for prayer and bible study by women who became known as The Brown Dress Society. Fluent in Greek and Hebrew, she assisted Jerome in his translation of the bible. She died from the injuries sustained at the hands of Alaric's men, searching her palace for gold.

Marcus: The grandson of Lady Galeria and brother of Claudia, who moved with his parents to London and joined the army in AD 393. Thirteen years later, just like the historical Marcus, *he was elected by the troops to be 'emperor' but was executed two months later when the soldiers changed their minds about his suitability.*

Marcus Antonius: In English, Mark Antony (84–30 BC), statesman and general, was one of a number of autocrats responsible for transforming Rome from a republic to an imperial dictatorship.

Maria: At about ten years of age this daughter of Stilicho and Serena, was married off to Honorius, the boy Emperor of the Western Empire. She died without children early in AD 408.

Martinus: Martinus, now known as Saint Martin of Tours, had spent some time in Trier, where he offered protection to Magnus Maximus's wife and daughter.

Meirion: Former stable hand at Garn Goch, whose talents as an equestrian, scout and messenger to Roman Britons had elevated his status in the new Celtic kingdom of the combined Silurian and Demetae tribes.

Melania the Elder (Valeria Melania): An extremely wealthy noblewoman from Spain; married at fourteen, widowed at twenty-two, she left her only surviving son and moved to Alexandria and became one of the first Christian ascetics to join a monastery in the Nitrian Desert in Egypt.

Melania the Younger: Daughter of Albina and granddaughter of Melania the Elder, she was pushed by her father into marriage to her cousin at a young age and lived in great splendour, much to her distress. After the infant deaths of their two children, the couple fully embraced an ascetic and celibate life and gave away their vast estates to the Church.

Milo of Croton: The most famous of the ancient Greek wrestlers and Olympic boy-champion in 540 BC.

Minerva: Roman goddess of wisdom.

Molio: An educated novice monk, literate enough to have gained employment at the Villa Arcadius to assist in the library. Monasteries as such were not yet established in the British Isles, but he had been schooled first at the villa and later at a Celtic Christian community in Strathclyde (south-eastern Scotland).

Nectan: The taller of the two mysterious hooded men who kidnapped Dilectus.

Ninian (AD 360–432): A Briton trained in Rome and sent by Bishop Martin of Tours to spread Christianity to the south Picts in AD 395. He built a church of whitewashed stone in what is now Galloway in Scotland. It was called *Candida Casa* (white house). He was later canonised as a saint.

Olympius: An officer of the guard in Honorius's court, in charge of the emperor's security and communications. He spread lies about Stilicho's intentions, organised a coup, killed Stilicho's leading officers, and then executed Stilicho himself on August 22nd, AD 408.

Orcinus orca: Roman name for killer whales. Orcus (also called Plato) was the god of the underworld.

Padrig: Celtic form of the name Patrick. Became a close friend of Dilectus after helping rescue him. Later, he felt a calling to go to Ireland to convert the people there to Christianity.

Patricius (Magonus Sucatus Patricius): Latin name of St Patrick (AD 385–AD 461). His actual birthplace is unknown, but the Welsh village of Banwen takes credit. His father was a well-off government official, and his grandfather was a priest. At the age of sixteen, he was captured by Irish slavers and taken to Ireland, where he was a slave for six years before escaping by ship to the continent. The ship was exporting famed Irish wolfhounds to wealthy buyers on the continent.

Paula: Paul, later sanctified, is an extremely wealthy widow of a senator; as a mother of five children, she would dress in silk and be carried around the city by her eunuch slaves. Strongly influenced by Marcella and the group of ascetic noblewomen in Rome, she was a friend of Jerome's and, with her knowledge of Hebrew, was able to assist him in his translation of the Bible into Vulgar Latin.

Pellicanus: Latin for pelican. *Dilectus had heard of pelicans on account of the Christian myth that female pelicans peck their own breasts to feed their young. He confused the word with the unfamiliar name Pelagius.*

Petroc: The second, slightly kinder, kidnapper.

Pheidippides: The Greek soldier who ran from Marathon to Athens to bring the news that the Persians had been defeated, whereupon he collapsed and died.

Plutarch: A first-century AD Greek philosopher, essayist and historian.

Potitus: Padrig's grandfather, a retired priest in the diocese of Viroconium, was named after the teenage Potitus, an early Christian martyr who was thrown to the lions, which refused to attack him. Living with the family in Banwen, he was hired by Flavius as a part-time priest at the villa.

Principia (died AD 420, date of birth unknown): A Roman virgin and nun who was Marcella's favourite student. Two letters that Jerome wrote to her have survived, one of which was designed to console her after Marcella died from her injuries.

Publius Ostorius Scapula: A Roman general appointed in AD 47 as the second governor of the Roman-occupied regions of Britannia.

Quintus Veranius Nepos: The fourth Roman governor of Britannia, who in AD 58 again defeated the Silures in battle and helped the military control of the region by building a network of roads, forts and small garrisoned watchtowers throughout Wales (Cymru).

Rhea Silvia: In Roman legend, she was the mother of the twin founders of Rome, Romulus and Remus.

Rhonwen: The chief cook at Garn Goch and Meirion and Sioned's mother. Elen and Meirion called their second child Rhonwen in her honour.

Rufinus (Flavius Rufinus): He was an East Roman statesman who served as Praetorian Prefect of the East under Emperor Theodosius I, as well as regent for his son Arcadius. After his murder by Gothic mercenaries, his role as advisor to Arcadius was assumed by the cruel eunuch Eutropius.

Rufus Lucius: He was Galeria's younger grandson. Like his brother Marcus, he'd joined the army and saw action under Severus in the Pictish war and later in Gaul, where he was killed in the Battle of Verona in June 402.

Sarus: A Gothic chieftain hostile to King Alaric. Known to be a skilful warrior, he was appointed a commander by Emperor Honorius, but his violence elevated him as a dangerous warlord.

Scipio Africanus: A Roman general (236–183 BC) who was never defeated in battle. His triumph over Hannibal led to the end of the Punic Wars.

Senica: Severus's wife. Their house was now incorporated within the aegis of the villa.

Serena: Stilicho's wife. After Stilicho's execution, she fled to Rome, where the Senate, with Galla Placidia's connivance, sentenced her to death by strangulation (garrotting).

Sevira (Flavia Sevira): The daughter of Emperor Magnus Maximus (Macsen Wledig). *Galeria helped arrange her marriage to Vortigern (Vitalinus).*

Sioned: Daughter of Rhonwen, the elderly chief cook of Garn Goch and older sister of Meirion.

Siricius: Bishop of Rome (Pope) from AD 384 until his death in AD 399, known for advocating celibacy for priests.

Stilicho (Flavius Stilicho) (b. 365, d 408): Stilicho, highly successful commanding general, he had a Vandal father and a Roman mother. The

Vandals were a Germanic tribe originally occupying lands now part of modern Poland. He married Serena, Theodosius's favourite niece.

Sulla (Lucius Cornelius Sulla Felix, 138–78 BC): Roman general is known for his cunning and for winning the first major civil war and the first to seize dictatorial control over the Republic.

Tacitus (Publius Cornelius Tacitus, b. AD 56–d. 120): A prolific and highly respected Roman historian and senator.

Telemachus: An ascetic monk who, in AD 404, ran into the arena of the Flavian Amphitheatre to separate gladiators and stop them from killing each other. The audience showed their displeasure by stoning him to death; the incident ended the games permanently by orders from Honorius.

Thermantia: The youngest daughter of Stilicho and Serena, who was briefly married (unconsummated) to Western Roman Emperor Honorius in May AD 408.

Thomas: One of the twelve disciples, he needed physical evidence of Christ's return to satisfy his doubts.

Valens: Roman Emperor of the East, based in Constantinople, from 364 to 378. Tolerant of Christians and pagans, he was killed at the crushing Roman defeat by the Goths at the Battle of Adrianople, which resulted in the Goths being allowed to settle within the boundaries of the empire.

Venus: Roman goddess of love, beauty and sexual desire.

Victorinus: A governor (vicarius) of one of the provinces of Roman Britain between AD 395 and 406. He was ousted in 406 when Marcus was nominated by the troops in Britain to be their 'emperor'.

Vigilantius: One of the many firebrand clerics in the Roman Church of this period. Born in France, he challenged the current practices of monastic asceticism, the virtue of celibacy and the veneration of relics of martyrs, which he described as superstitious idolatry.

Vitalinus: From the wealthy Vitalis family, powerful Romano-Celtic landowners in tribal lands of the Cornovii, living in a villa in Viroconium (modern Wroxeter). His Celtic name was Vortigern.

Vortigern: The name in Celtic means 'overlord'. It appears that in the Fifth Century he managed to unite many tribes under his leadership. He is best known for inviting Saxons to settle in Britain in order to counter incursions from the Picts and the Scoti. Various myths and legends surround this figure, but there's little evidence of his background; even the dates of his life are debated.

Places, Things, Events, Titles and Translations

Accipere locum: Latin for 'take the place of'.

Adrianople: The modern town of Edirne in northwest Turkey and the site of a major battle in AD 378 in which two-thirds of the eastern Roman army led by Emperor Valens was wiped out.

Amicus meus, inimicus inimici mei: Latin saying, meaning 'My friend, the enemy of my enemy'.

Angeln: A small district in northern Germany where the Angles supposedly came from.

Aquilam volare doces: Meaning 'you're teaching an eagle to fly' – the Latin version of 'don't teach your grandmother to suck eggs'!

Arelate: One of the most important ports of the later Roman Empire, now known as Arles, in France.

Armorica: Modern day Brittany, settled by many Celts from Britain.

Ariminum: The modern city is Rimini, on the Adriatic coast of central Italy.

ASP: Acronym for *absens sine permissione*; Roman army-speak equivalent to AWOL.

Assaria: Small bronze Roman coin.

Aqua Virgo: One of the eleven Roman aqueducts that supplied the city of Rome with water.

Autissiodorum: The Roman name for the modern town of Auxerre, central France. It is thought that St Patrick studied for the priesthood there and was consecrated by Bishop Germanus.

Bacauda (plural bacaudae, or bagaudae): Celtic name for the peasant rebels of northern Hispania and Gaul during the fourth and fifth centuries. Large revolts in Armorica further weakened Roman authority in the northern provinces.

Bajulus: Latin for steward or estate manager; the origin of the Middle-English word bailiff.

Banwen: A village near Neath in Wales. In Roman times, there were copper and tin mines nearby and an army marching camp and fort guarding the local road. It's a village tradition that St Patrick was born there. It is plausible that slavers from Ireland coming around the southwest coast of Wales could have landed at the nearby entrance of the Severn (Sabrina) Estuary.

Barritus: Roman army battle cry of the late fourth century, the volume of which was amplified by holding their shields to their mouths.

Benacus: Roman name for Lake Garda, the largest of the Italian lakes, between Milan and Verona.

Binica: Roman or possibly Celtic name for the modern village of Binic, on the coast of Brittany, France; it was once a major fishing harbour.

Bog myrtle: An aromatic plant whose leaves were traditionally worn or carried by brides in Celtic Wales.

Bononia: Modern name of the city is Bologna, in northern Italy.

Brewis: Celtic breakfast staple of bread or crumbled oatcakes soaked in broth.

Burdigala: The Roman name (with stress on the 'i') for the modern town of Bordeaux in France.

Caledonia: Roman name for that part of modern Scotland north of the Firth of Forth, named after one of the tribes, the Caledones.

Candida Casa: The monastic centre founded by St Ninian in Whithorn, Scotland. It means 'shining white house', as the buildings were made of white or whitewashed stone.

Candlemas Day: A Christian festival around February 2nd commemorating the occasion when Mary went to the Temple in Jerusalem to be purified forty days after the birth of Jesus. Pre-Christian Celts celebrated it as the day candles were no longer needed for early morning farm work.

Cantium: Modern day Kent.

Cervisia: Latin for beer.

Civitas: The key residential and commercial market town of a tribe, usually fortified.

Classis Britannica: The provincial Roman naval fleet assigned to waters around Britain, especially the English Channel, and based at Dubris (Dover) and Portus Adurni (Portsmouth). Originally involved in transport, by the end of the fourth century, its purpose was to combat pirates and Saxon raiding parties. By AD 409, it had been fully withdrawn.

Cleg: Today, a common Scottish word for a horsefly, but as it comes from Old Norse, you can be sure Severus actually called them something else.

Clepsydra: A device for measuring time by the gradual flow of water. The Romans invented a version consisting of a wall cylinder into which water dripped from a small tank; a float provided readings against a scale on the wall.

Coedwig o Daneg: A forest where Danes were once active; today called the Forest of Dean, in Gloucestershire, England.

Colonia: Any Roman settlement housing retired and disabled legionaries. Later, the term also became used for high-status cities.

Colonia Verona Augusta: Roman name for the modern city of Verona, in northern Italy, where a number of major military and commercial roads intersected.

Comes domesticorum equitum: A military rank – the commander of an elite cavalry unit of five hundred officers serving as a privileged bodyguard for an emperor at the royal court.

Comes Litoris Saxonici: 'Count (or commander) of the Saxon shore', one of the key military positions in the province of Britannia. The exact meaning is debated, but most think it referred to control of the line of forts along the eastern coastline designed to resist Saxon invasions.

Comitatus: Latin for 'retinue', but in the Roman army it referred to an elite company assembled to protect a senior commander.

Consentia: The modern name is Cosenza, and it is in southern Italy. Alaric died there towards the end of AD 410 of an unknown illness, possibly malaria.

Corieltauvi: A peaceful, largely agricultural tribe occupying an area now the East Midlands of England.

Corinium: A major Roman town and the civitas of the Dobunni tribe; now modern Cirencester in the Cotswolds.

Cornovii: A Celtic tribe occupying territory north of the Silures, covering what is new eastern Wales and the English counties of Cheshire and Shropshire. Their civitas capital was Viroconium (modern Wroxeter).

Corporal: The linen altar cloth that covered altars in fourth-century churches and chapels, which is blessed by the words of the Benedictio Corporalium.

Cucullus (plural cuculli): Latin for a hood, especially a monk's cowl.

Cucullus non facit monachum: An old saying meaning 'the hood does not make the monk', i.e., clothes don't make the man, or don't judge a book by its cover.

Cunomaglos: A Celtic hunting god prominent in the upper Severn Valley, north of Glevum (modern Gloucester).

Curialis: A Roman tax collector, often small landowners on whom the emperor tried to keep a firm grip. As imperial authority decayed in Britain, local chiefs taxed everyone in their orbit, and the curiales became even less popular. It is believed St Patrick's father was a curialis, but exactly where the family lived is not known, since the name he gives in his memoir ('*Confessio*') as 'Bannavem Taberniae' cannot be traced.

Cursus publicus: The imperial postal service created by Emperor Augustus, using relays of dispatch riders.

Cyhyraeth: A mythical Welsh creature, rarely seen, who makes a horrible moaning cry before someone dies. She is known to be very ugly, with long black teeth, withered arms and leathery wings.

Cymru: Cymru (pronounced *kəm.ri*) is the Celtic name for Wales. The Latin name for Wales is Cambria, but that was not used until much later. We don't know what the tribes called themselves, but it is very doubtful they had a collective or *national* name, so I have just taken the liberty of using the modern name in an old language to refer to the four or five tribes living to the west of the Fosse.

Cyparissus: A character in Greek mythology whose favourite companion was a tame stag he accidentally killed. The boy's intense grief turned him into a cypress tree, the symbol of mourning.

Damnatio memoriae: Literally 'condemnation of memory', a determination for a condemned 'traitor' whereby his name could never be used and would be erased from inscriptions, images would be destroyed, and if the person was of high rank like an emperor even coins showing his face could be recalled or cancelled.

Danubius: The River Danube, the north-eastern frontier of the Western Roman Empire.

Decurion: Decurion (plural *decuriones*) were the heads of local city or municipal councils appointed on the basis of modest means, community standing, reputation and service. As Roman control waned, these officials became the administrators under local chiefs and warlords.

Deva Victrix: Once one of the largest legionary forts in Brittania, it had been largely abandoned by AD 395, although the nearby town (civitas), modern Chester, survived as a Latin-speaking Romano-Briton town well into the Anglo-Saxon era.

Dim: Welsh Celtic for 'nothing'.

Dubris: Roman name for Dover.

Dumnonia: The lands of the Dumnonii tribe, occupying modern Cornwall and parts of Devon.

Duw amddiffyn Cymru: Welsh for 'God defend Wales'.

Duw Cariad Yw: Welsh (Celtic) for God is Love.

Eboracum: The Latin name for the modern city of York. A major military base, it was one of the largest and most important towns in Roman Britain.

Embrasures: The opening slits or loopholes in a fortified structure to allow the firing of weapons.

Eremos: Mount Eremos, a hill overlooking the Sea of Galilee, has long been suggested as the possible site of the Sermon on the Mount, where Jesus is said to have articulated the Beatitudes.

Foederati: Originally non-Roman groups bound by a treaty to fight on behalf of Rome. By the current period of the Empire, the term referred to the practice of allowing the settlement of entire barbarian tribes in exchange for their warriors joining the Roman army or fighting alongside them.

Fosse: Fosse Way was a major Roman road built in the first and second centuries, linking modern Exeter all the way to modern Lincoln. It originally followed the course of a ditch (fosse) that was the western boundary of Britannia for a while.

Frigidus River: Probably what is now the Vipava River that flows through western Slovenia and northeast Italy. The site of a major battle in AD 394 in the civil war between Emperor Theodosius and the usurper Eugenius. Theodosius was victorious, but in the battle, he sacrificed ten thousand loyal Gothic soldiers.

Fugit inreparabile tempus: A phrase from Virgil meaning 'it escapes, irretrievable time'; usually said in the modern era as 'tempus fugit' – time flies.

Garumna: The Roman's name for the Garonne River in the south of France.

Genii cucullate: They were the hooded guardians or spirits of the cult of Cuda. Their carved images have been found in many locations in Britain, but especially in the Cotswolds. Genii is the plural of the Latin 'Genius', a guardian spirit in Roman mythology.

Germania (Germanic Barbaricum): The area of Germanic tribes outside the boundaries of the Roman Empire, between the seas in the north, the Danube in the south and the Rhine in the west.

Glevum: Modern Gloucester.

Grain beetle: These insects were first introduced to Britannia during the Roman occupation and became a significant agricultural pest.

Hibernia: One of the Roman names for Ireland, all being derived from the earliest Greek geographers' name of *Ierne*, who knew of the island's existence from traders. The Old Irish name was *Eriu*; the modern Irish name is Éire.

Hispania: What is now modern Spain and Portugal was captured from the Carthaginians in 206 BC and by now divided into five heavily Romanized provinces.

Homoousios: The key Greek term, formulated at the ecumenical council at Nicaea in AD 325, to affirm that God the Son and God the Father are of the same substance (ousios). The addition of one letter, the Greek 'i' (homoiousios) changes the meaning from 'same' to 'similar' – which was the belief of Arianism.

Illyria/Illyricum: Roman province on the western part of the Balkan Peninsular (on the Adriatic), which was originally settled by Celtic peoples.

Imbolc: (sounds like im-olk), a pagan Celtic season of new beginnings around the second day of February, honouring Brighid, goddess of the hearth, who in this season is celebrated as the mother who has given birth, thus Christians later connected the season with Mary.

Isca Dumnoniorum: Modern day Exeter on the English south coast. The Romans established a fort there in AD 55 as the home of the 2nd

Augustan Legion, but twenty years later it moved to Isca Silurum. The Dumnonii were a Celtic tribe occupying what is now Cornwall and Devon.

Isca River: Modern name is River Usk. The harbour was between what is now Newport and Caerleon in south Wales.

Isca Silurum: Sometimes known as Isca Augusta, this was one of the three most important garrisons (*Castra Legionis* also *Castra Augusta*) of the Roman army in Britannia. Founded around AD 75 as headquarters for the Legion II Augusta, it is located in modern Caerleon, in South Wales. On the banks of the River Usk (Isca is Celtic for water), which flows into the Severn Estuary, the castra and its harbour had great strategic importance and its presence supported the development of the nearby market town of Venta Silurum, the civitas of the Silures, after this fierce tribe had been largely subdued.

Iutum: Roman name for Jutland, the home of the Jutes, now part of Denmark.

Latrunculi: Latrunculi (or ludus latrunculorum) was a board game of strategy played throughout the empire. The black or white playing pieces were called 'dogs'.

Laqueus: Latin for a garrotte, usually a wire instrument used in formal executions.

Lex talionis: Roman legal principle of exact retaliation as criminal punishment, based on the eye-for-an-eye concept.

Libra: Roman unit of weight, equivalent of twelve modern ounces, thus less than a modern pound (lb).

Lindum Colonia: The Roman name for a settlement near modern Lincoln, which was a legionary barracks at first and later used as a *colonia* to settle retired and injured soldiers.

Londinium: Modern day London.

Lughnasa: A pagan Celtic festival of feasting and ritual in early August, marking the beginning of the harvest season and often involving baking bread from the new wheat crop and offering other food to the god Lugh.

Magister militum: Title of a general in command of an army.

Magister utriusque militiae: Supreme commander of the Roman army, both infantry and cavalry.

Mare Friscum: Possibly the Roman name for the North Sea. Frisian troops were extensively recruited to the Roman army, and in Britain, they were particularly engaged as garrison troops at Hadrian's Wall.

Mare Nostrum: Literally 'our sea'; known now as the Mediterranean Sea.

Massilia: Modern name is Marseille, on the Mediterranean coast of France.

Mediolanum: Milan, which by the fourth century had become the administrative capital of the Western Empire and the location of the imperial court, rather than Rome.

Moesia: Modern-day Bulgaria and parts of Serbia, inhabited originally by Thracians and a colonised Roman province for many centuries. Goths were allowed to settle there as a barrier to the Huns.

Molossians: *Canis Molossus* was a now-extinct breed of fighting dog favoured by the Roman legions.

Mons Vaticanus: Meaning 'hill of prophecy', this area across the Tiber became a papal centre and had an extensive library with many scribes able to copy and illustrate important new writing as well as classical literature.

Nabataean horse: A breed now known as Arabians.

Navicularis: The title for wealthy businessmen in a powerful guild who controlled both cargo and passenger shipping in the Roman Empire. A ship owner was also called the *Dominus Navis*.

Nidum: A stone Roman fort, by this time abandoned for the last ninety years, located near the mouth of the River Neath.

Nodens: A powerful Celtic god connected with fishing but more probably healing.

Noricum: Roman name for a region once held by federated Celtic tribes, more or less corresponding to modern Austria and Slovenia. By this period, it was inhabited by Germanic tribes, had good agricultural potential and was a major source of high-quality steel for weapons.

Nova Roma: 'New Rome', an early Latin name for Constantinople.

Numerus fortensium: 'Many brave ones' – the name given to the garrison of Othona, one of the forts on the Saxon Shore.

Nummus: The smallest coin of the monetary denominations of the later years of the Empire, worth $1/7200^{th}$ of the most valuable coin, the gold solidus.

Oceanus Britannicus: Roman name for the English Channel. The open Atlantic was just called Oceanus.

Ostia: Rome's original port town.

Othona: A Roman army fort on the east coast of Britannia (the 'Saxon Shore'); its modern location is Bradwell-on-Sea in Essex.

Palace of Domitian: For three hundred years, this was the official residence of the emperor before the imperial court moved to Milan. It was the largest building on the Palatine Hill.

Palatini: (Literally 'palace soldiers') In the late empire period, palatini were elite units attached to an emperor or commanding officer.

Panegyric: A poem or a speech in praise of someone, usually highly flattering of someone important. The 'court poet' Severus was referring to is Claudius Claudianus, and what he did write about Stilicho's Pictish War was: 'Stilicho also gave aid to me [Britain personified] when at the mercy of neighbouring tribes when the Scoti roused all Hibernia against me and the sea foamed to the beat of hostile oars. Thanks to his care, I had no need to fear the Scoti arms or tremble at the Pict or keep watch along all my coasts for the Saxon'.

Pauloduobus: Literally, Latin for a small couple. The joke was that the two strips were like a couple together in bed. Peter's Basilica. The two great churches in Fifth Century Rome, one dedicated to the apostle Peter and one to the apostle Paul, were declared a safe sanctuary for Roman citizens by Alaric during the sack of Rome.

Pharsalus: The site in Greece where Julius Caesar won the decisive victory in the civil war against Pompey and the Senate.

Pillars of Heracles: Modern name is the Straits of Gibraltar.

Pollentia: Modern Pollenzo in northern Italy was the site of a major battle between Stilicho's forces and Alaric's Visigoths on the 6th of April, 402. The Romans claimed victory as they stopped Alaric's invasion of Italy for some years, but it was not a decisive defeat for Alaric.

Portus: The artificial harbour on the north side, the mouth of the River Tiber, serving the city of Rome.

Posca: Posca was a Roman drink made by mixing vinegar, water, wine and herbs. It was the soldiers, the lower classes and the slaves who mostly drank posca.

Praetorian Guard: Originally an elite unit of the Roman army designed to protect the emperor; later used to describe any bodyguard group for important officials.

Prefect of Rome: The prefect was responsible for maintaining law and order and, by 410, the overall governing of the city.

Priscillians: A Christian sect, followers of a Spanish bishop called Priscillian, whose ideas resembled Gnostic and Manichaean beliefs. He taught that matter (and bodies) were evil and that angels and human souls came directly from God. Their ascetic practices included forbidding all sensual practices, marriage, wine and meat.

Primus pilus: Literally the 'first spear', was the name given to a senior centurion who would be the equivalent of a modern army drill sergeant.

Procella: Latin for a severe storm, hurricane, gale, or tempest.

Procurator: Procurator was the title of certain Roman officials in charge of the financial affairs of a province.

Raetia: A Roman province northeast of Italy, roughly corresponding to modern Switzerland.

Ratae (Ratae Corieltauvorum): A Roman town in the English midlands, now called Leicester.

Rationalis: A high-ranking fiscal officer in the Roman Empire.

Regulbium: A Roman army fort on the Saxon Shore. The name means 'great headland', and the fort was near modern Reculver in Kent.

Rhedwch: Celtic for run, or gallop.

Rhenus: The River Rhine.

Rith: A small stream or brook.

Rodonus: The Gallic name for the River Rhone (Rhodanus in Latin).

Roman Camp: The fort Lestinus and the men from the villa rested at on the road to Glevum was at modern Lydney Park in Gloucestershire.

Sabrina estuary and river: Now known as the Severn, leading to the Bristol channel.

Sancta: Latin feminine of sanctus, meaning holy or sacred, and later meaning saint. There was no formal category of 'saint' in the fourth or fifth century.

Sarn y Leng: A Roman road built in Wales at the end of the first century, now known as Sarn Helen. Sarn is Celtic for causeway and leng Celtic for legion.

Saxonia: Roman name for modern Saxony.

Scoti: A powerful Gaelic/Celtic tribe originally from Ireland. Their frequent raids and occupation of lands north of Wales eventually established them as the dominant peoples of what is now southeastern Scotland. Before then, a few wealthy Scoti families had settled in parts of England.

Segontium: Modern Carnarvon in north Wales, was a major harbour for Roman troop movements until Magnus Maximus's defeat in AD 388.

Siliqua: A valuable Roman silver coin.

Sodalis: Latin for intimate companion, comrade, or buddy.

Spanish Legion: *Legio IX Hispana* – an elite regiment of the Roman army. Around AD 60, a large section was destroyed by British tribes under Boudica.

Strophium: A Roman undergarment like a tight strapless bra worn by young women when engaged in athletic pursuits such as riding, running, or swimming.

Subligaculum: Roman one-piece loin cloth that was folded like a baby's diaper and tied in the front to form underpants for men.

Stupidae (singular: stupidus): A type of slapstick clown in Roman amusement settings, wearing multi-coloured costumes and cracking jokes and riddles.

Syrinx: Panpipes, a wind instrument consisting of pipes of different lengths tied together in a row.

Tadcu: Celtic for grandfather.

Tamesis: Roman name for the River Thames (Tems in Celtic).

Tamium (or Tamion): Site near modern Cardiff where the Romans once had a fort and a small harbour.

Tawe Bay: The River Tawe runs into a sheltered bay (modern Swansea) that affords some protection from the open waters of the Bristol Channel (Severn estuary).

Temple of Jupiter: Built in 509 BC, was an enormous temple on the Capitoline Hill (one of the seven hills of Rome), symbolizing Rome as the centre of the world.

Tolosa: Roman name for modern Toulouse in France.

Torc: A neck ring and an important piece of Celtic jewellery dating back to the Iron Age and typically made of plaited silver or gold wires.

Treverorum: Modern Trier in southwest Germany, in the Moselle wine region.

Tuscia: Still called that in Tuscany, central Italy, home of the Etruscans who were conquered by Rome.

Turonum (Civitas Turonum): Roman name for the modern-day city of Tours in the Loire Valley of France.

Uncia: A Roman inch, one-twelfth of a foot, which was just slightly shorter than a modern foot.

Vallum Antonini: The Roman name for the Antonine Wall, a thirty-nine-mile earthen barricade north of Hadrian's Wall, between the Firths of Clyde and of Forth.

Venta Silurum: The *civitas*, or walled market town, of the Silures (remains are now in modern Caerwent, Monmouthshire, Wales), which grew in wealth and importance after the large Roman army garrison of Isca Silurum was established nearby (in modern Caerleon).

Vexillatio: By this time, a Roman cavalry troop was attached to infantry for a special purpose.

Via Devana: Important Roman military road running from Deva (Chester) in the west to Colonia Victricensis (Colchester) in the southeast.

Vigilare: Latin for 'be awake' – modern military equivalent is Reveille, usually a bugle or trumpet call.

Viroconium Cornoviorum: Modern Wroxeter, a Roman fort here, had been a major launching site for raids against the Welsh tribes, but as the Cornovii had been easily subdued, it had evolved into an important market town. It was here Elen and her husband Caradocus had hidden from the authorities and where Dilectus was born. The Vitalis family also had a town residence here, although many of their estates were further east, and once he was married, Vortigern set up his headquarters and lavish residence near the fort Venonis (in modern-day Leicestershire).

Notes on the Sources

There are a number of excellent books I consulted and enjoyed in an attempt to give my story a degree of verisimilitude despite having little evidence for how anyone other than a few erudite scholars actually thought. Fortunately, the theological works of Jerome and Augustine have all been translated and are readily accessible. There is much less of Pelagius's writings available, and most of our understanding of what he preached comes from rebuttals written by his harshest critics and enemies. However, for a reader wishing to learn a little more, a useful work is *Pelagius: Inquiries and Reappraisals* by Robert F. Evans (Wipf and Stock Publishers, 2010). An enjoyable account of the early Celtic church with entertaining details about the life of Saint Patrick (Padrig in the story) is *How the Irish Saved Civilization: The Untold Story of Ireland's Heroic Role from the Fall of Rome to the Rise of Medieval Europe,* by Thomas Cahill (Doubleday, 1995). Of course, my story is set in Wales, not Ireland (the Irish tribe, the Scoti, are the villains!), and there are many useful individual accounts of the extensive Roman remains in all the Welsh sites mentioned in the story, but I had to dig, excuse the pun, through journal articles (my sincere thanks to Massey University Library) and Wikipedia. For a general background on Celtic culture, *A Dark History: Celts*, by Martin J. Dougherty (Metro Books, 2015), has many fine illustrations. As for the Picts, I'm afraid no one knows very much except they painted their bodies before going into battle and became Scottish.

Historical writers commenting specifically on Britain during the fifteen years of this story, such as Gildas (an early Sixth Century Welsh monk) and Bede (who finished his ecclesiastical history of Britain in AD 731), only did so many years later. Modern historians, still challenged by a lack of data, always provide balanced perspectives. As a general account of what is called Sub-Roman Britain, I found Christopher Snyder's work *An Age of Tyrants: Britain and the Britons AD 400–600* (Pennsylvania State University Press, 1998) to be useful, with a strong emphasis on the archaeological evidence. The Roman and late Roman periods of Britain are well covered in the early chapters of *The Britons,* also by Snyder (Blackwell, 2003). Two older works, which cover the periods both before and after this story, were very helpful: *Roman Britain and Early England 55 BC–AD 871* (W.W. Norton & Co., 1963) by Peter Hunter Blair and the comprehensive *Britannia: A History of Roman Britain* (Routledge & Kegan Paul, 2nd ed, 1978) by Sheppard Frere.

To be as accurate as possible about dress, houses, lifestyle, foods and just about everything else at the time, I was constantly referring to the magisterial, beautifully illustrated, five hundred plus page work by Joan Liversidge, entitled *Britain in the Roman Empire* (Praeger, 1968).

As sound historical scholarship, two recent works by Adrian Goldsworthy can be highly recommended: *How Rome Fell* (Yale University and Press, 2009) and *Pax Romana: War, Peace and Conquest in the Roman World* (Yale University and Press, 2016). The latter work analyses how those conquered by the Romans responded and adapted, which is the subtext of this novel. For military history and conditions, I relied on Brian Todd Carey's book *Warfare in the Ancient World* (Pen & Sword Books, 2013) and the *Military History of Late Rome AD 361–395* by Ilkka Syvanne (Pen & Sword Books, 2018).

Two books in particular stand out as being thoroughly enjoyable to read as well as informative. Don Holloway's *At the Gates of Rome: The Fall of the Eternal City, AD 410* (Osprey Publishing, 2022) is detailed and thrilling as a story as well as history. And there is little as entertainingly and imaginatively written as *Alaric the Goth: An Outsider's History of the Fall of Rome* (W. W. Norton, 2020) by Douglas Boin, who provides a vibrant alternative narrative of the King of the Visigoths and a balanced view of the 'sack' of Rome. Being a professional historian, however, Di Boin could not have known that it was actually Dilectus who inadvertently allowed the Goths inside Rome on the early morning of August 24th, AD 410.

My sincere thanks to all these fine historians and apologies for my errors, either deliberate (novelist's licence) or accidental (novelist's confusion with hundreds of names, dates, places, battles, Roman names and Celtic mythology).

****